C000147613

AND THE DEAD

Over one of the tanks, a warrior hung by his arms from a metal spar, his muscles stretched taut as if they would split open like pods. His face wore a look of ghastly torment.

Dromator moved around the side of the vat, searching for a hold that would enable him to climb up to its broad rim. There were metal protrusions, and putting his weapon in his mouth, he swung upward. Once on the rim, he carefully inched his way around it to the suspended warrior. He could see that the man was secured by rope made from coarse fibers and that it would be impossible to part the rope without a blade. It was only as he reached for the man's arm that he realized the fibers had eaten into the flesh, as if they had *taken root*.

"Kill me," the man moaned.

Other Avon Books by
Adrian Cole

THE OMARAN SAGA

STAR REQUIEM *Series*

Avon Books are available at special quantity discounts for bulk purchases for sales promotions, premiums, fund raising or educational use. Special books, or book excerpts, can also be created to fit specific needs.

For details write or telephone the office of the Director of Special Markets, Avon Books, Dept. FP, 1350 Avenue of the Americas, New York, New York 10019, 1-800-238-0658.

Blood Red Angel

ADRIAN COLE

AVONOVA

AVON BOOKS • NEW YORK

BLOOD RED ANGEL is an original publication of Avon Books. This work
has never before appeared in book form. This work is a novel. Any simi-
larity to actual persons or events is purely coincidental.

AVON BOOKS
A division of
The Hearst Corporation
1350 Avenue of the Americas
New York, New York 10019

Copyright © 1993 by Adrian Cole
Cover illustration by Duane O'Myers
Published by arrangement with the author
Library of Congress Catalog Card Number: 93-90570
ISBN: 0-380-76889-5

First AvoNova Printing: November 1993

AVONOVA TRADEMARK REG. U.S. PAT. OFF. AND IN OTHER COUNTRIES, MARCA
REGISTRADA, HECHO EN U.S.A.

Printed in the U.S.A.

RA 10 9 8 7 6 5 4 3 2 1

He who is betrayed by his friend is capable of murder;
he who is betrayed by his god is capable of anything.

ZAER PHESMES—from the introduction to
The Book of Renunciation

PRELUDE

It has taken us twenty-two thousand years to realise that the gods have made a critical error in their shaping of our destiny, our genesis.

You may ask, how is it that you who have dispensed with day and night can measure a unit of time? What is a year? How long is twenty-two thousand years? You who have reduced time to a historical quirk, you who ignore the past, deny the future, and look to the moment, how can you speak of twenty-two thousand years?

There are no definitive records, as the Skryers will tell you. Some of them profess to be attuned to energy currents that they call memories, some of them claim to read currents that flow back from a time ahead. Their prophecies are as unreliable as their histories.

There should be at least one great work, one positive contribution to the recording of time. If there were such a record, we could see a pattern quite clearly; I am convinced of that. And it would be a pattern of error, of malfunction, of disarray, its threads stretching back twenty-two thousand years. I have unraveled something of them. I have used every art available to me and I have trawled every stream of energy that my position has opened to me, and more than a few that it has not.

There is no great work, no monument to time's treasures. In the absence of such a work, I begin this, my undertaking.

ZAER PHESMES—from the introduction to
The Book of Renunciation

PREFACE

It was high twilight, the time of maximum permitted light. Under the cloud ceiling that was Skydown, the land out here at the extremes was silent, even at this time. The air was empty and motionless.

Into the silence, from the direction of the heartlands, came the steady beating of wings; they stroked the air in comfortable, rhythmic sweeps. Pink and purple light underlit the belly of the clouds, suffusing the upper air, and in its glow a solitary creature could be seen, swooping effortlessly across the heavens, a great bird or flying reptile. But those who studied the skies from far below knew at once that it was neither.

The Foddaman turned to his two companions, gesturing for them to duck into the thick bank of reeds beside the path. ''Angel Guard!'' he hissed.

They moved at once, smothered by the reeds, holding their breath, their tiny eyes opening as wide as they could in fear, their bodies pressed together for comfort, like mice cowering from a diving bird of prey.

High above them, the Angel Guard had seen them. Its eyes were keener than that of any other creature under Skydown, and could view across remarkable distances; the same was true of its hearing. It had been bred for such skills, the product of countless generations of trial and error.

However, for the moment it did not flex its clawed hands. The farmers were unimportant to it. There were many of them in the outlands, although as this segment's edges were close to the rim of the known lands, there were fewer farms and communities below. Possibly the Angel Guard would drop down to the farmers later, to interrogate them, if it could not find what it sought.

So far there had been no sign of the runaway Externals. But the world under Skydown was alien to them: they would not be able to remain undetected for long.

The Angel Guard turned majestically, following a flight path that would turn it inside the perimeter of the rim, which was now no more than fifty miles away. As it banked, it caught a faint flash of light, possibly on water, an ocean perhaps, stretching beyond the rim. There were stories told among the dark brethren of the Angel Guard about this expanse, some said of sand. But the Guard had no desire to study it. It was unlikely that the Externals had found their way over the rim.

Something in the air caused it to pause, hovering perfectly still. It could detect the peculiar metallic smell that heralded the nearness of the Overlap, that curious irregularity in the physical fabric of the world. Whatever caused the Overlap and its utterly unpredictable appearances enabled it to tap the resources of other planes or dimensions, whatever they were. Even the Skryers, the savants, who attempted to rationalise the Overlap and its behaviour patterns, could not be sure of their definitions. The effects of the Overlap, though not completely known, were sometimes exploited by the rulers. They sent out their hunters to reach through the Overlap, to seize Externals, those other-world dwellers. The hunters were very subtle, careful how they chose, equally as careful not to leave a trace behind them. They had never yet been followed back into the world under Skydown.

It was rare that Externals, brought here, should escape and hide themselves in the outer lands. This time the Overlap seemed to have impinged itself on a remote region. The returning hunters may have been careless: a few escaped Externals, especially in these marshy farmlands, would soon be gathered in, or cut down. Usually they would be dealt with locally, but on this occasion there were to be no chances taken, it seemed. Nevertheless, a single Angel Guard would more than suffice. A message was sent to their Eyries. One such Guard had been despatched.

It used the subtle changes in the air to guide itself, eddying downwards, light as a leaf. To its exceptional eyes, the land below became perfectly clear. The marshes stretched indefinitely on all sides, but the Angel Guard was close to one of the enormous roads that reached out from the heartlands and the mother city of Thousandreach to the rim itself: this road was a mile-wide spoke, flattopped and bare, an elevated bank that towered fifty feet above the monotonous reed beds.

It dropped onto the stony surface of the road. Nothing grew on it. It reached back, shrinking to its vanishing point, featureless and grey. The Guard walked lightly to its edge, wings folded back over its shoulders almost to nothing, like a dark, insubstantial cloak. It studied the farmlands. Already it had seen the large farm some miles out across the marsh.

Yes, the Overlap had tainted this place before it slipped away like mist, closing over itself, sealing up any brief vent between realms. But three Externals had feigned near-death, tricked their captors, then slipped beyond the road to brief freedom.

Their deaths would be quick and merciful. Angel Guards lacked the cruelty of their masters. There was no honour in unnecessary suffering.

The Angel Guard had been told by the messengers that the three Externals were possibly dangerous, warriors stolen from a particularly bloody war. Something like a smile crossed its sharp, avian features. Dangerous? To one of the Angel Guard?

This place was far from Thousandreach and the comfort of his home Eyrie. Too far to herd these runaways. A quick death, then. It would draw out their blood and present it to the Providers as evidence of fulfillment of the act. It touched its belt lightly; the instruments had been prepared meticulously.

In the reeds, a hundred yards below the figure, the Foddamen hunched up, breathing very slowly, as if the very sound would bring the terrible creature winging over to them. One of them, Orf, had his mouth close to the ear of one companion.

"It hunts, but not for us. It must know we are here. The Angel Guard have no need of eyes."

"We aren't safe. Nothing is safe from these slaughterers."

"Rubbish, Strud. They have a purpose. They don't waste time. Not on Foddamen."

"Why doesn't it just piss off—"

"Shut your mouth!" Orf hissed in his ear, his coarse hand reaching up for Strud's throat. They could smell the stench of fear on each other, fear that blinded them, made children of them. The mutants of the outer marshes they could face, but the Angel Guard were the spawn of their worst dreams, terror incarnate.

On the road, the figure remained motionless for a while longer, ignoring the sibilant sounds from the reeds, the garbled hysteria of the Foddamen. To the Angel Guard, they were no more worthy of attention that the other things that slithered through the marshes.

High overhead, the clouds began to curdle, closing out what little light had seeped through the cover of Skydown. The Angel Guard looked up, frowning. Storms were common enough; one could sense them, smell their coming from miles away. This seemed a little sudden. A side effect of the Overlap, perhaps?

Normally the Angel Guard would have taken little notice, confident of its ability to negotiate a storm: it was part of its skill, part of its breeding. But it was wary of this place, marred as it might be by the Overlap. It might, after all, be prudent to seek shelter. And possibly the farm might hold clues to the whereabouts of the missing Externals.

Lightning crackled in the near-distance. Again the Angel Guard looked up. Strange hues lit the hanging belly of Skydown. Thunder rumbled uneasily. There was no intimation of rain, no telltale clouds towards the horizon. Thunder usually presaged a downpour. The air here was tight, oddly dry. The Overlap?

The Angel Guard tensed, as if it might be attacked, but still it did not take to the air, its natural element. It had never been near the Overlap, and this was the first time it had visited somewhere that it had passed. Like lightning, it was said never to strike twice in the same region.

The Angel Guard waited. Nearer came another flicker of lightning, a vivid white fork, jagged, searing the eye. In the reeds, the Foddamen had collapsed, whimpering, hands over their heads. The Angel Guard still ignored them, unfolding its wings. It would make for the farm, at least until this bizarre and blasphemous light had passed by. Strange that the gods permitted such forces to exist in a world where light was a sacrilege.

As it made to launch itself from the road, something crackled fiercely on both sides of it, as if the reeds had burst into flame. Light, more vivid and appalling than anything the Angel Guard had ever experienced, flooded the road and surrounding lands and a detonation of thunder resounded directly above him. Something, it may have been the fist of a god, punched the Angel Guard, and it was flung back by the force of the colossal blow, spinning in the air, eyes dazzled by showering sparks of light. Light, the ultimate heresy under Skydown, sacred to the gods above it, Absolute Light.

There was no time to think of sin, of punishment. The light seared all thought. Until, like the totality of midnight, the dark replaced it.

It may have screamed. As light was snatched away, so, too, was consciousness, as sudden as the executioner's blade.

While in the reeds, squirming like worms, the Foddamen would not raise their heads.

"I saw nothing!"

"Praise the dark!"

"Our shield and protector. Praise the dark!"

On their bellies, eyes closed, they wriggled slowly away from the vicinity of the road, searching for the path to the farm and dubious sanctuary.

ONE

RUARHI

Of course, there are no gods.

What we call gods are merely beings who wield more power than other beings: how jealously they protect the knowledge that keeps them puissant!

There are numerous methods of maintaining this self-styled godhood, though principally it is achieved through the use of fear. Absolute power has its roots in absolute fear.

Gods also sustain themselves through the faith of their subjects, for faith has its promised rewards. Belief in these rewards, this ultimate desire, drives all lesser beings upwards.

After all, what greater goal is there than to be one with the gods? Who would not be a god himself?

ZAER PHESMES—*The Book of Renunciation*

1

The man opened his eyes slowly, so that the daylight couldn't make his splitting headache any worse than was necessary. But mercifully it was night, or soon would be. The skies were tainted with a purple light: either the sun had just gone down, or it was obscured behind the canopy of massed clouds. Their formation was bizarre, like an assembly of gigantic spars or arches in an immeasurable cavern.

His arm throbbed. He could feel the crust of dried blood from biceps down to wrist. The flesh was stiff and cold. He tested his fingers: thankfully they moved. He raised the arm. An ache rather than a stabbing pain. The wound would heal.

He was a warrior. He needed to check his body over first, before he tried to comprehend the events of the day, this strange place he was in. There were cuts, a bruise on his side which would make him wince for days yet, and a throbbing head, but he'd had worse. And he was young enough to recover.

Satisfied, he studied his surroundings. A thick screen of reeds closed in on him, affording him a poor view. He had been crashing through them, ankle-deep in muddy water, falling here, dazed. It had been dark at the time, so there was no way of telling how long he'd been unconscious.

The reeds were tightly packed, but that was as well. He had them to thank for his being alive, or at least free. Strange, they didn't as much as waver. There was no breeze. Long grey stalks, with thicker upper stems, their true colour darkened by the twilight. He shifted his position. He was on a flattened bed of them, at least out of the cold water, but he couldn't remain here. Soon he'd move.

He closed his eyes. *Just a little more strength. Get me through this night and back to more familiar territory, out of this pitiless hell.*

His immediate memories crowded each other at once.

An army, cresting the hill, moving with confident stealth forward over scrubby terrain. Beyond that disciplined press of ten thousand warriors, the enemy had camped in the rough hill fort, hastily constructed as they retreated from an earlier defeat. The MagMannochs were coming for the final triumph, their blood up, victory a sweet smell in their nostrils. Up in the crumbling stones, their enemy King Kestegar of the Crummlaag, knew the days of his tyranny were over. But the old bastard wasn't going to surrender. He knew the MagMannochs would butcher him and his thanes. Still, he'd make a fight of it and leave the Crummlaagen families with some shred of pride.

Darrac could imagine the breathing of the MagMannochs around him now, as he lay back on his rough reed bed. He moved with the warriors, could smell their acrid sweat, as they came under the shadow of the fort. Beside him were Ruarhi and Dromator, his half cousins. Like him, they were daubed in mud, eyes gleaming in the first rays of the dawn. They were eager to bring down the despot, but this was the killing time, and fear flowed out of their pores as it did with every warrior.

Ruarhi, the youngest of them at twenty, spat on his flat

blade, grinning as though amused. Through the long weeks of killing and pursuit, his humour had sustained Darrac and Dromator when their nerves were rubbing raw. The boy was well muscled, his skin like cured hide, dark and rough, his flesh hard as stone.

He should have been a hunter, Darrac remembered thinking, as though he'd sensed before the battle that the youth was about to die. Not a warrior. He's no coward, but he has a better brain than the other MagMannoch killers. Too many of them are in this for the sport of it, using the blood god as an excuse for slaughter. And when the tyrant falls, what of them? How long before they become the scourge of the land?

But Darrac had his duty. He had returned Ruarhi's grin, though mirthlessly, and nodded to Dromator. The latter was tall and thickset: he had been battle-scared at fifteen, when he had been with his father, a mercenary, fighting in another land. He'd lost his father in some obscure tribal war, returning without the promised fortune. But his own god of war sustained him, his belief like a torch before him. Thirty now, he knew little but war, glad of the company of Darrac and the youth. He, at least, would survive the day, unless ill luck waited for him in the rocks.

It had followed the pattern of such things, that bloody affray. After the long wait, the creep forward to position, the bleeding of dawn light, the battle had raged furiously, everything a blur. So fast. Screams, blood, swords clashing, standards raised and cut down. Bodies hurling into one another. Madness and bloodlust, a frenzied joy, the release of something ancient and dark within them all, a grim craving satisfied. Blood for the god, crushed souls for the pits of Hellesvaar and its demons.

The slaughter on Hanging Tor had been terrible that day. Like a dozen battles in one cauldron. No quarter. The stink of blood, urine, and faeces had been overpowering. Darrac coughed where he lay now as he thought of it. The dead piled up, men of both armies, but the cornered king was fighting his last. The press of bodies to get at him and his remaining faithful few had been crazy. In the end, live men were trampled, men of both sides.

When Darrac and his two companions finally got down

from the hill, searching for a stream to clean themselves up, they were exhausted. Caked in filth, they resembled the walking dead. At last, beside the icy water, they looked into each other's eyes. The shame of the killing had died down. Instead they were able to laugh the false, loud laughter of relief, collapsing on the grass. Around them on the slopes lay the slain, and the living, for others had dropped with exhaustion, a grotesque partnership. The killing madness had passed.

Up on the hill, the burning had started, and already the fallen king had been tossed on to his pyre with a hundred other men. The stench was almost unbearable. Darrac wriggled to the stream and plunged his face under the water.

Ruarhi and Dromator were bruised, but had little more than aches and minor cuts to nurse. Darrac had taken a wound in his left biceps, a jagged rip. It was a blessing that it had come near the end of the battle. He bathed it and wrapped it as well as he could in cloth ripped from a dead man. Dromator, used to the rough physic of the field, made sure the wound was correctly tidied.

As they had stretched out on the grass, smoke billowed over them, thick and choking, but no one had the energy to leave that place of carnage.

Some hours later, partially rested, Darrac had seen figures moving through the billowing smoke. Looters, he assumed. Like the crows that always came, they were a part of any aftermath. He grinned as he saw some of the supposed corpses spring up, outraged.

Ruarhi was scowling down the slope. Darrac could see the youth's expression even now. Not one of horror, but one of unease, real surprise. Ruarhi pointed, slipping his blade from its sheath. Darrac looked to where he was pointing. The looters were almost upon them, veiled in smoke. There were a dozen of them. But they were no normal looters. They wore armour, metal? These were not waifs of the hills.

"Who in Hellesvaar are these?" snarled Dromator, getting up.

Out of the smoke came three of the strange warriors. Their armour was so closely fitted, it seemed like a second skin. They wore equally tight helms, with a single slit for the eyes, and where the mouth of the visor should have been there was a tube that reached back behind the shoulder into the armour suit. And the weapons that they held were unlike any the three men had ever seen before. Strapped to the arm, they were twin-pronged, knives with barbed edges.

These warriors gestured the men up. Their eyes were invisible. Behind them in the mist, others of their kind were rounding up fallen men, wounded and fit alike. There was something unnatural in the movements of the armoured warriors, something surreptitious, but confident.

Dromator leapt up with a curse, hacking with his sword. It took the first of the warriors by surprise and the blade clanged against the metal of his arm. But the being swung his own cruel steel and scored a line along Dromator's naked belly. Dromator toppled back, only to be clubbed by another warrior behind him.

"They don't want us dead," Darrac had told Ruarhi.

"Are they Kestegar's mercenaries? Don't they know we've roasted their king?" said Ruarhi.

The strange warriors made no sound, but they indicated what they wanted. Darrac and his companions were to follow them. Darrac nodded: they had better accede. Furious, but too tired to protest, they threw down their swords.

If anything, the smoke was thickening, turning the early afternoon into a gloomy evening, twilight. Darrac, Ruarhi, and a surly Dromator allowed themselves to be herded down the slope, away from the scene of the battle.

Herded. A curious word, but it had been apt, Darrac reflected now.

The unnatural darkness of the day had worsened, the limits of vision closing right in. But it was still not a time for heroics. These warriors had only to stand together and the prisoners, for so Darrac thought of them, would be cut to pieces, like so much meat.

There had been several groups of MagMannoch warriors: some of them glanced across at each other, utterly baffled by developments, others staring at the ground, nursing wounds, too worn out even to mouth a protest. Darkness came down again, like the blanket of a bad dream.

Darrac shuddered, opening his eyes. The motionless reeds were still before him. No dream. This land seemed comprised of nothing else. He listened. Silence. Perhaps a vague movement of water.

Where the land of the high moor around Hanging Tor had given way to these endless reed beds, Darrac could not say. He had known nothing of them, and wondered if the ancient gods of his people had sent their avatars to collect him and others. Maybe he and Ruarhi and Dromator had actually fallen in the fight? Not survived at all. This was the afterlife? But he had not believed it then, nor did he now. It was the sort of dark vision Dromator would have accepted.

Wherever they were, they were not safe. The warriors who were herding them and the two score other MagMannochs were not allies. They had come for blood and, in time, would want it.

Darrac, Ruarhi, and Dromator had made their break for freedom at a place where the narrow path curved. They had staged a mock fight with one another, each pretending to be mortally wounded, sprawling in the reeds beside the path. The armoured warrior ahead of them seemed to be taken in by the deceit at first. He bent down to examine Dromator, who rammed his elbow into the guard's abdomen: the warrior pitched off the path into the reeds. They tangled about him as he fell, snaring him for vital moments.

Darrac had not paused to listen to the growls of protest, though he knew at once that they were sounds that issued from no human mouth. Instead he was off into the reeds, smashing them aside as he ran. It was difficult work, and he could hear the rasping of his own breath. Close at hand he could also hear the trampling of reeds as his companions broke ranks and fled. There were howls of anger from the direction of the path: the hunt was on.

Darrac had been impeded by the reeds. His bandage ripped off, his arm bleeding anew, but he pressed on for as long as he had strength. Ruarhi and Dromator must have veered off; he couldn't hear them. But mercifully he couldn't hear the pursuit closing either.

Now, in the growing dark, he felt he had eluded those hellish warriors. Where were they from? And where in all the hells was this place? An underworld? Hellesvaar itself? But surely that was a myth. He studied the sky overhead. It was faintly striated with pink light, as if behind the ceiling of clouds, a bloody sun was hidden. The upper world, was that it? Was that where the rightful MagMannoch lands were?

As he watched, he felt a lethargy creeping over him. No, he must not let that happen! He must get as far from here as he could. He writhed to his knees.

Before him, the reed heads nodded. As he watched them, he saw their long upper stems begin to open, peeling back. He gaped at what followed. Narrow, white heads opened out, with slitted, blind eyes. Below each pair of eyes another segment of reed opened, to produce an orifice. Two dozen of them, each with a tongue that unfurled as he watched, pink and sticky, creating an illusion of serpentine malevolence.

Appalled, he turned, only to find that another line of reeds at his back had also opened to reveal the nightmarish minia-ture heads. Their tongues flicked out, and those pallid eyes, though seemingly blind, fixed on him.

He felt the first caress on his naked skin, spun round to meet it. There were dozens of the things. Every reed was a potential enemy. And they would feed. Something under the water caught at both his feet, dragging him onto his back.

The tongues wove towards him. Soon they were all over him, inside him, drinking, draining.

2

"Is it a camp?" whispered Ruarhi.

Beside him, hidden by the reeds and resting on his belly, Dromator peered from cover across the marsh to the strange buildings they had discovered on their flight from the path. The big man shook his head, though more in puzzlement than denial. "I can't see movement. No guards."

They both watched closely. The buildings were long and

low, unfamiliar, the walls featureless; they seemed to have been shaped from the dark mud of the marsh, hardened like resin. The roofs were, not surprisingly, woven from the endless reeds, almost flat. The men could discern four buildings, three of them apparently annexes to one broad central one. They were partly raised up from the reed beds on a bare expanse of soil or mud. There were various thicknesses of pipe protruding from the dull walls, some no thicker than the reeds, others as thick around as a man's waist. They all curled down into the mire itself, but there were no other features. No torches burned outside.

Ruarhi and Dromator were used to being patient. War had taught them how much their lives depended on the ability to wait. After an hour, they had seen nothing to suggest the buildings were in use. There were no sounds of pursuit, nor had Darrac found his way to them. He may have to take his chance alone in this alien terrain. There were many things the warriors wanted to discuss, but they conducted their vigil in almost total silence.

Dromator nudged his young companion, indicating with his eyes that he had at last seen something. Ruarhi followed the line of his gaze. Figures!

But they were so strange! Ruarhi scrutinised them in the poor light. There were three of them, trudging along what could have been a path towards the buildings. At first he wondered if they were overgrown children, but then saw that they were not. They were broad of shoulder, with misshappen faces, wrinkled like those of very old men, though the peculiarly muscular bodies suggested they were relatively young. Over their backs had been slung bundles of reed and rush, tightly tied. Now and then the last of them would turn and look out at the marshes, an expression akin to fear on his wizened face. Clearly he expected to see pursuit of some kind. But none showed itself, and the odd figures passed beyond the far end of the buildings out of sight.

Ruarhi and Dromator had no need of words. Again they would wait.

Silence and darkness closed in. They began to feel the cold of the marsh, seeping through their leggings. It was impossible to get dry, and there was no shelter other than the reeds.

But before they were forced to break cover and investigate the buildings, there was more activity. From out of the marshes some two hundred feet from their hiding place, the armoured warriors suddenly emerged, herding their prisoners. Those they had captured looked even more exhausted, coated in mud and filth, their heads bent as they staggered, knee-deep in mire, towards the buildings. Yet not so long ago they had been victorious in the field.

Ruarhi and Dromator shrank back as far as they could into cover. The alien warriors looked even more dreadful in this light. The skintight metal armour, with its tubes and fitted war helms, looked like the outer carapace of insects, and the twin-pronged weapons seemed far more effective than the puny swords the MagMannochs had carried. Ruarhi felt there was no denying the monstrous power of these warriors, no challenging it.

Their prisoners were moved through the marsh to the buildings, where, like the reed-gathers of earlier, they went out of sight, the last warrior pausing only to study the marsh briefly.

Ruarhi felt as though a cold serpent wriggled inside his belly. The only hope of comfort had rested in those buildings; now it was clearly impossible to explore them.

"Let's get out of here," he muttered. "There must be somewhere else, a way back to our own lands."

Dromator, surprisingly, shook his head. "Ruarhi, I don't understand what's happened to us. But the gods have manipulated us in some way. There may be no path back to the MagMannoch lands."

"What do you mean?"

"Look at the sky. D'you ever see the like? And these people. Half-men, warriors like demons. This is a land of legend."

"You think we died on Hanging Tor?" Ruarhi grinned. "Why, man, I'm not dead! I'm as alive as I ever was."

"Maybe we're between lives."

Ruarhi thought better of arguing. Dromator was far more superstitious than he was. He still made small offerings to the gods privately. It was not something a man mocked. Least of all where this fierce mercenary was concerned.

"So what do we do?"

Dromator shrugged. "There'll be food in those buildings. It'll be night soon enough. We need provisions. Who knows how far we have to travel? We can't risk leaving without food. The hunting might be poor. There'll be no meat in these marshes."

Ruarhi's grin faded. "Aye, you're right."

"So we wait."

"As long as we don't freeze first. There must be somewhere drier."

The twilight lasted far longer than they expected; but for the next two hours they watched the buildings. There were still no signs of life: the warriors and their prisoners might have passed on to another world. But at length Dromator was prepared to move.

Stealthy as hunting cats, he and Ruarhi slunk through the water, using the cover of the clumps of reed. They waited, wanting to be sure that they had not been seen, knowing that there was a chance that something watched from within the walls. Then, at Dromator's signal, they slid like otters up the mudbank and came under the shadow of the walls. Rather than take the path followed by the half-men and later the warriors, they crept around the other end of the long building to one of its annexes, a squat outhouse.

They could find no door. The annex had been grafted onto the long building, and like it, had no windows. There were several immense vats beside it, which they guessed to be water tanks, and what appeared to be unused pipes. They were cut from very hard material but were too big and unwieldy to make weapons.

"Maybe we could get on the roof and rip some of it open?" suggested Ruarhi.

Dromator nodded slowly. He inspected the vats for a foothold. As he did so, Ruarhi tugged at his arm, dragging him into cover behind another of the conical containers. They held their breath as a figure shuffled across the space between the buildings.

It came into sight and they felt their muscles relax slightly. It was one of the half-men. The light was very poor, but they could see its outline. It seemed to be deformed in some way, as though movement was an effort for it, and its face drooped, its misery undeniable. Such a creature could only be a slave, like a beast of burden, part man, part ox.

Dromator glanced briefly at Ruarhi, nodding, then stepped up behind the half-man and put an arm about his neck, the other about his mouth, dragging him back into the darkness under the eaves. The figure kicked and struggled, but when its huge eyes caught sight of Ruarhi, it stopped like a rabbit caught in the glow of a night flame. The being reeked of terror.

While Dromator gripped the creature, Ruarhi made simple gestures that made it obvious he wanted food, pointing to his mouth and chewing in an exaggerated way that made Dromator grin for a moment. At first it seemed that the half-man had gone into shock and would be incapable of doing anything, but at last he nodded understanding.

"Hold on to him," Ruarhi said, but Dromator gave him a look that suggested he had no intention of doing otherwise.

Ruarhi guided them to the wall of the annex beyond the vats. He again gestured to the prisoner, this time making it as clear as he could that he wanted to find a door. If not, they would kill him. The half-man must have understood, for he nodded.

Dromator allowed the being to approach the wall. Ruarhi took cover, wishing he had a weapon, but bunching his fists in case he had to use them. The little man reached out to the bare wall and touched it in a circular motion. Something within the wall groaned and, miraculously, an opening appeared. Faint light spilled out. Dromator pulled his prisoner aside, waiting. But nothing materialized in the soft glow.

Ruarhi waited for a few moments, then crouched and moved to the lip of the doorway. He could see vague outlines within, more pipes, and thick, tubular containers, packed close to the door, obscuring anything beyond. He slipped in, finding himself on a floor of beaten earth, a corridor that ran parallel to the wall for a few yards each side before turning. Quickly he gestured for Dromator to enter, and the latter did so, still not releasing the half-man, whose eyes remained wide in terror. They were milky white, with a dark iris almost as large as the eye itself.

Dromator made him close the door. At once the fugitives were aware of the sounds within the building. They were unusual, more like the sounds heard in a cave system: dripping sounds, the soft stir of water.

Ruarhi touched one of the pipes and recoiled. It was warm, and made of something that felt like leather rather than metal. A closer look revealed hairs sprouting on its surface, like the hair on the skin of a wild boar.

"Do you understand me?" Dromator whispered to his captive, but evidently the half-man spoke some other tongue.

"Either we kill him, or secure him until we've left," Ruarhi said softly. But he knew this was bravado. Killing in battle was one thing, but slaughtering a creature like this, in cold blood, was not fitting, even for Dromator.

"First we get him to feed us. Then we make sure he opens the door to let us out," Dromator grunted. "Fine leader you'd make."

Ruarhi flashed a smile, relieved. "Let's eat."

They made appropriate gestures to their prisoner and he seemed to understand what they wanted, nodding in a universal gesture. Dromator took his hand from the man's mouth and he did not cry out. Ruarhi used gestures to explain that if he did, they would kill him, and again the half-man appeared to understand. Slowly he led them through a maze of narrow pipes and conduits, some of which gleamed like steel, others of which hung like great roots. Both Dromator and Ruarhi felt uneasy in this unnatural place, with its sibilant sounds, its warm, clogged air.

Their guide, who showed no sign of rebellion, though his fear did not abate at all, trudged ahead of them, stopping at last outside a low chamber. He looked this way and that with his great eyes, but, satisfied that they had not been seen, beckoned the men to follow him within.

Soft radiance leaked down from somewhere above and Ruarhi wondered at the strangeness of the glow. What kind of torch could suffuse such even light?

The half-man pointed to what looked like troughs in the centre of the cramped room. Dromator kept by the door in case the half-man made a bolt for it, and nodded to Ruarhi to look.

Ruarhi went to the first trough. He frowned at the contents. They appeared to consist of yeast or something similar, pinkish in the light. A preparation for bread making, but on a large scale? he wondered. He reached down to touch it. It was warm, pliant. He motioned for the half-man to taste it first. Again, the latter understood and bent over the trough. He thrust his thick fingers into it and pulled something from beneath the surface. It was like a small branch, and as it came up, thick strands of dough stretched from it elastically.

Dromator's expression abruptly altered. He was watching the half-man in horror as he prepared to take a bite from the thing he had tugged free. Ruarhi, mildly amused at his companion's disgust, at last realised what it was. Shriveled and discoloured, but recognisable as a human arm.

3

Gurd the Foddaman realised that the men watching him were for some reason disgusted by what he was about to do. Of course, he suddenly thought, if they were newly acquired, they would not be used to fodda, the idea of human food. Ah, but they'd have to get used to it if they wanted to survive. Then something else struck Gurd, whose thoughts always came slowly and stickily, as if being extracted from mud. Could these two be the runaways that the Providers' huntsmen had lost out in the marshes? Must be. They had that familiar look of desperation about them.

He lowered the fodda. No point in incurring their anger. They would be warriors, chosen for that. They'd pull him limb from limb if it suited them. How to trap them? Must be done.

Ruarhi glanced at Dromator, his eyes saying, shall we kill him now and take our chances? There was no question now of being squeamish about killing the vile inhabitants of this world.

Dromator understood the unspoken question perfectly. He shook his head, gesturing for the half-man to lead them away from the chamber. The latter did so, falling into his stoop-shouldered slouch automatically.

"I think we should gag him," said Ruarhi.

Dromator grunted assent, tearing a strip of material from his shirt and tying it tightly around the half-man's lower face before the little being knew what was happening. His eyes widened, but otherwise he made no protest.

He led them through more intricate pipe mazes, the floor sloping downwards steadily, until it opened into a much larger chamber. They were now on a ledge above it, overlooking a long, broad area that must have been partly underground. It was brightly lit by glowing globes that were suspended from the ceiling beams, miniature suns that fascinated the warriors. But they drew back into as much shadow as they could in order to study the chamber. A cold gust of terror threatened them as they gaped at the vision below them.

Processions of tanks and vats stretched as far as the eye could see, all linked by the ubiquitous pipes, which twisted and curled, some rising to the ceiling, others burrowing into the earth. Some were jet black, like beaten armour, others were translucent as the stalks of plants, and fluids raced through them, varying in colour from a milky white to the dark of pitch. But it was not the alien machinery which horrified Dromator and Ruarhi. They had found their companion MagMannochs, and other survivors of the battle of Hanging Tor, though both wished they had been spared the discovery.

Some fifty of them were below. Tied—chained?—to the vats. Most of them were unconscious, possibly even dead, slumped back, their bodies naked, skin opened up at belly, arm, or thigh. And from their bodies protruded thin tubes, attached to the sides of the vats. Ruarhi gasped as he noticed some of the warriors had been suspended upside down, dripping blood, like butchered cattle, their arms pulled outwards by thin wires so that they made inverted crucifixes of their victims. Other men had been stretched out on metal sheets, their heads wrenched backwards so far that their necks had been completely exposed, opened up like gaping mouths. But there was no blood, as if the men had been leeched.

There was worse in this hellish place. A few of the warriors had had all their limbs removed; a row of arms hung from steel hooks at one side of the chamber. The real horror, Ruarhi saw, was that none of the warriors was necessarily dead. Some were evidently alive, their eyes wide, as if they were studying an even worse nightmare, if such a thing existed.

"We must get them out of there!" he said instinctively, though he almost choked on his words.

Dromator was thinking of the arm in the vat, the food that had been offered. Gods, was *this* where it had come from? He tried to shake the image from his mind. "Weapons, Ruarhi. We need weapons."

"Are those men drugged?" Ruarhi answered, trying to cling on to his reason, feeling it bend under the stress of this appalling place.

Dromator looked about him, his face glistening with sweat. Behind him there were a number of pipes, connecting two thick tubes, and some of the piping was made of thin metal. He gripped it and tugged. At first it resisted him, but then he felt it buckling. He heaved, his biceps knotting.

The half-man looked as though he would flee in horror at this sacrilege, but Ruarhi blocked his retreat, angry now, eager for a target. Dromator gave another great heave and the pipe burst, ripping free of the left vat in a shower of thick, dark fluid. Quickly Dromator dragged another length of pipe free. He held both up; they were no longer than swords, their ends splintered.

"It's a start," Ruarhi said grimly, taking one. As he spoke, one of the tanks ruptured, a wave of fluids cascading from it, and something solid, a shape that flopped on to the ground, writhing like a huge, leprous fish. But it was human in form, though its head was hugely bloated, features distorted beyond recognition. As it contorted, two white eyes rolled up in that face, blind but accusing.

"Gods of darkness, is it one of our men?" said Ruarhi, throat constricting.

Dromator was shaking his head. "I don't think so." He

gripped the arm of the half-man, gesturing for him to take them down into the chamber. He thought the being might argue or show greater fear, but instead it nodded.

They followed. Several yards further on there were steps leading down to the vat area. Dromator made the half-man lead the way. At the foot of the steps, other figures at last emerged from the chamber's interminable maze of pipes. There were three of them: two were very much like the half-man, squat and muscular, with faces that suggested great age. They could have been the beings that Ruarhi and Dromator had seen from the reeds.

The third figure was unlike any of them and far more disturbing. Tall as a man, for some reason almost naked, he was emaciated, his skin like wrinkled paper, his bones visible like knobs under it, so that his flesh was like a garment. His head was too big for such a frail body, his lips thin and bloodless, his nose a vertical gash. By far the most bizarre aspect of his appearance were the lengths of fleshlike tubes that hung from, *grew out of,* the back of his head and neck. Some of them swung freely, like so many thick tresses, but others fused with his flesh down their length, or curled out only to reenter the body below the shoulder and at the base of the spine. The eyes were as large and clear as those of his companions: they fastened on the intruders angrily, and he clenched his bony hands as if he might be contemplating an attack.

Dromator lifted his makeshift weapon. He would welcome the chance to split that horrific head open.

"You must be the missing ones," came the voice of the tall being, using their own tongue and completely taking Ruarhi and Dromator by surprise. "Where is the third?"

Neither man spoke.

The voice was soft but cold. As the man spoke, the cluster of strange growths pulsed like living organisms. His accent was slurred, though he controlled the language well, as if he used it often. "No matter. We'll find him. And you can throw away your weapons. You won't need them here."

"You speak our tongue," said Ruarhi.

"Yes," was the indifferent reply. "But I'm the only one here at the farm who does. A good reason not to kill me."

The voice had hardened; there was no real emotion in it, as though the creature merely said what was necessary, no more.

"Take that thing from Gurd's mouth," he said, pointing to the gag.

Dromator hesitated, but realised the gag would no longer be necessary. He removed it. But neither he nor Ruarhi had any intention of relinquishing their weapons.

"You called this place a farm," said Ruarhi.

"Yes. For fodda. Such farms are common in the outlands of the segments."

"Where is this place?" growled Dromator.

"You are under Skydown. The Overlap snared you. Don't expect to understand. No one understands the Overlap and how it works. This is not your world."

"And these men?" said Ruarhi. "What is being done to them?"

The creature shrugged. "The Providers will decide. Some will work, some will remain here—"

"As what?" snarled Dromator, suddenly stepping forward and clutching his weapon as if he would drive it into the strange man.

"If it is explanations you want, you can have them. It is all one. You are quite welcome here. There is a place for you."

"As prisoners?" cut in Ruarhi acidly.

"Under Skydown, we all serve. We belong to the Providers."

"I serve the MagMannoch clan," said Dromator caustically, and Ruarhi realised it was the first time he had ever seen the burly warrior losing his grip. The horrors of this place had cut him to the quick, even more so than they had Ruarhi. He had been in the worst kind of conflict, seen bloodletting that would turn a youngster's mind, but this realisation of his hell threatened him more certainly.

"Who are you?" Ruarhi asked the spindly figure. "And how is it you speak our tongue?"

"I am Sommoi. I have inner light," he added simply, gently touching the growths on his head as though it would explain everything. Seeing that it did not, he expanded. "Thoughts are like light waves. Sometimes they can be siphoned, absorbed, tasted. From the thoughts of the Mag-Mannochs I have filtered enough to comprehend language.''

"You listen to our *minds?*" said Dromator, bemused.

"Only certain things. If I let all the light into me, it would kill me. I have admitted enough to learn your language. I am not an Elevate," he added with a certain bitterness, though the reference was lost on the men.

Ruarhi tried to mask his suspicions: if Sommoi could read minds, and in this world, who knew that he did not? then he would already know that Ruarhi and Dromator intended to free their brothers. Sommoi would have tasted red murder in their minds. But it did not show on his face.

"Are you in command of this farm?" Ruarhi asked him.

"In a way. But I am no less a servant than these Fodda-men.''

"Release the men you have," said Dromator. "Those who are alive.''

"None of them are dead," said Sommoi in his dispassionate way. "Dead, they would pollute the fodda.''

Dromator lifted his weapon and brought it close to Sommoi's chest. "Some of them have been mutilated," he said, his voice like a knife. "They would be better dead. Those that can walk, you free now.''

"If they become unattached, they die within moments. They are part of the system now. Free them and their organs will cease to function.''

For a moment Ruarhi thought that Dromator would drive his weapon into the face of Sommoi: he could feel Dromator's fury like a blast of hot air.

"MagMannochs!"

The shout rent the air. Ruarhi and Dromator swung round as if they had been set upon, crouching like wolves about to fight to defend themselves. But it was not an attack. They saw at once who had shouted.

Over one of the tanks, hanging from a metal spar, one of the warriors had called out. He was partially immersed in thick, viscous liquid, only his chest and upper body free of it, glistening as if oiled. He hung by his arms, his muscles stretched taut as if they would split open like pods; his face wore a look of ghastly torment.

"Don't let him touch you! Hands of Hellesvaar! Keep them off you, or you'll suffer as we do! It's a trap!"

Dromator felt the movement behind him, swiveling with deceptive speed. Sommoi had been reaching out, his hand extending to become an elongated claw. Dromator reacted instantly, bringing his weapon down against the wrist with devastating force. He felt bone snap like dry wood.

Sommoi let out a piercing shriek, huge eyes almost popping from his head. The claw hung uselessly. He gripped it with his free hand, clinging to the wrist.

Ruarhi watched in fascinated horror as the damaged hand came away from the arm, dropping to the floor like the discarded end of a slowworm. Sommoi still held his wrist, trying to stem the flow of blood. He seemed to have succeeded, for only a little dark fluid ran out from his fingers as he doubled over.

"Watch him!" Dromator hissed, and Ruarhi nodded, holding his weapon up for the Foddamen to see. None of them moved, their utter bemusement gluing them to the ground. They were as useless in this affair as cattle.

Dromator moved around the side of the vat, searching for a hold that would enable him to climb up to its broad rim. There were metal protrusions, and putting his weapon in his mouth, he swung upwards. Once on the rim, he carefully inched his way around it towards the suspended warrior. He could see that the man was secured by rope made from coarse fibres and that it would be impossible to part the rope without a blade. It was only as he reached for the man's arm that he realised the fibres had eaten into the flesh, as if they had *taken root*.

He looked up at the beam, some twenty feet overhead. The rope had not been tied to it, but emerged from it like roots. He dared not break it, even if he could.

"Kill me," whined the voice of the man.

Dromator faced him, the dreadful look in the man's eyes. Slowly he raised his pipe weapon. One savage blow to the skull would do it. A merciful death. No MagMannoch should suffer anything worse.

"It will not kill him," said a voice almost beside Dromator. He turned, expecting to see Sommoi on the vat's brim, but he was still down below, guarded by Ruarhi. "No matter what you do to him, you will not kill him. Unless you sever the arterial cords. You are unable to do that."

"But you can!" Dromator shouted, abruptly walking along the brim. Ruarhi watched, horrified, as his friend almost slipped, careless of the danger now. But anger had given Dromator strange powers of balance; he made his way round the vat to the place above Sommoi and dropped, landing perfectly and straightening up.

"You can free them all, or I'll reduce you to pulp, by all the blackest gods in this hell!"

Ruarhi knew that Dromator was close to the breaking point. After all these years of war, of tireless bloody conflict, he had found his ultimate nightmare here. His reason was about to swing away from him. Ruarhi had already seen warriors buckle under the strain: Dromator was showing all the signs of disintegration. Ruarhi gripped his arm, fingers biting deep into the flesh.

"Hold down your rage, Dromator. We need this creature—"

Sommoi, who had been watching them closely, turned jerkily as footfalls came up the corridor behind him. Ruarhi could see another of the Foddamen arriving, breathless.

The squat figure paused to gape at the two men, but evidently even they were less of a concern to it than the news it brought.

"What is it, Strud?" said Sommoi.

The Foddaman spoke in words that were no more than meaningless grunts to Ruarhi and Dromator. But Sommoi listened keenly.

"We have seen—" began Strud, eyes bulging, "we have seen—one of the—"

"One of the what?" urged Sommoi, at last showing some sign of losing his calmness.

"Angel Guard," gasped Strud. He had seen Sommoi's severed hand, staring at it with an almost lunatic bafflement. Sommoi, however, appeared to have dismissed it. He was in no pain.

"Where?"

"It fell."

"Fell?" The word bit like acid.

Strud winched. "Orf and Trun saw it, too. On the road. There was light. Fire from the sky."

"Is it wounded?"

"We ran. Afraid."

Sommoi scowled, his face suddenly demonic. "You must take me there. At once. If we fail the Angel Guard, there will be retribution—for all of us!"

"What's wrong?" interrupted Ruarhi impatient to understand what was obviously a vital exchange.

"You want to meet someone in real authority?" said Sommoi tartly. "This will be an opportunity for you."

Dromator answered swiftly. "Is this person responsible for this—*farm?* Does he command those metal-clad warriors?"

"The Angel Guard are the elite," said Sommoi. "Their word is law to us all, and never disobeyed."

"Then we'll meet, and talk," said Dromator, though his mind could be read easily enough by Ruarhi, never mind the oddly gifted Sommoi.

"This is a trap," said Ruarhi. "But you'll be the first to die."

"No one need die," said Sommoi impatiently.

"We'll see. Bring him here."

"I cannot. He is injured. We must go to him."

Dromator swore obscenely. "Like the boy says, it's a trap!"

Sommoi unexpectedly stepped closer to him. "You can kill me with one blow. That is your guarantee that this is no trap. We must go to the Angel Guard."

Their eyes locked, and Ruarhi could have sworn that Dromator would go berserk, a mad hound unleashed. But he turned away, content instead to spit loudly.

"You will die if you betray us," promised Ruarhi.

Sommoi merely nodded.

4

Sommoi made no attempt to summon other servants to the search for the one he called the Angel Guard: it was enough that he had the lone Foddaman, Strud, as his guide. Ruarhi felt even more suspicious of his intentions, but Dromator had become so impatient to be on with the business that they agreed to start out at once.

"You will not need the weapons," Sommoi told them again.

"Just lead us to this commander," grunted Dromator.

Ruarhi was concerned that his judgement could be impaired by the effects of what they had seen. The buildings had yielded up an appalling truth, but this was no time to give way to the wild anger of battle. It would need a cold, almost cynical, calmness to get them out of this predicament. Dromator, however, looked ready to strike out at any passing shadow, almost as though he would invite death itself as a release.

Sommoi cloaked himself, covering his thin body but leaving his head with its growths free. He led the way out of the buildings, following a narrow path along a slightly raised mudbank, through the endless sea of reeds. Strud, his face a study of misery and apprehension, led off, with Sommoi behind him. Ruarhi kept close enough to him to use his makeshift weapon if he had to, while Dromator insisted on bringing up the rear, covering their backs. Though the light was poor, it now being night, neither Strud nor Sommoi seemed to have difficulty seeing their way, as if they were blessed with some form of night vision.

"Tell me something about this world," Ruarhi said.

"What do you wish to know?"

"Does it have a king?"

"No. Beyond Skydown, there are gods—"

"Skydown?"

Sommoi indicated the heavens, now a thick blanket, starless and impenetrable. "We are hidden from the gods by a shield, which we call Skydown. Absolute Light dwells beyond it. Very little of their gift ever penetrates, dependent on their will. We worship Absolute Light, which is why light is used only sparingly and for certain purposes. Some light is permitted at the foddafarm, but it is not a natural light, and serves the purpose of the rulers."

Ruarhi tried to grasp the concept of a world of perpetual darkness. Enforced?

"There are legends that once the world was brightly lit by the gods, before they imposed Skydown."

"Why was it done?"

"As a punishment. For the sins of the people."

"What sins?"

Sommoi snorted impatiently. "Better that others tell you. If you are to survive under Skydown, you'll learn."

Ruarhi waited for him to go on. The reeds almost enveloped them, strangely silent, like ranks of warriors waiting some signal to advance. They exuded the same atmosphere of tense expectancy that had clung to the warriors on Hanging Tor before the battle. Ruarhi suddenly thought of Darrac. Was he still lost out there?

"At the heart of our lands, lies the city of Thousandreach," Sommoi went on. "It is an immense place, far greater than anything known to your people, the Mag-Mannochs. It is where the Lightbenders rule the world under Skydown. The Lightbenders are the most elevated of our people: they are destined to become one with the Absolute Light beyond. Their families dwell in the higher bastions of Thousandreach, from which they maintain Skydown. Absolute Light works through them, providing them with great powers. All other life-forms are subservient to the Lightbenders. Their purpose is to keep the light from us.

"Thousandreach is said to rise up to the very clouds of Skydown. In its stepped magnificence there are many levels. It is possible for ordinary creatures of the world, such as myself, to be recognised as worthy enough to rise up through these social layers, though history suggests that such movement takes several generations. To become an Elevate, a servant of the Lightbenders, is the dream of all of us." Sommoi said this mechanically, but there was an edge to his voice, as if the words were distasteful to him.

"It doesn't explain why my people have been captured and mutilated," said Ruarhi coldly.

"We are in the outermost reaches of one of the many segments, far from Thousandreach. These are the lands of the foddafarms. It is our duty to harvest fodda for the Providers, who are, like the Elevates, privileged."

Ruarhi felt the stirring of a far deeper terror, something primitive and cruel, like a half-seen demon stalking the inner halls of his mind. Reaching upward. "Harvest?"

"The world under Skydown provides abundant fodda—"

"Fodda? What is fodda?"

"The lower orders. Those who are not Elevates." Sommoi said it with little show of emotion, but he was aware of Ruarhi's growing disgust.

"*Food?*"

"It is not so simple. Fodda can be used as nourishment. But there are many other uses to which it is put. You may yet learn of this, but not here."

Ruarhi felt again the reach of the demon, but closed it out. This world was a place of madmen! People as food! And worse?

"When the Overlap comes, the Providers sometimes send their huntsmen through it to find men of other worlds, such as yours."

"The Overlap?"

Sommoi shrugged. "An anomaly. It is not fully understood, but seems to be the result of an accident, a remote war, perhaps, which opens doors, corridors between realms. Certain Providers study it and its erratic movements."

"And my people have been their prey?"

Sommoi nodded, as though this was a natural thing and he saw no reason to try to justify it. "In the lowlands around Thousandreach, foddafarms abound, but in these remote segments there are fewer. Experiment is more common where the Lightbenders know least what occurs.''

"Then this hunting is illegal?''

"No. But it is harder to monitor here. Use of the Overlap is very dangerous. Some of the Lightbenders would forbid it altogether, in view of the potential threat to the world. If the wrong world was exploited, who knows what might be unleashed under Skydown?

"But the Providers cannot resist the lure of the Overlap. The Lightbenders accept it, up to a point, but watch closely. Through the Angel Guard.''

They had come to the edge of the reed beds. Ahead of them the raised path wove across an expanse of dark water to a bigger elevation, a sloping, fifty-foot embankment that had the look of a natural wall, stretching out into the night on both sides, though for how far, Ruarhi and Dromator could not see.

Sommoi pointed to the mound. It was only then that Ruarhi realised that Sommoi's hand, the hand that Dromator had so brutally chopped from him, had been completely restored, regenerating itself. Ruarhi looked carefully but covertly. It was true. Sommoi was in possession of both hands once more. How could this have happened? But in this bizarre world, there would be far worse surprises; he was sure of that much.

"The Angel Guards have many duties. One of them is to police these remote segments from time to time. Since the Overlap was recently active here, one of the Angel Guards has come.''

Dromator caught Sommoi by the wrist as the latter was about to move on. But before he could speak, he, too, realised that Sommoi's hand had regrown. He looked at Ruarhi, who nodded in confirmation. Dromator released the wrist as though he had grasped a serpent.

"We are not as you are,'' said Sommoi in bland response to the men's confusion.

"This Angel Guard, as you call him,'' said Dromator, not wanting to think about the hand. "Why should we come before him? What good will it do us?''

"If you do not, he may hunt you and kill you without question."

"Why?" said Ruarhi.

Again Sommoi shrugged. "I cannot predict the whim of an Angel Guard. You escaped the hunting party sent by the Providers. The Providers may have issued orders for your death."

Dromator swore obscenely, clutching the length of pipe as if he would use it on Sommoi's skull. "You thinking of delivering us to this executioner?"

Sommoi did not seem disturbed by the threat of violence. "If you are to survive under Skydown, I suggest you present your case to the Angel Guard. It may review your position."

"And do what with us?" said Ruarhi. "What are the alternatives?"

"There's no need to assume you would be killed, nor used as your fellows have been. There are other duties you could perform. The foddafarms need supervising. You may be given the opportunity to undertake such work. It will be up to the Providers. The Angel Guard will almost certainly want you presented to them."

"Where? In this city you spoke of?" said Dromator.

"I doubt that you will ever be privileged to see Thousandreach. Creatures like us, of the lower orders, could not expect to get close to the city. No, it would be somewhere along the road, closer in to the heart of the world."

"What about being returned to our world?" said Ruarhi.

Sommoi shook his head. "Unlikely. Who knows where the Overlap will appear next? And if it were to be found, what would the chances be of its opening a corridor to your world again? Very, very small. No, you are fodda under Skydown now. You must accept that."

Ruarhi grimaced at the thought. Sommoi talked of fodda as the MagMannochs talked of cattle.

Dromator looked up at the embankment. "What weapons will this Angel Guard have?"

"Even were it devoid of all weapons, all armour, you could not fight it."

"Why not?"

Sommoi drew in a breath as though having to explain

something to a child who could not grasp the implications of what he was saying. "Nothing can withstand the strength of an Angel Guard. A dozen of you, armed with all the swords you wanted, could not inflict the smallest wound."

Ruarhi shook his head slowly. "Then if this creature decides to execute us, we have little hope of defying it. It won't be interested in our arguments."

"Better that we take to the marshes," said Dromator.

Sommoi frowned. "No. You'll die for certain if you do. Better to risk the decree of the Angel Guard."

"What will you gain?" Ruarhi asked him. "Is there a price on our heads?"

"For finding you and presenting you to the Angel Guard, yes, I will receive commendation. It will help me in my search for promotion, of course."

Dromator spat into the black waters beside them. "I say we take to the reeds again, Ruarhi. And this time I'll open the bastard's skull—"

"We wouldn't get far, I think." Ruarhi's first instinct was to agree, to flee. Even temporary freedom was preferable to the uncertainty of the future with this grotesque culture into which they had stumbled. But would they be killed? Why should the denizens of this world bring them here just to cut them down beside a remote marshland?

While he debated with himself, something up on the embankment stirred. The half-man, Strud, pointed excitedly, the first sign of animation he had shown since leaving the foddafarm.

"What is it?" said Dromator, squinting into the dark.

Sommoi could see figures up above them. "Six others, up on the road."

"Who are they?" said Ruarhi, stepping closer to him.

"Foddamen, like Strud. And two others. Villagers, I think. A reedman and a girl. They have found the Angel Guard."

Dromator pulled Ruarhi aside. "Something is wrong. The half-man was concerned when he came to the farm, as though a disaster had befallen someone."

Ruarhi turned, but Sommoi was facing them both. Their words were no secret to him. Ruarhi smiled grimly. "The

Angel Guard is either wounded, or dead,'' he told Sommoi.
''Can you deny it?''

''You are no fool,'' replied Sommoi.

''You wouldn't have brought us here if the creature had
been unharmed.''

''I would not have had to. It would have found you easily.
The Angel Guards see everything.''

''Then why come?''

''If it is dead, we may all benefit,'' was the cryptic reply.

Ruarhi nodded in the darkness to Dromator. His friend
barely saw. It had to be a trap, they were both thinking. But
if it was, why so elaborate? What were Sommoi's motives?
But they could hardly discuss them, knowing that the strange
being could probably hear even their lowest whispers.

5

Ruarhi and Dromator followed Sommoi cautiously, climbing
the steep embankment up to the road. The figures that were
waiting were agitated, the Foddamen watching Sommoi with
a mixture of excitement and unease, like children caught in
some forbidden activity. Strud approached them nervously,
as if afraid to set foot on the road.

But it was the man who met Sommoi, the one he had called
a reedman. Ruarhi thought at first he must be from his own
world: he was of a similar build and of average height, his
hair cut to shoulder length, as was the fashion among many
of the MagMannochs and other clans. He wore a crude, one-
piece garment of coarse cloth, a long shirt that fell to the
knee. Yet as the man came closer, Ruarhi noted the strangeness of the eyes. They were far larger than a normal man's
eyes, protruding from their sockets in a disquieting way. Was
this a disease, or could it be a natural feature of men of this

wilderness? Ruarhi thought the latter, wondering if it had something to do with the poor light, in view of Sommoi's comment about the shield of the sky. In a world of almost perpetual gloom, men would need strong eyes.

The man glanced dismissively at Ruarhi and Dromator before speaking to Sommoi quickly, heatedly, pointing and gesticulating, punctuating his words with quick glances back along the road. Ruarhi could see nothing in the darkness. The man continued to ignore Ruarhi and Dromator, but the four Foddamen watched them furtively, all of them aware that the two men were armed with the broken pipes. Like Strud, they were docile, and did not ask questions, merely waiting to be told what was happening and what they were expected to do.

Sommoi was speaking rapidly to the man, ignoring the others.

Dromator nudged Ruarhi. "I can't see anything clearly. You think this is a trap?"

Ruarhi smiled grimly. "Seems like a lot of trouble to go to. And they look confused to me." He could see that Dromator was far more tensed up than he had been during the long wait in the reeds, his nerves as taut as they had been before the battle on Hanging Tor. It would not take much to pitch him into a fight. "Let's wait and see what—"

But Dromator grabbed his arm and pointed. There was another figure in the shadows, holding back from the group.

Ruarhi drew in his breath. It was a girl of about his own age. She wore a one-piece garment similar to the man's, the sleeves cut away to the shoulder, and her skin, even in this poor light, was bronzed, as if it had known proper sunlight. Eager to see her face clearly, Ruarhi stepped forward, but Dromator pulled him back gently.

"If this is the creature Sommoi spoke of—"

Ruarhi snorted. "I don't think so—"

Sommoi turned to them, his lip curling as if he might have been given news that pleased him. "The Angel Guard is not far from here. And he is wounded, possibly badly."

"Who are these people?" said Ruarhi.

"The Foddamen were working the reed beds, collecting.

The reedman's name is Festubul. He supervises Foddamen in the reed fields and his village is not far from here."

"And the girl?" said Ruarhi.

"She is Festubul's."

"His wife?"

Sommoi looked vaguely amused. "His mate, I imagine. Work in the reed fields is tedious and monotonous."

"He brought her to amuse himself?"

"So he says."

Dromator's brows knitted. "But you don't believe him?"

"Such things are done. But there is more to this." Sommoi shook his head slowly. "No matter. There are more important things to consider. The Angel Guard. Festubul will show us. I have told him you are overseers from a farm, my subordinates. Will you accept the guise for now?"

Dromator growled, as if about to protest, but Ruarhi answered for him. "Yes. For as long as it suits us."

Sommoi nodded, then turned to Festubul, motioning for him to lead them to the fallen being. Strud had joined the other Foddamen, speaking to them briefly as if they knew each other. Like obedient dogs, they plodded alongside the men. The girl emerged from the shadows and walked at the back of Festubul, using him like a shield. She had long, black hair that fell across half of her face, deliberately obscuring it, and Ruarhi tried again and again to catch a glimpse of her features. Would her eyes be the huge fish-eyes of the man she followed? She had a slim figure, her waist so narrow he thought he could put his hands around it, fingertip meeting fingertip. Her legs were bare and she wore nothing on her feet, her ankles slender, her calves thin but muscled, no doubt from the long walks she was forced to endure in this vast, open terrain.

Festubul glanced back at Ruarhi and Dromator occasionally, as if he did not quite approve of their presence, but he seemed to respect, possibly fear, Sommoi. Certainly the latter's word was law here; Ruarhi could see that much.

A short distance along the wide road, they stopped. The Foddamen hung back, and would undoubtedly have fled the place had they been allowed to. The girl, too, was clearly terrified of what lay ahead. Festubul pointed.

Ruarhi saw the figure, stretched across the road. He did not really know what he had been expecting. A monster, perhaps? But this was a man, or a sort of man, wasn't it? Darkness wrapped it, but it was no larger than a man, its shape and size exaggerated by the voluminous black cloak that spread around it, almost like a shroud.

"It may be dead," said Dromator.

"Let us hope not," said Sommoi.

"You say it might help us?" Ruarhi asked him. "If it lives and we help it recover, surely it would repay us?" He had assumed this must be the plan.

"I would expect as much. But these creatures are a law unto themselves. To them, you and I are the lowest of creatures."

Dromator spat impatiently. "Why do we waste time and words? Kill the creature and remove any potential danger! Here, I'll do it—"

"Wait!" hissed Sommoi, and there was power in the command. "If it is alive and you destroy it, others will know. Then we will all be hunted. Our fate then would be indescribably unpleasant, I assure you."

Dromator tapped the length of pipe against his free palm. "The situation is ludicrous! We cannot kill the creature, we can appeal to it, but it may still attack us. We cannot flee into the marshes because we'd be hunted down. Are we to risk everything on the whim of this creature? I say kill it and be damned!"

"If you had lived for any length of time under Skydown," said Sommoi patiently, "you would realise how dangerous that would be."

"Let's find out if it's alive," cut in Ruarhi, before Dromator did something foolish. "If it's dead, there's an end to the matter."

"I agree," said Sommoi. "But I cannot imagine what power under Skydown could possibly have felled an Angel Guard, let alone killed it."

Festubul said something and Dromator immediately asked for an explanation.

"He asks, who will go to the Angel Guard?" said Sommoi.

Dromator touched Sommoi's chest very lightly with the pipe. "You will. I will stand beside you. If I have to kill you, I will do it."

Ruarhi grinned at Sommoi. "Of course, being the low creatures that we are, no one would notice your death, Sommoi. No one would avenge you."

For a brief moment Sommoi looked mildly amused, but then he shrugged. "You are right. My status is low. I told you, I seek to improve it."

"So do we," smiled Ruarhi.

Dromator indicated the shape on the road. "Come on."

He and Sommoi stepped forward. As they went to the figure, Ruarhi found himself trying to see the girl's face again. Festubul noticed this attention, scowling furiously, and put himself between the youth and the girl, but Ruarhi ignored his indignant expression.

Dromator sensed the growing fears in Sommoi. Whatever these Angel Guards were, they had power.

Sommoi spoke in his own language to the figure, but there was no response. He bent down, squatting on his haunches, and spoke once more. Again there was no reply. Dromator was searching the ground for signs of spilled blood, but as far as he could see, there were none. There were what appeared to be scorch marks on the road, and for the first time, Dromator examined the broad road itself. It was constructed from a hard material, far neater and smoother than anything with which he was familiar. It must be the work of superior craftsmen.

"It is alive," said Sommoi. "But not receptive."

"Is it wounded?" said Dromator. He could see Sommoi hesitating. "Turn it over."

Sommoi reached out with great care, the fingers of the new hand touching the black material spread over the figure. It was not coarse, but smooth, almost rubbery. Dromator at last realised what it was. Not a cloak at all, but a *wing*. As Sommoi gently pulled the being over onto its side, Dromator understood. He saw the tendons of the wing, how they grew from the upper arm of the creature. Yet they were perfectly natural, beautiful. For a moment he felt a stab of envy.

Then he saw the face. It was human, but only vaguely like

that of a man. The eyes were slanted, like the eyes of a huge cat, glazed over, the iris huge, diamond-shaped. The nose was a blunt hook, more like the beak of a hunting bird of prey, and the mouth was a faint gash, the teeth that were just exposed like needles. The shape of the face was narrow, possibly evolved because this was a flying creature, the cheeks sunken, so that the whole aspect was that of a gaunt predator, a hunter well equipped for its work. One of the hands slipped from under the black wing as Sommoi moved the creature, and again Dromator caught his breath. It was a claw, a talon. There were four fingers and a thumb, but they were bony, the nail curving like a hook, but a closer inspection showed something at the wrist, a silver stud. Curious, Dromator reached down and tugged at it. He felt it give, and in a moment had pulled at the talon.

To his amazement he got it loose. It was a superbly constructed glove. Underneath, the flesh was white, the hand almost delicate, a complete contrast to the artificial claw. He stood up with it, examining it. Who could have made such a glove? It looked as if it had been grown rather than cast, its detail stunning.

Sommoi was loosening the tight tunic of the Angel Guard, revealing a thin shirt beneath it, probing the chest for, as Dromator assumed, a heartbeat. There was a wide, black belt, the buckle made of bright metal, possibly silver, and from the belt depended a number of lightweight tools or weapons. Some of them looked like the sort of implements a butcher or hunter would use for flaying or boning his prey. The craftmanship of these things was far beyond anything Dromator had seen before in any of his travels in his own world. He found himself wondering what sort of city this creature had come from. Thousandreach, Sommoi had called it. He gazed along the road, beyond the watchers. Already it called to him.

Sommoi looked up at him. "I cannot revive it, though it lives. Can you smell burning?"

Dromator nodded. "The earth is scorched."

"I heard thunder."

"If this creature was in the air—"

"Usually storms are the blood of the Angel Guard. They thrive in such elemental fury. But I wonder—"

The movement was so sudden, so incredibly fast, that neither of them had time to react to it. One black wing lifted, and in a blur, Sommoi was sent tumbling across the road. Dromator, still clutching the talon glove, gaped as the figure rose up before him. It was taller than he was, its face above him. The eyes were pure yellow, feral, and although he had no more than a second to look into them, he knew that something was wrong. Then he felt the stinging pain of his flesh being sliced open, as though a swordsman had slipped under his guard and found him.

He dropped both the glove and his makeshift pipe weapon: the latter clanged on the road. As he doubled, instinctively, another ripping cut took him, working from lower chest and up under his chin. He flung backwards in reaction, crashing down on the road, knocking the air out of himself. He could not move, his fingers groping upwards like the fingers of a baby. His eyes closed against the growing surge of acute pain, but he was vaguely aware of something standing over him, the sword of his gods.

Ruarhi had seen the sudden flurry of movement, the terrifying slash of talon. He pushed past Festubul and the cowering girl. Sommoi was sprawled on the roadside, dazed, trying to recover. But Dromator was in real trouble. Ruarhi stopped yards from the Angel Guard.

Its head swung round, but as its face turned to his, Ruarhi could see that it was relying on sounds to guide it. It was blind, or else its sight was so bad that it could hardly see. It had struck out at Dromator in confusion, perhaps. Now it waited, its one taloned hand held at its side. Ruarhi gasped as he saw the blood and shreds of flesh clinging to it.

Very slowly he inched closer to the fallen Dromator, who was gasping with pain. The Angel Guard made no move, but it was aware of Ruarhi and his edging forward. Its expression was vacant, but its manner was one of readiness. Gods, but it had been so fast! Sommoi had said it would be.

"Dromator," whispered Ruarhi, clutching his weapon in readiness for an attack. But the answer was no more than a strangled gasp of agony.

Abruptly the Angel Guard bent down, and Ruarhi readied for its spring. But instead it simply retrieved the fallen talon glove. It had not needed sight to find it. As the creature slid it on, Ruarhi glanced down at Dromator. Gods, but he was a mess! Blood soaked his chest and belly, and when he tried to turn his head, an incision in his neck and throat gaped, more blood leaking out.

"Don't move!" came a terse, whispered command from Sommoi, who had struggled to get to his knees. He did not take his eyes from the Angel Guard.

The creature looked his way and at last spoke, the voice another shock to Ruarhi. He had expected something bestial, the growl of an animal, deep throaty sounds in keeping with the manner of this monster. Instead, the voice was amazingly musical, rich and pure, like the voice of a trained bard, and although the words meant nothing to Ruarhi, he felt both their power and incongruous beauty. This was no monster, but a being of high intelligence.

Sommoi replied to its evident questions. As he did so, Ruarhi looked again at Dromator. He had stopped moving, and Ruarhi felt himself lurch. Dromator! In spite of Sommoi's warning, Ruarhi bent down to his friend.

The Angel Guard swung round, but did not step forward. There was anger in its cruel visage. But it waited.

Ruarhi felt the sudden welling of tears in his eyes. He had seen enough on Hanging Tor to know that Dromator was dead. He had been sliced up neatly and precisely by a master of his trade. His eyes stared openly at the dark canvas of Skydown, as though the last thing they had seen had been his gods coming to collect him, to carry him to yet another, final realm.

6

Had their situations been reversed, Ruarhi knew that Dromator would have thrown himself at the Angel Guard regardless of the consequence. However, he knew that to do so would mean a swift death, and he had no desire to die here. The warrior was powerful in a way that he did not comprehend. So instead he just looked up through his tears, wiping them away angrily and waiting.

Sommoi was the first to move. He seemed to have been waiting to see what Ruarhi would do. Seeing the youth was not about to attempt something rash, he got to his feet uneasily, again speaking to the motionless Angel Guard, which now seemed to be trying to orient itself.

Gradually Ruarhi rose: he could see that the warrior was aware of his movements, though it did not seem intent on attacking him as it had Dromator.

"It says it thought we were intent on harm," said Sommoi. "Otherwise it might not have defended itself so fiercely."

"Dromator is dead," replied Ruarhi flatly. It was condemnation: there was revenge in his voice.

"I don't doubt it," said Sommoi, without emotion. "I did not expect such an attack, but there is another reason for such unexpected aggression."

Ruarhi scowled. As far as he was concerned, it had been murder, cynical and brutal.

"The Angle Guard has been blinded."

Ruarhi almost released his bitter anger. Dromator was stretched out on the roadway like a butchered ox and Sommoi talked of the warrior's sight. Ruarhi's fingers tightened on the pipe weapon.

"You have to understand," Sommoi went on. "It was confused. It speaks of light, blinding light. Under Skydown, that is blasphemous, great evil. When it came to, it felt threatened. It struck out in its blindness. It did not judge your companion. It has not yet judged us.''

''What do you mean?'' hissed Ruarhi, his eyes fixed on the warrior, but it waited with stony patience.

''It may need our help, in which case it is unlikely to execute us. Thank your gods, whatever they may be, that it is in our hands.''

Ruarhi grunted. He doubted that anyone would get near the creature unless it allowed them to.

''So what do we do?''

''I must examine its eyes,'' said Sommoi, but there was no hiding the unease in his voice. He looked back along the road. Festubul, the girl, and the Foddamen were all rooted, none of them daring to move. ''I'll need the girl.'' He somehow made the words sound sinister, as though some dark intent lay behind them.

Ruarhi indicated Dromator. ''I must see to his burial.''

Sommoi frowned in confusion. ''I don't understand.''

Ruarhi gritted his teeth. ''It is the custom with my people that we bury our dead. The earth takes them back.'' For a moment he hesitated. Would his gods reach into the earth of *this* world and find Dromator? Would the bones be safe here?

''Where will you do this?''

Ruarhi looked into the darkness, to where the reed beds would be. No, that would be a bad place. ''Here, beside the road. The earth of the embankment will be his tomb.''

The Angel Guard broke its silence and said something to Sommoi, and Ruarhi guessed that Sommoi was explaining what Ruarhi intended.

''It says,'' transmitted Sommoi after another exchange, ''why cannot the dead one be given to the Foddamen? Why should the symmetry of the road be disturbed; why should fodda be wasted?''

Ruarhi felt his blood heating, his face flushing with fury. But he knew that only cold, calculated arguments would achieve anything with these creatures. ''Perhaps,'' he said, after some thought, ''it has been blinded by its gods, as a punishment.''

Sommoi looked offended by this suggestion, but Ruarhi went on. "If I did not bury Dromator and honour my gods, they might punish me."

Whether or not Sommoi passed this on to the warrior, Ruarhi would never know, but Sommoi did say something. The answer was brief.

"Very well," Sommoi said. "You may do as you say. But be careful not to damage the fabric of the road, It is a very ancient thing, and under Skydown, the older things are, the more deeply we respect them."

Ruarhi again had to choke back his sorrow as he put his hands under Dromator's shoulders and pulled him away to the side of the road, down the embankment, out of sight of the others. He found a place where the earth was relatively soft and used his weapon to dig into it. Now his tears fell freely as he worked. He told himself not to be a child, but there was no disgrace in such tears. Dromator had not deserved this terrible end.

Up on the road, Sommoi called to Festubul, who came forward slowly and reluctantly.

"Tell the girl to prepare a solution. I must bathe the eyes of the Angel Guard. He may have been blinded."

Festubul almost forgot his terror when he heard this. "But by whom? How is it possible—?"

"Don't argue! Just get the girl to do it. She must have some skills in these matters."

Festubul swallowed. "I'll ask her."

As Festubul went back to the others, Ruarhi worked the earth, a rich dark loam that was easy to scoop out from the grave he was making. When he was satisfied that it was deep enough, he placed Dromator's body in it, folding his arms over the bloody chest. Quickly he pushed earth over him, knowing as he did so that it was possibly the last contact he would ever have with someone of his own kind. But this was no time to feel sorry for himself. Instead he whispered the name of Dromator's god, asking that he be accepted. When he had finished, he beat the earth down, packing it, leaving a hummock of it, the only blemish in the unbroken embankment as far as the eye could see.

Wearily he trudged back up the road. A strange spectacle

met his eyes. The Angel Guard was on its knees and the girl stood before it. She was using a white cloth to wipe at the creature's eyes. There was an almost ritualistic look to the tableau, as though the three lesser beings were paying homage to a demigod. Behind her Sommoi and Festubul watched intently. They acknowledged Ruarhi's return with brief glances and he waited in silence.

When the girl had finished, she backed away, her eyes fixed on the face she had been tending, as if it held a deep fascination for her. Still Ruarhi could not see her own face. She turned away, her hair falling in such a way that he was still cheated.

Sommoi approached the Angel Guard as it rose. With what now seemed a lack of fear, he studied the face, particularly the eyes, then backed away. He said something and the warrior nodded curtly: it had lost none of its supreme arrogance. Then it swung round, blind eyes fixed upon Ruarhi as if they saw him quite clearly. It said something in that rich voice, none of which Ruarhi understood.

"It knows who you are, but you are to work with me in the farms," said Sommoi. "Do you know where your other companion is?"

Darrac! He had not been found? Ruarhi shook his head. "We were separated when we escaped."

"In the reed fields?" said Sommoi.

Ruarhi nodded.

Sommoi told the warrior. It listened, but did not respond. Instead it took several quick steps to the edge of the embankment, lifted it wings and was in the air. Seconds later the darkness had enveloped it. It left only silence behind it, and an afterimage of extraordinary beauty and grace.

Ruarhi caught his breath. In spite of his hatred for the thing and what it had done, he was stunned by its powers. Even though he had seen it in the air for no more than a few seconds, he had recognised its sublime empathy with the element, a natural flier more suited to sky than land. How could such a creature destroy a man so unemotionally? Perhaps it resembled the eagle in this.

"It has assumed your other companion lost," said Sommoi.

"Lost?"

"The reed fields stretch for as far as you can imagine in this segment alone. They are full of predators. You have been fortunate."

Fortunate! Ruarhi almost spat, as Dromator would have.

Sommoi listened to the darkness of the sky for a while, until he was satisfied that the Angel Guard had truly gone.

"What happens now?" said Ruarhi. "You don't expect me to go back to your farm? What happened to the discussion we were supposed to have with that creature?"

"From what Strud had told me, I had expected an advantage over it that did not, it the event, materialise."

"What advantage?"

"An injured Angel Guard, one that we could have captured—"

"For what purpose?"

"Power over such a creature would be purpose enough! You would have enjoyed a freedom unknown to your kind."

Ruarhi was certain Sommoi toyed with him, not giving him all the facts. He had his own purpose, but had no intention of revealing it. No point trying to beat it out of him. So what did he do now? He peered into the darkness, trying to see down the road, but the light was too poor.

"You are thinking your path leads down the road, towards Thousandreach, perhaps?" said Sommoi, close to his shoulder.

Ruarhi swung abruptly away from him. "I'll kill you rather than go back to the farm. Do you think I could watch those warriors, men of my clan, suffer its torments?"

Sommoi shook his head. "Of course not. But, tell me, what do you expect to gain along the road?"

Ruarhi tried not to let the feeling of despondency overwhelm him. "Maybe I'll find Darrac, the one who eluded your hunters."

"If he's in the reed fields, it will only be a matter of time before they claim him. He cannot survive them."

"Then I'll go on alone!" Ruarhi retorted. "If you try to prevent me—"

"I will not. In fact, I may go down the road myself."

"Why should you?"

"The Angel Guard spared us all, especially you. I assume as

payment for helping it when we could have killed it. But the Providers will not be pleased with this affair. Three of you escaped and although the Angel Guard will report two of you dead and one recovered, it will be held against my farm.''

"Why should it? Our escape was nothing to do with you.''

"I have enemies among the Providers. It is why I serve them in such a remote segment. My enemies may make something of this business.''

Again Ruarhi was sure Sommoi was holding back truths. But he did not say so.

"Better that I go on. At least to the villages. I may learn something. I'll send Strud back. He knows the work.''

"How far are these villages?''

"The nearest inward is ten miles. There would be no reason to go outward. Festubul has come from outward. Apparently he, too, is a pilgrim. I spoke to him while the girl tended the Angel Guard. He is not, as he first said, a reed worker. Not now. Like you, he is a runaway.''

"From what?''

"The villages have strict rules. Those who break them are punished brutally by the Providers. Festubul has committed at least three crimes. He had consorted with the mate of the village Drone. He has done more, he has abducted her, for this is she. And he has forced the four Foddamen to serve him on their flight inward. They are too afraid of him to disobey him.''

"What is the girl's name?''

"She interests you?''

Ruarhi looked at him in annoyance.

Sommoi shrugged. "She is Ukar-Tiri.''

"She seems unhappy to me. Did she leave her village willingly?''

"I think not. But she is in Festubul's hands now.''

"Where will they go?''

"Where there is work. Festubul is not lacking in skills.''

"And the Foddamen?''

"They are commanded by him.''

Ruarhi looked at them. They seemed like children, lost and forlorn, dependent on the others for guidance. He felt the stirrings of pity, but there was nothing that could be done for them.

Sommoi was staring out across the reed fields toward the lost path they had traveled to get here. Had he seen something? Ruarhi wondered. The Angel Guard returning? Strangely, a part of him wanted that, to see the magnificent, effortless flight.

"What is it?" he asked him at once. All he could see was the wall of shadows against the night.

"My imagination. There is life out there. But it leads a secret existence. So little is really known about those tracts. Our workers touch the edges of it, no more."

But Ruarhi was not convinced. Sommoi had seen or heard something. He was not going to reveal his thoughts on this. Instead he walked towards Festubul and the others.

They were leaving.

One figure had turned from the road, winding its long way back to the reed beds: Strud, following Sommoi's instructions without a backward glance.

Festubul, however, looked back once, his face surly, but then began the march inward, down the road. The girl, Ukar-Tiri, walked one step behind him and Sommoi and the three Foddamen fell into their trudging step behind her, heads down, oblivious to their surroundings. Ruarhi finally began his own hike, but he looked over at the marshes as he went, sure that there was a shadow among the reeds, stalking him, reflecting his steps. The ghost, perhaps, of Dromator.

7

Although the degree of darkness under Skydown varied, there was never true daylight. There did, however, seem to be a fixed periodic interval that corresponded with night. Ruarhi knew it would take him a long time to adjust to it, if he ever could. The death of Dromator had sent him into a kind of stasis, as if it had happened in his imagination and Dromator was really alive, but somewhere else. His frustration at being unable to do something about it, his confusion and sadness bent inwards. When Sommoi suggested a rest, he was suddenly exhausted and glad to stretch out on the side of the interminable road. Sleep claimed him almost immediately.

He woke like one drugged, rubbing a crust of sleep from his eyes. For a moment he expected to be on the slopes of a battlefield, but the shadow terrain was still before him, the slow, infuriating dance of the reeds.

To his surprise, the girl, Ukar-Tiri, knelt before him, holding something in her hands. It was the first time he had seen her face, for she had pulled back her thick tresses and tied them behind her neck. Her skin was dark, a natural colour, as if she had once known true sunlight. Her features were those of any normal human girl, though her eyes were a little larger: they made her look as if she had been startled. He could not help but watch her face; she seemed very nervous, afraid even, and he felt an urge to put an arm around her, tell her he was no threat to her.

He tried to say something, but his throat was dry. He felt stupid, embarrassed, but her expression did not change. What did she want?

He looked at her hands, what she carried, and she held it out. Beyond her, Ruarhi could see Sommoi and the Foddamen, squatting down, chewing at something. He realised at last what the girl was doing. Offering him food. Abruptly he felt famished. He pointed at the bundle and then to his mouth, pretending to chew.

She nodded, giving him the cloth, though she still did not smile. She waited while he undid the cloth. Inside it he found a chunk of what looked like cheese. He smelled it, but it was bland and unfamiliar. Slowly he bit into it. It was not unpleasant, but no more than edible. His hunger won him over and he chewed heartily. Ukar-Tiri watched him, and he thought he detected something like sadness in her eyes. What had caused such unhappiness? But then, under Skydown, who could be happy?

As he considered this, the pang of Dromator's death struck him, and he coughed out a piece of the food, shaking his head. The cough had brought tears. How easily they came! he thought.

At once the girl was beside him, showing clear concern. She must have thought the food had done this to him. Lightly she touched his back, as if not sure what she should do. She looked across to where Festubul was sitting, but for once the reedman seemed to be ignoring her.

Ruarhi again wanted to hold the girl: he needed the comfort himself. In this place she seemed the only familiar thing and he needed to clutch at such realities. But he pretended he was fine, that it was just the food. She looked at it with a kind of anguish, as if it disgusted her. Did it mean she was angry with it for bringing distress to him? he asked himself, though guessed he was being foolish.

He tapped his chest. "Ruarhi," he said softly, and then, to make her see what he meant, he touched her arm and said her name.

Her eyes widened in surprise. "Ruarhi," she said, awkwardly.

He couldn't think what else to say, so offered her some of the food, but she shrank back as though it was infested. As she did so, a sudden insight struck him. He stared at the food. Things Sommoi had said rang back at him. He got to his feet, tossing the food away.

Ukar-Tiri also stood, head bowed, as if waiting for anger to burst from him. But he forced himself to smile at her and walked over to the others.

"Have you eaten?" Sommoi asked him.

"What was it?" said Ruarhi through his teeth. The Foddamen could see that he was angry about something. They drew back like children witnessing adults in dispute.

"Simple fodda," said Sommoi. "Not particularly pleasing to the palate, but nutritious. The Foddamen always carry it."

"*Fodda,*" repeated Ruarhi. "You mean flesh?"

"No longer. It is a compound of many things. Regeneration is what sustains the world." To emphasise his point, Sommoi held up the hand that had replaced the one Dromator had struck off. "Can your flesh do this?"

Ruarhi shook his head.

"Fodda enables us to do this. For certain parts of our bodies, it is possible. But the dead are dead. They do not come back as themselves. But as fodda, they can be absorbed into others, reconstituted, just as plants sink into the earth, renewing themselves. Fodda is life, the blood of our world. You will eat it, too, or perish. In time, it will give new power to your flesh, new strength.''

Ruarhi considered the benefits of this, but the pictures it drew in his mind disgusted him. He thought of the MagMannochs at the farm, the horrible way they had been treated. No better than cattle. He pointed to the remains of the meal that Sommoi and the others had shared. ''Human flesh went into that?''

''Everything changes. Zerm,'' Sommoi answered, pointing to one of the Foddamen, who looked doubly frightened at being mentioned by name, ''is skilled in conversion. He will provide all the sustenance we need on our journey.''

Ruarhi could see that none of the Foddamen was carrying a pack, and if they had weapons, they were either small or concealed in their scant clothes. ''From where? The reed marshes? Does Zerm hunt?''

''There is no need. We have our food—on the hoof.'' As Sommoi said this, he looked directly at Ruarhi, as though challenging him to protest.

Ruarhi was gazing into the shadows of the middle distance. ''Is that what I have glimpsed? Something in the reeds, following us?''

''It is. But do not concern yourself. Zerm is the only one who needs to see the creature. He guards his skills jealously and would let no one else see him at work. Even Foddamen have their pride.''

''What sort of creature?'' said Ruarhi softly.

''That is of no importance. Fodda is fodda.''

''Could it be human?''

Sommoi paused for a while before answering. ''What you are asking is, could it have an identity, as once it might have had. A man. No. It is a beast, less than that. It has no mind, no feeling. In a way it is dead. It is fodda.''

''How does it move?''

''It follows the Foddamen. They control it. They draw what we need from it. It feels no pain, no distress, nothing. It is fodda.''

Ruarhi turned to the girl. She was watching him intently, as if she could understand Sommoi's words. Ruarhi was sure she knew what he was explaining. To show her his disgust, Ruarhi spat. Ukar-Tiri looked away, but she had understood.

"Is there no other food under Skydown?" Ruarhi asked.

"No, but there is no need. Where we are going, fodda comes in a variety of forms. You will acquire a taste for it. You will have to."

Festubul rose to his feet, growling something as he did so. He gestured to Ukar-Tiri. She drew back a moment, but then shuffled toward him. His skinny arm whipped out and his fingers caught her hair, tugging it, almost ripping it free of its knot so that it tumbled loose. Again he spoke to her, angrily, and Ruarhi felt himself flush. He pointed his pipe weapon at Festubul.

"Tell him," he said coldly to Sommoi, "that if he harms the girl, I will crush his skull. And there will be no miracle of healing."

Sommoi frowned. Festubul had paused, realising that Ruarhi must have made a threat of some kind.

"You have no dispute with Festubul," said Sommoi.

"If he harms the girl, I will have."

"What is she to you?"

"Tell him!"

Sommoi recoiled at the violence in the youth's shout. It was prompted by more than just the oafishness of Festubul. "Very well."

Sommoi spoke to Festubul, whose face clouded in fury. He let the girl go at once. She, too, seemed surprised by Sommoi's translation of Ruarhi's words. Festubul took out a weapon, a short, serrated knife.

"Yes, you son of a whore!" hissed Ruarhi. "Come forward. Try me." He realised just how much he wanted to drive his weapon into Festubul's flesh, to smash it up. The bloodlust of Hanging Tor sang in him anew, revenge for the MagMannochs, but more than that, revenge for Dromator's murder. He needed to free the poison of it from his system.

Festubul knew at once, and reacted quickly. He simply swung round and held his blade inches from Ukar-Tiri's face. She was frozen, unable to move. Festubul made the position clear to Ruarhi. One more step, one more threatening gesture, and he would draw blood. He had no regard for the girl's safety.

Ruarhi spoke again to Sommoi, but his eyes never left those

of Festubul. "Tell him again, that if he harms her in any way, I will open his skull."

Sommoi passed this on. Festubul's arm did not waver for a long time. Then he sneered, saying something sharp and abusive, but he slipped the knife away. He pointed to the remains of the food and barked a command to the girl.

Quickly, without looking at Ruarhi, she bent down and began folding the cloth that the food had been wrapped in.

"Are you content?" Sommoi asked Ruarhi. His tone suggested he had taken no sides in the matter.

"For the moment."

"We will be on the road for another nine sleeps at least. I anticipate that we will come to the village of High Crofels after that. There we can discuss what should be done. Before that, we would do well not to fall out."

"As long as Festubul understands my terms."

"She is his woman."

"Not by her own choice. You told me he abducted her."

"Be careful. If you are saying that you desire her for yourself—"

"I did not say that."

"But if you would take her from Festubul, either by force or by mutual agreement, she becomes your responsibility. She is the mate of a village Drone. But her abduction is her shame, as it would continue to be if you took her. If you tired of her and abandoned her, she would be an outcast. She would probably take her own life."

"And what would that mean?" said Ruarhi, appalled at the implied consequences of such an act. Under Skydown—

"You are beginning to understand our ways," replied Sommoi, as though reading Ruarhi's thoughts.

Ruarhi didn't respond, though he felt a renewed surge of emotion, partly anger, partly something else. Desire? She was a girl, no more desirable than others of his clan. Was it his loneliness that made her desirable, or her vulnerability? Or then, was it his own vulnerability? He shook himself. Dromator would have laughed at him, teased him. Fool to rationalise such things! You want her, boy. Nothing strange in that!

But Sommoi's counsel had been wiser. Responsibility. It was one thing horsing around with the girls in the camps of the clans, where a certain amount of self-education was tolerated, even encouraged. But not here. Ukar-Tiri was not for sport. He would not add to her misery.

Sommoi broke into his thoughts. "Our journey will be tedious, dull. I suggest there is a useful way for you to occupy yourself."

Ruarhi looked at him suspiciously. "Oh?"

"Learn the common language. It has many varieties, but a basic grasp of it will help you wherever you may be."

"You will teach me this?"

"I could do so quickly." Sommoi gently stroked the growths at the back of his head, the long tails of flesh, and Ruarhi shuddered, knowing what Sommoi meant. "But I have a better solution. Let Ukar-Tiri teach you. I am sure that Festubul will be intensely irritated by such a suggestion, but if it will satisfy you that he is not causing her grief, perhaps it is the best course. She would be skilled in such things, far more so than he is."

Ruarhi wondered if there would be some ulterior motive to Sommoi's suggestion, but he nodded. "Very well." He tried to hide his pleasure in knowing that he would have the close company of the girl on the journey, but knew that Sommoi would read that plainly enough.

When Sommoi approached Festubul on the matter a while later, after they had begun the journey anew, Festubul was oddly resigned, offering little resistance. Ruarhi's suspicions were reinforced, but when the girl came to him, eyes downcast in uncertainty, he smiled at her in an attempt to reassure her.

8

Ruarhi's education into the language of the people under Skydown began at once, although Ukar-Tiri was halting and uncertain. Ruarhi's patience with her, however, and the endless trek, enabled her to overcome her initial embarrassment and gradually she set about teaching him as well as she could. Their surroundings were so bare, the terrain still unbroken, that there were few things that she was able to use as examples in an effort to build up his vocabulary, but he was quick to learn, having mastered several local dialects in his own world. The clans there had been fiercely protective of their language, as they were of their lands, but he did not allow himself to dwell on that. It seemed that Festubul had accepted the loss of Ukar-Tiri's company during the equivalent of the day, spending his time instead with Sommoi and the Fodda-men, each of whom would occasionally leave the road in forays out into the reeds. Ruarhi tried to glean from Ukar-Tiri what their purpose might be, but she was either unable to explain it, or was afraid to.

After three days and nights, or sleeps as Sommoi called them, Ruarhi was able to speak the basic language crudely, enough to make himself understood, as least by the girl. Most of what they talked about was trivial; she remained reluctant to speak of the things which interested him most. He tried asking her what sort of place they could expect to find along the road, but she did not know. The thought of what was ahead frightened her. He asked about Thousandreach, but she shuddered as though he spoke of the equivalent of hell.

As they ended each period of march, resting beside the road, Ukar-Tiri went back to Festubul's side. Ruarhi watched to see if she was distressed at all, but Festubul, seemingly inhibited by the others, did not molest her. Ruarhi slept apart from them all and even Sommoi had little to say to him, as though he was deep in thought. Perhaps he regretted leaving the relative security of the farm. Ruarhi could not really understand why he had done so.

When the sky was at its darkest, Zerm the Foddaman would go down to the marsh. Ruarhi listened to his soft splashing as he entered the reeds. Each time he came back, he brought fodda. Ruarhi had no choice but to eat it. If it was having any effect on him other than curbing his hunger, he did not notice. He tried not to think beyond his hunger, but so many of the things he had seen in this world still repulsed him.

On the fourth rest, he had stretched out on the thin grass, staring up at the darkening sky, tired from yet another hike from nowhere to nowhere, when he heard something below the embankment, out in the reeds. He lifted his head casually, craning his neck. Something disturbed the reeds, a large animal perhaps. There was a snort, not something he could identify, but he sat upright, clutching his weapon. Up on the openness of the road, the party would be vulnerable if a predator of any size attacked.

Abruptly the four Foddamen came into view, standing at the edge of the road, pointing and gesticulating excitedly down at the reeds where the creature moved. Zerm hopped up and down as if he had been stung by a hornet, and for a moment Ruarhi was amused by the spectacle, until he realised that there was evidently danger of some kind. As he got up, dropping instinctively into a defensive crouch, he saw Zerm rush down the embankment into the edge of the marsh, shouting at the reeds. The other Foddamen followed him, though more cautiously.

There was no sign of Sommoi, nor of Festubul, but Ruarhi had no intention of disturbing them. If they were asleep, they could remain so.

He slipped down the embankment after the figures, curious to see what other creatures inhabited this realm. Zerm was already swallowed up by the nodding grey blanket of reeds. The other Foddamen spread out and went into them slowly.

Ruarhi had no trouble finding the trampled path that Zerm had made in his haste, and he followed it. Ahead of him, in the almost pitch darkness, he heard a groan, though it sounded more like annoyance than distress. Something crashed through the reeds, snorting as it went, the sounds quickly diminishing. Whatever it was, Zerm had frightened it off.

Ruarhi picked his way through the damaged reeds. Ahead of him there was a light, itself puzzling as the Foddamen seemed to treat light as vaguely blasphemous, especially at this hour. Peering through the reeds, Ruarhi saw Zerm, holding a small torch, cut from reed stems. Zerm must have used fire to frighten the creature: his nocturnal vision was good enough without it. Ruarhi had no time to wonder why the creature's presence presented such a threat to Zerm, or why he had seen fit to rush out into this wilderness to confront it. Instead he inched forward.

Stretched out on the flattened bed of reeds was a shape. Another figure! Zerm bent over it, shaking his head in evident annoyance.

Ruarhi glanced back down the rough path: there was no sign of the other Foddamen. Presumably they had elected to approach the intruder in a more subtle way. Ruarhi went forward until Zerm turned to see him. At once the Foddaman jumped up. He almost dropped his small torch. Smoke curled from it accusingly. He plunged it into the murky water.

Ruarhi ignored Zerm's ludicrously guilty expression and studied the fallen shape. It had the appearance of a man. Without torchlight, visibility was poor again, and distorted the figure, but it seemed as though it had no arms. A closer inspection showed that this was not so: they were merely tight to the man's naked sides. In fact, Ruarhi realised, they seemed to be stitched to them, the flesh smoothed over them in an unnatural way that made him scowl.

''Who?'' he asked Zerm.

The Foddaman also frowned, but it was in puzzlement, as though the question was meaningless. ''Fodda,'' he said simply. ''Follows.''

Ruarhi had to think for a moment before he understood the word, spoken in such a different voice to that of Ukar-Tiri. But yes, it made sense. *This* must be the creature that Sommoi had spoken of, the creature that followed the party, bidden to do so by the Foddamen. This was their food, on the hoof, like a cow. Ruarhi shook is head in bewilderment. It *was* human.

''That?'' he said, pointing to the direction taken by whatever it was that had fled.

Zerm tried a number of words, none of which Ruarhi understood, but his meaning came across better when he used gestures to explain himself. It had been a predator and would have eaten the fodda, leaving the party without food.

Ruarhi felt even more tired. He nodded, watching while Zerm tended to the figure. There was blood underneath it. The Foddaman tried to turn it, and Ruarhi insisted on helping him. His hands were sticky with blood: surely the man was dead. His face turned, obscured by muck. Whatever had attacked him had bitten into his neck and shoulder, ripping sections of the flesh away. Without thinking, Ruarhi wiped the muck from the face, which seemed oddly smooth, the skin as soft as a woman's.

Zerm grunted, shaking his head. He said something Ruarhi did not understand, but the youth guessed he meant the thing was dead. He was about to rise, when the face below began to look more familiar. As it did so, he realised what he was really seeing.

He recoiled, splashing backwards, stumbling to his knees, hand over his mouth. Zerm had also risen, rinsing his own hands in the dirty water, cleansing them of the blood of the fallen man. For man it had once been. It was Darrac.

Ruarhi felt himself going icy, his guts cramping. Abruptly he flung around, spewing out the contents of his stomach. Again and again he heaved, until there was nothing left, his eyes and nose streaming, his heart thundering as if it would burst under the strain of retching.

When at last he had finished, he plunged his head into the water, lifting it, shaking it, to find Zerm standing, bewildered, across the small clearing. Darrac's body lay between them.

Ruarhi managed to get to his feet, his head spinning the way it did when he had been stinking drunk. He pointed to the body, but when he tried to speak, his voice failed him.

Zerm shook his head. Ruarhi knew he had no idea that the body, the fodda, was the remains of Ruarhi's friend. To the vacant Foddaman it was simply meat, ruined by a marauding predator. He mourned the loss of the meat, that was all.

Painfully, Ruarhi got to his feet. He could not bring himself to touch Darrac. But before the journey resumed, he would drag him up onto the embankment and bury him as he had buried Dromator. For now, he lurched back down the path, Zerm following. He wiped at the tears in his eyes. Dromator had been right: this was Hellesvaar, the hell of their myths. Nowhere else could be so evil, as merciless.

Trudging through the edge of the marsh back to the embankment, Ruarhi drew air into his lungs, his gut aching, his chest tight as if from a wound. Where was Sommoi? He would kill him for this. Climbing the rise to the road, his anger began to wipe away the sorrow, the cramps.

But there was no sign of Sommoi on the road. In the darkness, now almost total, he could be anywhere, asleep somewhere on the embankment, oblivious of events. Ruarhi listened to the emptiness. Zerm had also disappeared. His fellows had not returned from the reeds.

A sound snared Ruarhi's attention. Close at hand, farther along the slope. Ukar-Tiri?

Softly he padded along the edge of the road. Somewhere beyond, he heard her. Strange, unfamiliar sound. The sound of—pleasure?

Squinting into the dark, he saw movement. In the grass. He was drawn inexorably. The sounds became clearer, more obvious, as he closed in. She was on her back, and Festubul was on top of her. Pushing himself into her. And she—she moaned with the pleasure of it.

Unable to move, no more than a few feet away, Ruarhi watched the two bodies as they coupled, oblivious to everything but the thrusting and grinding of flesh. And the girl called out encouragement to Festubul, her hands fastening into the exposed flesh of his buttocks, pulling them to her with each shunt.

Her eyes had been closed, but as she turned her head to let Festubul lick and kiss her neck, they opened. They met the cold gaze of Ruarhi, Her mouth dropped open, her eyes widening.

"Stop him!" she cried instantly. "Ruarhi, stop him!" At once she had transformed, fighting the man on top of her.

Ruarhi was thrown into confusion. But only for a moment. He rushed forward, hand tearing like a claw into Festubul's shoulder. He dragged him off, rolling him backwards, Festubul's member standing out in protest. Ukar-Tiri swung away at once, pulling her skirt down over her abdomen, as she scrambled to her knees.

Festubul was swearing and growling in fury, his eyes ablaze with a kind of madness. He, too, covered himself.

Ukar-Tiri was shouting something to Ruarhi, but he did not understand her words. She seemed to be directing her disgust at Festubul. Had he forced himself on her? Had her pleasure been an act? It had been convincing, but Ruarhi knew something about the ways of women. There were girls in the MagMannoch camp who teased the youths on their first efforts at sex, but others were far more knowing, pre-

tending pleasure to give the youths confidence. Sometimes
the pretence was obvious, but mostly it was a mystery, their
pleasure, though Dromator assured Ruarhi that it could be
very real, just as real as a man's.

As Ruarhi hesitated, Festubul got to his feet, pulling out
his knife. Ruarhi's mind clouded with another image of Dromator, then one of Darrac out in the reeds. His body reacted
as violently as it had when he had spewed in the reeds: he
stepped forward and rocked Festubul with a fierce blow to
the face. Festubul was flung back as if he had been struck by
a stone. He crumpled, moaning, rolling down the embankment into the darkness. Ruarhi did not pursue him. Instead
he swung round to meet Ukar-Tiri's frightened face.

He held out his hand. "Come on," he urged her. "We
travel on alone. Quickly!"

She nodded at once, no hint of doubt in her eyes, as though
she had only waited for him to say this. Swiftly they went
onto the road. There was still no sign of the others.

She held his hand tightly as they broke into an automatic
trot down the road, smothered by the darkness. He tried to
keep from his mind the image of the girl as she had been
coupling. Her hand burned him and he could not look at her,
forcing himself to glare at the black wall ahead of them. Their
pleasure equals a man's, Dromator had told him.

They had traveled well into the darkness before he realised
with a stab of guilt that he'd left Darrac's corpse out in the
reeds, unburied and exposed.

TWO

ARTERIEL

*They are single-minded creatures, these ferocious An-
gel Guards, but then, they were created thus. Such de-
votion takes many generations to perfect. Yet it would
be a dangerous oversight to imagine that they have no
feelings of their own.*

*Duty fetters them, deeply inbred, ingrained. They have
a sense of honour, of justice. One could almost consider
them noble beasts.*

*They freely sacrifice themselves that evil may be rooted
out. But how do we define evil? Surely it is relative.*

*Whatever threatens us, we call evil. Then are the
gods beyond evil? The Angel Guards would die pro-
claiming it.*

*However, convince even one that the gods are capable
of deceit, cruelty, or decadence, and what shape would
its anger take? That would be a weapon of a very different order.*

ZAER PHESMES—*The Book of Renunciation*

9

Nothing in his past experience compared to the total darkness
of his blindness. For with it came a confusion, a threat of
unaccustomed panic. This weakened him more surely than
the assault of any other potential enemy.

At first his instincts guided him to catch the thermals and
he flew, mastering his fear by allowing the currents he understood as only an Angel could to take him and carry him
on over the world. Inwards, ever inwards. Intuition guided
him, and as he flew, his other senses rallied. He heard sounds
with a fresh, exceptional clarity and felt every subtle caress
of the air, the passage of the dust within it. He was even
capable of judging subtle shifts in temperature as light

strained through the shield of Skydown, always seeking ways to puncture that shield. As it must have when it had struck him.

Gliding across mile after mile, high above the empty sectors, he had time to reflect on the disaster and its resultant confusion. It had been light, an intrusion. What—punishment? Had the gods sought him out for personal persecution? Such a direct judgement was unprecedented. But Absolute Light ruled beyond the skies, and all life bent to it. Had he not performed his tasks well? Was he not esteemed amongst the Angel Guard? He had his pride, as all his kind had it, but he had never considered himself worthy of punishment, at least not in the way that this had happened. To be blinded! But perhaps it was only temporary. A warning. Otherwise, what? An accident? Sheer misfortune that he had been in the vicinity when the light speared through the shield, a victim of coincidence. But he could hear the whispers of the Lightbenders already. They would discount such a thing. Had they been the ones who directed this bolt of fury at him? It was said they were at odds with one another, their great families vying for total control of Thousandreach and the inestimable powers it housed. All life under Skydown was subservient to the Lightbenders, subject to their whims.

The wind had no answers. But there was no further threat. As he flew on, the panic receded, though the uncertainty did not. He focused his mind on the place he had visited, the duty that had taken him there. The Overlap.

As soon as he thought of it, a fresh possibility struck him. Had it been the Overlap which had affected him? The Lightbenders did not control the aberration, nor was it thought, did the gods. But he could only speculate. Rather than waste his energy he turned his mind again to his duties.

He had been commissioned to find three runaway Externals. Such beings were not permitted freedom under Skydown because they were unknown quantities, potentially volatile. In the confusion of his accident he had almost forgotten them. Creatures of the lower orders had helped him. Normally he would not have given such vermin more than a glance, or shared as much as a word with them. But in the chaos of his pain he had been forced to communicate. One of them had even touched him, his eyes. But the girl had been gentle, her terror radiating from her like fire. Why should the image disturb him? Angel Guards fed on such terror, basked in it. But the girl's fears gave him no pleasure, only an unfamiliar unease.

Two of the Externals were no more, absorbed, fulfilling the destiny planned for them by the hunters at the outset, part of their harvest. The Foddamen had them and that was enough. But the third? He was there, on the road. *Why did I not kill him as I killed the second of them?* That kill had been, literally, a blind reaction, but it would have been done later anyway. *I let one of them go.*

Sommoi, the overseer, had spoken for the last External. He would find him useful at the Foddafarm. Such things were known. Externals were not always used purely for fodda. This was acceptable. The External was under the control of Sommoi. It would satisfy the Providers, who had charged the Angel with recovering the runaways. The situation was ironic: in the event, there had been no real need for an Angel Guard to be sent, but because one had, it was now blind. The Providers, of course, would emphasise what they always emphasised, that no chances could be taken with the Overlap and what it might discharge into the world under Skydown. *I agreed readily to the sparing of the External. Was I correct in that?*

How would the Providers react to his accident?

If it had been the wrath of the gods (for which he could as yet see no reason), they would surely condone it. Then what? Kill him? But he would have to be told why: they must grant him that. Although, as he knew, the Providers acted for the Lightbenders, and they did not have to justify themselves. They were the law, unquestionable and immutable.

Even so, I will ask them why I have been punished.

If, however, it was the Overlap that blinded me, they will restore me. No doubt they will show their anger and address the problem more thoroughly.

He knew that debates about the Overlap raged among the Providers. Some of them favoured experiment and relished the hunting of Externals. Others feared the Overlap and saw it as a threat to the stability of the world. On his return, the debate would rage anew. He would have to exercise great caution.

Although he could not see it, he sensed the proximity of Thousandreach as he neared the end of his return flight. He regretted his loss of sight now more than ever: the city was spectacular, rising up, level upon level in a series of titanic steps, tower upon immense tower, until it seemed to scrape the very belly of the sky. Whenever he approached it, he marveled at its workmanship, from the sprawling mass of the base levels, to the perfect sculpture of the uppermost levels, where the Lightbenders were housed in their magnificent, unseen palaces.

The penultimate level was ringed by the Eyries of the Angel Guard, set at half-mile intervals. These were sheer and smooth-sided, slender, hundreds of feet tall, their only entrances high up near their conical tops, accessible to the winged Guards alone. Above them and below, were other lesser towers, and the trees, the fabulous monstrous trees of Thousandreach.

In various parts of the city they grew, the largest of them reaching skywards like colossal pillars that held the sky up. Some were said to breach the clouds, the protection of Skydown itself, and go beyond. They were sacred, giving as they did, air to the world. Even the Lightbenders did not interfere with them, and they tolerated the many tree-worshiping cults in the city.

Now he was denied sight of these marvels. But they remained very clear in his mind. From a distance of scores of miles, he could imagine them as he swooped inwards, his unease of earlier dissipating. Below him he knew the roads were coming together, like the spokes of an immense wheel, reaching out from the hub of the city to the ultimate boundaries of the segments. Life would be thronging along them, an endless stream to the heart of this world, its pulsating core.

He approached the Eyries of the Angel Guard as he always did, from a vast height. He did not need his eyes to judge that distance: he could have done so had he been asleep on the wing. His body had become like a machine, part of the masterworks below him, synchronised by them, controlled by them. Spiraling down effortlessly, he swung towards the Eyrie that housed his own chapter. It would be to the chapter that he would report first, to its Praetor.

The Eyrie was not a living entity, but it had an unmistakable ambience. Clinging to its upper reaches were swarms of creatures the size of his fist; they were eyeless, their wide mouths agape to collect the insects of the air, their spatulate fingers gripping the stones, pressing their bodies to it almost lasciviously. He could smell them, hear their croaking. If he let them, they would eagerly fasten on him, sucking him dry in moments. All Eyries had them: they had never been cleared away: they were considered a deterrent to any climbing intruder, although only a madman would attempt to scale the Eyries. Some did it for wagers, for Thousandreach thrived on irrational dreams, but the prize was always a bloody death.

He alighted with absolute precision on a ledge, his ledge. His own private domain was within, a cavelike room. It contained almost nothing. A solitary stone seat, a table, a couch that was like a large nest, its material rubbery and crumpled. Foliage from the trees would have been more suitable, he had often thought, but to have taken it would have brought terrible retribution.

He saw none of the familiar things, but he knew where they all were, and moved among them unerringly. Outside the window he heard the grating arguments of the creatures as they took issue over territory. Sometimes their fights were quite violent and many of them were killed. Life in Thousandreach was often subject to abrupt termination.

He rested, sleeping through occasional dreams in which light speared at him, hurled by invisible, laughing deities.

Changes in light usually woke him. When he came to, he sensed that the same changes had still acted on him in some way, although he was still in absolute darkness. He rose, attended to his toilet, adjusted his attire, and left the bare room. Steps curled away downwards, passing other stone doorways. If other Angel Guards were stirring, he ignored them. Instinct was sufficient to guide him to the door he sought, although several times he almost tripped on the stone. It was as though the Eyrie, usually a part of him, was testing its own reaction to him. A blind Guard? Of what use could such a crippled thing be?

The door was not locked. He entered, trying to decide if there were others in the long, low chamber beyond. It was where reports were made, often heard by the Praetor. Guards sometimes gathered here before beginning their daily flights, though usually they were summoned if needed.

Somehow his body had adjusted to his blindness in such a way that it sensed other creatures in fresh ways. He knew unquestionably that no one was here at the moment. Perhaps, after all, he had risen too early. He reached the long table and sat at it, wings folded neatly behind him as though they did not exist.

Presently he was not alone. He should have guessed that it would be the Praetor himself who had come to join him. He could imagine him standing over him, fierce eyes glittering, a predator with its prize.

No one else had come. The door was closed, sealing the room with silence.

"Arteriel, are you rested?" said the Praetor.

The seated Guard nodded. Undoubtedly he had been seen arriving, during the sleep watch, was it? The silence of the Eyrie had suggested it. But no one had visited him. He turned his face up to the Praetor. He could not disguise the truth.

"I have no sight."

The Praetor may already have known this: his vision of things was far-reaching, uncanny. He did seem to react. "What of the three you were sent to find?"

"One I killed. The Foddamen had his flesh. Another took to the reed fields and succumbed to them. The last of them is under the control of an overseer."

"You killed only one." It was not a question, but he sensed that it might be an indictment. His blindness was, apparently, immaterial.

"I was not instructed to kill them. I exercised discretion."

"And was this before or after you lost your sight?" There was no pity in the voice, no emotion.

But he expected none. "After."

"You were influenced in your actions? Would you have acted differently had you not had the accident?"

"It is possible."

"What course would you have taken under normal circumstances?"

This discussion was not going well for him. He began to feel that he was being manipulated by these questions into an admission of incompetence. *I let one of them go. Why did I do that?* "I was not instructed to kill the Externals. I cannot say I would necessarily have done so."

There was a pause. "It's not for me to judge the issue, Arteriel. Others may wish to. I think we must report to the Provider who commissioned you."

"Of course." He stood, his hand touching the table briefly to steady himself. Blindness had not impeded his powers of flight, but his balance on the ground was imperfect. He would have to take every precaution to disguise the fact. Was he not to be quizzed on the accident? It seemed not by the Praetor.

"I will accompany you. Provider Hummal Goresch wishes to interview you promptly."

He nodded. So word of his return had reached Thousand-reach's many ears. He should have expected as much. The Providers were alert to every breath of air, through their networks. Goresch was one of their principal advisers, himself a servant of the Elevates who specialised in the study of the Overlap. Their position was a tenuous one: the Overlap was viewed by many of their contemporaries as blasphemous, an outrage. And the whim of the Lightbenders could always change. If they outlawed the Overlap, there would be many executions.

Arteriel took some comfort from the thought that the Angel Guard would be exempt from such recriminations.

10

"It will not be necessary for you to remain, Praetor."

The sharp voice of the Provider, Hummal Goresch, rang out across the stones of the chamber. It was a cold, ill-lit place, scrubbed and sterile. The walls were bare, except for their occasional carvings, symbols which only the Providers appeared to comprehend, part of their private mythology and language. It was a place at odds with their personal lives, which were said to be decadent and hedonistic. They saved their frugality for the conducting of business, and they were ruthless at it, demanding the highest output from their workers, meting out severe reprisals to those who served them poorly.

The Praetor bowed and left quickly, though he felt no fear before Goresch. The Provider was a client, not an employer. Even the Elevates did not command Angel Guards. But Goresch had commissioned an Angel Guard; he had his rights to an explanation.

"You stand uncomfortably," said Goresch to the remaining Angel Guard.

Arteriel had sensed the presence of the Provider on entering. He could recall him, how he looked. Very tall, with elongated arms and exaggerated hands like shovels, the fingers like something designed for scooping earth, grasping. Goresch moved with long, languorous strides, belying the ease with which he could spring, uncoiling with a power that could take an enemy by complete surprise, though Providers were not supposed to have enemies. His face was sharp and pinched, the chin jutting, teeth too large for the gash of a mouth; his eyes were hidden under thick folds of brow, his expression never clearly readable by those who faced him.

74

All these things the blind Arteriel recalled as though he had seen Goresch a few moments ago. How many sleeps had it been?

"I am blind."

Goresch frowned. There was nothing to show that this Angel Guard spoke the truth: his eyes looked no different than those of any other Guard. Odd that the Praetor had not mentioned this matter. But they were a proud race, and allowed nothing to come between them and their duties. Perhaps, Goresch reflected, sight was of secondary importance to them. Had some of them developed inner sight? It was a disturbing thought: Angel Guards were powerful enough as it was.

"It is not a natural condition," said Arteriel.

Was he lying? Had the Praetor put him up to this? Goresch tried to conceal his uncertainty. This entire business was unsatisfactory. He glanced across at the shadows near the wall of the chamber. Something moved there, subtle as a spider. Was the Guard unaware of what sat there? If he were truly blind, he would probably have assumed Goresch was alone.

However, Arteriel had already sensed the other presence. The slight movement had been enough. It surprised him to realise that his skin could be so sensitive to minute shifts in the air. Is this what blindness did? Had he merely traded one precious gift for another?

"An accident?" said Goresch.

"It seems so. There was a storm."

Goresch glanced at the darkness. The other being had not come forward. "You have flown in storms many times, though. You read their temperament as well as any other Guard."

"I believe so."

"Then, what accident was this?"

Arteriel felt Goresch's keen interest: it was in his voice, even though his words attempted to make light of it. But the silent presence locked on to Arteriel's words. It vibrated with the need to hear this.

"Light struck me down. Took me from the sky. As you say, I have flown amidst storms, danced with lightning. What Angel Guard has not?"

"Then this storm was unique?"

"I think it was. There was thunder, but no rain. Strange light under Skydown."

"Where were you?"

"Far out in the segments, near the very end of one of the many roads. Where the Externals were said to have escaped."

"Where the Overlap had opened?"

The Guard nodded. He could feel the breath of the other figure quickening. Curious how he could be so aware of its alertness. His words had stung it. He was beginning to form an opinion of what it might be. Though he had never been in the presence of a Skryer before, he felt increasingly certain that this was one of them.

"Is it possible that the Overlap had something to do with your accident?" said Goresch.

Arteriel imagined the Provider leaning forward almost hungrily.

"Yes."

Silence followed. Arteriel envisaged Goresch turning to the Skryer, a wordless conversation. Presumably this Skryer would be the one who had sanctioned the hunt that had brought the Externals here. Providers used the Skryers, who studied the vicissitudes of the Overlap, attempting to predict its occurrence and to approve a hunt. They were a strange sect, not outlawed, but not entirely blessed by the Elevates, nor indeed, the Lightbenders. If there were problems, if a hunt went wrong, or the Overlap in any way harmed the world under Skydown, the Skryers would wish to be informed. Hence this interview.

Goresch spoke again. "What of the victims of the hunt?"

"All but three were taken to a farm by the hunters, as had been their instruction. I met their overseer, Sommoi."

"These were the three you were sent to recover?"

Arteriel realised that this information was incidental: his listeners were concerned about the behaviour of the Overlap, not the Externals. But he played his role as instructed, and explained what had happened to the runaways. Was he to be chastised for not having seen to their executions personally?

Curiously, it seemed not. "If you are satisfied that the

Externals are accounted for, there is no point in discussing them further," said Goresch.

Arteriel bowed slightly, but the unease of the two beings was a palpable thing.

"Is it known," Goresch asked, "whether or not the loss of your sight is a permanent thing?"

"I have not had the opportunity to learn."

"No, of course not. In which case, I will not delay you. This accident concerns me. Send word to me if your condition does not improve."

"I would not wish to trouble you—"

"I insist," said Goresch, trying not to seem too demanding, though it was tantamount to an order.

"Very well."

"Shall I ask the Praetor to guide you back to your Eyrie?"

But Arteriel had already turned away. He went to the chamber door and put his hand on its bolt, sliding it open in one flowing movement as easily as if he had watched his hands perform the task.

He left without answering. The Praetor was not far away along the corridor. He studied the blind Angel Guard as he emerged from the Provider's chamber, the calmness, the complete self-control. Arteriel turned blind eyes towards him. The Praetor knew that Arteriel was perfectly aware of him. Other senses had leapt to the service of the damaged eyes. Remarkable.

"They seemed satisfied with my work," said Arteriel.

The Praetor frowned at the chamber door. "They? Did someone join Hummal Goresch? He assured me it would be a private audience."

In view of my condition? Arteriel mused. Pity? Would a Provider understand the meaning of such a word? Foolish to suppose it. And the Praetor knew better than that. Deceit was a rank stench in these corridors.

"He was not alone, Praetor. Did you not notice the Skryer?"

There was a pause before the Praetor commented. "I did not, but certainly it would have been his advice to Hummal Goresch that led to your commission."

"Well, it is done."

"You must have medical attention. We will see to it at once."

Clearly, thought Arteriel, *my blindness is less important than the satisfaction of those who commissioned me.*

As the Praetor was leading Arteriel discreetly away, Hummal Goresch brooded thoughtfully in the chamber.

"An accident," came the soft voice of the Skryer, barely above a whisper.

Goresch shuddered at its sound: it was like a caress. The Skryers had powers more seductive than many of the pleasures of Thousandreach. "No."

"Your conclusion?"

"If it was an attack, why wasn't he killed? Why blind him?"

"If it was an attack," came the susurrating voice, "who was responsible? Not Absolute Light, be assured."

"Has your art not told you?" snapped Goresch impatiently.

"It has not. The Overlap is as difficult to read as the gods."

"We have learned nothing!" Goresch snorted, banging his fist down on the arm of his seat.

"Oh, but I disagree. We have seen the beginning. This is merely the first step. A window has opened on a new dawn, if you will forgive my use of imagery."

Goresch saw the Skryer quivering. It was a few moments before he realised that it was registering amusement. *Damn the Skryers and their secrets! How can I serve Elevate Zaer Phesmes when things are kept from me! This Skryer had Zaer's confidence, but do I? I do not. This creature toys with me. What is their purpose, damn them!*

All the complex medical expertise that the Angel Guards had at their disposal could not help Arteriel.

"Will I see again?" he asked.

"I would say not," was the blunt reply. Instruments clinked in their trays. The smell in the medical block was overpowering.

"You will need further tests," he was told.

"Such as?"

"Your other faculties are unimpaired. You may think your

balance unsettled, but that is probably temporary. Your system will compensate."

"Fully?"

"Only the tests will show that."

"And if I fail those tests?"

"You will no longer be alive."

"Essentially we are assassins," said the Praetor. They had returned to his chamber. It had been a tiring period, the medical probes endless.

There was no pain in Arteriel's eyes, but his head ached. "Assassins," he nodded.

"Such other functions as we perform are supplementary. If we do not fulfill our role as assassins, we fail."

"You think a blind Angel Guard has no use?" The question was intentionally blunt, cutting through respect for the Praetor's rank. But there was no rebuke expected, nor given.

"It is not for me to deliberate. I need to be sure, one way or the other."

"They spoke of further tests."

"They did."

"Am I to rest first?"

"I insist that you do. When the sleep is over, you will undertake the testing. As you know, it is not customary for Angel Guards to fight each other, being contrary to our customs and wasteful. But if you are worthy of your role, you will have to demonstrate your worthiness."

"In what manner of combat, Praetor?"

"In open combat. The test has to be thorough. Survive it and you are as before."

The silence that followed was unnecessary: the dialogue was at an end. Arteriel quit the chamber, returning by the stair to his own. Twice on his way he stumbled, though he blamed fatigue. After a sleep he would be recovered enough. He would have to be.

At the head of the stairs, he listened to the breathing of the stones. Somewhere among them, another Guard slept, the warrior who had already been chosen for the combat. One of them would be opened up when it was over, his organs a gift to the hidden gods.

Are they testing me? he wondered. *Was it they who blinded me? Have I not served them well?*

The stones had no answer.

11

There were procedures governing combat between two Angel Guards, but as it had been a considerable time since such a contest had been staged officially, there was a delay while the appropriate records were consulted. It was a matter for the Guards alone, a private affair to which none other could be a party. Inhabitants of Thousandreach could expect a grim penalty for intruding on the event. After an intense study of the rules and rituals, the Praetor satisfied himself that he understood the protocol and that the conditions of the contest were as they stood be. Only then did he visit Arteriel.

The latter had been in his room, high over Thousandreach, his thoughts and movements absolutely private. He had been visited by no one since his return, apart from the Praetor. Blindness meant a kind of loneliness, just as flying on lone patrol meant isolation, but Arteriel was conscious for the first time of being utterly apart from his kind. Already he had been judged, ostracised.

The Praetor was no less blunt than before. "I will describe what has been done. Come to the ledge."

Arteriel had come to know his chamber well, its every dimension. He stood with assurance at the very lip of the drop, blind eyes facing the uppermost terraces of the city. He no longer walked with a trace of unsteadiness.

The Praetor looked out at the drop: the earth was several hundreds of feet below, lost in darkness. "You and your opponent will be confined to a specific area."

Arteriel's expression did not change, but he was thinking,

I will be advantaged by this. Blindness restricts me, but my opponent will also be restricted now.

"We have stretched a steel net between two of the Eyries, almost to their full height. And we have stretched other nets from the Eyries across to certain structures in the city. The area created inside the nets is triangular."

Then it would be a large area, Arteriel mused, trying to picture it. The work involved in stretching the nets would have been exceptional. Not long ago he had heard sounds beyond his Eyrie. Here was the explanation of those colossal exertions.

"We have not drawn a net over the ceiling. But you must not fly above the nets. If you do so, you will forfeit the contest and be brought down."

To my death. The contest is yet uneven.

"Have you all your weapons?"

"I have."

"You can utilise as many as you wish."

"May I know the name of the Angel Guard I am to fight?"

"It is permitted. He is a Flenser. His name is Syrakeil."

"I know him. An esteemed warrior."

"As are you."

Arteriel ignored the comment. He was facing oblivion. Any Angel Guard would be deadly, but Syrakeil was exceptional even by the standards of the Flensers.

"Are you ready to begin? The nets are cleared. Your opponent has already entered them."

"Very well."

"With your permission, I will watch the contest from this room. The view is commanding."

"Of course, Praetor. I am honoured."

"Then you may begin."

Arteriel tasted the air, felt the breath of the wind on his cheek. He could not judge the degree of light with eyes that no longer functioned, but he could feel the temperature of the air. His judgement had become very sharp, as if the accident had blessed the senses it had not impaired. He judged that there was good light. Syrakeil would benefit from that.

Arteriel glided gently out, spiraling down before hovering, beating his wings against the faint air currents and thermals.

He knew at once that many Angel Guard were watching from beyond the net. Some, like the Praetor, stood in the entrances to their chambers in the Eyries, while others clung to the outside of the nets. He could feel their eyes, hear their breathing, their muted words. If there was pity, it was stifled by the eagerness for conflict, the desire to see blood. This should have been a famous conflict, but most of them were anticipating a swift execution. And down below, in the lower levels of Thousandreach, where the buildings piled on top of one another like so much rubble, the Menials would be unaware. To them the death of an Angel was meaningless. All life to them was cheap. They had their own pains to bear.

A single cry, like the voice of a great eagle, came to Arteriel across the vault. Syrakeil was alerting him to be ready. It would be the only time either spoke. There would be no quarter.

It had begun. He could hear Syrakeil's wings, thrumming the air as he swooped for what would be a pass only, a test. Slowly Arteriel unsheathed a curved blade. He had longer weapons, but did not use them in aerial manoeuvring: they were light and beautifully balanced but a shade too unwieldy. The shorter blade would be easier to handle.

Syrakeil passed above him and Arteriel turned away easily, then climbed straight upwards as if he were making for the opening at the top of the nets. Syrakeil immediately flew upwards on a parallel course, curving across towards him at the last moment in order to intercept him. Arteriel could feel the Flenser's racing flight, surprised at the surety of his judgement. His sudden turn and dive caught Syrakeil totally unawares, it was executed with such perfection and beauty. The audience noted the move with amazement. It had taken great skill: this Guard was *blind?* That must be a mistake.

A pattern began to emerge quickly. Syrakeil was clearly the hunter, while his opponent made use of his phenomenal aerial dexterity to keep away from the thirsting hooks of his would-be killer. Twice Syrakeil almost snared his prey, but had to swing outwards to avoid a collision with the steel net.

His opponent dived down towards the darkness, testing it, knowing by the slight fall in temperature here that shadows festered. This would be the place to draw Syrakeil, though

like all Guards, his eyes would penetrate such gloom. Even
so, Syrakeil was wary of being drawn downward. It was obvious to him what his opponent wanted.

He flew slowly in gradual circles, closing in once more.
This time he was less eager to pounce, edging his prey back
so that Arteriel would be unable to produce another of those
stunning aerial twists that would take him clear. Syrakeil's
ploy worked well. He closed in, then dived with breathtaking
speed.

The two combatants met, weapons raised. Syrakeil would
have plunged his sword through the neck of his victim, but
the curved blade met his own, turning it with unexpected
strength: the strength of fear? But Syrakeil was not convinced
of that. He could smell no trace of panic on this blind warrior. For a second it unnerved him, and he found himself
deflected, fighting to break the hold. The clawed glove of his
opponent ripped into his side, dragging at the fabric of his
shirt. It held, but the skin beneath bruised painfully.

Syrakeil wrestled himself away as the two bodies began to
plummet. They broke apart and swooped upwards again, on
opposite sides of the net. It had become a fabulous dance:
the watchers were entranced, glorying in the skills of their
own kind, the absolute mastery of the skies. The kill was
unimportant.

It was not so for the contestants. With each rush of air,
their blood sang, and it sang with a need, a killing need.
Both of them were gripped now by desires that controlled
them, needs that had been bred into them over generations.
Mastery of the killing urge was the most difficult of all skills;
the tide could so easily flood, breaking through the superficial
barriers of restraint.

They clashed again, and Syrakeil marveled that his weapon
did not find its mark. How could his blind opponent be so
aware of its movement through the air? Yet an arm rose to
meet it as though that arm was imbued with its own senses,
independent of the body. But such magical resistance could
not last. Syrakeil adjusted his approach. He took another
blade from his belt. It would slightly restrict his flight, but
two blades would best the defence of his opponent.

Arteriel had used the space as well as he could, not allowing himself to be trapped in the angles of the net, but at long last Syrakeil found a way of edging him back. He came at him from below so that the only easy way out of the trap would be upward. But they were perilously close to the top of the nets. To go beyond was not permitted.

Syrakeil drifted upwards, both blades extended. He was certain that this would be the kill, that or he would drive his opponent over the top to disgrace, execution. He could hear the voices of the watchers. Some of them were not far below him on the nets. They knew the moment had come.

Arteriel waited, still holding the short blade. His other claw reached to his belt, but he did not bring out the long weapon, which would have been the obvious way to defend himself in this trap. Instead he clutched at one of the small hooks, a tool of the hunt. He was listening to every breath of his opponent, every faint creak of his wings.

Syrakeil plunged in, but it was a measured attack, swift and deadly. As he did so, Arteriel drew back his arm and cast the hook. Syrakeil ignored it, felt it bite into his side. It could not harm him. Instead he drove his twin blades towards the victim. The latter twisted, but could never have hoped to escape. His arm came up to take the first weapon, the second running into the wing and grating along its frail cartilage. But it had done enough to deflect the killing thrust.

Syrakeil knew that the kill was his for the asking. As he drew out his two blades, he let his opponent drop away, wing badly torn. The rest would be easy. He made to plummet himself, intending one long drop and strike. But as he did so, something wrenched at him and he felt his ribs grinding in his chest. He crashed back into the net, mouth gaping as his wings buckled, tangling in the fine steel mesh. Looking down, he saw the hook in him. It was attached to a length of thin chain, the end of which had been hooked securely to the net. Blood seeped thickly through the fabric of his ruined shirt.

As he struggled painfully against the snare, he saw Arteriel rise up before him. The empty eyes were on him. Did they see?

Syrakeil tried to tear his arm free, to raise his weapon in defence, but it was useless. He was pinned. Agony coursed through his every vein as his wings protested at the savage work of the mesh. It bit and tore.

Syrakeil's eyes misted as Arteriel at last drew out his long blade. They did not see it drive home.

Outside the nets, the Angel Guards watched in absolute silence as Arterial thrust his weapon through the neck of Syrakeil. The body of the latter twitched, legs spasming on the net for a moment, like a fly's last frantic exertion to escape the spider's clutch. Then it was over. The corpse hung limply and pathetically, like the cocoon of a huge moth.

The victor put away his blade, unhooked the chain that had trapped his victim, and flew without a sound across to his Eyrie. The Praetor had already departed.

This time he was allowed to have his wounds tended.

The surgeon who dealt with him had not witnessed the conflict. "Your wing will heal," he said coldly. "It will take time."

"And my sight?"

"I think not. They tell me you sacrificed your wing in order to trap your opponent. Is that so?"

"It was a calculated risk."

"In my view, an Angel Guard should make it a priority to protect his wings at all times. Without them, he is no better than a Menial."

"But my wing will heal?"

"I have said so," the surgeon grunted, his displeasure perfectly evident.

Arteriel left him abruptly. The Praetor, as promised, was waiting for him in his chamber. Arteriel could hear the sound of something held in his hands: it was, he suspected, a document, which was unusual, for the Angel Guards had as little to do with such things as possible.

"You are recovered?" said the Praetor. He had, so far, made no comment on Arteriel's extraordinary victory. He seemed neither pleased nor displeased.

"My wing will heal. It will be enough, I think."

The Praetor was not drawn by the implication of the remark. He held up the document. "I have here something from Elevate Zaer Phesmes."

Arteriel stiffened. Zaer Phesmes was a significantly powerful Elevate.

"Provider Hummal Goresch is his hireling. I am sure you are aware that Providers are far more answerable to the Elevates than they would like to believe. All Providers seek to become Elevates, though some act with more honour than others, who are inclined to be unscrupulous. Provider Hummal Goresch, in my view, eschews all values. He is selfish, but is careful to please Elevate Zaer Phesmes and dares not displease him. Goresch is a coward. Thus he has reported to Zaer Phesmes, fully. This is the result of that report. It is a directive to me, as Praetor of your chapter."

Again Arteriel stiffened. All that he had achieved so far could mean nothing.

"It is confidential," said the Praetor, "so I will not read it to you. But in my view you must be told its content. You fought well, Arteriel. You deserve respect. I promise you, you have mine."

"My thanks, Praetor."

"In the view of the Elevate, Zaer Phesmes, there should be no weaknesses among the Angel Guards, who are entrusted with the safety of Thousandreach, the lives of the Lightbenders. The document makes no reference to your blindness. Nor does it refer to the conflict with Syrakeil, your defeat of him. Thus there is no criticism of your combat ability.

"However, it does refer to events in the field, that is, your last commission. Your failure to adhere to instructions. In the view of Zaer Phesmes, you should have brought back the blood of the three Externals you were sent to deal with."

"I will fetch it."

The Praetor shook his head, knowing that somehow Arteriel was aware of the movement. "It is too late for that. It is the principle. You did not fulfil your duty. Zaer Phesmes is not content."

Arteriel waited. A coldness filled him, a knowledge that a greater darkness was reaching for him.

"You can no longer be an Angel Guard." The Praetor said this with no emotion. If he held views on the matter, he would not show them. It was his duty to be utterly impartial.

And duty ruled him; it was the air he breathed, the thermal he flew upon. He had said he respected Arteriel, and could say no more.

Arteriel heard sounds outside, the dismantling of the nets. It was as though his victory was already being put away, its value discounted. He waited.

"You are to leave this Eyrie."

"Am I to be executed?"

"No. Provider Hummal Goresch has been charged to give you further instruction. I regret that it is necessary." It was as close as the Praetor came to emotion, though the words were spoken flatly.

"If I have failed him, Praetor, why would he wish to use me again?"

"You will work in the city."

"As what, Praetor?"

"That is not for me to say. I will send for you when it is time to leave."

The room closed in after he had gone. It offered no answers, no mote of comfort. Work in the city? Away from the skies? It would be a living death.

He thought of fodda, the crawling masses of life that struggled into Thousandreach, cheap flesh. Surely the Provider could make better use of him, his proven superiority.

12

He waited, alone, at the foot of the stair. It debouched into a narrow chamber somewhere far down near the base of the Eyrie. Like much of the rest of the tower, the room was empty and airless. In the darkness and the silence his thoughts were like spoken words.

Protocol, duty, service. Words that had motivated the An-

gel Guard for centuries, the rocks upon which they built.
Each breath they took, each move they made had its roots in
that. There could be no deviation. They did not question.

*I will not question. I will not criticise my Praetor. Though
I have shown him and the gathered Angel Guard that, in spite
of my blindness, I am still able, still worthy, I must accept
the decree of the Elevate, Zaer Phesmes. It is not for my
Praetor to argue against him. I am not shamed. But the Angel
Guard cannot maintain me. Protocol is clear.*

They had taken his weapons, the instruments of his work,
and with them his rank, Blood Red. There had been few
words. Not one of them spoke against the decree, the excom-
munication.

But he would not be exiled, cast out. Since the charges
against his ability had arisen from the report of Hummal Goresch, it would be the Provider who must take over responsibility for him, find him work, however menial. There could
be no question of execution, not after the aerial battle. The
Provider would send other servants to collect their prize. And
there the matter would end.

Somewhere within his inner darkness, a shape began to
unfurl, writhing like a serpent under sluggish waters. A serpent of doubt, of resentment. *I proved my skill. There may
be a mystery in it, in a blind warrior defeating a sighted one.
But I am reduced to this.*

The resentment had not yet approached anger, bitterness.
It clung to the dark places in his mind, almost afraid to show
itself. Duty was all. It was not to be questioned. There was
only one code for the Angel Guard. To deviate was to risk
the damnation of them all, the collapse of their indestructible
power.

A door opened. He tasted air, the air of the world beyond
the Eyrie. It was sharp, tainted with the sweat of fear, the
ugliness, the press of base humanity, the lower reaches of
Thousandreach.

Three creatures entered: he felt them, one by one. The two
largest of them, which cast broad shadows, chilling the air,
were Transmutes, beings reshaped by the designers of the
Providers they belonged to. Arteriel had seen such beasts:
like ogres, bloated with muscle, thick-necked and primitive,

controlled by the smaller creatures that were their immediate wardens, the *goads*. The *goad* that had entered would be half Arteriel's height, and spindly, flesh shriveled, eyes sunken almost to nothing in an insect's head.

"They have taken your weapons?" came its reedy voice. Its teeth clicked. The Transmutes stood behind it like stone, their bodies exuding a sharp stench peculiar to their monstrous kind.

Arteriel merely opened his cloak to show that he carried nothing.

"I am to escort you to a place chosen by Provider Hummal Goresch. You understand?"

"Yes."

"I must ask you to hold out your arms. They are to be bound until we reach our destination."

Arteriel could feel the unease in the *goad*. Since his blindness, he had become astute at judging voices, detecting through the timbre shifts in emotion he had not been aware of previously. It was one of many arts he was rapidly acquiring.

The *goad* was partly afraid, seeing potential death before it. Arteriel watched its shadow materialise clearly on his inner eye. It pleased him. As it formed, it drew on the elusive anger that threatened his own equanimity. To be herded by these dregs! Bound!

He lifted his arms, placing his wrists together. But something of his resentment must have shown in his face. The *goad* exuded fear like stale perfume. It unwound the leather twine, slipping it over the wrists. The clawed gloves had been taken from Arteriel along with his weapons. Remarkably, the hands were pale and slender, nothing like the killing tools they became.

I could grip your neck and squeeze the life from you with ease, Arteriel thought, blind eyes fixed on the sweating face below him. His thought struck home; the *goad* worked furiously to finish. From the bindings, the excess twine became a leash.

The *goad* spoke to the Transmutes, who stood aside to allow the *goad* and Arteriel to pass outside. It was hot, deep down in the stone canyons of the lower city. They had emerged from the very roots of the Eyrie.

Arteriel again knew what it was to feel panic welling. He had never been so far from the sky. This place stank, the walls exuding filth, the earth rucked and broken. Life crawled here, swarming. It was cheap, expendable. If it aspired, it was upward, like rats emerging from a drain. Arteriel was relieved he could not see, as they trudged along, though the smells of this place became increasingly appalling in themselves. They fed his anger. It was no longer the secret thing it had been.

I do not deserve this. Whatever blinded me, chance or god, I do not deserve this. He closed out the stench, the brash sounds, the shrieks. There might have been a battle going on around him. He ignored it, entering his inner world, trying instead to make something of his future.

The *goad* took them to a bridge, a narrow span cut from stone. It was one of scores, radiating out from the narrow street across to the main wall of Thousandreach, which rose up, vast as a mountain beyond the abyss. Like the other bridges, this one was busy, its traffic streaming to and fro, ants scurrying ceaselessly. The *goad* pulled on the leash, Arteriel following mechanically. Behind him he could feel the slow tread of the Transmutes.

If he had not been bound, he would have opened his wings and taken to the skies, soaring up and away from this pit. What could they have in mind for him? What tasks could he perform, if not those of a Guard? He would be an inconvenience to the Provider, an embarrassment. Possibly he would be given a task so base, so depressing, they would anticipate the breaking of the will to live.

Halfway over the span, there were shouts, confusion. The way was congested, and no one was prepared to back off. It sounded as though a fight had broken out. The *goad* called the two Transmutes forward, and they brushed past Arteriel clumsily. Each of them wielded something, a club possibly. Arteriel heard them growl at the press of bodies ahead.

Someone screamed. A victim of the chaos. The bridge had become dangerous. Arteriel felt a gust of fear. Without his arms, he could not survive a fall. People had fallen: he heard them shrieking as they plummeted into the fathomless well to the very roots of Thousandreach. Something down there would be glad of their flesh, though. Nothing was ever wasted.

"Untie me," Arteriel told the *goad*. "At least until we can get off this span."

The *goad* was clearly confused. The press of bodies had become a weight, rolling forward, thrusting everyone back towards the outer ring. One of the Transmutes let out a bellow of agony as if someone had used steel on it.

"Hurry!" insisted Arteriel. "Untie me."

There was no answer. Angry, he tugged on the leash, meaning to bring the *goad* into his embrace so that he could force the creature to obey him. But there was no weight on the end of the leash. He lifted it and found its end. It had been cleanly severed.

He felt a hot mouth close to his ear. "Watch your step, blind one, or you'll walk off the span." It was a threat, not a warning.

He tensed, knowing that there was a weapon of some kind inches from his back. The *goad* had gone, probably to its death. Somewhere ahead, the chaos went on, and occasionally the two Transmutes could be heard, thrashing about in what had become a ferocious brawl.

"I will lead you to safety," breathed the voice. It was rich in treachery, in cruel enjoyment. A creature who took pleasure in the infliction of pain. But for the moment, the voice was the only path to safety.

Easing back, Arteriel followed where he was led. The crowd on the bridge understood the problem ahead, and no one was eager to join the riot. Like a flash fire, it would have to burn itself out. People backed away, the word going back down to the road. The situation eased, although in the middle of the span, the fighting had not abated.

Off the span, the silent man led Arteriel into a cold alley that sloped downwards steeply. Arteriel inwardly winced at the thought of moving farther from the sky, especially in this obnoxious place. But he had other things to consider. Why should this stranger take him anywhere? Why rescue him? But of course, this was no rescue. It was an abduction.

There would be questions, on both sides, but for the moment he could do no more than be led. Behind them, Arteriel heard other sounds of pursuit, slithering, ungainly sounds. The confusion on the span had been planned, the entire affair calculated.

Steps, down, down. Cold, bitter, and hostile. Fear took hold of him now. He was a creature of the upper air. This taxed him, his control. He, like all his kind, was proud of that control, a vital part of his ability to survive in a dangerous role. But this going down, this drift towards the underground was far worse than blindness. Gritting his teeth, he closed out the pressing walls of his terror.

His abductors knew, of course. It was the perfect way to disadvantage him. Blind, tied, far from the sky. Helpless.

But who were they? Who could possibly want him?

After interminable steps down through cramped corridors to the very bowels of the city, there was a chamber. The air was thick, almost unbreathable, so that Arteriel felt his chest rising and falling in an effort to draw air into him. He also sensed a number of bodies, possibly three of them. Whatever it was that had been following had remained behind, somewhere on the upper stairs. Transmutes of one kind or another, he guessed. If they were, then his captors served a Provider.

"So it is true what we were told," came a voice from the wall of dark. It was icier than that of the man who had brought Arteriel, barbed with hidden threats. A Tormentor, possibly, one of those trained in punishment. The worst of them were used by the Elevates. "You are indeed blind."

Arteriel said nothing. He would offer no advantage.

"Are you also dumb?"

Again, no response. They would tell him why he was here in their own time. He could wait.

"No, I doubt it. Confused, though. But safe. As long as Provider Goresch doesn't try to take you back. He's bound to, of course. Obviously you're valuable to him."

Arteriel noted the comment. Valuable? An odd choice of words.

"It surprises you?"

Had this man read his mind? Such things were possible. Tormenters were known to have bizarre skills.

"Had you not been valuable to him, he would never have brought those charges against you in order to take responsibility for you. Full control. He is a puppet, though. You understand that?"

For Zaer Phesmes, the Elevate, yes. But Arteriel remained still.

"Hummal Goresch is weak, contemptible. His master is not. He must consider you valuable."

As must your own masters. But why? Because I am the victim of an accident?

"You're of no value dead, so relax. I won't kill you."

But you'll torture me, try to drag every memory from me. For whom? Who is your own master? Another Elevate, a rival of Zaer Phesmes?

As these thoughts nudged him, Arteriel felt the twine binding him loosen slightly. The severed end had slipped through one of the knots. His captors would not expect him to attack them, not here, not where he ought to feel utterly vulnerable. They would be armed, confident. But what light was there? He concentrated. Light meant heat. Feel it, his mind told him.

There, in the wall. A sphere, light within it. The single source of light in the chamber. How large was the chamber? What furniture was there? Impossible to say.

The man who had brought him shifted slightly. He was a pace behind, to his right. He carried a weapon of some kind, almost certainly a dirk, a common enough blade. Two, possibly three, other men. One light. The maximum permitted by law. It would be weak, its globe fragile.

I will have to be fast. He eased his fingers. Would they notice? The knot slipped. He could free it.

Where is my anger? he asked himself. He summoned it, probing for the elusive bitterness. The time of repression was past. He must tap every vestige of outrage, use it, direct it. It was his only hope of survival.

13

As the twine parted, he felt a stab of decision, as powerful a shock to his system as the lightning had been. In a split second he saw his future, the coherent intention threading through it. And acted upon it. Very quickly.

From under his wrists to his elbow, serrated edges of steel sprang open, part of his regalia that had not been stripped from him. Perhaps the Praetor had seen fit to give him something in the way of protection, the nearest he had come to pity.

His right arm swung back and across the throat of the man who had brought him here. The movement was so fast that the man had no time to scream, only fall backwards, throat ripped out, blood pumping through clawing fingers. The weapon he had held clanged on the stone floor: at once Arteriel bent down, guided by the sound, and picked it up. As he had expected, it was a dirk. Already he had measured the distance to the heat source, the solitary light.

The dirk hummed through the air, the haft smashing the globe, which exploded noisily in the confined space. One of the other men did scream, shouting something about his eyes.

Then we are even, thought Arteriel. *And in the darkness, we are all equal.* He had rolled away silently and swiftly. He felt an object—a table? Using his strength, he heaved it upwards. It met with resistance, another of the men, who yelled obscenities. But Arteriel was far stronger than these men. He rammed the table backwards to where the wall would be, and felt the grinding of bones as he pushed.

Again he slipped away, moving with absolute stealth. The men were only just recovering from the shock of the attack, the sheer speed of it. One of them was groping for the door

94

in the utter darkness. Arteriel knew they would try for it and positioned himself near where he could feel a slight draft from the door. As the man came close to him, unaware of him, his arm shot out and down, the hooked edges tearing cloth and flesh in a deep rip.

Arteriel could hear shouts from above. Something was struggling down the steps, something unquestionably not human. He could hear the slither of its bulk, smell its acrid, reptilian stench.

Crossing the room, he sensed that he had dealt with all the men who had been here. Any he had missed had either fled or were crouching in a corner in dread of their lives. One still gurgled horribly, life gushing from his severed neck, while the one who had taken the injury from the exploding sphere of light was moaning close at hand.

Arteriel gripped one of his arms and his throat, forcing him backwards until he was up against a bare wall.

"Is there another way out?" Arteriel whispered.

The man nodded, knowing that the Angel Guard would be strong enough to wrench his head round, snapping his neck like a dry stick.

"Can you see?"

The man shook his head. "But there was a door behind where I sat."

Down the stairs came the others, snarling their rage. Had they seen the carnage? Arteriel swung the man along the wall until they came to the doorframe. The man frantically opened it and at once Arteriel thrust him through. Still keeping a grip on his throat, he twisted round and slammed the door shut. Something crashed against its other side almost at once, but Arteriel held it. There was no bolt, but he held it in place. It rattled as something hurled itself at it, but the Guard would not allow the door to open.

"What is it?" he hissed to the man.

"Transmute—"

"I know that! What is the beast?"

"Claw, reptile, carnivore. All that."

"Call it off."

"It's been unleashed—"

"If it wants food, it has plenty."

The man gasped as the grip at his throat tightened. Could this Guard be *holding* the door against the Transmute?

"Call it off!"

The man nodded. His face was thrust up against the door. He could hear claws raking the thick wooden panels. Raising his voice, he called on the beast to desist, using the commands with which it was familiar. Arteriel sensed that this was merely show: the man was using mental powers to control the Transmute.

It took a while, but eventually the door stopped rattling and whatever was beyond it calmed down.

"It will attack my men—"

Arteriel ignored him, again swinging him around. "Where does this lead?"

"Up into the hovels. A maze." The man's head swung round and Arteriel could sense heat above, another light source. Had the man seen it?

Something cold slipped into his mind, like the clammy touch of the Transmute beyond the door, and at once Arteriel realised what was happening. The man he held was a Tormenter, attempting to use his peculiar, warped powers.

"Can you see?"

"I—yes. I am not blinded. Dazed. But, yes, I can make out the steps."

"You are glad of your sight?"

The man nodded. The grip on his neck had not lessened. His muscles shrieked in protest.

"Remove your probe."

The Tormenter obeyed instantly, feeling himself on the brink of blacking out.

"Guide me upward and away, and you can keep your eyes." Arteriel did not need to elaborate. As the cold presence receded from his mind, he was able to lessen his grip, and the Tormenter's breath rasped as he dragged air into his lungs like a man almost drowned.

They went up the narrow steps slowly and cautiously. Arteriel could tell that they were still in the endless tunnel system that burrowed its way through the entrails of Thousandreach's lowest levels. If there had been a hint of the outside world, he would have sensed it. The air on his face would have proclaimed it. But it did not. Here it was oppressive, fetid. Dimly through the walls came sounds of gurgling water, of machines pumping. Creatures skidded away at their tread, others oozing back into the muck that dripped from the walls.

Arteriel clung to his purpose grimly. Much more of this and he could lose his reason. The sky seemed a world away.

They reached another level of tunnel that was cleaner and less evil-smelling than the one they had left. The Transmute was not going to follow.

"A few questions," said Arteriel.

"I guessed you'd say that," grunted the Tormenter, sagging down. He rubbed his neck, but Arteriel stood over him. This creature was supposed to be *blind!* His eyes were filmed. But down in the cell, he had been deadly.

"Who are you?" said the Guard. His hands, so slender! no more than inches away from the man's chest, ready to strike.

"Breboon is my name."

"You are a Tormenter."

The question was no surprise, as the Guard had sensed his attempt at a probe.

"I am."

"You serve whom?"

"I am undesignate."

"Someone paid you for my abduction."

Breboon knew that if he did not give up the information, the Angel Guard would simply kill him. At least the Guards were not known for torture. "It was one of the Elevates. But I do not know which one. He dealt indirectly with me, through his agents. It is usually the way."

Arteriel nodded. Breboon would not have been given the name. The Elevates were cautious. But whoever it was, he was a rival of Zaer Phesmes. Again, rivalry between Elevates was common. They vied for glory in the eyes of their overlords, the Lightbenders.

"What were you told to do with me?"

"I'm a Tormenter. I would have opened your mind on its past. They want to know how you became blind."

"Then I have something in common with them."

"You—do not know?"

Arteriel ignored the question. "When do you next meet the agents of your master?"

Breboon felt himself growing cold. "It would not be wise to meddle with them—"

"When?" The slender fingers reached out and touched his chest, the caress of a serpent.

Breboon answered.

"I want only one thing," insisted Arteriel. "The name."

"They'll hunt you. There is nowhere under Skydown that can harbour you, even down here. The walls gorge on secrets. They spew them out carelessly to those who know how to tap them."

"Only the name."

"You know they will not tell me."

"The agents will tell me."

"They will kill me."

"Probably."

Breboon shuddered. Death, it seemed, was to be his shadow. Unless he could trick this Guard somehow. But blind as he was, he was dangerous, so dangerous.

"First, we go up. I need to feel the sky."

"It's a long climb. We can't get that far up without being seen."

"You know these warrens. And doubtless most of the vermin that crawl through them. If I'm challenged, you die with me. It's that simple. I should already be dead. I've stolen time."

"Why don't you cooperate? Give them what they want?"

"I don't know what they want." *Just as I don't know what it is Zaer Phesmes wants.* Why should a blind warrior interest them? "When we are on more open ground," he told Breboon, "I'll select a place."

"Place?"

"To meet one of the agents you deal with. Send someone to fetch him."

Breboon agreed softly. This Guard was so cold, so confident. Or was he mad, his mind unhinged by the ordeal they said he had been through? But the word was that he had fought and killed one of his kind, in spite of his blindness.

No, not mad, Breboon thought. *Clinical, as his breed are. He wants that name. Why not get it for him? It is the only hope of safety I have, all that I have to barter with.*

Breboon had led Arteriel up through numerous levels. During the tortuous climb, Arteriel thought that for once he was better off without his sight. If he had been able to see the journey upwards they had made, he would probably have lost his nerve. He had not been prepared for the scale of the squalor. Fodda was little better than vermin, but the conditions in which it festered here were beyond all imagining. The sounds and smells alone had been enough to drive him close to the edge. What a cesspit this lower city was! Redolent with pain, misery, filth. Nothing but torment, suffering. Thousandreach's foundations were carved from such base things. Better that darkness obscured them.

Perhaps Breboon could have betrayed him: there must have been opportunities for him to signal secretly to men that knew him. If he had done so, Arteriel was unaware. But he held tight to his prize, breathed the threat of death close by Breboon's ear. No trap opened its maw as yet.

Breboon found them a place under the sky, an open place, though Arteriel was not wholly satisfied with it. But it would have to serve them. It was a small rectangle, a square, the buildings on all sides, Breboon swore, derelict and forgotten by all but the rats. There were many such places in this part of Thousandreach, at the very base of the central construction that was the massive plateau of the upper city.

The Tormenter sent someone, a scuttling, wheezing creature that Arteriel could only picture mentally, out into the seething streets of the lower city. He could take word to the agents.

Arteriel took Breboon into one of the abandoned buildings. It stank of rot and decay, the damp air laden with dust as if the very stone crumbled, cankered and withered. They sat in the rubble, on fallen beams riddled with worm. It was as though Arteriel could feel the stirrings of decay inside a huge corpse.

"What will you do?" Breboon asked, unable to bear the

silence that clamped down during their wait, broken as it was by no more than the steady drip of water somewhere within.

Arteriel always sat close enough to reach out and touch his prisoner. At first he said nothing. He was economical with words, as his kind were. They spoke when they had to. But he answered slowly.

"Like you, I am undesignate. I no longer have an Eyrie to fly to. I have no rank."

"What were you?"

There was more than an edge of pride in the reply. "I was a Blood Red. An elite."

"Will you serve Hummal Goresch, the Provider?"

"From whom you took me? Why should I serve the one who is responsible for casting me out of the Guard?"

"Defy him and you defy his master, Zaer Phesmes. He is very powerful among the Elevates."

"Would you say Zaer Phesmes was ambitious?"

Breboon pondered the question. How much did the Guard know? Were his kind party to the gossip that flowed like air through the lower city? Or did protocol forbid them to involve themselves in such things?

"He is an Elevate! They are all ambitious. They suck on power like a babe on a tit."

"And would you say Zaer Phesmes was ruthless in his pursuits?"

Breboon grinned. The Guard was in no way naive. Diplomatic. That was his code. But he knew how it was among the Elevates. How they grasped every opportunity. "I wouldn't know. But he's an Elevate, so is likely as cold-blooded a bastard as any of them. Having you discredited would have meant absolutely nothing to him. Not if he got what he wanted from you."

Arteriel nodded slowly. The Tormenter was afraid of him. That was good. It meant he wouldn't attempt escape unless he was absolutely sure he could get away. But he had spirit. Few men would have had the nerve to converse with an Angel Guard, much less question one. It made it easier to hold down his own contempt for the man, who was, after all, little better than the fodda that crawled through the maze they had just left. "And what is it Zaer wants?"

"The same thing my own master wants. The answer to one question: Who blinded you?"

The Guard's face was remarkably serene. He seemed unconcerned at the confusion he had brought back from the segments. "It was an accident," he said softly. "Chance."

"The Elevates don't think so."

Arteriel did not answer, nor react. But the words intrigued him. *No accident. But if not, where do I uncover the truth?*

14

Breboon winced: the Guard had been thorough, more thorough than his own henchmen had been when they tied the hands of their prisoner. The Tormenter's hands were now secured by the remains of the twine that had originally bound the Angel Guard. Arteriel had retained it when escaping from the chamber.

"There is no need for this," said Breboon, his back to a broken column. "As far as I'm concerned, you're free to—"

"Save your words," was the cold reply.

Breboon grunted. He heard the Guard move away. An utter silence followed. The winged ones were as silent as shadows. No wonder they made such deadly assassins. This one intended to leave nothing to chance. Breboon thought about trying a soft probe, just for the sake of knowing where the Guard was, but decided against it. Besides, the agent would be here soon, probably alone. This entire business had been conducted with an abnormal amount of secrecy. How interesting it would have been to be able to slide into the mind of the Elevates who were behind it all. Perhaps it was better not to know.

A sound among the rubble made Breboon peer out towards

the faint light beyond the ruin. He saw two shapes, the first the hunched rat-being that was his go-between. It sniffed the air, head poking this way and that, eyes gleaming, then ducked down out of sight. It had done its job. Breboon imagined it scuttling off back to its underground lairs until he summoned it again.

The other figure came forward, exercising caution. Robed, hooded, it slouched among the detritus, face leaning forward. The eyes were huge, twin moons that dominated the parchment face.

"Breboon?" a voice whispered, rasping on the still air.

"Here, Zwarfec. Come out of the street."

The figure hopped forward, picking its way over the jumble of stone as though afraid that one step awry would snap its hidden limbs. It moved like a crab, uneasy on this terrain as if out of its natural element. As it entered the darkness of the derelict house, a silent figure dropped behind it, light as a falling spider.

"I see you," Zwarfec said to Breboon. "Why have you summoned me? You were told to—" He would have said more, but cold fingers gripped a shoulder and he gasped in pain as though a bone had been snapped. Petrified, he hardly breathed. At his ear, a mouth spoke, the words soft but terrifying.

"Very still."

"Of course," Zwarfec gulped. The air rasped in his throat. Something touched the nerves of his brittle spine.

"Whom do you serve?"

"Why, Breboon, sir. I am the Tormenter's agent."

"That is clear already. To whom do you take your messages?"

"Tell him, Zwarfec," called Breboon. He could feel the pain in the agent's mind like the tolling of a bell.

Zwarfec's hood had dropped, exposing the globular head, the blotched skin. He glanced about him fretfully. "I am not obliged to—"

"With an Angel Guard on your back? Speak up, Zwarfec," said Breboon. "That or we're both meat for the kites."

The grip on Zwarfec's shoulder tightened. He cried out in

pain, but there would be no surcease. "I serve the Providers—"

"Which one?"

"Sir, Provider Sughai Orvech."

Arteriel slightly relaxed his grip. He knew the name among the Providers, but it was not one with whom he had had dealings. "What is he to Hummal Goresch?"

The creature squirmed, the nearest it could manage to a shrug.

"I can tell you that," said Breboon. "Orvech is very much a rival to Goresch. There is no love lost between them. Just as Goresch serves the Elevate, Zaer Phesmes, so does Orvech serve Elevate Yvane Sephir."

Arteriel considered this information silently. Yvane Sephir was a considerably powerful Elevate himself. Probably as ambitious as any of his contemporaries, and a dangerous rival to Zaer Phesmes. Any scheme in which Zaer Phesmes was involved would automatically be of surpassing interest to Yvane Sephir.

"Why did your master have me abducted?"

Zwarfec shook his head. "I was not told."

"To serve him?"

Again Zwarfec shook his head. "Sir, I merely pass information from the Tormenter to the servants of Sughai Orvech. I am told nothing."

"He can give you little more," said Breboon.

Arteriel was still for a long time. Breboon could almost hear the beating of Zwarfec's heart, like the heart of a small animal caught in a net, about to be killed. It was fascinating, that fear. He felt his own heart pounding in response to it.

"What purpose does this rivalry among Elevates serve?" said Arteriel abruptly.

Breboon realised the question had been directed at him. "You understand how the Elevates dream of higher things. They aspire to find favour with the Lightbenders."

"To evolve into Lightbenders themselves?"

"Naturally. Thousandreach crawls upwards towards Absolute Light. Fodda to Menial, Menial to—"

"Who does Yvane Sephir serve?" said Arteriel impatiently. "Which of the Lightbender Houses?"

"Ah, that I can tell you," answered Breboon. "It is the Da Sangravilles. The most powerful of all the Houses."

"And Zaer Phesmes?"

"He is loyal to the great rivals of the Da Sangraville House. The Des Aubach."

Arteriel listened to this with interest, though he remained absolutely motionless.

"It is safe to assume," Breboon went on, "that both Providers Hummal Goresch and Sughai Orvech, who have vied for possession of you, are intent on impressing their Elevate masters. Providers will do anything to achieve credit. Especially when it could lead to their own elevation."

"Are you saying that whichever of them possesses me, or to be more exact, the contents of my memory, will earn great favour, possibly *elevation?*" The notion seemed ridiculous, and yet—

"I think that must be right. Does Zwarfec have a view?"

The latter had slumped forward, head bowed. Arteriel lifted him easily, examining him.

"He is not capable of having a view on anything."

Breboon drew in his breath at the words, delivered so casually. But he knew what they meant. Zwarfec's mind was empty.

The Guard let the crumpled form of Zwarfec fall. "His heart has ceased."

Breboon gulped. Terror had done this. Or had the Guard exercised his effortless killing skill? There could be no mercy in such cold creatures. Death was their coin.

"So you think I am the means by which these squabbling Providers will win higher things?"

"Possibly. Elevate Yvane Sephir is known to bend his every effort to Kaizu, ruler of the Da Sangraville House. Kaizu is the overlord of all the Lightbenders, the most feared of them. In truth, he rules everything under Skydown. Subran of the Des Aubach is his great enemy, seeking to overthrow him. Zaer Phesmes serves Subran. So you see, the rivalry stretches from these base levels in which we huddle, up to the very halls of the Lightbenders.

"Anything that Elevate Zaer does is watched by Yvane. Yvane involves himself as a matter of course: if there is a hint of danger to the Da Sangravilles, Yvane leaps to defend his master, Kaizu. And when Yvane acts, Provider Sughai Orvech acts with him.

"Since Zaer Phesmes has shown an abnormal interest in you and what happened to you, Yvane has also taken an interest. But what does Yvane know about you? That you were blinded. He is hungry to know more. So he has used his servants to find a Tormenter. Secrecy was of the essence, so he commissioned an undesignate. I was to open your mind up."

Yes, mused Arteriel. *And had I been safely delivered into the hands of Provider Hummal Goresch, no doubt he would have had his own Tormenter waiting for me.*

"Your position is an unenviable one," said Breboon.

Arteriel ignored the remark. He bent down to the corpse of Zwarfec. For a while his hands slipped inside the robes. Breboon could not feel his own. If he remained tied for much longer, there was a real danger that he would lose them.

But Arteriel came over to him, reached out with only minimal clumsiness, and cut his bonds. As the blood rushed back into pinched veins, the Tormenter gasped with the agony, rubbing his hands in a desperate effort to combat the pain.

"I want you to deliver something for me," said Arteriel, ignoring his suffering.

Breboon nodded. If he survived, it would be a miracle.

"Since Zwarfec cannot act as an agent for Provider Sughai Orvech, you will have to do his work for him."

Breboon paled. He could smell more blood in this, his own death.

"I want you to take something to him, or to his agents." Arteriel held out an object that he had wrapped in strips of Zwarfec's clothing.

Reluctantly Breboon took it. It was wet, pliant.

"Don't open it. Just be sure that it reaches the Provider. And there is a message. Will you remember it?"

Breboon nodded. Then, realising the Guard could not see, grunted an affirmative. It was so easy to forget that this sure-footed creature was blind.

"Tell Provider Orvech that the blind Angel is his enemy."

"Is that—all?"

Arteriel nodded. "Just that. Give him that."

Breboon thrust the small bundle inside his shirt.

"Before you deliver it, I need something else."

"Yes?"

"They took my weapons from me. I am not defenceless, as you have seen. But what I have will not be enough."

"You want weapons? Give me a little time and—"

Arteriel interrupted Breboon's hurried speech by gently touching him on the arm. The effect was instant: Breboon stood very still, heart again thundering.

"Your own weapons are effective, but crude. All I need is some mesh. Is it possible for you to find me some?"

"Mesh?"

"The wire must be very thin, and strong."

"How much?"

"Enough to take a man, a large man."

Breboon was intrigued. But he dared ask no more. If the Guard had wanted him to know more, he would have told him. "Yes, I can obtain such an item. Will you trust me to fetch it?"

Arteriel paused, blind eyes fixed on the Tormenter. "If you try to betray me, I will find you. If you bring me the mesh and deliver my message to Sughai Orvech, you need never see me again."

Breboon considered this. It would be easy enough to agree and then to sneak off into the interminable mazes of the undercity. Probably the Guard would never find him, even if he did evade those who would be hunting him. But Breboon's emotions were mixed. He was afraid of the Guard. The death threat was not an idle one. But it was more than that; he respected the Guard. What he stood for, his rebellion, was a unique thing among his kind. To challenge one of the Providers, who were, after all, scum, less worthy than Tormenters. But was the Guard still loyal to Provider Goresch? It did not matter.

"I'll find you the mesh. And Sughai will receive your message, though I'd rather not deliver it in person."

"How you deliver it is your business. But don't fail me."

"Wait here."

"I'll dispose of Zwafec's body while I wait for you."

It was a dismissal. Breboon left quickly, melting into the crumbling ruins as though other eyes were on him.

Once Arteriel had disposed of the frail corpse, he hid himself in the upper storey of the building, where it was precarious but defendable. If anyone came near, he would hear them. If flight was necessary, he could get away before they hemmed him in. Breboon would be a fool to bring an attack, but there may be pressures on him to try. What did he stand to gain from this business?

It had become more complex. How far did the conspiracy, for such Arteriel judged it to be, extend? Rivalry between Providers was common enough, as was the power struggle between Elevates. Surely this had nothing to do with anything beyond that? Was it merely one Elevate trying to impress his masters at the expense of another? The Lightbenders could not possibly be interested in the lower life-forms. One Angel Guard blinded, whatever the circumstances, would mean absolutely nothing to them, particularly the Da Sangravilles. Kaizu was the most terrifying of them all, the single most powerful being under Skydown. What possible interest could he have in the scratchings of his lowest subjects?

Kaizu. Like a god, the supreme one, feared among even his own kind, second only to Absolute Light itself. His thoughts could only be on godhead, on union with the supreme powers.

15

Breboon approached the ruins carefully. He looked about him, reasonably sure that he had not been tracked, though in this part of the undercity it was always difficult to know. There were the curious, eager for information of any kind, as well as thieves, and there were the hunters, human and otherwise. Nothing could be taken for granted. Gently he cast about him with a mind-scan: it was a dubious business, sometimes prodding to alertness powers that had better been left dormant. But as far as he could tell, he had got back here alone.

He squinted into the darkness of the square. As he began to cross it, he felt the caress of something sinuous across his face and lurched back, stifling a cry. Many of the creatures that slithered and scrawled though the undercity were deadly.

"Are you here?" he called out, provoked by his sudden terror. He could see whatever it was that had touched his cheek dangling before him, inches away. It was not a living creature, nor its snare. It was the length of twine that had been used to tie the Angel Guard. It was above.

"Have you brought what I asked?"

Breboon grunted an affirmative, angry with the Guard for giving him such an unnerving reception.

"Tie it to the twine."

Breboon did so. The Guard did not trust him after all. Maybe he expected a dozen *goads* to come out of hiding at the Tormenter's call. Breboon pulled lightly on the twine, then watched the small bundle as it was drawn up towards the splintered rafters.

"Did you pass my message on?" the voice of the Guard whispered. He remained invisible, merged with the shadows.

"I contacted servants of the Provider. They took your offering, and your words. By now Sughai Orvech will have heard them."

Silence fell for a while. Breboon wondered if the Guard had abandoned him.

"Our business is concluded," came the voice, again making him start, though it had been soft.

"Listen, you'd better get away from the city as quick as you can. There's a hunt on for you. Agents in every quarter. From several camps. You've stirred them up good and proper."

"What have you told them?"

"That you've already flown."

Another long silence. In its stillness, Breboon suddenly realised what he was waiting for: another opportunity to serve this creature. To ensure his safety, and deliver a blow against the Providers. The Angel Guard had shown him little more than derision, and yet he could not help but be awed by him. Blind, abandoned, hunted, yet fiercely rebellious, unbowed.

Then the creature spoke again. "I'm grateful."

The silence that followed was a final one: after a while, Breboon knew that the Guard had slipped away. A little later, he, too, merged with the debris, a lonely ghost.

Estragel winged upwards in a perfect arc, wings curving as he made his swoop, his gaze haughty, his pride swelling within him. There were no other creatures like the Angel Guard: only the winged ones were exalted under Skydown. And he, Estragel, was one of the Bone Whites. As far as he was concerned, the Flensers and the Blood Reds could not compare with the immaculate Bone Whites. They were the true elite. Others might not admit it openly, but they knew the truth. The Flensers were mere workers, apprentices. And the Blood Reds were laudable, but were they truly as fierce and as productive as the Bone Whites? In his opinion, they were not.

Estragel dived, then swung upwards again in a dizzy climb, weaving from side to side in a manoeuvre that would have taxed the skills of many an accomplished flier. He had been given no specific orders for his watch, merely to pass over the Eyries and beyond, where the inner walls of the city rose up. It would be dull work, but an opportunity to revel in flight and exercise. Other Angels would see him: let them gape at his perfect mastery of the air.

Immediately beyond his present line of flight one of the immense trees soared upwards towards the ceiling that was Skydown. Its thick foliage and interwoven branches were forbidden places where only the mutant birdlife gathered. Worshiped by the lowest of the low and the highmost of the Lightbenders, the trees were sacred, older than the city, older than time. Their roots knew the forgotten secrets of the world's past, their uppermost branches the whispers of the hidden gods, Absolute Light.

Estragel swept close to the outer foliage. It was thick, the greenery sweet-smelling, almost alluring. Who among the

Angels had not felt the urge to drift among those branches and to land there, to drink in the secrets of the ages? But it was part of Estragel's duty to ensure that no one went there. Of course, no one ever had, and if any Angel had forgotten himself and gone there, he had not returned. The birds that used the trees were not the only creatures that dwelt there: deep down in the endless labyrinths of the foliage there were other creatures that had never been seen, but which surfaced in legend and in rumour, and had done over the centuries. It was said that the cults of tree worshipers that abounded in Thousandreach had carved likenesses of these creatures on the trunks of the trees, far below, where the Angels never went, together with the glyphs of their rituals. The Lightbenders approved of such activities and had not pronounced them sacrilegious. The preservation and sanctity of the trees was paramount, and next to the Lightbenders, they were the most honoured life-forms under Skydown.

Estragel was about to swing away from the outer leaves, when he saw a shape dropping below him. Its wingspread told him at once that it was one of his fellows, though from this height he could not be sure what kind. He dipped his head and began the plummet that would bring him closer.

As he swooped, the lower Angel did not seem to be aware of him. Estragel thought it odd, as the hearing of the Angel Guards was very keen. Perhaps this Guard was concentrating on something else. Certainly it was flying very close to the branches of the great tree. Had it seen something?

Estragel came within a short distance of the Guard, when it abruptly veered into the branches. It must be flying perilously close to them. Estragel dropped, hovering as he tried to see beyond the outer leaves. Within, there was a long tunnellike cavity, a natural shape formed by the branches here. He could just discern the shape of the Guard, but what was it doing? It seemed to swing round, then stop, hovering perfectly in the utter stillness. Estragel moved forward slowly. He was conscious of the density of the leaves around him. They kept out even the slightest breeze.

"What is it?" he called out. His voice was oddly muffled by the leaves, their conspiracy of silence. The other Angel was farther away from him than he had realised, and probably hadn't heard. He still couldn't make out what kind it was, which might have given a clue to what it was doing here. Surely it had seen him. Gliding easily, it swung downwards towards the branches underneath it, as though it would land on one of them. But it hovered, feet away.

Estragel drew out one of his weapons. Something was wrong. This was no sanctioned entry into this place. He dropped down slowly, but as he came closer to the other Guard, it suddenly plunged downward, narrowly avoiding the greenery, paralleling it in a dramatic and dangerous swoop as it made for the open. Estragel smiled grimly. There would be something to enjoy after all.

As he swooped, using his wings to speed him rapidly in pursuit, he struck the unseen mesh at an angle and was catapulted around viciously, caught like a moth in a huge web. He swung back and forth, shrieking with pain as he felt one of his wings fold up, the other snaring him. His speed had been his undoing. The mesh bit into flesh, tightening its hold as he struggled. If it had been thread, he would have been able to tear free. But the mesh was made of steel, the cruel workmanship of the undercity and its specialists in pain.

Beyond him, beyond the cloud of pain that closed around him as tightly as the mesh, Estragel sensed but did not see the other Angel Guard. It had set this trap deliberately. But for whom? Not him, surely. What possible purpose could it serve?

The other Guard was on the mesh, working its way down to the trapped Estragel, climbing as easily as a fly across a wall. It avoided the traps of the mesh, the invisible barbs.

"Cut me loose!" hissed Estragel. "My wings are damaged. I'll lose them if you don't free me!"

The other had come down to within inches of him. It hovered, its own face close to Estragel's so that he could see it, the strangely clouded eyes.

"Do you know me, Estragel?" it said coldly.

Estragel nodded. It was the Blood Red, Arteriel. He was *blind*. What did this mean?

"I have been cast out, Estragel. My Praetor delivered me into the hands of the Provider who called for my dismissal. It was his duty to do so."

Estragel felt the mesh swaying. He could see the thick foliage beyond, and felt the shuddering sensation of being closed in, crushed. "The laws cannot be changed," he gasped.

"Of course not. But they took my weapons, Estragel, my claws, my instruments."

Estragel closed his eyes. That was it. Arteriel wanted his weapons. But if Estragel lost them to him, he himself would be disgraced. His Praetor would cast him out, perhaps even have him executed.

"You understand?" said Arteriel softly, pitilessly.

There was nothing to say, other than to agree quietly. This was death, a sure sentence. A life for a life. Arteriel had chosen survival over dishonour. Why? Revenge? But Angel Guards did not stoop to such base emotions. They were all aware of the codes. Failure had to be faced, the penalty paid. Arteriel, for some reason, had spurned the ancient codes. Estragel would not. He grinned in spite of his pain. The Bone Whites were the elite: they understood what honour was. No Bone White would betray the codes as this crippled Blood Red was doing.

Estragel felt his belt sliding from him, his harness. In the mesh he was powerless to prevent Arteriel from stripping from him all that he required. Lastly the Bone White's clawed gloves were removed. His pale hands hung limply.

"I am sorry that I must add your death to my disgrace," said the voice, though without emotion.

Estragel stiffened. His own position had become hopeless. To die now would be the only solution for him. "I am a Bone White. Be swift."

The dark flared to blinding light for the briefest of instants, then closed in like a fist, shutting out everything.

"Who is it?" said the Praetor gruffly. The watch was almost over and as was common, there had been no reports. It had become habit, this screening of the Eyries and the skies around the trees. Who would ever disturb these skies? The Praetor had been about to rest. Now it seemed he was to be interrupted.

One of his Bone Whites stood at the door, a look of dismay

on his handsome face. The Praetor ushered him in, closing
the door.

Before he could speak, the Bone White held out a bundle.
It was partly clothing, the ripped remains of the shirt of another Bone White. The tatters of its insignia clung to it.

"What is this?" said the Praetor, not taking it, anger stirring in his breast.

"It was found in the chamber of Estragel. It is his."

"Has he not returned from duty?"

"Praetor, we think he is dead."

The Praetor's eyes narrowed. Fury gleamed in them, but
he took the bundle without a word of anger. He studied it,
opened it out. The shirt had been cut away neatly from Estragel's back, but it had been lacerated by something else
first.

"There was a message, Praetor." The Bone White looked
appalled, but remained stiffly at attention.

The Praetor waited, mouth tightening. Someone would be
skinned alive for this.

"Praetor, Estragel was last seen near one of the great trees.
We are—"

Again the door shook as someone outside pounded on it,
ignoring protocol.

The Praetor flung it wide, eyes ablaze. Two more of the
Bone Whites stood outside, wings folded. Their faces were
ashen. It was a rare sight among these cold warriors.

"You have found him?"

They both nodded. "In a steel net, Praetor," said the first.
"His weapons had been taken, as had his harness, his
gloves."

"Who *dares* to attack the Angel Guard! *Who dares?*"

"Praetor, we know who it was."

The Praetor stepped very close to them, eyes brimming
with hatred. "You do?"

"Estragel's corpse bore the killer's message. It had been
cut into his flesh. It said, 'Know this, Angel Guard. The
blind Angel is your enemy.' "

"The blind—"

"We saw him strike Syrakeil down, Praetor. Blind though
he was, he used a trick to snare him."

"And *this* is his revenge?"

"Perhaps, Praetor," said the Guard behind him, "he has lost his reason."

The Praetor's lips thinned as he spoke slowly but venomously. "Send word to all the other Praetors. And gather the watch. I'll have Arteriel's wings pinned to my Eyrie walls."

16

Provider Hummal Goresch stared at the remains of the shirt, its dark stains. It had belonged to one of the Bone White Angels, a proud warrior, worthy of his rank. But now disgraced and destroyed.

"You heard the message that was sent with this? Inscribed in the Bone White's flesh!" He snarled. He was addressing the shadows where the Skryer sat. "The blind Angel declares himself our enemy! The effrontery!"

Goresch moved uneasily about the chamber. Something was far from right in this affair. *How can I operate unless I am given the facts!* his mind protested. This Skryer knew far more than he did, had the ear of the Elevate, Zaer Phesmes. It was infuriating! Goresch wanted to shout. This business would not have gone so far adrift had he been kept informed! *Damn the Elevates and their power games!*

"You seem unduly disturbed," came the soft voice, as though the Skryer refused to be moved by events. "A single warrior, maddened by blindness—"

"What is his purpose?" There, I've come out with it. Why can't he be open with me? They know *my loyalty is unquestionable. He's a Skryer, can't he read it?*

"You see something in this? You fear a plot?"

"You said Arteriel's blindness was an accident—" *And lied! damn you.*

"Perhaps it was. Whether it was or not, he is simply re-acting to the way he has been treated. He has his pride. And no desire to work as a Menial would. But I think he has gone a little far. Most of his kind would have chosen suicide. I am sure his Praetor would not have anticipated this act of vengeance. It does not become the Blood Red Angels."

"Gone a little far! The Angel Guard are furious. The Praetor of the Bone Whites is demanding that he be allowed to sweep the entire city—"

"I assume the Blood Reds are less hysterical, although they will be no less angry at the murder of any Angel Guard. The honour of their chapters will be tarnished."

"And rightly so."

"Arteriel is no longer in Thousandreach."

Goresch drew in his breath. "You have seen?"

"One of my colleagues. Even if he had not been aware of Arteriel's flight, we could have deduced the obvious. He could not remain here in safety. All Thousandreach will be alert to him."

"Who is protecting him?" *Come on, give me the facts, curse you! What are you hiding from me? Is Zaer responsible for this duplicity?*

"If he is protected, it is a superbly hidden secret. But I would say that he has fled because he no longer has a master. If there is to be any safety under Skydown, it will be far from here. And only temporary."

"We must find him. Elevate Zaer is furious."

"Yes, I know," mused the Skryer, and Goresch detected amusement in his tone. It infuriated him further, but he kept his patience. They were all Zaer's fools, manipulated in darkness. How could they be expected to operate effectively if they were not given the facts? What was this really about?

"I have sent word to as many of our agents as I dare," he told the Skryer. "I could not delay."

"Good. What about Sommoi?"

Goresch frowned. "Yes, I included him. Why do you ask?" Was this a clue? Sommoi had once been a rival Provider, a colleague of Sughai Orvech, but he had fallen from favour and had been demoted and exiled. Paradoxically his anger, his private lust for revenge on Sughai Orvech now bound him to Zaer Phesmes. But Sommoi's contact was directly with Zaer Phesmes and he was even more secretive than the Skryer.

"I think Arteriel may fly back that way. The segment where this began for him will draw him. He possesses great curiosity."

"Is Sommoi in danger, do you think?"

"No one who goes near Arteriel can consider himself out of danger. The blind Angel trusts no one. From now, everyone will be his enemy. As he has been at pains to tell us."

Then why wasn't he killed at the outset! Goresch again wanted to shout. But he merely nodded calmly. The Skryer was not necessarily possessed of mind-scanning skills. He would not be reading the Provider's torment.

Provider Sughai Orvech, principal servant of Elevate Yvane Sephir, walked through the last of the guards that lined the walls of the antechamber. There were a hundred of them, and though they were little more than sentient statues, he knew their skills. They were trained in a single art, the art of slaughter, and only the command of their master motivated them. They were machines, contemptible but magnificent, infallible. It was ostentatious of Yvane Sephir to parade them, although they served to underline the Elevate's position. They were there to intimidate guests, although, on reflection, Orvech could hardly consider himself a guest. Yvane Sephir was one of the most powerful of all Elevates, surely on the point of promotion to the palace of the Da Sangraville Lightbenders, while he, Sughai Orvech was merely a Provider, and thus hardly better than fodda in Yvane's eyes. Even so, this matter was important enough to warrant an audience. To be able to meet with an Elevate was a singular honour, even for a Provider. To Orvech, it presaged his own coming to greatness and, dare he think it, Elevation? Perhaps when Yvane was drawn to the palace—

"Do they frighten you?" The voice was rich and deep, but would have shocked had it not been familiar. It belonged to the synthetic creature that Yvane always used as a spokesman at interviews, the Dolus.

Orvech watched it emerge from the ranks of warriors and

motion the way to a more private chamber. It wore a sweeping robe, clasped at the throat, which hid its body. The head was a curious colour, unnaturally pink, the flesh as smooth and unblemished as polished marble.

"In a conflict they would terrify the most resilient opponent," said Orvech. "But as a loyal servant of Elevate Yvane, I have no need to fear them."

The Dolus was incapable of expression, its eyes wide but glassy. Yet its voice contained all the inflections of a human voice. Orvech had surmised on earlier visits to these halls that the voice was a projection, possibly Yvane's own. But he had never met the Elevate.

They entered a room that was beautifully decorated, lavish in its carpets and murals, and extravagant in its light: entire clusters of crystal hung from the curving ceiling, lights blazing in a profusion of colour. It was the gift of the gods that the Elevates and their most favoured servants enjoyed, a hint of the glory of Absolute Light. No fodda ever experienced exposure to such as this. Splendid though the chamber was, Orvech knew it was nothing to the luxury beyond, in which only an Elevate would be permitted to indulge himself.

The Dolus sat on a broad couch, and Orvech took a seat opposite. "You have news for Yvane?" said the Dolus.

"From the Tormenter, Breboon."

The Dolus remained as impassive as ever, but Orvech knew that Yvane would be alert, eager for this news, possibly listening.

"Does he have the Angel Guard?"

Orvech shook his head. "Arteriel was taken as planned, but he escaped his captors and killed one of Breboon's agents. He has left evidence of the agent's murder, and a curious message."

"For whom?"

"For Yvane."

The Dolus stiffened uncharacteristically. "What is it?"

"That he is Arteriel's enemy."

"That is all?"

"Yes."

The Dolus stood up calmly, but the voice was angry. "Where is the Angel now?"

"Hunted but not yet found."

"There must be no delay. Find Arteriel swiftly. If Zaer Phesmes recovers him first, it will be disastrous."

Orvech stood up, nodding politely, as if Yvane himself stood before him. So it was not to be a personal meeting after all. Perhaps it was as well: Yvane would be incensed by the irreverent message.

The Dolus began to glide away silently, though it had not officially dismissed the Provider. Orvech wondered if the bad news had confused its master. He made to go, but found himself confronted by another figure.

It was Annaxion, Yvane's personal Skryer. "An inauspicious meeting," he whispered. He was an emaciated creature, face white, eyes rimmed as though he never slept, and his form suggested he rarely took little solid food. His robes hung about him limply. But for all his sorry appearance, he was rich in power. He had not been chosen by Yvane for being weak or incompetent.

"What are you doing here?" Orvech asked him, though not without tact.

The Skryer coughed, adjusting his loose robes. Orvech guessed they hid a frail, skeletal body. The Skryers were creatures of shadows, their art even more secretive than that of the Elevates.

"Yvane summoned me. I am instructed to work with you."

"To recover Arteriel?"

Annaxion nodded. He had a curious head, with its wide brow, short hair, and sallow complexion. His eyes were deep set, their expression almost dreamy, careless. "Yvane knows that his enemy, Zaer Phesmes, plots on behalf of Lightbender Subran. Yvane senses that this Blood Red Angel is the key to considerable upheaval. We have to find him."

"Are there any clues?"

"He's left the city. As far as I can see, he's gone back towards the outer segments."

"Can you track him?"

"I am bending my efforts."

"I'll have my agents alerted."

"There's a further complication," added Annaxion, eyes

widening as though he had caught sight of something on the edge of vision. ''The Angel Guard want him, too.''

''For whom? Zaer Phesmes?''

Annaxion shook his head lazily. ''Oh no. Their Praetors want justice. Arteriel's acts have brought disgrace to them all. They demand a kill for a kill. Already there are Angel Guard seeking the renegade. When they find Arteriel, they will tear him to pieces.''

Orvech swore. ''We must prevent it.''

''We must.'' Annaxion said no more, but could easily have added on both their behalfs, or Yvane's anger will know no limits.

Far from Thousandreach's towers, the lone winged figure sped on into interminable night.

I scorn you all, Arteriel thought, his only consolation the coolness of the racing wind. There was no greater pleasure than that, so what more should he ask.

Do you watch me from beyond Skydown? he thought, imagining the unspoken question penetrating that dense shield, reaching the minds of Absolute Light.

See my flight. Why don't you use your bolts to bring me down again? I am your enemy, too.

There was no sound beyond the rush of the air, no answering thunder from the heights. Arteriel was alone. Ahead of him there was only the darkness. He considered the irony that, with his sight restored, that darkness would remain.

THREE

HIGH CROFELS

One of the prerogatives of the gods is deviousness.

It is not enough for them to obscure themselves in mystery or to obfuscate truth in ritual. They relish subterfuge, and permit a degree of it among lower orders. They savour the irony which thus enables them to spy upon the perversity of their servants.

High Crofels is the perfect example. It seethes with intrigue, with deceit, with plots and counterplots. And, it goes without saying, heresy. So why has it not been leveled in a demonstration of divine omniscience?

The answer is that it is far too valuable. Without such a place, it would be so much more difficult to monitor the stirrings of rebellion, the rumbles of discontent.

In High Crofels, all these things can be bought, sifted, and considered. High Crofels is the universal ear.

ZAER PHESMES—*The Book of Renunciation*

17

They had run a long way into the darkness, breaking into a natural, easy pace that covered mile after mile along the endless expanse of the road. They assumed they would be followed, but they had no way of knowing if they were. Everything was silent behind them. Sommoi could be miles away, or mere yards, the darkness was so deceptive. Ruarhi was surprised by the girl's stamina: she seemed to run as comfortably as he did, as though familiar with this sort of exercise. MagMannoch women were hardy, used to living on the move, but somehow Ruarhi had not expected Ukar-Tiri to match his stride. She had more spirit than he realised. Each time he glanced at her face, which was almost obscured by the darkness, he could see a determination there that surprised and pleased him.

"Where are we going?" she asked him after a silence between them that was becoming uncomfortable.

He shrugged. "I don't know anything about this road. Except that it leads eventually to Thousandreach."

She looked appalled at the mere mention of it. "We dare not go there. I have heard such terrible things about it."

"Do these reed beds go on forever?"

"There are settlements."

"Towns?" he said, unable to stifle his suspicion. There were towns in his own world, but they were places he visited infrequently. They had their own kind of madness.

To his surprise she smiled at his grimace, her teeth perfect, her face transformed. For the first time since he had met her she seemed less nervous, though the tension in her was still palpable. He had always found it difficult to get very much out of her. She had taught him the language well, and he had astonished himself at the speed with which he had picked it up, but she had always neatly evaded any probing questions. Perhaps now, away from the immediate threat of Festubul, she would open up to him a little.

"Why do you smile?" he asked her.

"You have no love of towns."

"I'm a hillman. At least, in my world. And you?" He suddenly realised he wanted to know her story, her background, more so, perhaps, than he wanted to learn about this hostile terrain.

"Like you, I am not from under Skydown."

Her reply took him aback. It was something he had not considered. He stopped running, but they walked on quickly, glancing briefly back.

"I was brought here with others from my own lands. That was a long time ago. I was very young."

"The armoured warriors?"

She nodded. "I lived with my people on the shores of a great sea. There was a village, and others farther along the curve of our bay. There were small fishing craft. Many of them, covering the water. I used to watch them from the dunes. My father had a boat and he used to return in the evenings with a huge catch. The waters abounded with fish.

Traders used to come from inland, from towns, to barter for the fish at our market.''

He was picturing it as she spoke, seeing it vividly.

"I remember the sun. Always there was the sun. Not like here. There is no sun under Skydown. If it broke through, it would kill us. Light is revered, but feared."

"A sea," he mused. "I've glimpsed the sea from the highest of the foothills, like a sort of glass in the distance." He abruptly caught himself, embarrassed. "And sunlight—by the gods, I'm used to light. This place is like an underworld."

"I thought so at first. Certainly it is peopled by demons, full of cruelty and contempt for human life."

"Why did they bring you?"

She looked away. "There are settlements here. I was taken to one. Put to work. I was young and not very big, so they made me and other children crawl through the ducts under the settlement, clearing the deposits that clung to their sides like weed on the rocks—"

"I don't understand—"

She sighed awkwardly, looking down. "I'm sorry. I had almost forgotten my world. I haven't talked like this for so long."

"You don't have to—"

"I want to. I've grown so used to punishment. The slightest gesture, a word out of place. I've been a prisoner most of my life. And we don't have much time like this."

He pulled up, staring at her. The silence closed in on them, its darkness made more alien and hostile by the visions she conjured. "What do you mean?"

"There's no escape from under Skydown. The chances of finding the Overlap are as remote as they would be of finding one grain of sand on a beach."

"Maybe." He looked sullen for a moment, then turned away. "I can't believe these reeds go on forever."

"No. But we can't escape. They'll find us. Someone will. We are fodda. We have no rights. No one does under Skydown. Only the Providers, or the Elevates."

"Who are they, the rulers?"

She nodded. "In a way. Everyone is accountable to them."

"You don't think we can avoid them? Don't you want to try?"

She could see the anger behind his gaze and it was her turn to look away. "Forgive me. Of course I want to. It's just that I've seen—"

He took her arm, more roughly than he'd meant to. "What? What have you seen?"

There were tears in her eyes. "The suffering!" She shook herself loose. "You have only been here a short while. It is easy to be confident, eager to escape. But when you taste their cruelty, when you understand what they are capable of—"

He would have retorted, poured out his bitterness at the deaths of Dromator and Darrac, but her own despair was like a fist brandished in front of him. He was uncertain what to do. Take her in his arms? Argue with her? He waited.

In a moment she turned, wiping the tears away quickly with an annoyed toss of her head. "You see? I can still cry. I thought I was beyond tears now. That's two things you've made me do. Smile and cry."

He began to let the unease drain out of him. "This must be an evil place if it can't tolerate a smile."

"You will see few smiles here. Foddamen never smile, did you notice that? And the only tears are tears of pain. In the settlement where I lived, there were many. We learned obedience, thralldom."

"Sommoi told me you were the mate of a Drone. What does that mean?"

She shook her head slowly. "In the village, the Drone was the overseer. His purpose was to see that the quota was met. Fodda. Everyone served him. He did nothing. Just supplied the Providers." She paused for a moment, wrestling with a particularly painful memory. "I will not describe him to you. He was partly human, like other creatures under Skydown. But hugely misshapen—"

"You don't have to—"

"No. You are a warrior. You cannot know what it is for a woman to have to endure abuse. But at the hands of a Drone—"

"And Festubul?"

"He wanted me. I no longer had feelings. I had become a machine. It was the only way to avoid madness. He told me he would free me, work me to death if I resisted. He had that power over the workers. I didn't care one way or the other."

"He abducted you?"

She nodded. "He risked everything because of his infatuation with me. It was a disease with him. He took me from the village. He put himself at risk. Forced Foddamen to serve him, but they wanted to flee him. You saw how he used me." This time it was she who challenged him with her gaze.

Embarrassed, he could not meet her eyes. The image of her coupling with Festubul sprang quickly to his mind.

She knew what he was seeing. "You think I enjoyed that?" She barked a sharp, scornful laugh, another unexpected sound. "Once we were out of the village, I soon gave up any faint ideas I had of fighting him. Festubul knows about pain, humiliation. He is a master of it. Better to pretend pleasure than suffer such indignities. Under Skydown, submission is survival."

He could see the anger rising in her, a bitterness that had been locked away, deep down inside her, for years. It must come out, drawn like poison. His own was nothing compared to it.

"It they find us," he said coolly, "I will kill him."

Again she laughed caustically. "You think that will restore my dignity, my pride!"

He shook his head. There were no comforting words he could give her.

"They'll find us," she told him. "It'll be Foddamen. They're like dogs, sniffing through the reed beds."

"If you knew it was hopeless, why did you come?"

She dragged her hand through her hair, pulling it back off her face. For a moment she looked arrogant, defiant, someone she had not allowed herself to be other than in secret moments of rebellion. But then her shoulders sagged and a sudden tiredness crept over her. "Instinct, perhaps. What little of it remains." She laughed softly. "I'm sorry. I annoy you with my lack of spirit."

"You want to sit here and wait for them?"

She looked at him. "No," she said, though almost resignedly.

"You think I'll make the same demands as Festubul?" He had uttered the words before he could control them, wishing at once that he hadn't.

"You're a warrior, but you're young."

"Two years your elder, at least!" he snorted, suddenly feeling like a boy of thirteen, and very childish. He was not a warrior, but how could he tell her than! If she thought he was a mere hunter, she might scorn him further.

"You're not equal to Festubul's cruelty. You have your codes, I suspect, even for a fighting man."

The conversation was drifting uncomfortably close to matters he did not want to discuss. Of course he desired her. And she would know it. "I just want to get back—"

"I can't help you—"

"You know more about this world than I do. I need your help. But I won't force you to stay with me. Go if you wish to."

"Since we fled together," she said less stubbornly, "it would be sensible to go on together. But I warn you, Ruarhi, you mustn't build your hopes. Not under Skydown. Expect only the worst."

He nodded, confused by her changing moods. She did have spirit, her anger had exposed it, but she seemed to lack the will to fight.

She was listening to the sounds of the night, as if she might have heard trackers on the road behind them. But she shook her head before he could ask about it. "They'll come."

"I meant what I said about Festubul. If he comes after us, I'll kill him."

"Because of what he did to me?"

"Would you rather I let him live?"

She looked away. "I've had enough of his abuse."

"Sommoi will be harder to deal with, I think."

"Who was he? I've not seen anyone like him before. Those growths—"

"Don't you know?"

She shrugged. "Another overseer, as far as I could tell. I thought you and the other man were his servants."

"Was he—like the Drone?"

But she shook her head. "No. But Sommoi had authority. Festubul was afraid of him. I could tell that much. They say there are creatures here with the power to enter your mind. Maybe Sommoi is like that. But Festubul didn't fear him as much as he feared the Angel Guard."

"What do you know about them?"

"Almost nothing. They are extremely dangerous. Festubul was staggered to see Sommoi interfering with the one we found, even though it was injured. They despise us and would kill us as soon as look at us. I pray we never see one again."

"Sommoi had some dark purpose, something to do with that flying creature. I couldn't fathom it."

"I think Festubul was right to fear Sommoi. If we are followed, you would do better to kill Sommoi. Festubul doesn't matter. Nor I to him. Not enough for him to hunt me. He would treat me as lost. He has his own life to think of. But Sommoi may not let him go."

Ruarhi scowled. "Why should Sommoi concern himself with you?"

"I don't think he would. Except that he assumes I will be with you, since you took me with you."

"Sommoi hunts me because I escaped him? His superiors would punish him for letting me escape? One warrior, when the armoured warriors took so many?"

"You are important to Sommoi. He will follow you." She said it with complete assurance.

But he grinned. "Then I'll take your advice. And kill him."

She shrugged. "It is what warriors do."

18

They had crossed over to the far side of the road, but the view, limited though it was, was identical to that on the side they had left: endless reeds. Parts of the reed fields were obscured by mist; it drifted sluggishly in white bands, yet somehow avoided the road, as though the embankment had properties that kept it away. Ruarhi asked Ukar-Tiri about the road, but she said no one spoke much about it. It was very old, part of a civilization that had perished in the forgotten past. She seemed to feel no curiosity for such things, whereas he was intrigued by them.

She pointed out into a thick bank of mist. She had seen something. "It must be the settlement Sommoi spoke of."

Ruarhi stood at the edge of the slope and tried to see. As the mist rolled, occasionally breaking apart before re-forming itself, he caught sight of dark shapes etched against a further backdrop of milky mist. Built out in the reeds, the village was the most bizarre settlement he had ever seen. It was raised on stilts that reached upwards for hundreds of feet, seemingly precariously balanced, waiting for one strong gust of wind to send the entire structure crashing to the ground. The buildings themselves were more like nests, woven tightly into spherical shapes, all caught together in an untidy cluster, swaying high above the reeds as though mirroring their movement below.

"Sommoi called it High Crofels," she said beside him.

Listening, he thought he caught the mingled croaking of birds. They reminded him briefly of Hanging Tor, his dead friends. A bad omen.

Ukar-Tiri sensed his sudden tension and put her fingers on his arm. "What is it? You fear this place?"

He closed out the terrible images of Dromator and the bloody corpse of Darrac. "I'm all right."

Her grip on his arm tightened. "We'd better go there. We need water. And food."

He swung round to face her. "Food! And what does that mean in this stinking hole? Fodda? Human flesh?"

She pulled back from his anger. "There may be alternatives in the settlement," she said softly. "But we can't avoid eating fodda."

"How can you—?"

"I know! You think I feel any differently? Eat it or die. I had no choice. I was a child. They forced it into me. After a while you—"

She hesitated, but he gripped her. "You what? Tell me!"

"You cannot refuse it. Your body—needs it."

He released her, turning aside. In spite of his disgust, his hunger had become overpowering. He would have to eat something soon.

"I think we should go there," he heard her say.

He nodded. After a while he drew himself up, annoyed with himself for showing his weakness. She would think him a boy. "Is there a path?"

"I don't know."

"Then we'll go down and look."

They did so, traversing the foot of the slope carefully. The water was murky but shallow, and shortly they were able to thread a way across to the reed beds and force a path into them. Ruarhi pulled the length of pipe from his waistband, wishing he had a proper weapon.

"I hate the reeds," Ukar-Tiri said behind him, but he motioned her to silence, as if her words would encourage malevolence in the growths.

It was a struggle to forge through them, and the poor light did little to help them judge their direction. More than once Ruarhi thought they must have lost their way. The reeds here were far taller than any others he had seen, towering over them, at times folding across, blotting out the sky. Ruarhi would have used his weapon to beat at them, but something held him back. On and on they trudged, their search endless, exhausting.

At last there was a break in the reeds and they had arrived at a natural break. In front of them a strange, flexible growth rose up from the mire. At first Ruarhi thought it must be a tree, smooth and branchless, but then saw that it was like no trunk he had ever encountered before. It was some twenty feet around, pale as the stems of the reeds, as though it could almost be a gigantic version of them. Beyond it, other similar growths loomed from the mist. The village was high overhead. But looking up, they could discern only the vaguest of outlines in the shifting vapours.

"Is there a way up?" Ruarhi asked aloud, though he knew Ukar-Tiri wouldn't know.

Instead of replying, she walked on ahead, peering this way and that as if expecting guardians of this place to appear. Ruarhi followed her, equally as cautious. But a clammy silence had shut down over them. The huge structure moved gently, like a giant beast stirring in its sleep.

Deeper into the grotesque forest they traveled, until at length Ruarhi saw a way upward. It was some sort of net, woven from fibres, reeds perhaps, which stretched between two of the growths and swung upwards out of sight like a huge web. But there was still no sign of people. Did they watch from higher up? Or was there a need for them to guard this village at all? Ruarhi knew that in his own world, no settlement went unguarded. The MagMannoch encampments were likewise always patrolled.

Ukar-Tiri was studying him. She pointed to the swaying net.

"Can you climb it?" he asked her.

"There are worse things to fear than high places," she said, but he thought she looked uncomfortable at the prospect of an ascent.

"I'm used to stranger climbs than this. Keep close to me," he told her.

He swung up on to the net lithely, offering her his hand and tugging her up with him. In a moment they were ascending. The net swung to and fro as they climbed, and Ukar-Tiri had to grit her teeth against her increasing fear. But Ruarhi, himself quite at home on the net, was patient with her, pausing to make sure that she was all right.

The mist closed in, mercifully blanketing out the view so she could not see how high up she was. The net became more tightly woven, breaking up into a number of distinct ladders, which stretched away to a number of other growths. Ruarhi chose a ladder at random and climbed it, Ukar-Tiri keeping as close to his heels as she could, but her arms were beginning to ache. He turned and gripped her, pulling her up to where he stood on a platform woven from the ubiquitous reeds. She sagged down, glad of the rest, while he looked upwards. He could see the bulk of the village, not far overhead now, though there was still no sign of habitation.

"A little farther," he told her. When he reached for her hand again, he realised she was shivering. He got her to her feet and she clung to him, trembling like an animal. Automatically he stroked her hair and her grip on him tightened.

"You'll be all right. A few more rungs. I can see the village." He had been weaned among lofty crags, his clan often on the run. Heights held no terrors for him. They exhilarated him. A sudden desire made him dizzy: he would gladly have had her, there on the swaying platform, and for a moment he struggled to shut out the image that was forming. Her thighs were pressed tightly to his: she must have felt his hardness, realised his desire for her. She did not move, too afraid to object.

"Come, climb." He pulled away. She said nothing, gripping the ladder when he showed her, concentrating on mastering her growing terror. Step by step they went on up. This time he made her go first, his arms on either side of her, his face close to her flesh. His desire increased. Gods! to have her here, on the ladder itself! What was to stop him? Dromator would have laughed encouragement. He would have done it and laughed with pleasure. Dromator. Poor dead Dromator—

Ruarhi realised they had arrived at the top. Ukar-Tiri had scrambled onto another, far bigger, platform, and was reaching down to him. He managed a weak smile, forcing his desire away. He did not need her hand, but he took it anyway, clambering over the lip onto the platform. He stood up and looked about him, but Ukar-Tiri crouched down, catlike.

Ruarhi's view was obscured by more coils of mist, but he

could see that the platform wriggled its way between several of the clusters of buildings. It was not possible to say what they had been woven from: the materials looked alien to him. There were more ladders, more walkways above, and several different levels. The overall effect was one of a gigantic hive. There were birds out in the mist, flapping and cawing noisily, as if they, at least, were insulted by the intruders.

"Perhaps it's deserted," Ruarhi mused.

Ukar-Tiri shook her head, but didn't speak.

"We'll find out." He didn't put out his hand to her this time. What were her thoughts? His desire had betrayed him; would she be angry? You're a warrior, she had kept telling him on the road, as if she could expect nothing less from him than his abuse. He walked along the swaying walkway. She followed, gripping the rope guidelines tightly.

The first of the buildings he came to seemed to have no means of entry, and others were the same. Perhaps they were storehouses. But on this level, none of the buildings had doors that he could see. They would have to climb still higher.

He was beginning to feel exasperated, when voices came from the mist ahead. Two people talking. He motioned Ukar-Tiri back out of sight and clutched the pipe weapon.

They were in front of him before he knew it. They were thin, almost sticklike, but men, as far as he could tell. They had the unnaturally large eyes characteristic of people under Skydown, and wore brief tunics, their skin pale and loose. Both of them gaped at Ruarhi, as though a demon had dropped from the sky. But they did not challenge him.

It was a moment before he realised that they were puzzled by his weapon, his threatening attitude. Slowly he put the pipe back into his waistband, nodding to the two men.

"Is this High Crofels?" he asked in the language Ukar-Tiri had taught him.

The two men both nodded. They had hardly moved, but since he had put away his weapon, they seemed less edgy. Even so, Ruarhi was unsure how to go on with this.

It was Ukar-Tiri who got him out of difficulty. Slipping beside him, she smiled at the two men. "We were told we could find refuge here for a while."

At last one of the two men smiled, half his teeth missing.

"Refuge? Sure, that's why the place was constructed, girl. Refuge. No one will want to know your business, don't worry about that. Just climb up to the middle level. Plenty of room." The man gestured with a skinny arm.

Ruarhi and Ukar-Tiri thanked him and passed him and his silent companion. Both nodded, then walked on, continuing their conversation as though nothing unusual had happened.

Up in the higher levels, Ruarhi and Ukar-Tiri saw more people, though most of them paid them no heed, going about their errands quietly. High Crofels was evidently an open village, where all were free to come and go as they pleased.

The middle level seemed to be one huge construction rather than a number of buildings. And it was unexpectedly crowded inside. Light burned, torches perhaps, though Ruarhi couldn't be sure, for the lights were encased in some kind of membrane. This light had a curious effect, casting dancing shadows on the curved walls. The room was cavernous, with numerous doors leading from it, apparently into other huge rooms. People thronged here, most of them seated at long tables, some eating, others drinking or simply talking. Some slept, either tilted back in their chairs, slumped over the tables as if in a stupor, or curled up on the floor like dogs. They were strange beings, for the most part men and women, though all hybrids. Ruarhi had seen no one yet who looked like himself, or like the girl.

"Shall we ask for food?" she said beside him.

Ruarhi had seen a place across the hall where an enclosed fire burned, smoke curling up to what must be a vent overhead. "Let's try there. It looks like an oven."

A few heads turned as they passed, but no one evinced more than passing curiosity. In High Crofels, everyone was a stranger, it seemed.

"Newly arrived?" said a burly fellow by the fire. He was by far the most muscular inhabitant of this world Ruarhi had yet seen, though his arms were somehow out of proportion to his body. He was stirring a vat of thick, souplike substance, and seemed to have some authority.

Ruarhi nodded, his interest in the food obvious.

"Help yourselves to platters," said the big man, wiping sweat from his greasy face.

"How do I pay for this?" Ruarhi asked him.

"Time for that later. I'll get someone to take you to the Emeschi in a while. You can explain your circumstances to them. If they want anything, they'll tell you."

Ruarhi watched as he ladled out food onto platters for him and Ukar-Tiri. It was thick and glutinous, chunks of something in it, and it had a spicy smell that made Ruarhi's mouth water in spite of his misgivings. The man handed Ukar-Tiri a platter that steamed with the stuff and she took it eagerly. She and Ruarhi found an empty table and sat down.

She watched his face; he waited, still not committing himself. She bent down and with the rough spoon provided, began wolfing the food.

"Is it good?" he asked her.

She nodded, but didn't look up.

He controlled his hunger with an effort, slowly dipping his own spoon into the mixture. He tasted it. At once he was scooping the stuff up as quickly as she had done.

The big man stood over them. "Plenty more. Those who arrive here for the first time usually haven't eaten for several sleeps. And don't worry. No one is eager to ask too many questions. If you're not on the run, then you're damned unusual. Most of the crowd in here are in trouble of some sort or another." The big man snorted with amusement at his own joke.

Ruarhi let him ladle more onto his platter. He looked at Ukar-Tiri, but she would not meet his eyes.

Fodda. It was unavoidable. And the temptation was too great. He dipped the spoon into it again.

19

After they had finished eating and had been given water to drink, Ruarhi and Ukar-Tiri were joined by another man. He was small and rodentlike, his face pinched, his eyes as unusually tiny as most other men's here were large. But he seemed quite capable of seeing clearly. He sat opposite Ruarhi and Ukar-Tiri, hands clasped together under the table, gently rocking to and fro like a child. Most of the time he looked at Ukar-Tiri. There were other girls and women here, but none of them like her: they were either old or strange to look at, skins parched, hair thinning, as though all of them suffered from some wasting disease.

Ukar-Tiri felt uncomfortable under the scrutiny of the little man and scowled at him. At once the fellow looked away, but he would not move from his seat.

"You want something?" snapped Ruarhi, finally losing his patience, but had to repeat it in the language he had learned.

"There's a cell for you," piped the man. "When you finish here." He indicated the huge man who had given them the food. "Ogost says."

"A cell?" grunted Ruarhi.

"I think he means a room, somewhere to rest," said Ukar-Tiri softly. "They seem to make strangers welcome in High Crofels. It must be a haven."

Ruarhi frowned, but then nodded. "All right. But I'm not used to this. In my world, we'd have been treated with distrust, probably chained up."

"High Crofels is for misfits," Ukar-Tiri smiled. "The runaways, the miscreants."

Ruarhi snorted. He got up, stretching his arms. "Show us

137

the cell," he told the little man, who slipped off his stool
and bowed, apparently eager to be of service.

They had to force their way through a press of bodies to
keep up with him. People studied them with more than a
passing interest, Ruarhi thought, but it was hardly surprising
in view of the fact that they stood out in such a strange gathering. But they reached the far end of the huge chamber and
followed their diminutive guide up a stairway that appeared
to have been woven out of tough fibres onto a landing. They
traversed a number of these landings, until the man stopped
outside the promised cell.

Ruarhi looked inside. It was empty, mercifully clean,
though it also had the look of a nest.

"You rest," said the little figure. "I fetch you later."

"For what?" said Ruarhi.

"Emeschi."

Ruarhi would have pursued this, but Ukar-Tiri dissuaded
him gently. "Let him go. He can't tell us much. Can't you
see he's terrified of you?"

Ruarhi watched the little man scurry off down the corridor.
"There'll be a price for this hospitality."

When he turned, the girl was already in the room. She was
feeling the floor, which looked to have been woven from
dried wood stems, possibly even the rushes, which were evidently used for every conceivable purpose. It felt hard and
uncomfortable, but Ukar-Tiri sat down, leaning back.

"I didn't realise how exhausted I was," she yawned.

He squatted down, her yawn infectious. "Is it safe to sleep?"

But she had already stretched out, closing her eyes. She
muttered something incomprehensible. He determined to stay
awake for a while, but moments later both of them had succumbed to their tiredness.

She was already awake when he opened his eyes. She was
using a rag of some kind to wipe her face and arms. Beside
her was an earthenware jug.

"Is that water?" he asked, rolling over on his side to watch
her.

She nodded. "Not as clean as I would have liked it."

"Where did you get it?"

She indicated the doorway. "Our companion has returned," she said softly. "He is outside."

Ruarhi got up and looked. The little rodent man was hunched up, back to the wall of the corridor. When he saw Ruarhi staring down at him, he gasped, almost toppling. He scrambled to this feet at once.

"You are rested? You need more food?"

"No." Ruarhi went back into the room. Ukar-Tiri had finished her ablutions, her hair bound up behind her. She had found something with which to tie it in place, though Ruarhi preferred it loose. He did not say so.

Behind him the little man stirred. "You go to Emeschi now?"

Ukar-Tiri shrugged. Ruarhi nodded in agreement to the little man. "Yes. Take us."

The little man seemed relieved, and scampered off at once. Ruarhi paused only to slop a handful of water over his face and rub the sleep from his eyes. He had no idea how long he had been asleep, but he felt surprisingly refreshed.

In the corridors, they followed the little man upwards. The cells they passed were closed and silent. The only sound was the sound of the floor creaking underfoot; otherwise, they might have been in a tomb.

Abruptly another figure stepped into the confined corridor ahead of them. Larger than their guide, it was broader, almost gross, wearing little more than a harness, its white skin etched with curling designs, purple and pink, that stood out garishly, almost like a disease. The man's face was huge, as if a head too large for the shoulders had been squashed out of shape, the eyes bulging in the characteristic way of men under Skydown. Sharp splinters of wood had been thrust through its topknot, and wisps of greasy hair trailed down the man's shoulders. In the wide belt at his protruding gut, the hilts of several weapons stood out.

"Gulhaag will take you to the Emeschi," piped the little guide. He didn't wait for a response, turning and disappearing in his ratlike way.

The squat figure beckoned Ruarhi and Ukar-Tiri forward, its brows knitting in a ferocious glare. Ruarhi could feel the girl trembling beside him. She knew better than he what these creatures were capable of.

"We'd better follow it," he told her. She kept close to him, using his body as a shield.

They had not gone far when the figure swung open a wicker door to yet another chamber. Light spilled out, almost as bright as the light Ruarhi was used to. The gross figure made it clear he wanted Ruarhi and the girl to go in.

Ruarhi led Ukar-Tiri slowly forward, pausing at the threshold of the chamber. It was larger than the cells, but no higher, enough to accommodate a dozen people. A rough table was at its far end, and it was on this that the source of the light had been placed. Ruarhi looked at it for a moment, intrigued by it. In his world, light came from fire. But this was a globe of some kind. Whatever fire burned within it, it was self-contained, as though it might be a living creature.

He felt Ukar-Tiri tense, her fingers tight on his arm, as the wicker door closed. The gross guard Gulhaag had withdrawn.

"You are an External," said a surprisingly musical voice.

The light shifted to one side, moved by one of the beings seated at the table. Ruarhi saw that there were four of them. They wore drab grey robes, and three of them looked almost identical, their faces very pale, narrow, with tattoos on either cheek, odd sigils, possibly marking them as part of some cult or religious brotherhood. Such things were known to the MagMannochs.

The one who had spoken also had the facial markings, embossed and picked out clearly by the light, but unlike the other three he was not totally bald, his hair cut very short, the widow's peak a knife-shaped shadow. His eyes were narrow, lined, a cold ruthlessness gleaming in them. Ruarhi had seen such coldness in the priests of his world. It seemed to be embedded in the single mindedness of their beliefs.

"You are an External," the man repeated, his lips curving downward in a false smile.

"This isn't my world," nodded Ruarhi.

"It is now."

Ruarhi glanced at the others. They watched him fixedly, no warmth in their gaze. They might have been drugged.

"If you say so."

"The girl was an External, too. But she has been under Skydown for most of her life."

Ukar-Tiri was shivering, but she nodded automatically.

"We are the Emeschi," said the central figure.

"You rule High Crofels?" said Ruarhi.

"In a manner of speaking. Even the lawless need codes. We attend to such things. You have eaten, rested?"

Ruarhi nodded.

"Now that you have fled your masters, what do you intend? High Crofels is content to harbour you. It was created for just such a purpose. You need have no enemies here."

"But I must earn my keep?"

The man's eyelids drooped as he slowly nodded. "Of course. We Emeschi negotiate such things."

"I may not want to stay here long—"

"As you wish. We must calculate your value. What do you need?"

"Food, a cell, enough for a few sleeps. A weapon."

"What sort of weapon?"

"I am used to using a sword. Do you have such things here?"

The figure smiled, its teeth white. "In High Crofels we are able to obtain all manner of things. A simple sword would be easy to acquire. Is that all you wish?"

"For now."

"And the girl?" The eyes turned to Ukar-Tiri. She shrank back. "Do you speak for her, or does she barter for herself?" The others were watching her with interest.

Ruarhi turned to her. She looked imploringly at him but could not speak. She had become as afraid as she had been when he had first met her. The spirit that had returned to her on their journey was in danger of disintegrating. What did she know of these creatures?

"I speak for her," he said.

The central figure nodded. "We need to know such things. Her value depends on them."

"Value?"

"Yes. You have a high value. A Provider used an Angel Guard to hunt for you. He must want you very badly."

Ruarhi's eyes narrowed in spite of himself. "The winged being? But it flew off. It killed my companion, but left me."

"If we gave you to the Provider," the man went on, ignoring him, "he would reward us well. Thus you are valuable in that respect. The question is whether or not you would be more valuable to us in other ways.''

''Such as what?''

''You are a warrior, fresh from a war.''

Ruarhi didn't ask him how he knew this, but nodded.

''We need fighting men. We have many enemies. In truth, the Providers would like to raze High Crofels and crush all of us. But we are too useful. Too valuable a source of information.''

''You want me to kill for you?''

''Perhaps. Would you do this?''

''I have no other skill.'' *Nor is this my skill. But I have nothing else with which to barter,* he thought. *And I am not a warrior by choice. I am a hunter. MagMannochs are not mercenaries. Yet Dromator became one. Must I?*

''We can offer you what you wish, if you put yourself at our disposal.''

Ruarhi nodded.

''The girl is very beautiful, as many of the Externals are. What is it she wishes?''

''The same.''

''Who pays?''

Ruarhi looked askance at his interrogator. What did the man mean, who pays? What game were these people playing with them?

''You speak for her,'' said the man. ''But is she yours?''

''Mine?''

The man's eyes narrowed, and something akin to amusement gleamed in them. He seemed to take pleasure from Ruarhi's discomfort. ''Her position is not clear to me. If she is her own woman, then she earns her keep here in High Crofels as many of the other women do. She is beautiful. There are many pleasures she can offer to those who dwell here. I assume she was originally destined for better things, though. A fine woman such as she could bear many offspring, and she would be best suited to a proper breeding programme. Any eminent Drone—''

''No!'' cried Ukar-Tiri. ''Ruarhi, I cannot go back to that—''

He steadied her. ''If she refuses?''

"What are you saying? That she refuses in her own right, or that you decree it?"

"I?"

"Is she yours?"

Ruarhi began to understand. He recalled the words of Sommoi, telling him that if he took Ukar-Tiri from Festubul, she would be his responsibility. The same questions arose here. If he put aside the responsibility, Ukar-Tiri was to be a whore in this place. Or what? Used for *breeding?*

"If she is yours," said the man, "then you work harder for both your keep. It is all the same to us. But we need to understand the arrangement. The choice is yours, of course. We pride ourselves on freedom of choice in High Crofels."

"I will earn her keep," Ruarhi said bluntly, but he could not bring himself to look at the girl.

"Tell me," said another of the men, leaning forward, his talonlike hands folded in front of him on the table, "would you truly kill for us? Did you mean it?"

Ruarhi paused, watching their eyes. He saw no emotion amongst them. "Possibly."

"We'll see," said the first. "In the meantime, we need to be sure where your loyalties lie. You'll indulge us?"

Ruarhi knew he had no choice, in spite of their words, so he waited. Still he did not look at Ukar-Tiri, but he could feel the beating of her heart as if it pressed next to his skin. They knew something of her past, and that much scared her. Would they betray her?

20

They had separated him from Ukar-Tiri and put him in another chamber. There were, they said, a few last things they had to understand about him. He had no alternative but to indulge them. He had seen the anguish in Ukar-Tiri's face, but tried to smile reassuringly, though he felt anything but reassured. Since he had come to High Crofels, he felt only confusion; he was at the mercy of people he did not understand. But if he were to survive this world, he had to bite back the fear.

The cell he was in was small, the light from above poor. He had been sitting in it for a long time, when he noticed the light beginning to fade even more. He got to his feet, his head inches from the curved weave of the ceiling. The door had been secured: no doubt the huge guard was outside.

"Do not be alarmed," came a quiet voice from beyond one of the walls. The light went out, throwing him into darkness. It was like being far underground, something he hated.

He faced the wall from which the voice had come. They had not taken his weapon; he clutched it now, in anticipation of an attack.

"You are from a world that is very unlike this one, a world where the division between light and darkness is clearly marked, is that not true?"

He nodded, which seemed enough for whoever was watching.

"Day and night, you call those periods. There is no day or night under Skydown. Only degrees of darkness. Light is for the gods. We indulge in it sparingly. If we were to use it unwisely, too liberally, the gods would punish us. But it was not always so.

"Are you a creature of light, or darkness?"

Ruarhi did not know how they wanted him to answer. He kept very still. In the total darkness, he began to feel the onset of disorientation already. He had friends in his own world who had been below the earth, boasting of their exploits in the deep caverns, but he was happier high among the crags where the eagles soared. If he was kept in this darkness for long, he knew his mind would slide into panic.

Perhaps his observers sensed it. They did not speak to him for a long time, though the darkness made it impossible to measure its passing. But he refused to cry out. He felt a cold sweat breaking out over him, trickling between his shoulder blades. Why must they do this?

The time dragged on inexorably. He tried to close his mind to his circumstances, thinking of other things, but the darkness was only too eager to release images that haunted him, added to the persecution. Dromator, stretched out in his earth grave, his belly ripped open, Darrac in the reeds.

Ruarhi smashed his pipe weapon down into the floor and felt the snapping of the weave. Again and again he did it, but the floor held.

The spasm of fury passed, but it had left him shaken. He slumped down, shutting his eyes. What do they want from me? Why not just kill me?

He opened his eyes. The darkness was less intense, unless he was imagining it. But no, there was a degree of light. Suffused from all around him, the source invisible. Growing. He felt a flood of relief. Straightening, he watched as the light grew even more powerfully. Now it seemed to come from a point somewhere in the centre of the room, but was too intense there to look at directly. It became extreme, and with it the temperature increased. He could not look at the light, closing his eyes again.

Yet it was far more bearable than the darkness had been. He endured it without fear. This time he waited. If they kept him in the light for as long as they had in darkness, he could not tell.

As before, the light changed. It dimmed from its brilliance, settling to something like the normal daylight of his own world. His tormentors must have know what that was, otherwise how could they be so precise?

"A creature of light," said the voice.

"What did you expect?" he snapped.

"Our enemies have taught us to expect anything. They have power. They use it in devious ways. You might be their tool."

"I am not your enemy," he spat. "I don't even belong here. I just want to get back to my home."

"That is impossible. No one goes back."

"What do you want of me?"

"We'll tell you now."

The voice went away, and more silence followed. Ruarhi was too drained to feel any more anger.

A while later, the door opened and the huge guard beckoned him out. Ruarhi followed him to another chamber. There was food and water on a crude table, and a simple bench. He was far too hungry to resist the food, fodda or otherwise, and ate it greedily.

When he had finished, he noticed a figure beyond him, seated on what could have passed for a chair, though its design was strange, cumbersome.

He looked up from his food. The man was one of the Emeschi, his skin glowing pale in the artificial light of the chamber. It was the one who had been their spokesman on the first meeting.

"Is this light more comfortable?" he said.

Ruarhi folded his arms, nodding.

"In your world, light is taken for granted. I expect you never think of it. It probably does not seem precious. Here under Skydown it is almost forbidden, the prerogative of the gods, Absolute Light. They have lowered Skydown, preventing life from enjoying the light above the world. They say that it is because Absolute Light kills. To expose us to it would destroy us utterly."

"Why should it?"

"Ah," said the Emeschi, opening his pale hands. "Why should it? Skydown protects us, so the Lightbenders tell us. But suppose this is a lie. Suppose Skydown is a relic of a long forgotten past, when it was needed. A time when the light above threatened our world. Fire storms, unbearable heat, scorching winds. Legends speak of such times."

"In my world," said Ruarhi, his mind reaching for vague, half-remembered images, "there were traveling men who claimed to have seen vast tracts of sand, deserts where the sun was unbearable in the day."

The Emeschi nodded. "We have legends which talk of an ocean beyond the rim, and some say it is an ocean of sand. Destroyed by light."

"But you think Skydown is no longer necessary?"

The Emeschi nodded. "It was needed once. But no more."

"Then why does it remain?"

"Our gods are Absolute Light. Their supreme servants are the Lightbenders, the highest order of life under Skydown. They revel in their powers. And they control everything else.

Skydown is the means by which they exercise that control. All life is subservient to the Lightbenders. They are the glory to which all life aspires. Fodda, Menials, Providers, Skryers, Elevates, and all the others. All crawling upwards towards the golden palaces of the Lightbenders above Thousand-reach.''

And you, thought Ruarhi, *are the rebels*.

''For their amusement, the Lightbenders commission the Providers to use the Overlap, a peculiar quirk of the fabric of our world. It is unpredictable, whimsical, and uncontrollable. But it opens passages to other worlds. The Providers hunt. You and many like you are the victims of such hunts. Sport for the Lightbenders and their servants.''

''They use us for meat,'' breathed Ruarhi.

''Oh, yes. Fodda takes many forms. But you'd be foolish to suppose it ends there. Fodda is life, energy. Fodda is pleasure.''

Ruarhi felt a stab of unease at this last.

''Yes, well might you start. You cannot imagine how fodda is put to use in Thousandreach. How life is tormented and abused. Since your arrival under Skydown, you will have noticed how life is treated with utter contempt. Fodda is cheap, plentiful. The Providers have access to unlimited supplies of it. The Lightbenders indulge themselves indiscriminately and ceaselessly.''

''Then how have they endured?''

Again the brief flapping of hands. ''Power. Total control.''

''But you'd overthrow them if you could?''

The Emeschi smiled patiently. ''It is our purpose. But it may take us many lifetimes. The Lightbenders have ruled our world for as long as we have records.''

''What do you want of me?''

''I cannot say precisely. We have no specific task for you, not yet. But you are strong, far stronger than most of our people. In our work, there is a real need for men like you. We will house you, feed you, give you what we can. High Crofels is large, carefully preserved. It is a centre of learning,'' the Emeschi laughed softly. ''Many secrets are exchanged here.''

''And the girl?''

''She is under your protection. Your service pays for her.''

"I think she, too, would be glad to rebel. She has suffered."

The Emeschi nodded. Then he rose and walked slowly around the table, apparently thinking about something else. He paused close to Ruarhi's side. He seemed frail, delicate, hardly fit to be a warrior, a rebel.

I could kill him with one swift blow, thought Ruarhi, but then scorned the thought.

"Tell me, when you were on the road, fleeing, did you see anything unusual?" the Emeschi asked him.

Ruarhi snorted. "Everything I have seen in your world is unusual!"

The Emeschi smiled indulgently. "Of course. But were there any creatures, other than Foddamen, you saw?"

Ruarhi wondered if he meant the Angel Guard. Should he tell him?

"You are understandably reticent. You don't bestow your trust lightly. Why should you? But I think you need to be honest with me. There are things I must know. If I am to protect you."

"From what?"

"You have escaped from dangerous enemies. They will come here."

"That sounds like a threat."

The Emeschi shook his head. He stood very close to Ruarhi. "We cannot work together that way. Help us. You could be most valuable to us. And we could help you."

Ruarhi shrugged, but nodded.

"What did you see?"

Ruarhi spoke slowly, choosing his words carefully. "You call them Angel Guards. One of them was on the road. Injured."

"Injured?" The Emeschi looked intrigued. "How?"

"The Foddamen said it had been hurt in a storm. Lightning."

The Emeschi cocked his head, birdlike. "Is this so? An Angel Guard? Such a thing is unprecedented. Storms are nothing to them."

"Well, the thing was hurt. Blinded."

"Blinded?" echoed the Emeschi. His hands gripped the edge of the table, the bony knuckles jutting as though he had to steady himself. The information had come as a shock to him.

"Ask Ukar-Tiri. She'll confirm it."

"Do you know where it is now?"

"It took to the sky." Ruarhi looked away angrily. "But not before it had struck down Dromator, my companion. For that I will kill it—"

The Emeschi shook his head. "Do not talk of killing an Angel Guard. There is no more dangerous a creature under Skydown."

Ruarhi could not believe that it was the thought of the killing power of the Angel Guard that had disturbed the composure of the Emeschi. Something more significant attached to this. "What is wrong?"

The Emeschi walked slowly back to his chair. "We were told that an Angel Guard would visit this segment."

"By whom?"

"We have agents in Thousandreach. They keep us informed. I cannot divulge more than that to you at the moment. But you say the Angel Guard was blinded?"

"I'm quite sure. By lightning, or so it seems."

"Incredible."

"Men have been cut down by lightning in my world. To be exposed or in a high place is dangerous. The Angel Guard was either foolish or unlucky."

"No. Neither. It was planned."

"By *lightning?*" scoffed Ruarhi. "Surely not."

"Yes. We were promised this. We were *told* the Angel Guard would be blinded. Though we doubted."

"I don't understand—"

"I spoke of power. This was a demonstration."

Ruarhi's curiosity struggled with his irritation. "What are you saying, the Lightbenders did this?"

The Emeschi closed his eyes, but his face wore a look of relief rather than anxiety. "No," he said softly. "No, not them. Mercifully not them."

21

Ruarhi was taken back to his room, escorted by the gross Gulhaag, who still said nothing. Ruarhi wondered if the creature were mute.

In the cell, Ukar-Tiri was waiting. She had been sitting on the floor, legs crossed, head bowed, but when he entered, she got up quickly as if she was about to come to him and embrace him. But she pulled back, though she could not hide her relief at seeing him.

"What did they do to you?" he asked her, listening to Gulhaag positioning himself outside in the corridor.

"They took me to where there was food."

"Were you questioned?"

She shook her head. "And you?"

"They offered me work," he said humourlessly, then explained.

When he had finished, she turned away. "You told them you will work for my keep?"

"It was that, or give you to them. You know more about that than I do."

She swung back to him, her face darkening. "And what do you expect of me? You expect me to serve you, is that it? Couple with you as I coupled with Festubul!"

The sudden violence of her outburst stunned him. Why did she not react this way to others, show them her steel? He stood with his mouth slack for a moment, then realised he must have looked oafish. "Don't be stupid," he snapped.

"What else am I to expect? Why should you bring me—?"

"Why did you come?" he said automatically. She had a way of making him stammer out words where silence would have served him better.

"You cannot imagine what it was like with Festubul! You gave me a chance to get away from him—"

"Then be grateful!"

She bunched her fists, her cheeks glowing. "Grateful! By letting you take me, I suppose—"

"I've never asked that!"

"No, but how long will it be, now that you think you have a claim on me?"

"You do not have to stay," he said through his teeth.

"I have no choice. I will not give myself to the Emeschi, nor anyone else in this place."

"Then you don't have to. I make no claims on you."

She frowned. "So what are the terms of this arrangement?"

"Can't you just accept that I'm willing to protect you?"

"For nothing? You have no desire to use me?"

"You have no desire to be abused, as you put it."

"Why should I tolerate something which gives me no pleasure?"

"It isn't necessary, I've told you!"

"Under Skydown, nothing belongs to itself. Humanity is fodda. Flesh is for consumption, one way or another."

He swore obscenely. "I'm not of this world! It's a disgusting place! In my world, men choose what they desire, and so do the women. There are laws to protect us both! Here I eat because I have to."

"And couple because you have to."

Her persistence amazed him. She seemed determined to infuriate him. Again he gritted his teeth on his anger. "If I must couple, then I must. What man doesn't desire such pleasure? It is not something fit only for a man! But in High Crofels it seems such things are automatically provided. Especially for those in the hire of the Emeschi."

She took in a slow, deep breath, as though she had not yet finished her tirade, but she spoke quietly. "You heard the Emeschi. They consider me beautiful, just as Festubul and the others in the village did. They would take pleasure from me. Or better, use me to breed from. How many brats would they sire on me? How many litters? I've seen the women in the village! Fifteen children and more."

"Fifteen?"

She ran her fingers through her hair, which served only to enhance her beauty, though she must have known that. "Oh, yes! Flesh is fodda. They use it in many ways. Breeding is so important to them—"

"Who?"

"All of them! Foddamen, Emeschi, Providers, all of them! I am valuable to them, but only on their terms. In terms of what I could provide, either in pleasure or in offspring."

"You assume that all men would treat you that way?"

She laughed derisively. "I have played the part, and may have to again. The choice will not be mine to make. But no one can dictate my feelings to me."

Mercifully further discussion was not possible as Gulhaag appeared, gesturing for them both to follow him. Ruarhi was too relieved to argue, falling in step behind the gross figure as it led him and Ukar-Tiri up to another landing and deeper into the endless maze of the settlement. Its structure was deceptive, a warren of corridors and cells, a labyrinthine confusion of walkways and stairs. It had been so skillfully made that it could have been a natural growth; certainly in parts it seemed more living organism than artificial construction. Even the light that seeped from its walls seemed a composite part of it.

They were taken to another chamber, which opened out like a small cavern, its ceiling made of curved arches that looked like wooden beams, though Ruarhi wondered if they were yet more variations on the amazing reeds, which seemed to be the sole plant life in this part of the world.

Several of the Emeschi awaited them, including the one who had last spoken to Ruarhi. Gulhaag stood back, but for once did not exit, standing docilely to one side, eyes fixed ahead of him.

Ruarhi felt Ukar-Tiri close to his arm, where she always stood in the company of others. Where was her anger now? Why didn't the little vixen raise her voice here? Why not give these creatures a piece of her mind? Oh no, she would let it fester within and then discharge it at him when they were next alone! *And I thought the MagMannoch girls were difficult to understand!* he mused.

"Ruarhi," said the spokesman. "We can exchange names

now. I am Inkulke. We have called you again sooner than we had intended. But we find that we are called upon to act quickly.'' He held out a slender hand, and one of the other Emeschi stepped forward. He was holding a leather bag which contained a number of weapons. He offered them to Ruarhi for his inspection.

There was a sword: Ruarhi pulled it from its scabbard. It was the kind he was used to, short and double-edged. Well balanced, though he was no expert. The steel from which it had been cast shone like silver. He nodded approval, as if he were familiar with such quality, and studied the other weapons, most of which were knives, though there were also hunting tools, suitable for skinning and the stripping of bone. These would have served any MagMannoch hunter well.

''They are yours,'' said Inkulke.

Ukar-Tiri's eyes widened as she watched Ruarhi strap the belt to his waist, fitting each weapon into it with care. He took the pipe weapon he had carried thus far and grinned at it. Then he slipped it into the belt as well. ''It will remind me of certain things,'' he said.

Inkulke nodded. ''There is information you must have, people you must meet. One of our most important agents has come here. There is urgent business. It will concern you.''

Ruarhi waited.

Inkulke turned to one of the others, saying something that Ruarhi did not catch. There was a door beyond, and the Emeschi Inkulke had addressed left by it.

''The girl saw the Angel Guard, you said.''

Ruarhi looked at Ukar-Tiri, who seemed to have shrunk under the eyes of the Emeschi. They were looking at her openly, but did not use her name, and seemed to treat her with minimal respect. Was it as she had said?

She nodded, but did not speak.

From the door, other figures came into the room. The Emeschi had brought them and they faced Ruarhi and Ukar-Tiri in silence for a moment.

Ukar-Tiri gave a moan and clung to Ruarhi's arm.

Instinctively he drew out the killing sword, a curse forming on his lips.

Sommoi and Festubul stood before him.

Ruarhi said nothing, waiting. He had told Ukar-Tiri he would kill Sommoi.

"Put away your weapon," said Inkulke. "Sommoi is the agent we spoke of."

Ruarhi did not know how to take this news. "And Festubul?" he said. "Is he also in your pay?" He barely managed to conceal his contempt.

Festubul pointed accusingly at Ukar-Tiri. "Give her to me."

Ruarhi could not tell if Festubul spoke directly to him, or to the Emeschi.

Inkulke glanced at Festubul. "She is under Ruarhi's protection, just as you are under Sommoi's."

Sommoi spoke for the first time. "This is correct, Ruarhi? You claim her?"

Ruarhi grinned coldly, Ukar-Tiri's words ringing back to him. "I earn her freedom in High Crofels. No one owns her."

Festubul stepped forward, his face twisted with loathing and resentment. "Then if you have no claim on her—"

"If you touch her," said Ruarhi, "I'll open you up before these people." He lifted the sword a few inches.

Festubul's eyes shifted to the blade. It must have struck him then that the Emeschi had given it to the External. He was theirs!

"Well?" said Inkulke to Festubul. "You have a claim on this girl? If so, we seem to be in dispute."

Festubul moved back slowly. The Emeschi were not going to support him. They had not admonished the External for his bloody threat. Thus they would allow him the freedom to use the sword. He shook his head. "No. I have no claim."

"Then your business here is ended," said Inkulke flatly.

Festubul glanced at Sommoi, as though expecting support from him, but Sommoi would not even look at him.

"Stay in High Crofels by all means," said another of the Emeschi. "But go your own way. Find other pleasures."

Again Festubul looked to Sommoi, as though challenging him to speak on his behalf, but Sommoi ignored him. With a muted curse, Festubul swept out through the door. It was closed quietly behind him.

"We will impart certain knowledge to you, Ruarhi," said Sommoi. "Is the girl to share your knowledge?"

The question took Ruarhi by surprise. But he would not be rushed into an answer this time. If he agreed, then Ukar-Tiri would be even more tightly bound to him. His responsibility to her would be doubled. Any danger to him would fall on her. And clearly she neither enjoyed danger, nor the thought of being beholden to him.

"No."

At once he felt her stiffen, but she kept her silence.

Inkulke nodded to Gulhaag, who stepped forward.

"Take her to Ruarhi's quarters."

Ruarhi would not meet Ukar-Tiri's gaze, not knowing if it would be one of relief, anger, resentment, confusion, or what. But at least she must be glad to have been officially freed of Festubul. The Emeschi would not have supported the reed-man, Ruarhi was sure of that. He would have used the sword: had they known that? He thought so.

Sommoi had been studying Ruarhi. "So you are hired," he said wryly.

Inkulke cleared his throat. "Explain what you know. And tell him who you are, Sommoi."

Sommoi shrugged. "What I am and what I once was are two very different things. Now I am an agent, a rebel, a dissident. But once I served the Lightbenders, gave my every effort to their whim. I was a Provider."

"You were one of them?" said Ruarhi, puzzled.

"With considerable estate. I was a colleague of Provider Sughai Orvech, and we were slaves of Elevate Yvane Sephir and through him the master of the Da Sangravilles themselves, the formidable Kaizu. Who could have wished for a better path to glory?

"My fall from grace is known to the Emeschi: I won't dwell on it here. Suffice it to say, it concerns Provider Sughai Orvech. I owe him a telling blow. How better to deliver it than to transfer my loyalties to his avowed rival and bitter enemy, Provider Hummal Goresch, who serves Elevate Zaer Phesmes and the House of the Des Aubach.

"The Lightbenders would destroy each other if they could," he went on, his strange eyes fixing Ruarhi. "They fight a perpetual war, though it is principally a war of intrigue and silence, fought down below them in the pits of Thousandreach and across the segments in whispers, the cut of a knife in darkness.

"Subran of the Des Aubach longs to destroy Kaizu. He concentrates his will on that, just as Kaizu plans to wipe away all other Houses. While they develop their strategies, high above the world, other powers seek their fall. And while they amuse themselves with endless acts of barbarism, life under Skydown writhes in torment. Does not all you have seen disgust you, Ruarhi?"

Ruarhi was surprised by the sudden outburst of bitterness. He nodded slowly.

"Are you not outraged?" Sommoi went on. "You have seen what it is to live under Skydown. You have seen how your own kind are brought here, used as fodda, cut down mindlessly. Your friends who—"

"You were responsible for that farm—"

Sommoi shook his head. "No. My punishment was to run it for the Providers. But I have other masters." He turned to Inkulke. "What does he know?"

Inkulke spoke only briefly, outlining what he had told Ruarhi.

"Our rebellion centres on an undisclosed power," Sommoi continued. "He is our real hope, for without power, true power, the fall of the Lightbenders is unthinkable."

"Was it this ally who struck down the Angel Guard?" ventured Ruarhi.

"Yes. We were promised this. Provider Hummal Goresch was told to commission an Angel Guard to come to this segment to recover three Externals after a hunt. He acted on the instruction of Elevate Zaer, who was told by our faceless ally that he would blind the Angel Guard as a demonstration of his power. It was no small thing."

"You don't know the identity or the nature of this ally?"

"Safer for him if he remains unknown at this time."

"He is in the city, Thousandreach?"

Sommoi shook his head. "We think he is above it. In the place of Absolute Light."

Ruarhi frowned. "Where your gods dwell?"

"He may be one of them," said Inkulke. "We pray that he is."

22

"Until now," said Inkulke, "our rebellion has been a small thing, a beast of stealth, slow-moving and cloaked in darkness. Not until our ally made himself known to us did we begin to consider delivering a real blow against the powers that control our world."

"We were like children," said Sommoi. "Tossing stones at a wall. Our enemies knew nothing of our efforts. But with such an ally, we have become potentially more effective. The Lightbenders would never expect true rebellion, and certainly they would scorn a rising of the lower orders. They would be highly amused by such lunacy."

"It seems incredible to me," said Ruarhi, "that you are considering challenging your *gods*. What will you use?" He held up the sword he had been given. *"This?"*

Inkulke smiled indulgently. "Rebellion has many stages, many degrees. The sword is one weapon. Between it and the power of our ally, there will be others."

"How is this rebellion to take shape?"

Inkulke looked at Sommoi, but the latter nodded, as though satisfied that Ruarhi should be fully party to their intentions.

"Our first task is clear," said Inkulke. "We have to find the Angel Guard who was blinded."

Ruarhi waited. He understood very little of the implications of this. Blinding a warrior seemed a bizarre way of demonstrating power. Why not simply kill him, or capture him?

Inkulke read his confusion. "I should explain things more clearly. When Elevate Zaer was told to send one of the Angel Guards to this segment, he had to cover himself and his actions carefully." He turned again to Sommoi. "Are you aware of the complications that have arisen?"

It was Sommoi's turn to frown, but he nodded. "I know that the Angel Guard is still alive."

Inkulke went on, speaking for the benefit of both Sommoi and Ruarhi. "Our ally got word to Elevate Zaer Phesmes, the leader of our conspiracy, that an Angel Guard should be commissioned and sent to this sector. Zaer Phesmes gave the instruction to Provider Hummal Goresch, who is a master of the hunt, reputed for sending his hunters into the Overlap. Provider Goresch works closely with the Skryer, Verusion, who is also recognised for his work with the Overlap.

"Provider Goresch had the Angel Guard, Arteriel, commissioned and sent, as instructed, though he knew nothing of the real purpose. He was told that three Externals had escaped and were proving particularly difficult to retrieve."

Ruarhi felt his cheeks flushing with renewed anger. "Was the winged man told to kill these runaways?"

Inkulke recongised the bitterness in the young man's voice. "We had to avoid suspicion falling on any part of our plan. It had to seem regular, even though it is not common to use Angel Guards to hunt Externals."

Sommoi interrupted. "Did you think your escape from the hunters was real?" he asked Ruarhi.

Again Ruarhi felt the stab of anger. "It was contrived—?"

"Of course," nodded Sommoi. "The three of you were the bait for the Angel Guard. You survived by your wits. But I have to say, your friend who died on the road was unfortunate. The Angel Guard struck him down in defence. It was not a calculated kill."

But you used us, and would have let us die like animals, Ruarhi was thinking. *And have your plans changed so much now? Am I to trust you?*

"After Arteriel flew back to Thousandreach," Inkulke went on, aware of Ruarhi's controlled fury, "he had to be disposed of quickly. Otherwise the power that had blinded him would have been questioned by others, undoubtedly including Elevate Yvane Sephir. Our plot would have been uncovered, our ally exposed. Arteriel was therefore called before his Praetor, the commander of his Eyrie. Provider Goresch had informed the Praetor that the search for the three Externals had ended in failure. Verusion had used his skills as a

Skryer to determine this. The Praetor was obliged to answer Provider Goresch's charge that the Angel Guard in question was not worthy of his wings. It led to a trial by combat.''

Sommoi was watching Inkulke as he spoke, his attention rapt.

"A particularly skillful Angel Guard, Syrakeil, was chosen to test Arteriel's right to continue in service. Syrakeil should have killed him. It would have served us well, and given Arteriel an honourable death. But Arteriel defeated Syrakeil,'' said Inkulke softly. "It must have been a glorious contest. But it did not further our cause. An alternative plan had to be effected quickly. Elevate Zaer Phesmes sent a written document to the Praetor, telling him that in view of the blind Angel's failure in the field, he was to be sent to Provider Hummal Goresch, for a new posting. There would have been nothing unusual in such a command; Elevate Zaer Phesmes was merely exercising his rights. Once he had Arteriel, he should have been able to dispose of him. Not as tidy as death in combat, but at least the conspiracy would have been protected.''

Sommoi shifted uneasily. "Why was Arteriel not delivered to Provider Hummal Goresch? What went wrong?''

Inkulke massaged the bridge of his nose as though trying to prevent the onset of a headache. "Provider Sughai Orvech, prompted by his insufferable greed for power, abducted Arteriel, killing a number of Provider Goresch's servants.''

Sommoi swore. "They would have used a Tormenter, opened Arteriel's mind—''

"They tried to. But this is no ordinary Angel Guard. Arteriel seems to have taken strength from his blindness.''

"What do you mean?'' said Sommoi.

Ruarhi was intrigued. He was puzzled by the numerous references to people in the remote city, the intricacies of the plot, but somehow the elusive powers of the blinded winged man struck a chord of sympathy in his heart, until he recalled that the same winged warrior had ripped Dromator open and left him gutted like a calf on a block. It may have been a reflex kill, but it did not stop the hate.

"He escaped Provider Orvech's henchmen,'' said Inkulke. "He killed his captors and left a clear message for Provider Orvech. *The blind Angel Guard is your enemy.* And he left the same message for Provider Hummal Goresch.''

Sommoi drew in his breath. "Is that everything?"

Inkulke shook his head. "No. Not content with that, he took the life of another Angel Guard. A Bone White. He himself is a Blood Red."

Sommoi looked appalled. "He *took the life* of a fellow Angel Guard?"

"He needed his weapons. And he wanted to show contempt for those who had spurned him."

"Then where—?"

"Wherever he is," said Inkulke, "we must find him before anyone else. He is hunted by the Angel Guard, as well as by Elevate Yvane Sephir, who is now most anxious to find and interrogate him."

"If that happens," said Sommoi, "we are all damned. Our ally will be revealed to Absolute Light."

"We want Arteriel alive," said Inkulke.

Sommoi shook his head. "The sooner he is dead, the better. Everything is compromised otherwise."

Inkulke looked even more grave. "I have received word from our contacts with Elevate Zaer. He says our ally is aware of the dilemma, and has clear instructions for us."

"And?"

"He prefers Arteriel alive."

"Capture him?" Sommoi laughed derisively.

"Our ally thinks we can use him. He would be a superb weapon."

Sommoi looked even more outraged. "Win the Angel Guard to our cause? An ally? He would scorn us! We are ordure to him. And already he is enraged by what has happened to him."

"He is lost, totally alone," said Inkulke. "Everything under Skydown conspires against him. He has a little time, that is all. Death is at his shoulder."

"Inkulke, he is an *Angel Guard!* A Blood Red. Bred as a killing machine with nothing in his heart but utter contempt for all life-forms other than those protected by his duty."

"His anger has direction. Our rebellion will give it focus."

"What are you saying?"

"I told you. Elevate Zaer says our ally wants us to attempt to win him to us."

Sommoi snorted. "Impossible! Even if we found him, how would we get near him? He will be far more dangerous than usual."

Inkulke looked at Ruarhi. "Zaer feels that Arteriel will lack a cause now. He will not consider revenge, that is, returning to Thousandreach in a hunt for blood. Not as a lone hunter. He knows the impossibility of avoiding captivity. The only thing left for him will be his personal honour."

"What honour? He has been cast out, disgraced."

"He is an Angel Guard. They are all the same, arrogant and haughty. Pride burns like a fire in Arteriel's breast. He will put right what he can." Inkulke pointed to Ruarhi. "You were the cause of his failure. Elevate Zaer Phesmes's communication to the Praetor confirmed it. Arteriel failed to kill the three Externals."

"He killed one," said Sommoi. "Another is dead, and Arteriel would have assumed as much. Survival in the reed beds would have been unthinkable."

They talk about Darrac and Dromator with no compassion, thought Ruarhi. *Fodda. So much flesh to them.*

"But he knows you are alive," said Inkulke.

"You think Arteriel will seek him?" said Sommoi.

Inkulke nodded. "I think he will do two things. Hunt Ruarhi, with a view to killing him."

"And after that?" said Sommoi.

"He will have nothing left. He will take his own life."

Already Ruarhi could see how they intended to use him. It was how the MagMannochs would have operated, had they been in the field. He had already been unwittingly used as bait. This time they were at least asking his approval.

"I was used once before," he said. "And you've already told me I have to earn my keep," he added caustically.

Sommoi paced slowly across the floor, thinking over Inkulke's words. "A trap? Using Ruarhi?"

Inkulke nodded slowly. "It is the only way we can get near Arteriel. But we don't want your life sacrificed, Ruarhi. All life is valuable. It is the creed we seek to uphold. The very reason we would see the Lightbenders brought down."

"How will you draw Arteriel to us?" said Sommoi. "He might be anywhere if he's fled Thousandreach."

''The Emeschi have eyes and ears in strange places. The passage of a lone Angel Guard, no matter how well disguised, will not go unnoticed.''

''You've word of him?''

''We have left information in key places. We knew he would return to the road, to the place where he was blinded. The trail will lead him here.''

Sommoi scowled. ''He'll not enter High Crofels. He'll despise the company of fodda. And he'll be very cautious.''

''It is unlikely he'll link Ruarhi with his enemies, though he may well anticipate that his enemies have agents here. Who does not?''

''He won't come here,'' Sommoi repeated.

''Then we must take the bait to him.''

''How?'' said Sommoi. ''Stake Ruarhi out?''

''In a manner of speaking.''

Ruarhi watched them coldly, wondering if it would be better to look for an opportunity to kill them both. But he quickly smothered his thoughts, knowing that Sommoi possessed strange powers, his mind like an ear, attuned to things no MagMannoch could detect.

Inkulke thought for a moment then spoke. ''If Ruarhi was to be protected in some way, so that Arteriel cannot reach him, so that Ruarhi could speak to him—''

''Speak to him!'' Ruarhi cried. ''What could I say to this killing machine!''

''Detain him long enough for us to take him—''

''As soon as he suspects a trick,'' said Sommoi dismissively, ''he'll take flight. He's an Angel Guard. Even blinded, he'll be hard to deceive.''

''Yes,'' agreed Inkulke. ''Clearly his blindness has made him more dangerous. It is why our ally wants him, his help. Our enemies would be taken completely unawares if we had such a warrior acting with us.''

Sommoi turned to Ruarhi. ''Ruarhi, all that has befallen you have been consequences of this world, this decadent regime. I have subjected you to misery, despair. I had to. You perhaps think I did nothing to prevent the deaths of your companions. I could save none of them. You are not here by chance. If the world under Skydown revolts you as it does others, you must help us.''

Willingly, or at swordpoint, Ruarhi mused. *Unless they decide to torture Ukar-Tiri as a means of persuasion.* A tiny shiver of apprehension ran down his spine. *No, I couldn't let them do it. They have me. But Sommoi is right, curse him. How can I scorn a cause which professes horror at this vilest of worlds? My loathing of it merely reflects theirs. And if there is truly no way back, I have no other course. I must face the winged killer.*

23

Two figures sat in the shadows at the outer edge of the eating hall. The place was crowded, scores of people packed together, drinking the cheap, strong beer of High Crofels. The noise level was high, higher than it would have been in other settlements, where the threat of the Providers hung over everything. But no such threat existed in High Crofels. Its inhabitants enjoyed what freedom it was possible to snatch, though they knew that the limits of their safety extended no farther than the stilts of the reed town.

One of the two figures carried a cloak, which he had only now discarded and draped over his seat. His face was badly scarred, the skin etched deliberately by a cruel knife, marking him as property, though now he had chosen exile. His eyes were dead, the lids drooping as if the man was always on the point of sleep. It gave him a deceptively lazy outlook. He nodded at two passing women, slatterns who were making for another table where a group of men awaited servicing.

''Plenty of women in this hole, Festubul,'' he said softly. His voice was as cold as his eyes. ''Can't understand why you don't make use of them, instead of chasing one.''

Festubul glowered at the man, though he would never have dreamed of voicing disagreement. He was a dangerous killer, a highly skilled hunter who had been in the pay of the Providers, though since his defection he kept his loyalties to himself. There were very few who could afford his services: anyone who could not had no need to know who he was or what he did.

"Just find her," growled Festubul. "You'll be paid."

The hunter drained his beer. "Before I begin, I'll need some information, in advance. What assurance do I have that you can pay me well?"

Festubul snorted. "Try this. A Provider sent an Angel Guard to hunt for three Externals, runaways."

The hunter frowned. "Extravagant. Externals often attempt flight. Waste of effort. No need to send an Angel Guard to drag them back."

"There was an accident," Festubul went on, his voice very low. "A storm, lightning. The Angel Guard was blinded."

The hunter's left hand idly stroked the scars of his face, as though taking pleasure in them. "Strange fate."

"Two of the Externals are dead. The other is alive."

"Interesting."

"His name is Ruarhi. I know where he is. And who protects him."

"Why should I want this External?"

"Ask the Provider who sent an Angel Guard to look for him."

The hunter sat back, lips pursed. "You think they'd pay me well for him, or rather, his head?"

Festubul grinned. "Is that how you would deliver him to them?"

The hunter shrugged as though it were nothing. "It is how I always deliver. Tidier and more economical than delivering a carcass."

"Then you accept my commission?"

"The woman for this External?" The hunter yawned, exposing sharp teeth that were unusually white. "It seems a poor exchange. How do you gain? The woman can have little value."

"She is not as the women you see here."

The hunter laughed quietly. "Then I may be tempted to use her myself before returning her to you."

Festubul gripped the table to control his anger, a gesture that was not missed by the hunter, though he pretended not to notice.

"Where is she?" he said idly.

"She is here in High Crofels. The External has her."

The hunter's eyes narrowed suspiciously. "Together? Then it should be a simple matter. Men disappear in High Crofels."

"He is protected."

The hunter yawned again. "High Crofels protects us all."

Festubul shook his head. "You don't understand. The External has the special protection of the Emeschi."

The hunter's expression never flickered. He merely shrugged. But he gave this information careful consideration. Who was this External? An Angel Guard sent to hunt him, and now protected by the Emeschi. Such peculiar circumstances. There were Providers who would relish this information, even if the External could not be taken.

"I'll find them."

"The girl is called Ukar-Tiri."

The hunter nodded, though he was already looking through the gloom at other women in the hall. He found none of them desirable.

Ukar-Tiri was waiting for Ruarhi when he got back to his cell. At first she looked apprehensive, unsure of herself, like the girl she had been on the road. But, like a disguise slipping from her as easily as a veil, the mood changed almost as soon as he closed the door behind him.

"How dare you treat me this way! My hands might just as well be tied together! High Crofels is supposed to be a haven. But I'm a prisoner, just as I was under Festubul—"

He stared at her, then lifted his hand. "You're not a prisoner. You're free to go."

"Where? To the halls below? To *serve*? Or out into the reeds, to be devoured?"

"I'm leaving for a while—"

"Leaving? Where are you going? To serve them? The Emeschi?"

"Never mind. You can stay here if you wish. No one will harm you. But you can't come with me. I'll be back. When I return, tell me what you want, because I'm damned if I know what it is!" He shouted this last and she reacted as if he had slapped her across the face.

She didn't speak for a long time, watching him sullenly as he bent down to the earthenware dish that had been put in the room, and dipped his hands into the cool water. He ran them over his face.

"Where are you going?" she asked at last, though more softly.

"On a hunt," he said.

"For what?"

"Never mind."

"It's the Angel Guard, isn't it? The blind one?"

He looked up at her, then thought better of arguing. "Yes."

"Then you're a fool! Don't you realise how dangerous those creatures are? Haven't you seen enough blood—"

"There'll be no killing this time—"

She swung round to the wall, leaning on it and laughing derisively. "No killing? You don't understand this world at all! No killing. It is all the Angel Guards are bred for."

He stood up. "You can wait if you wish." He opened the door and saw her surprise that it had not been locked from outside. "If you decide not to, the door is open." He stepped through it, closing it before she could answer.

She may have called him, but he did not hear.

She did open the door, but not until much later. She looked up and down the corridor. It was dark and empty, but this time there was no guard. She had half thought there would be. She stepped back into the cell, closing the door, cursing quietly. Far safer to remain.

They'd bring food and water at intervals, but she knew that it was close to a sleep period. The body soon adjusted to the artificial night under Skydown: Ruarhi's had. She sat down, her mind going over again the journey across the reed beds.

As she was thinking, she heard the creaking of the woven walls. The reeds dominated everything. Used for so many purposes. There was no escaping them. Reeds and fodda,

they seemed to be all that the world under Skydown consisted
of. She thought again of prison, the reeds her bars.

Something stirred outside the cell. It was far too late for
any more food to be delivered. The door suddenly swung
open. Light filtered in. Limned in its poor glow stood one
of the gross guards. It was not the familiar Gulhaag.

Ukar-Tiri shrank back against the wall, making herself as
small as she could. Ruarhi had said she'd be safe. But no one
was safe under Skydown. The guard's bestial face was
screwed up in an expression that could have meant anything.
But she could only assume he intended to take advantage of
Ruarhi's absence. He took one ungainly step forward, then
to her amazement toppled to one side, crashing to the floor
as if unconscious. Maybe he was drunk. But as he rolled on
to his side, away from her, Ukar-Tiri saw why he had fallen.
A long length of metal had been thrust through him, narrowly
missing his spine. Thick blood dripped down the metal.

Another figure materialised in the doorway, then entered,
shutting the door without a sound. It held a cruel flaying knife.

Ukar-Tiri was too stunned to cry out. The figure was
dressed in a dark robe of some kind, its head wrapped in
black cloth, only the eyes showing. A gloved hand indicated
roughly that she should get up, and the wicked blade emphasised the command. She shuddered at the sight of the
grim weapon knowing what it could do: she had seen the
Drone's servants strip living dissidents with such steel.

Quickly she scrambled to her feet. She felt her gut clamping as the terror gripped her. Her mouth had dried up; she
could utter no sound. The figure ignored the guard, assured
of its handiwork.

Quickly the figure gripped her wrist, snapping something
cold over it and tugging so that she was pulled through the
door into the corridor.

"Not a sound," breathed her captor. He slipped the hook
of the knife under her skirt with practised ease. She felt the
cold metal against the inside of her thigh.

She nodded, fighting back tears. He prodded her in the back
and she moved up the corridor at his instruction. They were
rising. The corridor twisted around the upper levels of the woven building, until at length another door opened onto a ledge

outside. The darkness was almost total, broken only by a few lights below. A breeze stirred. Ukar-Tiri began to feel giddy, conscious of the huge drop into darkness only feet away.

Her captor took the end of the small chain attached to the wrist-lock and secured it to one of the thicker strands of weaving beside her. The wall curved upward and then gently away, a domelike roof exposed totally to the sky.

Fear had disabled her mind. She could not think properly. This was no ordinary abduction. The man was a trained hunter. He had not brought her here to abuse her. He would hardly do such a thing to spite the Emeschi. As she tried to shut down her panic, she began to go over the possibilities.

Her captor was watching a narrow bridge swinging below them. Like the web of a huge spider, it spanned a gap to the spherical building opposite, another of the bizarre nestlike constructions. Screwing up her eyes, she could just discern a second figure making its way over the precarious walkway, rising up towards them. The hunter waited. This was a planned rendezvous.

Ukar-Tiri felt her heart chilling as she recognised the figure. It reached the ledge and swayed there, eyes fixed hungrily on her. It was Festubul.

"So you thought you'd got rid of me, you bitch," he growled. "Well, you'd better think again."

Ukar-Tiri looked at the other figure, but it was motionless, face still hidden. How could Festubul possibly have been able to employ such a creature? What had he used to buy its service?

"She's yours, Festubul," it said, the words almost taken by a gust of wind. "She was alone. Where's the External?"

"She'll tell you that. Speak, girl, or you'll suffer the worse for your deceits."

"Gone to the Emeschi," she managed to say, her teeth chattering. Her hands gripped the rail for support. The wind was blustery up here, threatening to buffet them all from the platform. Festubul was about to say something else, taking a step forward, when a huge shadow swooped past him in a blur of speed. He held up his hand, his eyes bulging for a moment as if he had seen something terrifying. Ukar-Tiri tried to see what it was, but the darkness had swallowed it as swiftly as it had disgorged it. Her captor leapt back, knife flashing as if he were under attack.

Festubul seemed to stagger, hands going to his neck, flapping at it. Then he stumbled over onto the walkway, head flung back to reveal a white expanse of flesh under his chin. A dark stain spread across it.

Ukar-Tiri dropped to her knees as the wind again cuffed her. It was gathering, possibly for a storm.

Behind her she heard her captor unchaining her from the roof. "Get down, girl!" he called. "To your belly."

She did as bidden at once. Festubul was very still, one arm hanging limply over the walkway. The dark stain was blood: she could smell it.

The walkway suddenly shuddered as if something had been dropped on it. Beyond Festubul yet another figure appeared, as if formed from the very night. She lifted her head, but could only see the legs. They were sheathed in dark leather boots. Craning her neck, she recognised the figure. This time she almost screamed.

The Angel Guard reached Festubul, and with one kick sent the corpse tumbling down into the murk below.

The hunter watched the Angel Guard close in. Its eyes were open, but there was something wrong with them. This was the blind one he had been told of. Its head moved gently from side to side. Blind it might be, but somehow it registered everything.

"What do you want?" said the hunter, barely able to get the words out. No one bargained with these monsters. He kept as still as he could. Silence might possibly aid him.

The Angel Guard was equally motionless. The wind had no effect on it.

"The girl? Take her."

There was no reply. Why didn't the cursed creature speak? Why were they so inscrutable, so unreachable? This one was no different. But it was blind. That could be the one chance the hunter needed. With infinite care, he drew back his hand. He was an expert with the knife. One accurate throw could end this. He chose his moment carefully, timing it perfectly. The knife flew towards its target.

But the Angel Guard was impossibly quick. The darkness

seemed to shimmer as the Guard turned aside from the knife, which bounced somewhere beyond on the walkway and was lost to the drop. The hunter gasped. He was dead. There would be no mercy, not a word exchanged. One sweep of those claws and it would be ended.

In desperation he swung out over the walkway. No time for thought, calculation. He simply let himself drop, leaving himself at the whim of chance.

Ukar-Tiri watched as the Angel Guard opened his wings and glided out over the drop, then swooped out of sight at incredible speed, like a loosed arrow. She thought she heard a scream below. She waited, keeping flat to the walkway. Silence closed in again, broken only by the murmur of the wind as it again prepared to unleash itself.

At last she rose to her knees. The walkway was clear. She got up, turning back to the doorway. Faint light seeped over its portals. As she stepped closer to its sanctuary, she glanced up.

The Angel Guard was crouched above the door on the curving roof. She froze. He slid down easily over the wicker and landed a few feet from her. She would have sworn that his eyes studied her. Had he recovered his sight? "You were on the road, with the others," he said in his rich, deep voice. It was not the voice of a killer, a beast that drew blood as freely as it drew breath.

She nodded.

"One of them was an External, a runaway."

Again she nodded.

"Is he below, in these wretched slums?"

"He's . . . gone with the Emeschi. Looking for . . ."

The hooked beak of a nose lifted, as if the Angel Guard was catching at a scent in the darkness. "For?"

"For you. They seek you."

He seemed to consider this for a moment, as though he might challenge it as ridiculous. "Go and find them. Send word to them if you have to." He pointed to a lone tower across from them, almost obscured by the shadows. One of the walkways crossed over to it, swinging violently in the gusts. "Tell them I'll be up there. I want the External. Make sure they understand that."

"I'll try—"

"If you try to run, to cheat me, I'll find you. You know that?"

She nodded, not doubting it.

"I'll be waiting for them. Tell them!"

He lifted his arms, his magnificent wings, and she bit her hand to prevent herself crying, toppling back, only denied a fall by the guide ropes. By the time she had got her balance back, the Angel Guard was gone. She thought she caught the sound of a beat of wings, but it could have been the wind once more.

Quickly she fled into the building.

24

"It would be far too dangerous up on the road," said Sommoi. "If others are hunting Arteriel, a chapter of the Angel Guard for instance, we would be discovered and eliminated easily. I say we must organise something in the reeds." They had been discussing the matter for some time, but no realistic strategy had presented itself.

Inkulke was about to comment, when he was interrupted by voices at the door. Another of the Emeschi entered and Inkulke would have waved him away, when Ruarhi, who had until now contributed very little, spoke up.

"What is it? I thought I heard Ukar-Tiri—"

Sommoi looked round impatiently. "We must leave High Crofels soon. We have no time for any other considerations."

The Emeschi who had entered took Inkulke to one side. Inkulke listened attentively to him, his eyes narrowing. He nodded and the Emeschi again went out.

"You are right, Ruarhi," said Inkulke. "It is the girl. She has strange news for us."

"What is it?" snapped Sommoi, irritated by the interruption.

"Let her speak for herself," said Inkulke.

Ukar-Tiri was brought in. Her face was streaked with tears, her eyes red. At once she flung herself at Ruarhi, her arms closing around him, her head falling on his chest. She was trembling as if something dreadful had happened to her. She began to sob and he looked away from the others, as mystified by the girl's behaviour as he was embarrassed by it. He wanted to soothe her, but felt constrained by the presence of the others.

Fortunately the Emeschi who had admitted her came to his rescue. "She was found wandering in the corridors. She says the guard on the cell where she has been kept has been killed. When we looked, we found him, just as she said."

Ruarhi took her shoulders and gave her a gentle shake. "Is this true, Ukar-Tiri? The guard is dead?"

She nodded, controlling her sobs.

"Who did this?" cut in Sommoi.

Ukar-Tiri took a few more deep breaths, steadying herself. "It was a man who disguised himself. He wore a cloak, and a mask. I never saw his face. He took me up onto the roof. Festubul was as there. He hired the man."

"*Hired* him? said Sommoi. "With what? Festubul has nothing with which to barter."

Ukar-Tiri looked up at Ruarhi. "He said he wanted the External. He meant Ruarhi; I'm sure of it."

"Where is this man now?" said Sommoi.

"I think he's dead."

"What do you mean?" said Inkulke. "I don't understand this."

"We were attacked on the roof. By the one you are about to hunt. The blind Angel."

"Arteriel!" gasped Inkulke. "He has come here?"

She nodded. "He killed Festubul with one pass. The other man leapt off the walkway to save himself, but the blind Angel flew down after him. I think he killed him."

"How did you evade him?" said Sommoi.

"He didn't want me. He wants . . . he wants Ruarhi."

Ruarhi stiffened, cursing under his breath.

"As I feared," mused Inkulke. "It is his own strange way of atoning for his faults. But to come here—"

"Where is he now?" snapped Sommoi.

"Waiting. He told me to bring you and Ruarhi to him."

Inkulke shook his head in bafflement. "This is a strange business. First the hunter: why should he seek Ruarhi? For whom does he operate? He must be in the pay of someone."

"Are we sure he's dead?" said Ruarhi.

Sommoi laughed dryly. "The Angel Guard are thorough—"

"This one's blind. And he's already failed once," retorted Ruarhi.

"We'll search carefully," said Inkulke. "Meanwhile, what should we do? Go up to Arteriel? Find out his terms?"

"Terms? What terms?" said Sommoi derisively. "He wants Ruarhi. There will be no compromise."

"And if we refuse him?" said Ruarhi. "He can't take on the whole of High Crofels."

"He has no need to," said Inkulke. "Not if we can talk to him. At least we have the chance. It is what we wanted."

The simple statement silenced them all for a moment. It was what they had planned for, the chance to communicate with the blind Angel.

"We won't capture him, not on the roof," said Sommoi. "The position favours him."

"It is not a matter of capture!" said Inkulke. "If we can make him listen to us."

"Yes, we have to try," said Sommoi. "Ruarhi? You understand the risk?"

Ruarhi shrugged. He had already decided.

Ukar-Tiri gripped his arm. "You can't mean to go! He will kill you. He's an Angel Guard! He is in disgrace because you are alive—"

"We could have killed him, on the road."

Sommoi nodded slowly.

"Ruarhi—" began Ukar-Tiri, but he gently loosened her grip. "I have to see the Angel Guard."

Sommoi and Inkulke stood at the threshold of the door to the ledge, high over the settlement. Inkulke insisted that they bring three warriors with them as a precaution. To Ruarhi they looked identical, and no different from the guard who had been cut down in his cell before Ukar-Tiri. They were gross, faces screwed up in fixed grimaces that made it almost impossible to decide what they might have been thinking. Fear seemed an alien emotion to them as they stepped doggedly out onto the terrace.

"This is where you saw him?" Inkulke asked the girl.

She nodded, new terror flooding her. She pointed through the wall. "Over there. A single tower. He said he'd be waiting."

Ruarhi pulled her back gently. "There's no need for her to remain. Go back to the cell," he told her.

Inkulke nodded, and behind him another of the Emeschi prepared to escort her. She looked as if she might protest, but Ruarhi tried to give her a reassuring nod. Why did the danger to him so distress her? Simply because he was her protector, the only one she had encountered who had not treated her cheaply? Did it matter? He would like to have thought not, but he knew it did. It served to make him more defiant of the Angel.

Sommoi called softly to the warriors. "Do you see anything?"

They had drawn their weapons, crude, spiked clubs. They peered out into the darkness that now shrouded everything. But each of them grunted a negative. Inkulke and Sommoi stepped carefully onto the ledge, shielded by the bulk of the three warriors. Ruarhi glanced back once at Ukar-Tiri as she was led away. She was shaking her head at him, but he said nothing.

Then he, too, was on the ledge, but he ducked down, doing as the others had told him. They knew how fast the Angel Guard could be if it did choose to attack.

"Ease along the ledge," Inkulke told the warriors.

They did so, the others following. They reached the walkway that led to the solitary tower. It swung to and fro in the gathering wind.

"What tower is it?" said Sommoi.

"A warehouse," said Inkulke. "Arteriel has not chosen it by accident. There is a large door, but it is lowered from within when fresh supplies are stored. It will be secured. This is the only way across."

Sommoi nodded. They would not have been able to surprise the blind Angel anyway. They would have to meet him directly, under his terms.

"Movement," whispered Inkulke as they stepped onto the narrow walkway. As he spoke, a shadow detached itself from the darkness on top of the lone tower. It coalesced into the form of Arteriel, standing at the edge of the roof.

"Keep absolutely still," came his voice. After that the silence clamped down, broken only by the stirring of the wind. The brewing storm that Ukar-Tiri had sensed still brooded.

"I cannot believe he is blind," whispered Inkulke. "He looks directly at us."

Arteriel was holding two of his small instruments in his hands: they shone like silver. Abruptly he flicked his wrist and there were sparks. He leaned over towards something on the roof and again struck the instruments against each other. Flames took, and the torch he had erected in the roof burned, a vivid tongue waving against the backdrop of darkness. Arteriel moved to his left and ignited two more of the torches. In their golden glow he was clearly visible.

"Light?" said Ruarhi, puzzled. "Maybe he's no longer blind?"

But Arteriel called out to them, and his purpose became clear. "Fire," he shouted. "You know what it can do."

Inkulke drew in his breath in horror. "He could set the entire settlement alight! It would go up in moments! Is he mad?" Panic vibrated through his words.

"Don't think to attack me," called Arteriel. "One step in defiance of me, and I overturn the torches. High Crofels will be a pyre to you all."

"Gods of light!" gasped Inkulke. "He's right—"

"What do you want?" Sommoi called back.

"Somewhere in this settlement you are hiding an External. A runaway. You know him. Bring him to me."

"Why do you want him?" asked Sommoi.

Arteriel cocked his head, as though evaluating Sommoi's voice, recognising it.

"Keep down," Inkulke warned Ruarhi. "He doesn't realise you are here."

"I was commissioned to find him. I have a duty to discharge."

"For Provider Hummal Goresch?" called Sommoi.

The Angel Guard did not answer for a moment. In the guttering glow, his face looked terrible, demonic.

"You've surprised him," said Inkulke softly.

Sommoi hardly moved. Again he called out. "Provider Goresch has servants here, too, in High Crofels."

"High Crofels serves as many masters as it has towers," came the blunt retort.

"Some of us are capable of loyalty," Sommoi insisted.

"You serve Provider Goresch? In what way?"

"We would speak to you about it."

Arteriel's face showed his disdain. "Perhaps you would like to kill me, present me to my enemies. I have many."

"You are safe where you stand," said Sommoi, beads of perspiration breaking out over his face. "We cannot harm you while you threaten us with fire."

"Be assured of that."

"We would not dare to challenge you. But will you hear us?"

Again the Angel was silent. Its contempt for them radiated from it. "Why should I hear you?"

"Provider Hummal Goresch is not your enemy," Sommoi went on.

"In that you are mistaken. I have sent word to his master, Elevate Zaer Phesmes, that he, too, is my enemy."

"Elevate Zaer Phesmes has sent word to us that you are not to be considered his enemy. He would still make use of you."

"In what way?" said Arteriel, the suspicion clear in his voice.

Sommoi looked about him. The skies were impenetrable. This was no place to discuss rebellion. "It is too open here. Will you not speak with us more privately?"

Arteriel answered by plucking one of the blazing torches from its place. He held it aloft. "I can feel this light, even though I cannot see it. My hearing is excellent. I hear the wind, the coming of a storm. That is all. The storm is not my enemy. If you want to exchange words with me, I hear you perfectly well." It was a threat. He would not relinquish his advantage.

Sommoi muttered a curse and bent down to Ruarhi. "We'll have to do as he says."

"So what do you want me to do?" said Ruarhi.

"Go to him. Tell him what you learned. Tell him about the rebellion."

"How he was blinded as a sign to you?" snorted Ruarhi. "He'll thank me for that!"

"If he kills you," said Inkulke, "he'll follow your death with his own. He has no choice. By rejecting the rebellion, he has nothing left to live for. All under Skydown would hunt him. But if you convince him there is a way to defy those who betrayed him—"

"Why do you think I can achieve this?" But Ruarhi knew the answer. He was expendable. Fodda.

"You are the only one he will allow up there with him. Because he came here for you."

"If I refuse?"

Sommoi glowered at him. "The fire is no idle threat. He'll gut the entire settlement. It'll be reduced to ashes in moments. We'll all die."

Ruarhi felt a stab of helplessness. He had to face the winged killer. Circumstances would allow for no other solution. If he was to survive this nightmare, he would have to speak to the blind Angel Guard first.

Slowly he stood up. He said nothing, pushing his way through to the walkway beyond Inkulke. He looked up at the winged figure. He knew instinctively it had sensed his presence.

"You are here," said Arteriel, as though he had scented him.

"I'm coming up," said Ruarhi. He didn't look back, awkwardly crossing to the tower and clambering steadily up to where the figure waited.

Arteriel took a step back as the man stood before him. He could feel that this External was not cowed by the height, nor the wild elements.

Ruarhi found himself staring into the blind eyes.

"I let you live on the road," said Arteriel. "I don't know why. I should have killed you."

"Perhaps we should have killed you."

"Unquestionably you should have."

"It's well that we didn't." The old images rose up, ugly

spectres. Ruarhi tried to forget that this creature had ripped the life from Dromator.

"I will spare you any suffering," said the blind warrior.

"Before you waste my life," said Ruarhi, his eyes straying to the strange weapons in the belt of the Angel Guard, "will you hear me?"

"Be swift. The others are right: this place is too open, though it is not the coming storm that concerns me."

"There's more than a storm gathering. War is coming."

"War?" Arteriel repeated, and Ruarhi could see that the Angel's cold composure was momentarily moved. "That is a strange word to use. War under Skydown? Foolish talk."

"War among your gods, Absolute Light."

Arteriel's expression turned to one of utter disdain. "Even more preposterous."

"You're its first victim."

Arteriel tensed, as though his patience was exhausted and he would use his weapons.

Ruarhi was thinking and talking as quickly as his reflexes would allow. He was a knife's slash from death. "You were blinded. It was the first move in a far greater game. Now you have to retaliate. But not by killing me, or these below us. We have to become allies."

"I was blinded deliberately? You *know* who blinded me?" The anger in the voice was terrible.

Ruarhi felt as if he was in the presence not of a human creature, but a wild animal, a huge predator, his words slowly reducing its humanity to fuel the beast within it. "Yes, it was a deliberate act."

"Why it was done?"

"They know. Talk to them."

Arteriel was again silent. It was impossible to gauge his feelings, whether he was angry, intrigued, or suspicious of deceit. Then he slipped a twin-edged knife from his belt and touched it lightly. Ruarhi knew that his life balanced on the edge of its blades at that moment. He could hardly breathe, waiting for the Angel Guard's judgement.

FOUR

THOUSANDREACH

Inescapably, we are all slaves to the flesh that houses us, no matter what we do to it. It is both our prison and our temple, our pleasure and our pain. We cannot deny its needs, its cravings. And it is a hard, insatiable master.

The gods who rule us have capitalised on this, controlling evolution ruthlessly, shaping it to their own ends. They have enhanced our weaknesses, made us dependent on our desires: they feed us the things we crave, and promise us more. Survival depends on compliance.

We have become corporate; we do not act as individuals; we cannot swim against the torrent that flows to them, their bloodstream. We are their lifeblood.

How to break the cycle? How to open the vein?

ZAER PHESMES—*The Book of Renunciation*

25

Provider Hummal Goresch sank into the couch with a deep sigh. It was almost voluptuous in its extravagance and uncommonly comfortable. Goresch closed his eyes in anticipation of the pleasures that would shortly be his. He would not have admitted it, but he lived for the Gratifications. Here, in the private retreat, fashioned with such cunning expertise by the Pleasure Guild, a Provider could forget for a while the rigours of office.

Although it was permissible for light to be varied in intensity in the numerous individual chambers of the retreat, Goresch usually chose to have it as subdued as it could be while still allowing him to see the entertainments. He also preferred to take his pleasures alone, though he would have scoffed at anyone who suggested he might be ashamed of his practices.

Fodda was fodda. How could anyone be ashamed of how it could be treated?

He tried to relax, but was too eager for release. Officers of the Guild came to him discreetly and asked him if he would be requiring instruments of any kind, or if there were other specific services he wished.

He asked that a male be brought, drugged, but not deeply. He waited, trying not to think too elaborately about how he would spend time with the victim of his pleasure.

When the offering arrived, eyes slightly lidded, steps uncertain, Goresch studied the naked, oiled body with mounting interest. It was muscular, the body of a worker. Goresch disrobed slowly, eager to begin.

In a domed hall not far from where Provider Goresch amused himself, his rival, Provider Sughai Orvech, was sitting with other colleagues, enjoying some particularly fine wine. He had been careful not to overindulge himself, something which his colleagues commented on out of his earshot. Orvech usually drank excessively. But in the House of Sighs, no one was castigated for such behaviour. There were no boundaries to indulgence here, and the only significant rule was that Providers, however great their rivalry might be, did not in any way harm or discredit each other while within these walls. No matter how depraved they might wish to be, it was not proper to comment. The Pleasure Guild was pleased to encourage excesses. The fodda, after all, had been obtained through the offices of the Providers.

Provider Orvech was, as anyone studying him would have noticed, looking out for something. An agent, possibly, for this was the perfect place to exchange information. Bizarre tales flourished here, and among the deceits and lies, myths and fables, useful truths circulated. Deciphering them was an art, however, and Orvech was known for his skills.

Another Provider was approaching the group where Orvech sat. Most of them had succumbed to the wine, subsiding lethargically on the couches. A few waved tolerantly as the newcomer stood before them. It was Provider Goresch. Clearly he had been availing himself of his own special pleasures. He had only partially robed his skeletal body, his eyes were glazed, his flesh mottled, suffused with pleasure. The others could not help but compare his physique with that of Orvech, who was equally as thin, typical of his kind, though Orvech exuded strength and had a less emaciated face. His cheeks in contrast to those of Goresch were far less hollow, his eyes more alert, perceptive, and in his face anyone could read a fierce, uncompromising ambition. Goresch did not have that energy.

Orvech waved a glass airily at him. "Hummal Goresch, honourable rival! Please, sit with us. Enjoy some of this wine. There is none better."

Goresch would have as soon spat in Orvech's face as looked at him, had he been elsewhere. But in the House of Sighs, such things were put aside. He inclined his head politely, a little unsteady on his feet, as though he had already partaken of strong wine. But he dropped into a vacant seat, stretching out with studied indifference.

"A pleasure," he sighed.

"No better reason to be here," nodded Orvech agreeably, flicking his fingers at one of the hosts, who slid from the shadows with practised ease and poured wine for Goresch.

"I trust you have been enjoying your time here?" said Orvech.

Goresch lifted his glass awkwardly, almost spilling the pink liquid. But he got it to his lips and took an immoderate gulp. He nodded. "Oh, yes. Quite superb. I feel wonderful. I raise my glass to you all, colleagues." He drank again.

The others hid any amusement they might have felt. Goresch was known to be a slave to his weakness, his love of flesh. It would, they knew, forever be a barrier to his Elevation. The Elevates took their pleasures far beyond the bounds that mere Providers could dream of, but they were not slaves to them. Lust was their weapon. They exercised perfect control. Goresch possessed little of that, nor would he. His flesh was barely stronger than fodda. It happened occasionally: a Provider slid backwards.

"There must be few pleasures of the flesh you've not tasted," said Orvech casually.

Goresch shrugged modestly. "One searches for new experience. But as you say, colleague, I have tried them all."

"I would wager you'd not turn away an opportunity to savour a new pleasure. Something unique, a sublime delight," Orvech went on. He still spoke casually, as though none of this was of any real importance, but already some of the Providers caught the intimation of something behind the facade.

"Only show me this pleasure!" snorted Goresch, emptying his glass and holding it out. It was instantly refilled.

"What would you give me," said Orvech, "if I did offer you such a diversion?" He leaned forward.

Goresch paused before lifting his glass. The flush of pleasure he had worn when he joined the group had gone. In its place he now wore a look of unexpected longing, a dreadful thirst.

How easily it is drawn out, thought Orvech. *I have his measure.*

"I would give much, if such a thing existed."

Orvech sat back, smiling. "But it does! I assure you. Listen, I spoke with Provider Ramman Lurish on my last visit. You know what an insatiable appetite he has! Well, he swore to me that he had found immeasurable pleasure in a certain creature that was brought here recently. A hybrid, it seems. Something fashioned by experiment, but of no practical use to the Elevates. Of course, you know Lurish. Never the same pleasure twice. But even he despaired finding anything quite like it again. You should ask him, Goresch."

Goresch leaned forward, his eyes fixed on his rival. "Perhaps I will ask him. Where is this creature now?"

Orvech sipped his wine slowly, savouring it. "You would not believe how difficult it was to persuade the Pleasure Guild to sell it to me."

"Sell it?" said Goresch. Anxiety crept into his face.

"Come, come," said Orvech, almost shyly. "You know my own obsession. I am a collector. Hybrids are my speciality. I simply had to have the creature."

"You . . . have taken it from the House of Sighs?"

"I have. It is kept safely, and I should add, legitimately, in my own estate."

Goresch rose, gripping the side of the seat for support. His face was suddenly grey. But he bowed, his skin slick with perspiration. "I have an appointment," he said abruptly.

The Providers watched him go, though they were too full of wine to make anything much of Orvech's behaviour.

"I'll wager I know who you're looking for," murmured Orvech, but the others hardly heard.

Provider Ramman Lurish was unusually fat for one of his kind. Provider metabolism usually dictated a thinness, coupled with a litheness that made them deceptively quick in a contest of arms. Lurish was no slouch, but his flesh hung loosely on him, his face puffy. For this reason he was easy to find in a crowd. In the House of Sighs, he was often in a particular hall, where wine was always available, and where scores of naked creatures danced imaginatively and provocatively for the pleasure of those who watched.

Provider Goresch was almost out of breath when he confronted the bigger man. "Lurish, I have to talk to you," he murmured.

Lurish didn't even look at Goresch. He was too busy studying two naked mutants who were writhing together, their sleek skins painted, their hair entangled. They seemed more beast than woman. "Better be quick, Goresch. I've a mind to take both of them soon."

"I spoke to Orvech—"

Lurish nodded. "I can guess what you want."

"You can?"

"Goresch, you are so transparent! The hybrid."

"Yes."

"What about it?"

"I have to know—"

At last Lurish's eyes flickered towards him. "There's only one way to *know*. Otherwise you would not believe."

"Orvech said you found it unique—"

Lurish nodded. "I have come close to breaking my rule. I never go back, you see. But that hybrid, ah, unique is right. Go back to Orvech."

"He has *bought* the hybrid?"

"So I believe. Such a waste! Orvech is a collector. He'll never use it for the purpose it serves best. Mind you, he could pleasure his guests with it. Or even impress an Elevate. Yes, that's probably it. He'll make a gift of it to Elevate Yvane Sephir.''

Goresch looked appalled.

Lurish grinned. ''Why don't you ask Orvech if there's anything you can do for him, eh? He might let you try the hybrid as a reward.''

''You know Orvech is my rival,'' Goresch hissed. ''As you say, he serves Yvane! My own master is his sworn enemy.''

''Elevate Zaer Phesmes? Yes, there is no love lost between them. But then, Yvane serves Kaizu. As does my master. It is wise, if you ask me, to serve the interests of the Da Sangravilles. Oh, I admit the Des Aubach have power, as do the Spiritores. But safer to be with the Da Sangravilles, eh?''

''What do you mean?''

Lurish was watching the mutants again, but with less interest. ''Kaizu rules. Right down to the deepest holes in this city.''

''You think I should defect?''

''Abandon Elevate Zaer? Are you dissatisfied?''

Goresch drew in a deep breath. ''Since you ask, Lurish, I am not entirely happy.''

Lurish turned to him. ''We're in the House of Sighs, Goresch. Don't be afraid to speak your mind. I'm not after your blood. I enjoy scandal as much as anyone. What's worrying you?''

''Between ourselves, Lurish, Elevate Zaer and his Skryer don't take me into their confidence.''

''Which is his personal Skryer? Verusion isn't it?''

Goresch nodded. He had caught the eye of one of the servants, who brought two glasses of wine. He handed one to Lurish.

''Thanks,'' said the latter, gulping it and waving for more. ''I'm not surprised! Verusion is a scheming bastard. Even his own Guild doesn't know half the things he gets up to. He's been walking dangerously where these hunts are concerned. You know, the Overlap? The Lightbenders themselves get a bit touchy about the Overlap, I gather. Mavericks like Verusion usually end up at the mercy of the Tormenters, or here, fodda for the likes of us.''

Goresch was surprised at Lurish's openness, though the

Provider had a reputation for it. Goresch drank more of the wine. "They are scheming something. But I'm not informed. How am I supposed to serve them? How can I function correctly?"

"Sounds to me, Goresch, as if you want to get out before they kick you out. If they do that, you'll end up like Provider Gundra Sommesch. Disgraced and sent out into some remote segment to look after a farm. Humiliating."

"Sommoi—"

"Eh? Sommesch. You knew him, didn't you? He served Elevate Yvane. Worked with Orvech."

Goresch nodded. "Yes, I knew him."

"Sommesch became too powerful for Orvech's liking, so Orvech had him compromised and virtually exiled. Now Orvech is Yvane's particular favourite. And we know how utterly ruthless Yvane is. He'd eat his own arm if it meant entering the Lightbender palaces. So it's up to you. But I tell you, sooner or later there's going to be trouble between Elevates Yvane Sephir and Zaer Phesmes. And it'll be Yvane that survives. Zaer is soft in comparison! Be wise. Think about it."

Goresch opened his mouth to speak, but Lurish had already walked off, openly bored with his company and even more so with the cavorting mutant dancers.

It was much later when Provider Lurish prepared to quit the House of Sighs. He was moderately satisfied, but at least there had been some pleasures to be had. He was stopped near the exit by a tiny figure. He would have brushed it aside contemptuously, but he recognised it and bent down to it.

"You spoke to Provider Goresch?" it whispered in his ear.

"I did," he answered as softly. "Tell your master he's ripe. And have the hybrid ready."

"Elevate Yvane shall hear of this."

"Happy to serve, eh?" grinned Lurish, straightening and walking steadily out of the place of pleasures.

26

Goresch woke feeling unusually tired. His dreams had been tormented by visions of Provider Sughai Orvech and a legion of demonic creatures, all lasciviously tearing his vitals from him under the watchful, amused gaze of Provider Ramman Lurish. Goresch dressed himself clumsily, muttering curses. By the time he was ready to leave his private chambers, there was a knock on his outer door. He swung it open angrily, glaring at the messenger, a dull-eyed youth who cowered beneath the Provider's gaze.

"The Skryer, Verusion, would have words with you, sir."

Goresch grunted, waving the messenger away. The youth was quick to scuttle off. Goresch pulled his coat around him, feeling unduly cold. Perhaps he was sickening with something.

The Skryer had already made himself comfortable in Goresch's chambers of office. He had taken his accustomed place among shadows, his frail shape almost masked by them, his face invisible, as though it was marred by some secret too terrible to show. Goresch had seen it few times, a pale blob that had few features to distinguish it from countless others.

"I trust your efforts to locate Arteriel are responsible for your exhaustion," said Verusion softly.

Goresch drew in his breath, seating himself and dabbing at his brow. "Doubtless," he grunted. "Have your own arts produced anything?"

"No," said Verusion coldly. "I would have expected your hunters to provide answers. My arts are for other purposes."

Goresch was already tired of criticisms and considered a retort. How dare the Skryer give him orders! Elevate Zaer

Phesmes was his master, not this accursed prophet! But he held himself in check, recalling his conversation with Provider Lurish. Yes, he could still hear those words, so clearly.

"Well, my hunters are out in the segments. My resources are stretched to the full. When I have word, Elevate Zaer will be the first to hear."

Verusion made a rustling sound as he stood up. "Don't fail him, Provider. We must recover Arteriel. The consequences of failing—"

"Yes, yes, I know!" snapped Goresch.

"Good. Bear it in mind."

As the Skryer left Goresch remained seated, fists gripping the arms of the seat in frustration and anger. Lurish had been right. Why should he have to tolerate this insufferable situation?

His mind drifted to thoughts of the hybrid. He licked his dry lips. Foolish to be obsessed by such a thing. But he must find out if what Lurish said was true. Unique.

"He's here," said Annaxion.

Provider Sughai Orvech put down the chart he had been studying and looked up at his Skryer. "So soon? Well, well. I hope he was circumspect."

Annaxion's pale features creased in a smile. He looked as though some wasting illness held him in its fatal grip, but Orvech understood only too well how much energy coursed through the Skryer's pinched veins. Perhaps it was the mental powers he possessed that so leeched him.

Annaxion inclined his head. "I'll leave you to your discussions."

"Send Provider Goresch in."

Orvech seated himself, again studying the charts. A few moments later a servant ushered in Goresch.

Orvech could see at once that the Provider had been sleeping badly. Orvech took delight in the fact, though it did not register on his face. He did not get up, pretending deep interest in his charts.

"An unexpected visit," he said bluntly. The politeness he had shown on their last meeting was gone.

Goresch expected no different. This was not the House of

Sighs. "I took some pains to prevent being seen coming here."

"Indeed? And why are you here?"

"You know why I am here."

Orvech leaned back, trying not to smile. It had been ridiculously easy. But he must not be too eager to close the trap. "I didn't expect such a rapid response. There would have been plenty of time to discuss the matter in the House of Sighs. But now, while discharging our functions as Providers—"

"I have good reason to come to you now."

Orvech nodded. "You want the hybrid?"

Goresch had begun to perspire. He mopped at his face. He did not have to answer.

"Forgive me, but it is foolish to let one's desires rule one's head. Aren't you taking a great risk in coming to me? Elevate Zaer Phesmes would consider this meeting highly dubious."

"I don't care," Goresch blurted.

Orvech's brows rose. "Really? An extraordinary admission."

"What do you want for the hybrid?"

Orvech snorted, waving aside the question as if it were not the issue. "I won't consider selling the hybrid. I told you, I'm a collector, Goresch. You understand passion. Collecting is mine. And this hybrid is unique."

"I'd pay you well."

"You couldn't afford my price if I asked it."

Goresch leaned forward, his face a sheen. "Try me."

"Goresch, the only thing I value more highly than my collection is Elevation. Thus I serve Elevate Yvane Sephir to the best of my ability. I allow nothing to interfere with that. If Yvane were to ask for my entire collection, I would give it to him. Anything to secure that step to glory."

"Then let me help you."

Orvech pretended to be deeply surprised. "You, Goresch? Be realistic! We are deadly rivals! Our Elevate masters would bring each other down at the first opportunity! Are you saying you would ignore all our disputes for the hybrid?"

Goresch realised the trap he was creating for himself. He

had gone too fast. He straightened, trying to restore something of his dignity. "Perhaps."

"But you've not even seen the hybrid."

Goresch drew in his breath. "No. Could it be arranged?"

"How soon?"

"How soon do you want me to help you?"

Orvech rubbed his jaw. "Goresch, how can you help me? What do you have that would interest me?"

"Information, perhaps. Perhaps more than that."

Orvech smiled hungrily. "How interesting," he said, as though something had just occurred to him.

"You will find it so."

"Does it concern a certain object of dispute that was recently the cause of some confusion?"

"Yes."

"Then you are right. I am interested."

Goresch leaned further forward. "Show me the hybrid."

Orvech seemed to contemplate the matter for a while, but then nodded. "You won't be disappointed."

They were in another part of Orvech's chambers of office, near to the place of torment, where he brought dissidents for questioning, or fodda for amusement. It was a gloomy region, lit poorly, the walls cold stone. They oozed with suffering, and the air had an acrid reek to it.

Orvech's servants unlocked a door for him and stood back while the two Providers went through to a small chamber that was entirely out of keeping with the unpleasant corridors and cells they had passed through to get here. It was sumptuous, lined with couches and silks, and there was even a small pool. The air was perfumed, the light subtle, pleasing. It was, Goresch noted, not unlike the House of Sighs.

"I am sure," said Orvech, seating himself casually, "that you have such rooms in your own chambers of office."

"Of course," said Goresch thickly. It was true, though nothing so lavish as this. The wealth of his rival far exceeded his own, a further comment on service to Yvane rather than Zaer.

"Well, then. To business. You want to see the hybrid." Orvech nodded to one of the armed guards who had been standing at one end of the room. The man bowed and left through another small door.

Goresch felt himself shaking with anticipation. This was ridiculous. And to unman himself before his enemy! He was a fool to let himself come to this. Where is your control? he told himself. He sat uncomfortably.

Orvech feigned indifference. *How trapped he is by his own desires!* he thought. *We could not have known. This is excellent!*

The velvet curtain through which the guard had disappeared swung gently aside. The guard reentered, holding a thin silver chain. It was attached to the neck of a creature that at first could not quite be seen in the shadows.

As it came into the room, Goresch gasped, his eyes widening. The hybrid was naked, a male of medium build, with golden skin. It had long, slender hands that had never known harsh treatment, a thin, girlish waist, and unusually long legs. Its hair had been allowed to grow very long, a mass of thick, black curls, and it had a rich, sensuous mouth.

Orvech rose and went to it. Its eyes were a rare shade of blue, and not the wide, staring eyes of much of the fodda under Skydown. They looked at Orvech, but might have looked through him. The creature had an air of dreaminess about it: Goresch wondered if it had been drugged.

"The texture of the skin is quite singular," said Orvech, running his fingers down the hybrid's arm and across its belly. It shivered, its eyes lidded. Goresch saw the genitals twitch, as though roused by Orvech's touch. He stood up slowly, aching to touch the hybrid himself.

"Come," said Orvech. "Feel how soft it is."

Goresch almost stumbled forward. His hand groped, fastened on a shoulder. To his amazement he could hear the hybrid purring. Its skin was beautiful. It turned to him, breathing close to his face, and its breath was clean, alluring.

Orvech watched as the hybrid's hand slid over Goresch's chest and stroked his neck. Goresch was mesmerised.

Orvech gripped the chain and pulled hard on it. The hybrid staggered back and twisted, falling to the floor. At once it crawled to Orvech's feet, pawing at him. "Be still!" Orvech hissed.

Goresch stood, mouth open, saliva running from it. "I . . . must experience . . ."

Orvech's eyes narrowed. He tightened his grip on the chain. "You can use it, Goresch. But I want something from you."

"Name it."

"Where is Arteriel, the blind Angel?"

Goresch looked bemused for a moment, but shook himself. "Uh, Arteriel? We don't know yet. We're searching."

"I want him, Goresch. You hear me? *I want him.*"

Goresch nodded dumbly. "Yes, yes. When we find him—"

"If you find him, the hybrid is yours. In the meantime, I want to know everything."

"Everything?"

"About Arteriel. Why is he blind? How did it happen? What is Zaer Phesmes planning? Tell me these things, Goresch, and you can use the hybrid now. A taste."

Goresch's mouth had dried up. He could not speak. He nodded frantically.

Orvech handed him the chain. "Here. Pleasure yourself. When I come back, I want answers."

Goresch took the chain, fingers slippery with sweat. He saw the hybrid stand, its body eager to please him.

The Skryer, Verusion, waited calmly before the broad flight of steps. He had never climbed them and wondered if he ever would. They led to the antechambers of Elevate Zaer Phesmes, whom he had never been permitted to meet. Very few Elevates allowed themselves to be seen by the lower orders, and to Elevates, even the Skryers were lesser beings. They acknowledged the Lightbenders alone as their betters. Verusion did not let it concern him. He knew his own worth. He had long ago mastered patience.

A robed figure descended almost carelessly. It was a Shadowguard, one of Zaer's particular intimate protectors. It had been carefully bred, its genes selected from the banks which Zaer guarded with such pride. Zaer's passion for breeding exceeded those of all other Elevates, and he was known to be obsessed with the creation of the perfect form. Others

laughed at the irrelevance of such experimentation, such
wasted energy.

The Shadowguard bowed to the Skryer, who returned the
bow.

"You have word?" it said in its hollow voice. Its eyes were
misted, the mouth a lipless gash. Evidently it was functional
and no doubt an exceptional killing unit, but it was not an
example of the perfection for which Zaer reputedly strove.

"Provider Ramman Lurish sent a message to me," said
the Skryer. "Tell Elevate Zaer Phesmes that the bait is taken.
Provider Hummal Goresch will soon be the slave of Provider
Sughai Orvech as we planned."

"Is there anything else I must say?"

"Only that we shall prime our unwitting Provider very
soon. Matters progress better than we could have hoped."

27

Consort Nu-Ko-Te examined herself for the last time in the
huge mirror, twisting and turning to be sure that the garment
fitted her precisely as it should. She had a very slight build,
her skin the perfect tone of pale pink that Elevates so strived
for in their breeding programmes. She might have been a
child, she was so lacking in height, and she smiled at the
thought. No child could have been party to the knowledge
she possessed.

She flicked her hair: it swished to and fro across her shoulders and down her spine, a shimmering black cascade. Yes,
he would be pleased. A final smile, then she was ready. She
left her room, walking calmly and with rigid dignity down
the marbled hallway. No one saw her: this was the most private of all the inner quarters. There were servants, naturally,
but these never appeared unless summoned. Even the Shad-

owguard would not trespass here unless expressly commanded to do so.

It would be today: he had promised. *Consort Imprimis*. With control over all the others. She savoured it, repeating the title over and over, as she had done before she slept, even during her dreams.

She pressed the golden stud on the great arched door and it opened at once, registering, she knew, with her master beyond. Elegantly she went into the chamber, pausing to take it in. It always amazed her with its deceptive angles, its bright, hallowed light. Elevates were permitted such luxury, a sign that Absolute Light approved of them, their service. When her eyes had adjusted to the glare, she gazed at the geometric ingenuity of the walls, the artefacts. Fodda never experienced such things. Indeed, would fodda understand them? The lower levels of humanity were fit only for the darkness, their eyes unable to assimilate splendour. So had she been taught.

"Do not be shy, little one. Enter in."

She drew in her breath. Already he was watching her. Would he take pleasure in what he saw? But of course he would. Had he not told her already that she was magnificent?

The voice was barely above a whisper, sibilant but seductive, with more than a hint of affection. She could feel his attention, his being focused on her. Surely he could not be like this with his other Consorts? she asked herself.

"I was afraid I would arrive before you were ready," she said, her voice picked up by the perfect acoustics of the chamber and amplified gently. "I did not wish to incur your wrath."

"Impossible, Nu-Ko-Te."

She shivered. When he spoke her name, he used it like a charm, as if weaving his art around her, binding her more tightly to him. Elevates could do such things, she felt sure. Elevates knew true power. The Lightbenders invested them with it.

"Come closer to me. Let me see what you have chosen to wear for me on this special occasion."

He had not forgotten! Consort Imprimis. The honour was to be hers, truly it was.

She stood before his throne, at first lowering her head, but then she raised it so that she could look at him. He was the most beautiful creature she could ever have imagined. Elevate Zaer Phesmes was immense, the size of five ordinary men, his huge abdomen bulging before him, his massive arms folded across it. He wore a brief harness that hid only his loins and parts of his upper body, and jewels shimmered where they had been set in its leather. His skin was a vivid pink, heaped in folds like thick coils about his trunk, his shoulders sagging under the vast weight. But there was only a supreme dignity about him. His face was similarly huge, the full lips curving in a smile that he always wore for her. He was completely without hair, but the shining dome of his skull had been intricately etched with designs, a maze of colour in which she had often lost herself in concentrated study. His eyes were hidden behind a curved sheet of reflective material that had been polished so thoroughly that it was painful to look at for more than a moment at a time. But she knew that the invisible eyes gazed on her.

"You have never looked more divine," he said, confirming her thoughts. "Come closer."

One of the huge hands dabbed at his side. Nu-Ko-Te smiled and went up the steps to his throne. It was a unique artefact, cultivated from living materials that appeared to form a part of Zaer's body, as if he had made it one with himself. It was like a chair, its contours matching his, yet he was able to make it glide over the smooth floors of his chambers, easing his weight. She had no idea how he controlled it, but assumed it was as easy for him as it was to raise an arm or turn his head.

With slow and deliberate skill, she positioned herself beside one of his huge legs, her skin touching the curve of his calf. She leaned back to look up at him, her hands stroking the flesh behind her.

"How could I refuse you the prize I offered you?" he said. She could feel his body relaxing under her touch. None of the others, he had told her, touched him as she did. Her flesh was his flesh. His own fingers, thick as her wrist, reached down and, light as air, caressed her spine.

"Consort Imprimis," he breathed.

She sucked in her breath, closing her eyes and shuddering.

"What do you desire?" he asked her.

They remained very still, like one form, one mind.

After a time, she spoke. "Tell me about the Lightbenders," she said. "How powerful they are, and how terrible."

"They interest you?"

He lifted her in his huge arms and cradled her. She pressed her face to his chest, listening to the blood coursing through him, the roar of its power.

"Tell me about them," she repeated.

He sighed, and she rose and fell as he breathed, delighting in the sensation of movement, the closeness of that inestimable heart. "Yes, as you are Consort Imprimis, it is time you learned certain truths."

"Consort Imprimis," she whispered.

"You have special power," he said, lowering his voice, his breath in her ear. "My thoughts are your thoughts. Your desires are mine. You alone share this."

Her lips pouted. "What of the many other Consorts?"

"I am an Elevate, Nu-Ko-Te. Elevates are expected to indulge themselves. I must retain my Consorts, as I retain other things that I have no desire for. The Lightbenders expect this of me. You are jealous?"

She nodded.

"Then I am pleased. Ordinary Consorts are not constrained by emotions. They serve and respond as expected to, being bred to obey, never to question. Thus none of them could ever be Consort Imprimis. I chose you because of your emotions, your desire for answers. I, too, have such strong drives. It is my peculiar nature. I have bequeathed some of it to you."

"Are not all Elevates thus?"

"All are fueled by emotion, yes. But in me, I sometimes think, another strain is at work."

"Did the Lightbenders make you thus?"

"No. Lightbenders enhance Elevate power. But all power derives from Absolute Light. As all power returns to it."

"Will you become a Lightbender?"

He laughed softly and again she rocked deliciously. "How eager you are for knowledge! Well, you must share it. It is your destiny to know."

"Tell me about the Lightbenders," she said once more.

"The first thing you should know is that the Lightbender families are at perpetual war."

"With whom?" she gasped, her perfect eyes widening.

He stroked her hair. "With each other. They vie for absolute control of our world. They are very jealous of one another. Each House is very inbred, as mixed breeding between Houses is anathema to them. They pride themselves on their lineage, but there have been a few lapses, and very strange progeny has been produced.

"The most powerful House is that of the Da Sangravilles, which is ruled by Kaizu. He is a single-minded genius who is steadily shaping the fate of this world. His obsession with pleasure and power is carried to the extreme and he allows nothing to obstruct his pursuit of it."

"Kaizu," she breathed, imagining a monstrous but invisible force.

"The other Da Sangravilles are weak beside him. There is Immarne, an insipid creature who rarely leaves the confines of his immediate fortress. Also there is Pholhadrun the deformed, unashamed slave of Kaizu, and Thestermon, the youngest and most independent, but a dangerous madman, prone to fits of destructive violence, used by Kaizu as a killing instrument to chilling effect. Mother of the entire brood is Shezrool, who never leaves her palace. She is fused into it, her alien shape fed and sustained by the human flesh and bone on which she gorges herself. She once ruled the House, but she knows now that she is only kept alive by the whim of Kaizu. Her principal daughter, Zendrakil, lusts for sovereignty and is the most powerful of Kaizu's enemies. Yet he desires her, a passion that overrides all others with him at times, though she has thwarted all his efforts to subdue her. Servants of Zendrakil and Kaizu often secretly slaughter one another in their private war that is never mentioned in the public halls of office. But we Elevates know that it goes on."

Nu-Ko-Te watched his face, enrapt. These monstrous creatures came to life when he spoke of them, and she felt the weight of the city above her, groaning to their terrible ministry.

"Second most powerful of the Lightbender Houses is that

of the Des Aubach. They are no less cruel than the Da Sangravilles. Subran rules them, a cold, dispassionate being, who
thinks of nothing but the fall of Kaizu, although he is loyal
to Absolute Light.''

"He is your master, is he not?''

"In name. But he is as corrupt as Kaizu.''

Nu-Ko-Te murmured her surprise. "You dare say such
things? Will Subran not strike you down?''

"I am too far beneath him, though I am wary of his agents.
Lightbenders have many eyes, many ears. Here, with you, I
am safe.''

"I am content.''

"Subran has used the Skryers and the Overlap in his at-
tempts to find a means to overthrow Kaizu, and as a consequence certain parts of his citadel contain obscure and terrible
creatures, a danger to all families if not controlled. Subran's
brothers, Imahal and Denehul, are as temperamental and aggressive as he is. It is their lack of unity as a family that
weakens their opposition to Kaizu.

"There is only one other major House, that of the Spiritores. They are mainly concerned with administration and
ritual, and have no specific desire to rule as the others do.
They believe themselves to be the elite and that internal strife
is beneath them. Anything less than a Lightbender is nothing,
of no value. Vesporzi is their ruler, a quiet, dignified being,
gifted with secular powers that even the Da Sangravilles are
reluctant to interfere with. If history has its secrets, Vesporzi
may have the key.

"Luiggis is the only one of them who looks beyond his
citadel, and he has cultivated his private assassins, the Twilight Hand, killers driven by their cause like machines, killed
only to be reanimated time and time again. Some of them
are Angel Guards that Luiggis has secretly mutilated. He derives great pleasure from destroying and reshaping animate
things.

"Karlas, his sullen younger sister and Hesperida, her aunt,
a fiery-tempered creature, are only mildly ambitious within
the family and seem unconcerned about the other Lightbender struggles for power.''

Nu-To-Ke opened her eyes. The serene face of Zaer

Phesmes hovered over her. He had become very thoughtful, as though his long monologue had opened up new avenues of contemplation for him.

"When you become a Lightbender," said the girl, "will you take me with you?"

His thick lips pursed in a smile. "I have no desire to become one of those monsters."

She gasped. "Again you mock them! You shock me—"

"I have one desire, sweet Nu-To-Ke. That is, apart from my union with you."

"I am nothing," she said, eyes dropping. "I am little better than fodda."

"You must not say such things," he said, a suggestion of annoyance in his tone which she perceived instantly. "You must not think so little of yourself. And you must not speak derisively of fodda. In fact, it is a word I wish you to avoid."

"Once more you confuse me."

"Our world is a living sin, a monument to the evils of the Lightbenders. Fodda is the unit on which the world is built. It is their sustenance, their nutrition, their prime source of energy. Almost all other life-forms are extinct. Once, there were many."

"This is wrong?"

"Yes, it is evil. The Lightbenders are parasites. I told you I have one desire—"

"Other than union with me," she added at once.

He smiled, caressing her gently. "Other than that. It is to destroy the Lightbenders. All of them. Skydown will be broken. Light will return to this world."

"But will light not kill the fodda? The . . . other life?"

"No. Absolute Light will raise life up from the dark well in which it flounders."

"How will you destroy the Lightbenders?" she asked calmly, as though the real implications of such an act were beyond her.

"By deceit, cunning, treachery."

"And war?"

"Silent and hidden. As a disease courses through the body. Virulent and remorseless. It has already begun. And you, my

Consort Imprimis, are part of the fall, the most important
component in my machine of destruction.''

Destruction, she mused. It was a word that brought a de-
lightful shiver to her. A word so full of possibilities.

28

The Dolus wore black, trimmed with scarlet flame, the personal colours of Elevate Yvane Sephir. Its cloak reached from
under its throat in a wide sweep to the floor. Only its pink
head and hands were exposed. Gliding across the marble
floor, it paused before Annaxion, eyes fixed on him like glass.
The Skryer imagined the tubes and wires of machinery that
were hidden by the cloak: the Dolus was not alive in any
usual sense of the word.

''You are privileged,'' it intoned in its deep, impersonal
voice.

Annaxion bowed, unsure why he had been ordered to
this place, which was high above the usual haunts of the
Providers.

The Dolus turned and led the way along the hall. As usual,
there were guards, as mechanical as the Dolus, but they had
been programmed to allow Annaxion through. They did not
move. Beyond them, in a hall of glass, the Dolus paused.

''Elevate Yvane Sephir will see you. But he is Receiving.''

Annaxion gathered his composure as best he could. What
did the Dolus mean, precisely? Surely not that Annaxion was
to be ushered into the actual presence of the Elevate. Yvane
was the least likely of all Elevates to permit himself to be
seen by the lower orders. Nevertheless, Annaxion followed
the Dolus as it left the glittering splendour of the hall of glass
and entered a maze of corridors which were poorly lit, thick

with shadows. They were cold and depressing, not at all what the Skryer would have expected in such corridors as these.

When they came again to a place of light, it was of scrubbed stone, though the unnerving smell of blood and flesh clung to it. Annaxion knew he was in Yvane's pleasure sanctuary, where the slaves of the Elevate spared no effort to provide gratification for their master. The Providers' House of Sighs could not compare with this realm. Annaxion himself had no desire for pleasures of the flesh and was not subject to the same cravings that drove the Elevates and lesser beings: it was his mind that sought satisfaction, as was the nature of Skryers. They had been fashioned in a different mould.

The Dolus paused before a curved arch that looked as if it had been chiseled out of bone. Annaxion knew this must be illusion: no life-form possessed such a bone. Yet he knew that life took many strange forms in these regions, where Elevate Yvane imitated his master with his ceaseless experimentation.

"Yvane is beyond," said the Dolus.

Annaxion caught his breath. It did not matter that the Dolus saw his consternation. But to be brought to Yvane's presence? It must be for good reason. Or the worst. Annaxion felt himself growing cold, unable to exercise the mental composure that would be a barrier to fear. But the thought of meeting the Elevate was too difficult to bear without the onset of terror. Was he to be executed here?

The Skryer watched the Dolus as it withdrew, sliding across the stone without a sound, as though even it had no wish to disturb its master. Annaxion forced himself to go under the arch into the huge chamber. It was like a cell carved from naked rock, the lights low, the colour of blood. In the centre of the chamber was a sunken area several times the size of a man, and on three of the concave walls of the chamber, creatures had been stretched out and suspended above the stone floor.

The Skryer's face betrayed no emotion in the grim light, but he felt his heart judder at sight of these wretches. Long strips of twisted ganglia hung from them into the pit: and other parts of their bodies had been neatly opened to expose the organs. Pipes were attached to them, and thin tubes which ran down into the pit. They were fodda, alive still, though they could hardly be thought of now as men.

As Annaxion watched them, pulsing to the beating of their own hearts like fish caught on a line, something stirred in the central depression. A face rose up from it, eyes glaring. But such a face! Dominated by the eyes, it was contorted with a wild hatred, skin drawn down to a mouth in a malign rictus, as if it had been deliberately fashioned to offend the sight. And those eyes were bloody orbs, filled with a nameless animosity. It was impossible to imagine why such cruelty should be housed in a single being, what terrible purpose it could serve.

For this was Yvane. His skin was extremely pale, almost corpse white but riddled with veins. As he lifted his massive shoulders, Annaxion drew back. The veins were like the roots of a tree, standing out starkly against the white flesh, spreading repulsively like some infinite, embossed tattoo.

Yvane's mouth was full: a number of the tubes from the three spread-eagled fodda ended there. Others sank into his arms and chest, pumping fluids into him. His huge eyes glared balefully at Annaxion for a moment. Then he spat out the tubes, wiping his mouth on the back of a hand that could have crushed a man. The pipes dangled obscenely, like entrails, dripping with the last dregs of life of the victims.

"You are the Skryer, Annaxion?" whispered Yvane, leaning on the stone edge of his pit as if with an effort.

"I am, Elevate. The Dolus brought me. Surely this meeting is inconvenient—" Annaxion blurted, in danger of revealing the starkness of his terror. He could never have imagined that his master would take such a repugnant form.

Yvane snorted. It might have been a laugh. Or his bloody feast had made him drunk, Annaxion thought.

"I told him to bring you," said Yvane. He looked at the three fodda, then abruptly used the back of his hand to smash one of them from its bindings. The chains snapped and the body was knocked across the chamber to slap against the far wall. It slithered to the floor.

Yvane spat. "Traitors. Note well how I treat them, Annaxion. Providers or not. Anything less than an Elevate is fodda.

Only the Elevates have the right to make decisions. You understand?''

Annaxion nodded at once, though his heart was pumping. This broken flesh had been *Providers?* Yvane treated them with such utter disdain?

The Elevate showed no sign of dragging himself from his stone bath, as if the Receiving had been a tiring ordeal. "I am surrounded by traitors," he hissed. "You know that."

The Skryer bowed. "We bend our efforts to root them out, Elevate."

"And? *And?*"

"Elevate?"

"Haven't you any news?"

Annaxion knew precisely what Yvane meant. "Elevate, we have not yet recovered the blind Angel Guard, Arteriel. But we believe we have the means to do so."

Yvane glowered, but then nodded.

"As you know, your mortal enemy, Elevate Zaer Phesmes, set in motion some bizarre plan, implicating the Angel Guard."

"Yes, yes. Have you uncovered the plan?"

"Not yet, Elevate. But we have succeeded in suborning one of his Providers, Hummal Goresch. Goresch has a particular craving. We used it to enslave him."

The obese face leered. "Providers are easily manipulated. They sell their loyalty cheaply, especially those who do not serve Kaizu."

"Goresch was party to the affair with the blind Angel. We have dredged his mind for the truth behind the matter, but he has limited knowledge. Elevate Zaer Phesmes did not trust him with the full facts."

"Zaer is unfit to be an Elevate! His very name offends me!"

"Goresch has returned to his place, serving the Elevate. The Provider will seek out what we wish to know, and give the knowledge to Provider Sughai Orvech. We will solve this mystery, Elevate."

"If I have enough evidence, Kaizu himself will instruct me to bring down Zaer Phesmes and all who serve him. I'll absorb his vitals myself."

Annaxion bowed, shuddering at the thought of what Yvane could do.

"Fail me, Skryer, and I'll drink yours."

"Elevate, we do not contemplate failure."

Yvane snorted. He pointed to the slumped flesh by the wall. "You're a Skryer, which is why I summoned you. You practice the art of divination. There, pick through the carcass. Tell me what you see."

Again Annaxion felt himself shudder, this time his revulsion almost too much for him. Necromancy! But it was not his chosen path. Such obnoxious pursuits were for other Skryers. Why choose him? But he nodded, not daring to voice his disgust, and crossed the slippery floor to the fallen body. It leaked blood, tubes poking from it like ruptured arteries. He bent to it, trying to affect calmness. This could never be his art, his prime skill, though he knew how it was done. He was conscious that those huge eyes were watching him; he dipped his hands into the pulped flesh. Slowly but with growing pressure, like water flowing sluggishly, the body spoke to him. He could not halt the racing images.

The victim's former pain transmitted itself, the agonies it had endured under Yvane, so that Annaxion winced. The Elevate's thoroughness in his using of the body, his total abuse of it, ran like shocks through the Skryer. He experienced Yvane's lust, its true depths, but had to veer from them as the darkness threatened to snap his own mind, as surely as it had burst the mind of the Provider. The monstrous visions closed around him, opening doors to regions he could never have realised existed.

Eventually Annaxion sagged back, his clothes soaked with perspiration, his body shaking. He wanted to vomit, but dared not, controlling himself with an effort. He could not as much as hint at the depth of his disgust.

"Well?" said Yvane, his impatience like a poised knife.

"I . . . saw shadows, Elevate. The future is always opaque."

"But there were details?"

"Of sorts."

Yvane indicated the other two bodies. There was no life

in either of them. ''Use these if it will consolidate your vision.''

''There's no need, Elevate. I have seen enough.''

''Then impart it to me!''

Annaxion bowed. ''The blind Angel cannot avoid us. That is, I have seen that he does not. Through Provider Goresch we will discover what Elevate Zaer Phesmes plots—''

''And take the Angel?''

Annaxion nodded. He was finding it hard to speak.

''You saw these things?''

''They were hinted at—''

Yvane coughed, spitting blood, though it was not his own. ''Did your art tell you how soon?''

''Divination is imprecise, Elevate.''

Yvane glared at him. ''Is it? Very well. But my time draws near, Skryer. Kaizu will take me beyond this level of existence. If I deliver to him the treacheries and deceits of the Des Aubach vermin, my destiny is assured. As is yours and all who serve me well! You understand that?''

''Of course, Elevate. All flesh bends to you.''

''Find the Angel. I want his blood.''

Only after he had stripped and scrubbed himself did Annaxion visit Provider Sughai Orvech. The feeling of being unclean persisted: he knew that he would not be able to erase from his face all of the horror he had felt during his visit to Yvane. It had been beyond nightmare, a reason to die, to quit this horrendous Elevate. How could the gods permit this? How?

He was right about Orvech. The Provider saw his emotional turmoil at once.

''Forgive me, Annaxion, but you seem to lack your usual passivity. You are by far the most immaculate of Skryers. Is there an urgent matter?''

Annaxion pulled his cloak tighter about him. ''I have come from Elevate Yvane.''

''He spoke through the Dolus?''

Annaxion shook his head. ''No. I was seen by Yvane himself.''

Orvech looked stunned. "You—went before him? You were given an *audience?*"

Annaxion nodded.

Orvech scowled for a moment, but then hid his envy. Surely this Skryer was not to be favoured with Elevation? And not before him, Sughai Orvech! "A unique privilege. You are honoured."

"It was a little disturbing. Yvane is eager for results. If we do not provide him with them soon, he will be angered. I have seen the consequences of his anger."

"Share them with me."

Annaxion sat down, which Orvech knew was unlike him. He was usually far more formal. But he let it pass without comment. The Skryer spoke quietly for long moments. He shielded his emotions and was careful not to dwell on the details of what he had seen and experienced.

When he had finished, Orvech sat back thoughtfully. "For you to have been seen personally is highly significant. A show of power, or rather, as I'm sure you rightly surmise, anger. Yvane is not pleased with us and the delay in bringing his affairs to a head. In view of that, I'm relieved that it was you and not I who was summoned," he added, trying to dismiss the matter lightly.

"I had no choice."

"Of course not. We obey Yvane in all things. What about the divination?"

"Others are better at such things. He should have chosen more appropriately. But I could hardly deny him. I saw only vague outlines."

"You elaborated?"

"I dared do nothing else."

"You predict success?"

"It is true, I saw the blind Angel. He stood in a lake of blood."

Orvech nodded slowly. "I assure you, he will. And it will be Zaer Phesmes and all his vermin who fill it."

29

Verusion took his seat quietly amongst the gathering of Skryers, settling back in the gloom of the hall. Below him was the semicircular seating where the Directors sat, waiting for the gathered brotherhood to quieten down. Elevate law dictated that they meet regularly, sharing information, knowledge, discoveries: their findings had to be scrutinised and approved by the Elevates. Verusion was well aware, however, that not everything was discussed in this forum. He contemplated his own devious involvement in his master's affairs and almost smiled at the thought of the panic that would have been caused had he brought the truth before this gathering. But his mild amusement faded; the Skryers lacked unity. Ironic, he told himself, that these so-called visionaries are so shortsighted.

The business of the meeting followed its usual dry pattern. The Directors concentrated their discussion on the Overlap, its interminable vicissitudes. They were at least united in their dream of predicting its movements, but were forced to conclude that so far their efforts had met with only partial success.

Verusion glanced to his left. There were a few empty seats, but he noticed one of his colleagues paying him unexpected attention. Polite inclinations of the head were exchanged.

Well, well, mused Verusion. *Odd that Annaxion should as much as credit my existence. Surely he doesn't suspect anything. We've been so very careful over the Goresch affair. Yet Annaxion looks strangely uneasy. No, it isn't that: he looks ill.*

The meeting was a dull one, but mercifully did not take long. When it was over, Verusion made his way quietly back up the aisle to the exit. He had not contributed to the talks. Neither, he noticed, had Annaxion, which was unusual: Provider Orvech's Skryer usually had more than a little to say, though Verusion knew that it was the Provider's instruction.

In the room beyond the hall, Verusion felt a touch at his elbow. When he turned and found himself face-to-face with Annaxion, he was not surprised, as though the meeting had been inevitable.

"Your pardon, Verusion," said Annaxion. "A word with you, if I may."

"Of course," nodded Verusion. There were drinks served for the Skryers after their meetings. Verusion ushered Annaxion towards them. Annaxion declined to take one.

Verusion feigned mild interest, sipping the wine slowly before allowing himself to be gently shepherded to a quiet niche at the side of the hall. It was common for Skryers to discuss personal matters after the meetings, and in fact, Verusion knew full well that any fruitful discussion could only be had this way.

"What is it you want of me?" he said.

Annaxion looked about him with a most uncharacteristic nervousness. His face was pale, his eyes red, rimmed with dark shadows. But of course, all this could be a trick, a superbly planned strategy. Elevate Yvane was the grand master of deceits.

"It is difficult for me to know where to begin."

"If I may say so, Annaxion, you seem a little, uh, distressed."

"I am. I have been subjected to things that have unsettled me, colleague."

"Forgive me again," replied Verusion, lowering his voice. "But I have to say that it surprises me that you are telling *me* this. Our masters are particularly hostile to each other, after all."

"They are. Elevate Yvane Sephir is the enemy of all other Elevates. Many serve Kaizu, but even so, they are mindful of Yvane. And with good cause."

"I know this."

"Have you ever seen your master, Elevate Zaer Phesmes? I mean, have you been in his presence?"

Verusion smiled indulgently. "Of course not. As you know, Elevates do not show themselves to the lower orders."

"Some of us have been privileged," said Annaxion, but the irony in his voice was clear.

Verusion's smile melted. "What . . . to see?"

Annaxion nodded, gazing around him. "I have been before Elevate Yvane."

Verusion remained calm. Yes, this was undoubtedly a trap. But did they know about Provider Goresch? "I am astounded. You are very honoured." *Or lying. Clever though: your feigned unease is quite brilliant.*

"Verusion, I know you are Yvane's bitter enemy. Zaer would kill him if he had an opportunity. I know you are loyal."

"As you are, colleague. We all have our duties, our ties."

"Tell me, are there limits to these duties? Would you deny your master anything?"

"I am a Skryer. I do not pass on everything. Which of us does? Who knows what chaos they would create if they knew everything?"

"I don't mean that. I agree that Skryers possess sacred knowledge that even the Elevates should not have—"

"Then you do subscribe to the brotherhood's rights—"

"I do. For the stability of our world. But that is not what I mean. Are there demands that your master would make that you would question?"

He cannot expect an honest answer from me, thought Verusion. *Unless this is an attempt to seduce me away from Zaer.* "He has not made any such demands on me. Can you be more specific?"

"Do you have the skill of divination?"

"There are many paths. I have some small talent in the reading of atmospheric conditions—"

"There is power in bones, in flesh and blood, even in the dead." Annaxion looked even more grim.

Verusion began to feel more certain that Annaxion had had some kind of shock. This was not, after all, an act. "I have no skill in necromancy. But such arts are practised. Obviously we have colleagues who are adepts."

"I am not one of them. My skill lies in the use of the

Overlap. I cannot predict its movements, but I know how to use it, how to direct power into it and back from it. I make gates. It is a dangerous business, and demands life. I was chosen by Yvane for my skill. I am not a necromancer. He should know that!'' He seemed angered by something. Again, it was no act.

"It would be unreasonable of him, or of any Elevate, to expect a Skryer to perform duties that were beneath his capabilities.''

Annaxion looked hard at him. ''You believe that?''

Verusion nodded. ''Unreasonable, and foolish. If an Elevate wanted an assassination performed, he would not employ a Skryer, he would select an Angel Guard.''

"I was asked, *forced*, to perform an act of divination.''

"By Yvane?''

Annaxion nodded slowly. ''With one of his victims, a Provider who had displeased him.''

"Again, I have to say I am puzzled as to why you should impart such information to one of your rivals!''

Annaxion clutched at Verusion's robe. ''I was not unsuccessful.''

"The dead spoke to you?''

"That is not how it happens. Their emissions are like dreams, fractured and disparate. But they are not inchoate. Certain truths lie in them. Particularly in respect to death. I must have a degree of skill. Perhaps, as Skryers, we all have.''

I have to ask him, thought Verusion. *It is what he expects of me. Though how can I be sure he will tell me anything but lies?* ''You saw the future? But what did you foresee?''

"Blood, slaughter. Unimaginable horrors. And greatest of all was my own death.''

"Your own?''

"At the hands of Yvane.''

Verusion said nothing, looking into the tormented eyes of the Skryer. What did he really want? To *betray* Yvane? Surely that was too much to hope for.

"I pray,'' said Annaxion, ''that the divination is only a partial truth, one possibility of many.''

"You could find out more.''

"From an adept?"

"Quite so."

"That was my thinking. Tetraven is reputed to be the master."

"Yes." *He draws nearer to his point.*

"You have a close association with him?" Annaxion said it as if he already knew the answer.

Verusion smiled grimly. "No one has that! As you know, Tetraven has shut himself away and is a law unto himself. But I know him and have had dealings with him."

Again Annaxion gripped Verusion's arm. "I have to learn more about what I saw. I need Tetraven's help. I dare not approach him directly for fear of offending him. He holds Yvane in contempt. But you could speak to him on my behalf."

Verusion shrugged. "But, Annaxion, in theory we are enemies. Zaer and Yvane are at *war*. It has almost become an open affair! We cannot pretend otherwise."

Annaxion would not loose his grip. "If you win me an audience with Tetraven, I will allow you to be present. You will share in all my visions. My mind will be open to you."

"You would make yourself that vulnerable?"

"Yes."

"I still cannot understand why."

Annaxion looked about him carefully before he spoke, lowering his voice until it was almost lost. "How else can I convince you and Zaer Phesmes that I am no longer the servant of Yvane, that I would be his enemy?"

Provider Ramman Lurish pushed aside the empty dish. He had, as usual, fed well. He wiped his mouth and lifted his glass of wine. His guest waited patiently for him to finish. One did not disturb Lurish at his pleasures.

"Delicious," the gross Provider pronounced. "Well, my friend, what do you make of it? Trap?"

Verusion almost smiled. Lurish had a deceptively relaxed manner, as though all the plotting and deceiving in the world were little more than a game to be enjoyed. "I can't relate it to the planting of Hummal Goresch. Orvech cannot suspect Goresch. He's in their power!"

"Oh, I agree. Goresch is their slave. They have him. But we'll feed him with enough spurious information to throw them off the scent of Zaer's real plans. Perhaps Yvane has wit enough to have thought it out, eh? In which case Annaxion becomes Yvane's plant and they play us at our own game."

"Yes, the meeting was so open, I wondered about that," said Verusion. "But if Annaxion subjects himself to Tetraven, he will be absolutely exposed. He couldn't hide his true plans."

"Unless Tetraven has become Yvane's slave."

But Verusion shook his head. "Impossible. He's too independent. His power lies in that freedom. He would never relinquish it. I am certain he would rather die than submit to Yvane."

"So why should he help us, eh?" said Lurish sceptically, leaning his bulk forward.

"Oh, he indulges me."

"You play on some secret lust of his, do you?"

"Lurish, not everyone is prey to lust. Certainly not carnal lust, as you imagine."

"I can't see why not! What else compares to the raptures of the flesh?"

Verusion laughed gently. "You will drown in a pool of flesh, Lurish—"

"I hope that isn't something *you've* divined, Verusion."

"I don't need to be an adept to predict what might await someone with your tastes."

"No, you're right," Lurish laughed. "Let me drown in my particular desires. But what about Tetraven, eh? Why does he deal with you?"

Verusion pretended to examine the garish but arresting paintings displayed on the walls of this part of Lurish's apartments. "Tetraven," he said at last, "does have a weakness."

"Ah, I knew it! Then he's not an artificial being, or a genetically contrived machine."

"He is an adept at divination. But the future and its secrets have been, in a way, forced upon him, a gift from the gods. In his case, an unwanted gift. Hence his seclusion. What he really enjoys is the past. There lies his fascination. History, Lurish. Where a thousand secrets lurk.''

"You do disappoint me. History! There's no pleasure in a corpse. What's gone is gone!''

"Not to Tetraven. History is the true key to power. Zaer is convinced of it.''

"You believe this?'' said Lurish, amazed.

"Not necessarily. But I know enough to understand that tremendous knowledge has been lost over the ages. The Overlap sometimes provides answers, keys. I share some of these with Tetraven.''

"In exchange for what?''

"Let us say, we exchange information that broadens our understanding of the sciences. But in this case, I will have to provide Tetraven with something quite lavish if he is to help us delve into Annaxion's mind.''

"Such as?''

"He'll have to know the truth about Arteriel. About the coming rebellion.''

For once Lurish lost his insouciant grin. "Recruit him?''

"I admit, it will be a difficult task. Tetraven trusts no one. But it is only a beginning. We may, before long, have to recruit Annaxion.''

Lurish grimaced. "We'd have to be sure of him.''

"If we can't be sure of him—''

"I'll kill him.''

Verusion knew this was no jest. For all his mirth, Lurish was as dangerous as an Angel Guard. And he would not employ anyone to do his killing for him.

30

Provider Lurish watched from the seclusion of the balcony, completely hidden by its darkness. Below him, within earshot, a number of figures had entered the circular room. They were all Skryers, their drab robes neutral, though they served different masters. Lurish often wondered if any of these strange beings were truly capable of more than lip service to the Elevates. Nevertheless, Verusion had been as good as his word. He had arranged this unusual meeting, here in the private tower of Tetraven. It had obviously been difficult for him to persuade the elderly Skryer to permit a Provider to be present, especially as he had to be secreted somewhere where Elevate Yvane's Skryer would not be aware of his presence. But it had been done. Lurish wondered what promises had been made; Verusion had not specified to him what bargain he had struck. Lurish smiled; he admired intrigue on any level, and the Skryers were well skilled in it.

For the time being he listened as the words drifted up to him clearly, the acoustics of the tower excellent.

Tetraven addressed Annaxion. "I understand that you wish to make use of my services." Tetraven was amazingly frail and stooped. His eyes were watery, but there was deceptive energy in the small frame. He clung to life with an obdurate tenacity. Both Verusion and Annaxion loomed over him, but he was not intimidated.

"I do," said Annaxion.

"For whose purpose?"

"For my own."

"Yet you serve Elevate Yvane Sephir. I am not bound to him."

Annaxion glanced at Verusion, who nodded discreetly as

if to say, I have already settled this matter with him, but humour him.

"Not in all things. I have been abused," Annaxion said cautiously.

"All Skryers are abused. We are treated no better than fodda by some of the Elevates. Particularly by the execrable Yvane," Tetraven snorted. "So—what do I gain out of this audience?"

Verusion coughed. "Tetraven, we have discussed this."

"I know, I know," growled the old Skryer. "But I want to hear it from him. Is he committed?"

"Tell him," said Verusion. "But be careful, Annaxion. This old demon is probably listening to your mind."

"If there is any duplicity," said Tetraven, "I'll sniff it out. If this is one of Yvane's treacherous—"

"It is not," said Annaxion firmly. "As you will learn. I am committed. Are you, old man?"

Tetraven scowled. "Verusion here tells me I should ally myself more fully with his master."

Up in the balcony, the silent Lurish stirred with unease. It was a little too soon to let Annaxion have any details. If there was any chance of his being a plant, he must be told nothing.

"Perhaps you should," said Annaxion.

"Oh, do you deny Yvane in favour of Zaer?"

"I will answer you after we have concluded this matter. And whatever knowledge Verusion has promised you, I will not ask for."

"You want an interpretation of the divination you performed for Yvane?"

"I must have it." Again Annaxion wore the haunted expression that Verusion had seen and been so puzzled by when they had met after the concourse of the Skryers. And again Verusion was sure it could be no guise.

Tetraven turned away and went to the circular slab of stone at the heart of the chamber. There was a shallow impression in the smooth stone, shaped to take a body. Tetraven ran his hands over it, closing his eyes for a moment, muttering something to himself. Then he turned back to Annaxion. "Disrobe."

Slowly, Annaxion did so. Provider Lurish watched with keen interest, amazed at how skeletal the body of the Skryer was. How could it sustain life! Pale as the dead, skin stretched tautly over the bones, arms and legs elongated strangely, almost as if pulled out of shape. But Annaxion held firm to his dignity, climbing up onto the stone. Tetraven directed him and he stretched out in the depression, limbs spread.

He is at their mercy, thought Lurish. If this is a ploy, he has uncanny nerves.

Tetraven came close to Annaxion. "It will not be pleasant."

Annaxion took a few deep breaths, as though about to plunge into chilling water. "It can be no worse than it was."

"Perhaps."

Tetraven motioned Verusion around to the other side of the stone. "Take his arm and hold it firmly. When this begins, he will try to pull free of us. Do not permit it. His life will be in our hands. You understand, Annaxion?"

Sweat was breaking out in a sheen on Annaxion's white face, but he nodded. "I am committed," he said.

Tetraven took his other hand, locking it with both of his own. He had a grip like steel.

Now, thought Lurish. *Now we'll see why Yvane's favourite has come running to us in fear. What is he hiding?*

Annaxion heard a sudden roar. It was a moment before he knew it for what it was: the rushing of his own blood, pumping like a torrent through veins and arteries. He could feel his heart pounding, a massive engine, its throb driving the energy through him, the centre of the world. Everything else closed out, light fading.

He no longer felt Tetraven's steel grip, nor the hands of Verusion, as if both Skryers had released him. But he felt something else, immediately reacting to it. The blood and vitals of the Provider Yvane had tortured and flung aside, the victim whose flesh he had been forced to study in that bloody chamber. It was as though his hands were again dipping into that ruined meat. And flowing up into him like a current, the visions came. But this time they were far more potent, far more sharply focused.

Lurish gripped the seat on which he sat, his fingers numbing. What was happening below? Annaxion's body thrashed, the two Skryers barely able to hold it. Tetraven had his head flung back, eyes rolled up to show the whites as if having some sort of fit. What did he see?

Tetraven saw what Annaxion had seen and was seeing again.

Visions of stark terror. Walls of blood, torn aside like curtains to reveal huge shapes, lumbering monstrous beings, hybrids that were grotesquely mutated, shaped by powers that delighted in a random fusion of flesh, or its dissipation. Madness seemed to have guided the hands of the sculptors, a madness that knew no bounds. Nothing was too extreme. Shape after shape writhed and slithered through the vision in a procession of chaos. Figures rose up in the mire of blood and melted flesh on which they fed, distorted and confused. But among them were faces, strained but familiar. Annaxion's was one of them.

Around him there were conflicts breaking out, a cosmic battlefield, as if a number of mad visions were superimposing themselves one on top of another, overlapping and intersecting. Towers burned, or toppled, while beyond them, rising over all, the horrendous shapes continued to writhe and distort, sucking up into them the endless sea of flesh.

Elevate Yvane Sephir appeared, his own bloated bulk slithering through a lake of blood. His lower body had been truncated, his limbs hacked and bleeding, and from the dark pools, the teeth of a score of mutants snapped at him, ripping chunks from him. He bellowed, beating about him, but from the skies other shapes fell, winged demons, tearing at him with vicious claws, ripping his head and shoulders.

Annaxion's own figure was knee-deep in blood, and from the filth a further shape rose up, an Angel Guard. It turned its empty eye sockets upon him. Light speared from them, striking at Annaxion's figure. Flames sprouted.

Annaxion screamed, and both Verusion and Tetraven almost lost their grip on his arms. They felt the heat of the fire, as if he were charring on the stone. A sudden blanket of darkness dropped over them all.

Lurish watched in astonishment as all three Skryers screamed. Verusion and Tetraven fell backwards, slumping down on the flagstones. Annaxion had gone limp. Something dripped from his dangling arm. It hissed as it hit the floor. Lurish stood up. Should he go to them?

He waited.

At last it was Verusion who moved first. Lurish watched anxiously as the Skryer got to his knees. Shaking himself, Verusion used the stone block to heave himself to his feet. He glanced dazedly at Annaxion, but then went around the block to Tetraven. He bent to him. The old Skryer stirred, then sat up. Presently he nodded and was able to get to his feet.

On the stone, Annaxion rolled to one side and vomited.

"Did you share the visions?" Tetraven asked Verusion.

"Partially. There was a veil over it all. Shapes came and went. I'm not sure what it meant—"

"Rest. There is water over there." He pointed to a ewer. "Bring it. Annaxion will be exhausted."

While Verusion did as bidden, Tetraven went to Annaxion. He felt his pulse, then listened to his heartbeat.

"Is he all right?" asked Verusion, passing the ewer.

Tetraven dipped a cloth into the water and used it to mop at Annaxion's brow and mouth. The latter came to, groaning.

They got him to sit up and helped him dress. After he had drunk, he got off the stone, leaning on it to steady himself. He looked very shaken, like a man returning from the brink of death.

"You were right," he told Tetraven. "I saw much more clearly. But I only half understood. Did you see—?"

Tetraven nodded. "Everything. Rarely have I shared such clarity of vision. It is a sign."

"A sign? What do you mean?"

"Such visions are not experienced by chance. Divination is an art, a skill given to certain of us. But you, Annaxion, were chosen."

"By whom? The gods?"

"Perhaps."

"Absolute Light?"

"I think it probably was."

"Can you interpret what I saw? Yvane—"

"You saw his fall. Much of it may have been symbolic. The shapes, the huge denizens of the dark. They represented power. The gods, possibly."

"You saw—my death?"

"A blind Angel killed you."

Annaxion looked at Verusion. "Arteriel," he said hoarsely.

"You know why he was blinded. Do you know why he seeks my life?"

Verusion shrugged. "Arteriel has left messages for all of us. He says we are all his enemies."

"Why should he single me out?"

"What you saw was a possible future," said Tetraven. "It was confused by the past."

"I don't understand."

"The conflict you saw. You were witnessing the awesome wars that brought about the fall of a world, millennia ago. The atrocities that were spawned, devouring natural life, churning the earth into a charnel realm. A deep memory that must be in all of us. Who has not suffered nightmares in which such chaos swirls? Out of that chaos was born the darkness under Skydown. Skydown, the shield that protects us from Absolute Light. Absolute Light, which has shown you, through the visions, the folly of war. And what continued conflict will bring."

"Your interpretation?" said Annaxion, his voice almost inaudible.

"Serve Elevate Yvane Sephir and the cause of Kaizu, the Da Sangraville slaughterer, and you will fall."

Annaxion shook his head. "Yet if I serve any other Elevate, no matter who, I will be embroiled in the Lightbenders' private wars. There is no avoiding them."

"It is a time of change," said Tetraven, as though he was reviewing the visions. "You have been given a sign. Perhaps we all have."

Annaxion looked at Verusion. "You want me to serve your master?"

"I serve Absolute Light," said Verusion.

Annaxion looked puzzled. "Through Zaer Phesmes—"

"Zaer does not serve Subran first. There are greater powers. This is the truth, Annaxion: Subran, Kaizu, Vesporzi, and all the other Lightbenders are unworthy of Absolute Light. Their greed, their arrogance, have set them apart from all other life-forms. To them, even Elevates are fodda. To be consumed."

Annaxion's frown deepened. "You speak of rebellion on an impossible scale! Vilify the Lightbenders? Are you mad?"

Tetraven was listening coolly, but his eyes never left Verusion's face.

"Possibly I am," Verusion went on. It had to be said now. "But you told me you went before Yvane. You saw him. Now Tetraven and I have seen him in your vision. Did he not disgust you?"

Annaxion was taken aback, his face betraying the truth.

"There is no need to answer," said Verusion. "Your disgust gave fuel to your vision. Yvane is a monster in a world of monsters. But it is his contempt for all other life-forms that makes him so. There can only be one end to this if it goes on. The world under Skydown will rot: already it is withering, shrinking to nothing. The Lightbenders are forced to drag their sustenance from other worlds. Our own is full of horrors, of hybrids created by cruel masters. They cannot help their shapes, their deformities. Why should they suffer? Why should flesh be fuel, sport?"

Annaxion dabbed at his face. "But *how* is this change to happen?"

Verusion looked at Tetraven.

The old Skryer returned his level gaze. "Tell us, Verusion," he said. "Where is our power to bring down the Lightbenders?"

"It comes from above. It has touched you, Annaxion. As it has already touched another."

Annaxion saw again his death at the hands of the blind Angel. "The Angel Guard, Arteriel," he breathed.

Verusion nodded.

"Who blinded him?"

"Our suffering has been acknowledged," said Verusion.

Above him on the balcony, Lurish watched Annaxion closely. In his hand was a slender blade. From this range he could throw it with stunning accuracy.

31

Provider Sughai Orvech looked smugly at his victim, who was slumped down on the seat despondently. How quickly his deterioration took its course.

"I've told you all I know," blurted Hummal Goresch, repeating the statement as he had been doing since his arrival.

Orvech knew that, for the moment, he had exhausted the poor supply of knowledge that Goresch possessed, but it amused him to torment the insufferable creature. "You enjoy the pleasure of the hybrid?"

Goresch shot him a venomous look, but then remembered where he was and turned away, nodding. "You know that I do."

"Excellent. Continue to do so. You have been as good as your word. But we are still no closer to finding Arteriel."

"I have told you, Verusion does not inform me fully. But there are signs that he is becoming more forthcoming."

"Ah."

"We are to meet with the Praetors of the Blood Red Angels and the Bone Whites."

Orvech frowned. "A commission? But I understood the Bone Whites have a priority kill on Arteriel."

"They do. Elevate Zaer wants it withdrawn. Hence the meeting. Zaer wants Arteriel alive."

"So does Yvane."

"Believe me, Orvech, I have other servants working for me. They come to me, not Verusion, not to Zaer, or any of his other people. They are the ones who will find Arteriel. Word crosses the segments through them. Give me a little longer."

"If I must," said Orvech testily.

"The hybrid—"

"Not now. Perhaps after your meeting with the Praetors."

Goresch looked suddenly haggard. His fists clenched, but Orvech was already waving him away, the meeting over. Goresch stood up, watching Orvech's disappearing back as he left the chamber. There had been a time when Orvech would never have dared to turn his back. It was now a measure of his confidence that he could do so.

"Provider Goresch," came a soft voice.

Goresch jumped, twisting about to see another figure in the chamber with him, emerging from behind an arras. It was Annaxion, the Skryer attached to Orvech.

"What do you want?" muttered Goresch.

Annaxion came to him and gently led him by the arm from the room, listening for the sound of Orvech's return, but the Provider had disappeared into an inner chamber.

"Provider Orvech asks that I be fully informed of all developments regarding the blind Angel Guard, Arteriel. You are to come to me first, do you understand? I have complete control of the mobility of Provider Orvech's forces."

Goresch grunted. It did not surprise him. If Annaxion was as close to Elevate Yvane as Verusion was to Zaer, then it was no surprise that he had more power than the Provider.

"I also have a considerable amount of persuasive influence over Provider Orvech," Annaxion went on.

Goresch's face brightened for a moment, but then he covered his emotions as if he had betrayed himself.

"Unlike Provider Orvech, I take no interest in tormenting and torturing," said Annaxion. "I have seen how he abuses you with the hybrid. It is unnecessary. You have shown your change of loyalty, albeit under duress."

"I keep to my part of bargains."

"I am sure you do. Consequently I will see that you have access to the hybrid whenever you wish it, within reason."

Goresch was unable to contain a smile. "You can do this?"

"Oh, yes. Provider Orvech will indulge you if I ask him to. But I must insist that anything you learn about Arteriel, anything you hear, no matter how small, comes to *me* first. Is that absolutely clear? I promise you, no ill will befall you because of this. On the contrary."

"Yes, I understand."

"You detest Provider Orvech, do you not?"

Goresch hesitated.

"I can see that you do. No matter. He is not important. To move on, upward, one must serve the Elevates. Yvane is far more important than Provider Orvech."

Goresch saw things clearly at once. The Skryer was ambitious. He saw this as a chance to overleap Orvech in Yvane's eyes. "Of course. Yvane."

"Keep me informed. Between us we can see that Provider Orvech is given what he thinks he needs. You and I will see that Yvane, and hence Kaizu himself, are served well."

"If you can promise me access to the hybrid—"

"Do as I tell you, Goresch, and I will ensure that you own the hybrid. In good time."

Goresch felt himself quivering at the thought of it. His mouth was drying. All he could do was nod.

"Nothing must go to Provider Orvech without coming through me. Absolutely nothing."

Again Goresch nodded. "Nothing," he croaked.

Verusion watched from the shadows. Goresch was sitting in the centre of the chamber on a raised seat. The Provider looked distinctly lacking in composure. If Verusion and Provider Lurish had not set Goresch up, it would have been evident to them that something was wrong with him. His bones stretched his skin taut, skin that had become a sickly grey pallor. His obsession with the hybrid had completely ruined him. Verusion wondered if Provider Orvech had deliberately interfered with the hybrid in such a way that it was infusing or injecting drugs into Goresch. He was becoming more gaunt, his mind less capable of focusing attention. He would have to be watched carefully.

Still Verusion asked himself, could Annaxion be trusted? He would be the filter for all information Goresch gave to Provider Orvech. Some of that information would not come to Zaer. Goresch had his private channels, as all Providers did.

The door to the chamber swung open and two Angel Guards entered. Their faces were sharp, predatory, their manner not hostile, but hinting at a will to attack any suggestion of aggression. More like beasts than men, they scanned the room expertly and glanced at the shadows, knowing that the Skryer would be watching them but did not acknowledge him.

"Praetors," said Goresch, not bothering to rise.

The two Angel Guards bowed slightly. But they waited, saying nothing.

Goresch made an effort to pull himself together. The strain he was under was not lost on his two visitors; they glanced briefly at one another but still did not speak. Verusion could read their contempt.

"I have summoned you to discuss the renegade," said Goresch.

Still the Praetors waited.

"Well?"

The Blood Red Praetor broke his silence. "Arteriel is no longer my concern, as far as I am aware."

Beside him, the Bone White Praetor contained his evident annoyance with as much dignity as he could muster. He gave Goresch an icy stare.

"Not your concern?" said the Provider.

"I delivered Arteriel to you as instructed. Subsequently he left Thousandreach, as I understand it. My Blood Reds have not been commissioned to recover him."

Goresch's face twitched with annoyance. His hands gripped the seat, knuckles whitening. "Are you telling me, Praetor, that your Blood Reds have done *nothing* to find Arteriel?"

"That is correct," said the Praetor calmly.

The Bone White was unable to remain silent. "My own Bone Whites are out in force, Provider. One of them was murdered by the renegade, as you are both well aware. Although my colleague does not deem it fit to avenge the death of my warrior, I am duty bound to seek the killer."

"Had a Blood Red been murdered," interrupted the Blood Red Praetor calmly, "then it would clearly have been my duty to take steps to bring the killer to heel. As it is, I cannot interfere without a commission. As you are aware, colleague."

"This slight upon the Bone Whites has been noted," said the Bone White Praetor.

Verusion spoke into the curdling atmosphere. "What course of action is the Praetor of the Flensers taking?"

It was the Bone White Praetor who answered. "None. Presumably he does not feel it is his duty—"

"Clearly it is not," said the Blood Red Praetor.

Goresch stood up, his fists balling, his body quivering. "I will not tolerate this! Arteriel *must* be brought before me!"

The eyes of the Bone White Praetor narrowed. "I presume, Provider, you expect only his corpse?"

"I want him *alive!* Elevate Zaer Phesmes has demanded it. Alive. If he is killed, there will be recriminations. *Where is he?"*

The Bone White Praetor stiffened. "Is this a commission?"

"Call it what you like—"

"I need to understand you," said the Bone White Praetor chillingly. His total lack of respect for the Provider was clear to them all, though he must have known such derision also slighted Elevate Zaer.

Verusion answered him from the shadows. "It is a commission. And for the Blood Reds, and for the Flensers. Arteriel must be taken alive. He will be dealt with, be assured of that. But your vengeance, Praetor, counts as little next to the law."

"The *law?"* said the Bone White.

"The law of the Elevates, handed down by the Lightbenders. Their word is as sacred as the great trees."

"Thank you for reminding us," Goresch said to Verusion.

The Blood Red Praetor again bowed. "You are saying this is a fresh commission? For *all* Angel Guards? Do you have the papers?"

Goresch's eyes widened as if he would unleash his wrath, but Verusion stepped from the darkness. He carried three rolled parchments, one of which he handed to the Blood Red.

"They are here. And for you, Bone White," said the Skryer, handing over another of the parchments.

The Bone White looked surprised, taking it with bad grace. He read the scroll, nodding reluctantly. "Very well. A commission. Arteriel alive. But tell your Elevate that the Bone Whites will want assurances—"

"Surely this is not a threat, Praetor?" Verusion asked him calmly.

The Bone White's eyes filled with anger. "Arteriel has

committed the ultimate crime against us. There must be an accounting.''

"I am sure," said Verusion, remaining very calm, "that Elevate Zaer Phesmes understands this. He, too, has been gravely insulted.''

"Arteriel," said the Bone White, focusing his anger on the Blood Red, "is a disgrace to his kind. I am amazed that the Blood Reds do not feel dishonoured by his actions.''

The Blood Red did not rise to the bait. "Arteriel is no longer a Blood Red, nor indeed, an Angel Guard. He ceased to be an Angel Guard the moment he was handed over to Provider Goresch's servants. Whatever actions he has taken since were not carried out on behalf of my Blood Reds. I assure you, Praetor, that my Blood Reds will not provoke enmity between us.''

"Your squabbles don't interest me," snapped Goresch, losing his patience altogether. "Just find him. *Find him!*" He spun round on his heel, staggered as he passed his chair, then, to their amazement, had the audacity to leave the chamber.

Both Praetors watched him go with withering looks of disgust on their faces.

"I must apologise for him," said Verusion, sensing the raw hatred of the two warriors. "He is under severe strain. This business has gone very badly.''

"If this commission," said the Bone White, holding up the parchment, "was from that vermin, rather than an Elevate, I would tear it up before his eyes and make him swallow it!''

The Blood Red smiled without humour. "The Provider has shown considerable contempt for all Angel Guards at this unfortunate meeting." He turned to the Bone White. "Since we have been given an identical commission, Praetor, perhaps we should consider combining our resources, together with those of the Flensers?''

The Bone White was still glaring at the empty doorway where Goresch had exited. *"Squabbles,* he said. How *dare* he? This is an intolerable insult—''

Verusion held up his hand. "The matter will be dealt with. But we have another priority. You must find Arteriel. I urge you to consider the commission carefully. You will see that Elevate Zaer offers you a rich reward.''

The Bone White turned to his fellow Angel Guard. "You have seen?"

The Blood Red unrolled the parchment and read silently for a moment. "Can he do this?" he said to the Skryer.

Verusion nodded slowly. "Zaer can open many doors. He will do what he promises in the commission."

"Then I agree," said the Bone White. "Unite the warriors for this mission. No one else must take Arteriel."

"Alive," said the Blood Red. "Whatever your views are on revenge, colleague."

The Bone White stiffened, but held up the parchment. "For this, we put aside vengeance."

Verusion watched them leave. Goresch's foolish outburst had worked well to his advantage. The Angel Guard united? Surely it would preclude anyone else getting to Arteriel first. And they would not kill him, in spite of the Bone White's livid fury. They would respect the law, the commission of an Elevate. Pride, duty. Gods, what terrible weapons they were, and every bit as strong as greed, lust.

32

"You use my language badly," said Arteriel, though he spoke with indifference rather than scorn. He had been listening as Ruarhi spoke haltingly of events that had befallen him since his arrival under Skydown, of all that he had been told by Sommoi and Inkulke. Not once had the Angel Guard broken his silence, until now. He had been as still as an eagle and as impervious to the shuddering gusts that shook the tower.

Ruarhi did not answer. He had finished, the bitterness in his own voice not lost on the Angel Guard. But his anger at the loss of Dromator and Darrac, the terror he felt at being exposed to this winged demon, seemed to mean nothing to the blind warrior.

Arteriel's attention fixed momentarily on the gathering winds. Then he went to the first of his torches and smothered it. He did the same with the second. The last of the brands he lifted, as if its heat guided him.

"They are coming," he said, though he seemed to be thinking aloud, ignoring Ruarhi.

Ruarhi could see only darkness beyond the guttering flame. "Who?"

"Angel Guards."

"They hunt you?"

"Bone Whites. To avenge Estragel," Arteriel added, almost as an afterthought.

Ruarhi listened to the mounting fury of the elements, but heard only their raging.

"I will not give them satisfaction," said Arteriel.

"Will you talk to the Emeschi?"

Arteriel's face seemed to tighten in a sneer. "About rebellion? This so-called war that you speak so ineloquently about?"

"I was brought here against my will, just as you were blinded without explanation. Doesn't that anger you?"

Arteriel did not answer, but Ruarhi could see the fire in him, held in check. Surely it must break soon. Arteriel turned to the skies, listening. Then he swung back to face Ruarhi.

"I'll come. Tell the Emeschi that I want two things. Sanctuary, and an answer. Otherwise I will destroy the entire settlement."

Ruarhi had no doubt that he would do it. "I will go and tell them."

"I will follow you."

Ruarhi was relieved to clamber down over the curved roof, dropping onto the walkway below. He watched as the blind Angel carefully lowered himself, holding the brand away from the crude bridge. Arteriel listened to its creaking as it swayed, then he motioned Ruarhi along it.

Ruarhi began the precarious trip back, the construction rocking in the winds as they rose. He could make out the shadow figures of Sommoi, Inkulke, and the others by the buildings. He glanced back. Arteriel was walking across the divide, but he showed no sign of stumbling, his balance perfect. The wind whipped at the torch, smoke pluming from it.

Sommoi was waiting, sword in hand. "What does he say?" he called, his face grimacing with uncertainty.

"The Angel Guards will be here soon. He seeks sanctuary."

Inkulke was nodding furiously. "Of course! He shall have it."

"And an explanation. If not, he's going to destroy High Crofels."

"We'll give him what he asks," said Sommoi.

They waited as Arteriel crossed the span and stood several yards from them, blind eyes turned on them. It still seemed remarkable that he could not use them. He held aloft his torch.

"Has the External told you what I expect from you?" he shouted above the wind.

"In exchange," said Sommoi, "will you help us?"

"In your ridiculous rebellion? What do you expect me to do?"

"You will have a part to play," said Inkulke.

Arteriel emitted a sound that could have been a laugh. "I have already outlawed myself. I have commissioned my own death."

"We will provide you with sanctuary," insisted Inkulke.

"From the Angel Guard? Again you delude yourselves."

Ruarhi could not contain his amazement at the blind warrior's utter fearlessness. It was not simply that the Angel Guard no longer cared about his life, it was his sheer contempt for beings he considered beneath him. They offered no threat to him, even though he was blind.

Arteriel indicated the doorway. "Let us go within. I will put out this torch. I realise how dangerous fire is to your settlement. But understand me well, I can ignite it again very easily." He snuffed out the torch as if by magic, passing a clawed glove over it as a shaman might have. From his belt he took two short knives. He flicked one blade against the other and a tiny shower of sparks flared. Inkulke drew in his breath in evident dread.

"The merest hint of treachery, and High Crofels burns," said Arteriel.

Inkulke's face looked pained. His eyes never left the knives, as though nothing could be more terrifying to him. Ruarhi knew how much the blind Angel was testing him. If the Emeschi could overcome his terror of fire enough to allow the Angel Guard in, he must be desperate for his cooperation.

"So be it," murmured Inkulke, but Arteriel heard him. The Emeschi and Sommoi led the way back into the buildings, and Ruarhi followed them. A few steps behind him, the blind Angel crossed the threshold, and Ruarhi realised that the winged warrior was as uneasy in buildings as Ruarhi was in caves or underground. They shared a love of high places, though Ruarhi knew they could have nothing else in common after his ordeal on the tower.

The procession was a strange, almost ethereal, one. It moved in single-file silence downwards, winding and twisting through the convoluted weave of the building, which might have been deserted. The word must have gone on ahead, news of the potential fire spreading. The inhabitants kept away: no one intended to be responsible for provoking the blind Angel. If he began a fire, it would turn into an instant conflagration.

Ruarhi was relieved when Inkulke finally found a chamber that suited him and led the party into it. It was neither small nor large, though it had a domed ceiling some twenty feet high at its apex. Arteriel stood away from the walls. There was light, and in its glow, Arteriel's twin knives gleamed menacingly.

Arteriel stood very still, the brand no less alarming than the knives.

"Is there anything you need?" said Inkulke.

"Describe this room," said Arteriel.

Inkulke did so.

"You consider it safe from the Angel Guards?"

"We will lead your enemies away from High Crofels."

"They may not wish to enter," said Arteriel. "Like me, they are creatures of the air. But not only Angel Guards seek me. They may have others with them."

"Elevate Zaer Phesmes himself protects High Crofels," said Inkulke.

"You serve him, so this External tells me."

"Like us, Elevate Zaer is part of the rebellion."

"Who is behind it? Lightbender Subran?"

Inkulke looked at Ruarhi, as if to admonish him for not furnishing the blind Angel with enough information. "We are opposed to all Lightbenders. Elevate Zaer does not support their regime. It must end."

Arteriel's features drew themselves into a semblance of a smile, as though he were listening to the defiance of children. "Really?"

Sommoi shook his head silently at Inkulke. "We are minor players. But the rebellion should not be taken lightly."

"So you intend to bring the Lightbenders down?" said Arteriel. "Who is behind this ambitious rebellion?"

"The one who blinded you," said Inkulke.

Arteriel nodded very slowly as if, at last, he would hear something of genuine interest. "The External said that it was the first move. It was deliberate?"

"It was. A sign to us. Something to show us that such powers do exist. Powers greater than those of the Lightbenders."

"Who blinded me?" said the Angel softly, though Ruarhi had never before heard such subdued venom in a voice.

"There is a renegade among the powers of Absolute Light," said Sommoi, reading Inkulke's mounting fear. "We could not hope to identify such a being. But he has communicated with Zaer Phesmes. It is he who seeks to bring great changes to our world."

Arteriel turned his attention on him as if he might strike him for his apparent insolence. But the Angel kept perfectly still, weighing the issues. "Absolute Light blinded me? Why?"

"We were told it would happen, as a sign of the rebel power. And now we understand there were other reasons," said Inkulke.

"Which were?"

"To win you to our cause," cut in Sommoi.

"By *blinding* me!" Arteriel almost snarled. "This god thought to woo me by crippling me?"

"You are here. How else could he have brought you to us, to listen? You could never have been persuaded to come had you been as you were. No Angel Guard would deign to speak to us. We are fodda." Sommoi barely held his own anger in check. Ruarhi was staggered by his audacity.

Arteriel considered the heated words. "So you prepare—what? An army? Led by a crippled Angel Guard?"

"You are blind, but not incapacitated," said Sommoi. "You have already put terror into the hearts of the servants of those we would bring down."

"One Angel Guard?" snorted Arteriel.

There was a sudden commotion outside, and moments later another of the Emeschi entered. Arteriel had positioned himself carefully, allowing for any attack to his rear: now he swung round easily, the twin knives ready to be turned into weapons if need be.

The newcomer glanced nervously at the Angel as he addressed Inkulke. "The settlement is surrounded. Angel Guards have come. There must be several chapters of them."

Arteriel was motionless. The news did not seem to surprise him. "And you will protect me?" he said sardonically.

"You knew they would come," said Sommoi.

"They will know I am here."

The Emeschi who had entered nodded. "They assume so. They are demanding you be sent to them."

"What Persuasion are they?" said Arteriel.

"There are Guards of All Persuasions."

This took Arteriel by surprise. He frowned. "Blood Reds, Bone Whites, and Flensers. *Together?*"

"What are we to tell them?" asked the Emeschi, shivering with dread. "They say they will enter and search if we do not give up the blind Angel."

"How well can you hide me?" said Arteriel to Inkulke.

"Well enough. But who commands the Angel Guards outside?"

"Each flight is under the direct command of its Praetor."

"Indeed? Then they have given me a unique priority," smiled Arteriel. "I should be flattered."

"If we hid you," said Sommoi, "and they did not find you—"

"They'll destroy High Crofels as I would have."

"But if not?"

"They will. They are Angel Guards. They meet defiance with bitter reprisal. You should know that."

"They want you alive," Inkulke insisted. "How can we prove that to you?"

"They have a commission," said the Emeschi who had brought the news.

"They need no commission! I killed a Bone White. Their Praetor has obviously appealed to all Angel Guards to rally to the avenging of Estragel's death."

"But they have a signed commission," repeated the Emeschi. "I have seen the papers. It is true, they want you alive."

"Who signed this commission?" said Arteriel.

"Elevate Zaer Phesmes."

"He has commissioned *all* three Persuasions?"

"Can you imagine the price?" said Sommoi.

"You understand such things?" replied Arteriel.

"I was once a Provider," said Sommoi. "I know precisely how much such a commission would cost. It would be beyond even an Elevate to commission all three Persuasions. Besides, the Lightbenders would consider such an action an affront to their powers. No single Elevate is permitted control of the entire Angel Guard. The Lightbenders would consider such power dangerous."

"Does Elevate Zaer Phesmes, then, have access to unique bargaining skills?" asked Arteriel.

"The commission is in his name," said Sommoi. "But it is funded by another."

Arteriel considered this in silence. Ruarhi could see that it had impressed him. It was the first time in all these discussions that the blind Angel had been even modestly convinced by any of the arguments.

"Your invisible ally," he said.

"He is not without power, as we told you," said Sommoi.

"Bring this commission to me," said Arteriel suddenly. "I will test its veracity."

"If you are convinced?" said Inkulke.

"If it is genuine, I will listen to their demands. Presumably they are to deliver me to Elevate Zaer Phesmes?"

"You will be safe with him."

"And if I go to him?"

"He will instruct you personally."

Arteriel frowned. Clearly he had serious reservations about the affair. But Ruarhi guessed there were few choices left to him.

"Fetch the commission," Arteriel said at length.

* * *

Ruarhi found the patience of these people extraordinary. For all their fears, the uncertainties that ruled their lives, they were able to stand in silence for long periods, to him almost unendurable, waiting. They waited now, all of them, motionless. Ruarhi wanted to scream at them, conscious that he alone among them fidgeted. The blind Angel was like a statue. By far the most terrifying of them, a warrior with powers beyond anything Ruarhi had previously seen, he was yet able to control his emotions to such a degree that he became almost a machine, switched off, dead. Yet there was never any doubt that he was in control of the situation, absolute master of it.

The Emeschi eventually returned. He had brought a roll of parchments. He looked askance at Inkulke, who nodded. The parchments were offered to Arteriel. He took them in his clawed gloves. Slowly he removed one glove and began to feel around the parchments with his pale hand. He found the seal on each scroll, nodding as he pressed his fingers to it. The seals were one thing, but Ruarhi wondered how he could possibly expect to read the scrolls. He soon had his answer.

"These will have to be read for me," said Arteriel.

"Of course," said Inkulke, taking a step forward.

"Bring the girl."

The words fell like stones into a still pond. Ruarhi knew instinctively whom the Angel meant.

"The girl?" echoed Inkulke.

"The one who was with you on the road," said Arteriel to Sommoi.

Sommoi looked at Ruarhi as if trying to prevent him from reacting, as if to say, I have no choice.

Inkulke spoke softly to the other Emeschi, who left at once. Again there was a silent pause. Ruarhi was very still, though his heart and mind raced. *Should I kill him? Risk my life for her?*

When Ukar-Tiri entered the room, ushered in by the Emeschi, her terror was evident. She looked at Ruarhi and he felt a sudden stab of guilt. If he harms her—Ukar-Tiri drew back from Arteriel, but the Emeschi blocked her retreat. Arteriel turned, sensing her arrival.

"Stand before me," he told her.

Ruarhi's hand fell to his sword haft, but he nodded in an attempt to reassure Ukar-Tiri. Slowly she went to the Angel.

"You are safe as long as you tell me the truth," he said to her.

She watched his blind eyes for betrayal of his thoughts, but they gave her no clues. He handed her the parchments. "What do they say?"

She looked only once at Inkulke and Sommoi, who both nodded, then she took the parchments.

Arteriel could smell her. He knew, as he had known before, that she was not a creature born under Skydown. Bred elsewhere, she had a sense of the alien about her. Perhaps she was beautiful. Unexpectedly, he reached out with his ungloved hand and touched her hair with his pale fingers.

She jerked, but immediately went very still. Ruarhi's hand tightened around his sword haft.

"You are an External," said Arteriel.

She nodded, but it was enough. He felt the air stir, knew her answer.

He had not yet been matched, his mate not yet chosen for him by the complex Angel Guard rituals, though he was ready for the ceremony and all that followed it. His exile had lost him that privilege. Should he, then, take this exceptional child? Even if it was to be for a short time, before his enemies closed in? He could feel her terror: she wore it like a mantle. It both pleased and displeased him. But it would force the truth from her. She would not read falsely. It would be cruel to take her. He was a Blood Red Angel: what was cruelty to him? This was fodda. *Already I have let one live.*

Angry with himself, he withdrew his hand, resheathed it in its claw. "Read."

Trembling, she began, her voice very low, but then lifting as she continued. There was an amount of verbosity in the documents, but she read it accurately, her command of the language excellent, far better than the youth's had been. She paused, sensing Arteriel's attention.

"You are surprisingly lucid," he commented.

"I was the mate of a village Drone," she said, as if it

would dispel any displeasure he might have felt. "I had to learn many things."

It explains your self-loathing, he thought. "Read on." This was not the time to be contemplating pity.

She continued. "That the former Blood Red Angel, Arteriel, be brought before me, unharmed—"

"You are sure those are the words?" he challenged her.

"Yes," she murmured, scanning over the lines carefully, afraid that she had made a mistake.

"Go on."

"For this service I, Elevate Zaer Phesmes, envoy to the Lightbender Subran of the House of Des Aubach, will provide to the commissioned parties the following." Ukar-Tiri paused, aware that the others were watching her intently, possibly even more intrigued than Arteriel. Ruarhi had been following the words with difficulty, but the implications of what she was about to say were not lost on him.

"Through the manipulation of the phenomenon known under Skydown as the Overlap, I will open a way for all those chapters, of whatever Persuasion, who wish to remove from the world under Skydown to an alternative, benign world."

Sommoi caught his breath. Arteriel's head turned at the sound, recognising it at once.

He knows it was no act! Ruarhi realised, astounded at the warrior's perception.

"A unique commission, I think," said Sommoi.

Arteriel said nothing. He knew that Ukar-Tiri had finished. She stood in silence, hardly moving, not understanding what the Angel wanted next.

"Your life is precious, Arteriel," said Inkulke. "Those who seek to injure you will be severely dealt with."

"Will you go with the Angel Guard?" said Sommoi.

Arteriel considered it in silence, his body very still. At last he spoke again. "Each Praetor was promised this. It cannot be a lie. If Elevate Zaer Phesmes could not do as he promises, the Angel Guard would be at liberty to seek him out in his palace and destroy him. No Lightbender could forbid it."

"What he promises," said Inkulke, "he can provide."

Arteriel felt their anxiety, their desire to win him over. Could it be possible? That Zaer had found a way to control the Overlap? And set the Angel Guards free? It would spite Subran, Kaizu, all of the Lightbenders. But if Zaer was truly a rebel, he would do this! *Freedom for the Angel Guard, in exchange for my services. One Angel Guard for so many. Why?*

"Let us ascend," he said at length.

This time Sommoi, Inkulke, and Ruarhi were the only ones to accompany Arteriel up to the towers above High Crofels. They climbed in silence, but fear clung to the Emeschi.

A single Angel Guard waited on the far tower, though the darkness held the promise of many more. Ruarhi watched, baffled, as Arteriel seemed to scent him. Without another word, the blind warrior crossed the narrow walkway to join the waiting Angel. Arteriel handed over the scrolls. There came a beating of wings, and then only darkness and silence.

After another long silence, Ruarhi felt something stir beside him. It was Inkulke. "You seem bemused," said the Emeschi.

"He seemed to accept his fate so easily in the end. I thought he'd run."

"They knew he was here. He understood we had no choice but to tell them. They would have captured him, unless he took his life. Which was what he had planned, of course. Your death, then his."

"The commission changed his decision?"

"He knew the girl could not lie to him. She read what was written. He recognised the seals and knew they were genuine. He has to return. It will put him closer to the one who blinded him. One thing still drives Arteriel. He is an Angel Guard. They have their honour to think of."

"Will he serve the rebellion?"

"As long as it suits his cause."

"Which is what?"

"Revenge. Nothing more. He would penetrate Skydown itself if he thought it would give him the opportunity to avenge himself."

Far beyond them, in the perpetual night, the blind warrior was not thinking of revenge. He thought of a path, the flight of warriors along it, the world beyond, the light, the clean light.

FIVE

THE ELEVATES

Beauty is many things. Like evil, it is relative. It is a form of power, and like all power, it can be wielded in many ways.

The world under Skydown is without beauty. Light is almost totally forbidden: it is for the gods. And what could be more beautiful than light? Our warped evolution shapes us to a dull conformity, a uniform purpose. Fodda. The crawling masses, groping up towards Absolute Light, the ultimate beauty, perfection. We have been created without beauty: we are deliberately grotesque. It fuels our need to aspire.

Thus a desire for beauty drives us all. We would invoke beauty at every opportunity, if permitted. We would, for example, give ourselves to love, for love is a form of beauty that the gods have driven deep down into the darkest parts of us, perhaps in recognition of its power. The gods see love as disruptive: it deflects the mind of the slave away from his master.

But the gods have never been able to exorcise love from us, try as they have done.

Love, like beauty, has power. Power means fear. We are afraid of power, of giving ourselves in love, of being controlled. The gods know it, thrive on it.

I have tasted love. I have created beauty and I have cherished it. Those who love are the true rebels.

ZAER PHESMES—*The Book of Renunciation*

33

Ruarhi watched the never-ending reeds, part of his mind shrieking silently at the monotony. Was the whole world covered with the beds? For the equivalent of days, the party had moved on through them, the reeds weaving and dancing in the winds that sprang up suddenly, promising a storm only to disappear, the only changing factor in the environment. Overhead, the twilight sky pressed down, oppressive.

It was a small company. The Emeschi themselves had not come out of High Crofels. Instead it was Sommoi who led the party. There were a dozen silent warriors: they seemed to Ruarhi no more than larger versions of the foddamen, muscled, armed with clublike weapons that he thought would have limited use in a fight. They spoke only in low grunts, and rarely to him, though they bore him no ill will.

To his surprise, Ukar-Tiri had come. He did not know whether this annoyed him or pleased him, though he had been greatly relieved when Arteriel had taken his pale hand from her hair and showed no further interest in her. She seemed both desirable and unattainable, something to tempt him, then mock him. He refused to be tormented by her presence, but could not ignore it. Sommoi told him she was here because she was Ruarhi's responsibility. She was angry, and would not speak, turned away from him, always keeping to the rear of the party as it trudged through the sea of reeds. Ruarhi could not understand but he had made up his mind to speak to her: she was the only hint of sanity in this realm. But each time he prepared to go back to her side, something prevented him—pride, perhaps. He brooded sullenly, waiting for the ghosts of his dead companions to leer at him from the reeds, as he knew they would.

The trek seemed interminable, the drudgery of it chafing at the spirits. How easy, Ruarhi thought, to give in to this greyness, to accept the soulless life of fodda. But at last the party came to a break in the reeds that opened out on to a narrow lake, its far shore clogged with yet more reeds; at least the expanse of dull brown water was a welcome change.

Sommoi joined Ruarhi. "The Providers utilise this stretch of the marshes for loading."

"Loading?"

"A craft will come. The Emeschi have made arrangements with its Collector, Ubanik. We go to Thousandreach."

To Ruarhi's surprise, Ukar-Tiri had pushed forward. "Under whose protection?" she snapped. The warriors looked at

her sleepily, though none of them made a move to thrust her
back.

Sommoi spoke patiently. "The Collector Ubanik strikes
many bargains with the Emeschi. This segment contains vast
tracts of unknown land, and thus yields up many unexpected
things. The Collector is something of a maverick and enjoys
a reputation among Providers for gathering the bizarre. He
relies on the Emeschi to help him sustain his reputation. We
will be under his protection. He will deliver us safely to the
servants of Zaer Phesmes, though our journey will be uncomfortable."

There were, as usual, many questions that Ruarhi would
have asked, but Sommoi deflected them, urging patience. Exasperated, Ruarhi turned to the girl as Sommoi moved away
to supervise the warriors.

"You know anything about this Collector?"

She shook her head. "Almost nothing. As a Provider, he
delivers fodda to Thousandreach. I suspect we will be shipped
as fodda. As such, we won't bring suspicion on ourselves.
You had better hide your sword," she added, with more than
a hint of scorn.

He gritted his teeth on a retort. Did she see herself as
betrayed? He tugged his cloak more tightly about him, again
watching the reeds.

They broke the monotony of the wait by eating. Hunger
had forced Ruarhi to take the food given to him, even though
he knew what it was. If it was affecting him, he was unaware
of any change to his system. He felt healthy enough. But he
was too jaded to fight against eating.

Eventually he caught sight of something breaking through
the reeds on the far shore. Dark and huge, it swung out onto
the lake, an enormous black craft. It was featureless, its bow
rounded, its sides curved. There were no sails, just a long
humpbacked ridge running down the centre of its deck. There
were no figures, no crew. Like an immense, dead fish, it
drifted over the water, barely touching the surface. Ruarhi
watched in astonishment as a section of its keel dropped
down, seemingly of its own volition. Pale light spilled out,
blotching the murk. It was as if the craft bled to death.

As Ruarhi turned, looking for Sommoi and some indication of what was expected, he realised that the reeds behind him and along this shore of the lake which, moments ago, had been silent, were now teeming with life. Abruptly the movement began, a surging exodus that threatened to engulf Sommoi's party. Scores of beings lumbered through the reeds and shallows of the lake to the craft, making for the ramp that had dropped for them. They trudged up it to the waiting maw of the craft.

"What are they?" said Ruarhi aloud.

Ukar-Tiri pressed herself close to his arm. "Fodda. Dwellers in the reeds, from all parts of the marshlands. See, there are hunters among them." It was true, for Ruarhi could make out a number of armoured warriors, herding the lines of creatures, using long poles to goad them forward, into the water. The exodus from the shore was the more eerie as it was conducted mostly in silence. Like cattle, the fodda plodded to an unknown destiny. The creatures themselves were bizarre; to Ruarhi, unnerving. Some were human in shape, smaller versions of warriors from his own world, though they looked hunched and dejected, their faces grey, eyes dull. Others crawled on arms that were obscenely huge, dragging lower quarters that were mercifully hidden by the water. Some hopped, uncomfortable in the water, falling but pulled up by the watchful hunters: still more flapped inadequate wings, or flopped, part fish. There were a number of foddamen, or beings like them, some of which herded other creatures that were either quadrupeds or amphibians, half-finished creatures that belonged to the darkness. All moved in silence, as if they had been drugged, or beaten into submission, like an army humbled by a terrible and final defeat.

To his right, Ruarhi saw other creatures break from the reeds. These were much larger, like overweight oxen, though they did not resemble oxen in any other way. Their heads were eyeless, mouths a drooling gap, their shoulders vast. Several had been harnessed by foddamen, who were driving them towards the huge craft. On the backs of the beasts of burden were tied a number of thick lengths of pipe, and as the creatures waded out to the ramp, Ruarhi saw that these pipes extended back into the heart of the reeds. The proces-

sion halted as the beasts dragged the ends of the pipes up
into the hold. Hunters watched until the operation was done.

The loading continued, and Ruarhi saw the pipes twist with
movement as whatever flowed through them was pumped into
the craft. He was reminded of the foddafarm and felt a shudder of revulsion: it was as if the land itself was being sucked
dry of its vital fluids. Like a feasting maggot, the immense
craft was gorging itself.

Ruarhi made to draw back, Ukar-Tiri clinging to him now
as she always did in times of fear. He put an arm around her,
drawing her close under his cloak. Her flesh was warm, vital.
For a moment they were like children, aware of their total
alienness in this world. He felt her arm encircle his waist, an
affirmation of her need. But it was a false situation, he told
himself. Fear created her need. It was not real. But he was
distracted by the reappearance of Sommoi.

"It will be dark inside the Collector's craft. Keep close to
me. We are protected."

There was no time to respond. Sommoi was already going
to the water's edge and the ramp. He waded in, beckoning
Ruarhi and the girl to follow. They had little choice. Loosening their hold on each other, they followed.

The water of the lake was unexpectedly warm, which made
its caress all the more repulsive. It was like wading through
congealed blood. Around them the bodies pressed, though
harmlessly. Sommoi's warriors closed in, protecting their
charges. The ramp itself was soft, fleshy, and Ruarhi again
felt himself shuddering. His fingers closed over Ukar-Tiri's
hand: it seemed the only link with humanity he had in that
hellish place.

As they climbed up to the black opening, they could feel
the compression of flesh within, the stink of it. Ruarhi's mind
urged him to vent a roar of outrage, but the flow of the creatures could not be denied. Darkness enveloped him, and
Ukar-Tiri's grip tightened so that he thought she would crush
his fingers.

Within, they went upward, shuffling now, edging forward,
wanting to release their fears in a cry. Sommoi suddenly
pressed close to Ruarhi. "Endure it, Ruarhi. It is harmless.
You are in no danger."

"It is vile, worse than any slaughter yard—"

"We are hidden from enemies. When we enter Thousand-reach, we will be secreted away. Then we can begin."

Ruarhi felt the darkness closing over him like a weight of water. He was able to sit on a compressed mat of reeds, Ukar-Tiri close beside him, Sommoi on his other side. "Will you tell me then what it is you expect of me?"

"I will. I know you do not trust me."

Ruarhi snorted. All around him he could feel the panting of strange beings, as though their hearts beat uniformly in uncertainty. It was not blind terror that bound them, but blind obedience. Even so, something in their unnatural bodies must have rebelled against their circumstances.

"Surely they feel nothing," said Sommoi, as if he had pulled Ruarhi's thoughts from the air. "They are fodda."

"You cannot believe that."

"I admire your anger. It is vital to your strength, vital to our cause. It is well-founded. So few creatures under Sky-down question the laws of this world. The Emeschi are almost unique. You feel sorrow for these creatures around us, or if not, at least you are moved by their plight. It is another component of your strength. No creature under Skydown compares to the men of your world in this strength. Hence you are invaluable, though you do not see it. You are a weapon, Ruarhi. Like Arteriel."

"And you?"

"I am a weapon of a different kind. I do not have the terrible killing hate of Arteriel to fuel me, nor his speed, his powers. Nor do I have your strength, your adaptability. But I share your disgust, and I am committed to ending this vileness."

In the pressing darkness, Ruarhi could see nothing, not even his hand before his eyes, but he could sense for the first time an element of humanity in Sommoi, who had hitherto never spoken so openly. Perhaps it had taken the utter dark to enable him.

"The Lightbenders are literally devouring this world, and all that's in it. They will have it all if they are not stopped. They will become the only life, and they are changing, preparing for their next phase of existence. Godhood, we call it, in our ignorance. Absolute Light. Once the Lightbenders transform, there will be nothing left under Skydown.''

"What lies beyond Skydown?"

"Too few of us have asked that question. But Zaer Phesmes asks. Prompted by whatever it is that blinded Arteriel. We will know, Ruarhi. We will confront it. But not with an army, not with a tide of angry warriors, rushing headlong to doom. We travel in darkness. We use the shadows they have put upon us. You, me, Arteriel. A few others. Together we are a weapon, tipped with the poison that will seek out these blasphemies.''

Ruarhi felt Ukar-Tiri's flesh beside him quiver. "What of me?" she whispered, but Sommoi had either not heard or had moved away to consolidate some other aspect of his strange purpose.

"I am not strong," said the girl. "Why should I be part of this crusade?''

"I think I understand why," Ruarhi told her. "But it would only anger you if I tried to explain." He imagined her face, the indignant look.

"To please you?" she said.

He was silent for a moment. The mass of bodies around them might have been far away, in another hold. "Yes," he said at last. "Sommoi can sense emotions. He told me when we met that he had certain powers. I don't think he reads thoughts, but he is strangely alert to feelings.''

"And what are yours?" she said, barely keeping the edge from her voice.

"I don't know."

"Desire?"

The darkness made it easier for him to be honest. "Yes."

"Love?"

The bluntness of the question surprised him. "I don't know.''

"What is more important to you, Sommoi's cause, or your own?''

"It may be that they are the same. It's true that I'm appalled by all this. I'd gladly strike at those responsible.''

"If I told you I would give myself to you, even now, here,

provided you took me away from these creatures and their insane rebellion, would you do it? For me?''

"You would sell yourself for freedom?"

This time she was taken aback by his words and he sensed her unspoken anger.

He had not meant to retort so sharply. "I could ask for your freedom," he said. "Sommoi would not deny the request. Do you want me to?''

She wouldn't answer; a damning silence closed in. And again he cursed himself. He could hear Dromator's crude laugh, teasing him. Such fuss over a simple wench!

34

Arteriel was accompanied by two Angels, one a Blood Red, the other a Bone White. He knew neither of them, but had been told their rank. They had been with him for most of the flight back from the outer segments. Now they marched in silence down a corridor of the citadel that smelled empty and disused. Arteriel could smell also a hint of fear on the two warriors, faint but unmistakable. His reputation had gone before him. But they should not have concerned themselves: warriors of their stature should have been able to overpower him if they had needed to. *Already I am a legend.*

Their step was purposeful: though they were not in one of the Eyries but in Thousandreach itself, they had an appointed rendezvous. Arteriel had quickly learned to interpret such things. He could read much in a man's tread, in the drawing of his breath. These two were growing more uneasy, but it was not necessarily only his presence, he realised, that made them so.

As with all visits to Thousandreach, this one involved an endless walk along corridors and up and down stairways, some narrow, a few broad. They met no one. This affair, Arteriel was not surprised to note, was being conducted in absolute secrecy. That this was achieved at all was testament to the immense power that must have been wielded by the Elevate who had commissioned the combined flight of the Angels. Such an Elevate would be an extremely dangerous adversary.

The Angels halted, and Arteriel heard one of them knock softly on a thick door. It creaked open, emitting a waft of unpleasant air. Perhaps the Angels did not notice. Arteriel sensed that he was being observed. Approval must have been given: he was gently urged into the chamber beyond the door.

It was warmer than the corridor, the air thick, cloying. Carpets muffled sound. Food had been eaten here. But the room did not feel sumptuous. It was the chamber of an underling.

"You may leave us," said a soft voice, though one, Arteriel could tell, that was used to commanding. The Angels were gone within moments, the door closed. A silent presence bolted it.

"Arteriel, former Blood Red Angel?"

Arteriel inclined his head slowly.

"Let me introduce myself. I am a Skryer. My name is Annaxion. I doubt that you have heard of me."

Arteriel did not answer, waiting patiently. He heard the soft tread of someone leaving through another door. He sensed no one else but the Skryer. The conversation was to be private.

"You will, however, know of Provider Hummal Goresch."

"He serves Elevate Zaer Phesmes," nodded Arteriel.

"You have called him your enemy, I believe?"

Arteriel snorted. "When I left Thousandreach and the Eyries, I left many enemies behind me. Now I find myself outlawed by some, wooed by others."

"Goresch is a traitor. He betrays Elevate Zaer Phesmes. Which is why you have not been delivered to him. I, too, have betrayed my master. I served Elevate Yvane Sephir."

"Is Provider Goresch his toy now?"

"He is. The Da Sangraville claws reach deep down into

this realm. Goresch gave you over to me, thinking I would deliver you directly to Yvane.''

"Clearly you have other plans.''

"Yes. We are both in extreme danger. Yvane is desperate to take you and doubtless rip your secrets from you. He suspects Zaer is involved in a plot, and has assumed you have a key role. So we are to secrete ourselves well away from him and his spies. Until we are called by Zaer.''

Annaxion kept his distance from the Angel: Arteriel could sense the Skryer's uncertainty. It mirrored his own.

"You are my passport, Arteriel. Zaer Phesmes needs proof of my loyalty. I give your safety over to him. You, too, must trust me.''

Arteriel nodded. "Yvane is powerful. Yet you desert him for this strange rebellion. Am I unreasonable to question your faith in such a reckless cause?''

"Of course not. But you have to believe me. There are places prepared for us. They are as safe as any in Thousand-reach. Later, we begin Zaer's work. You'll meet others who share the cause. And Sommoi will come here. His journey will take longer, and will be even more devious. We have to take such pains. Yvane is exceptionally dangerous, as you say.''

"Do I meet Elevate Zaer?''

"I can't say. But he has thought long and deep on the rebellion. He is no fool. He does not move without considering every consequence.''

Again Arteriel nodded. "And I will not act until I am satisfied of his intentions.''

"Of course. Will you wait here until I return? I have business to finish before we can go to the sanctuary prepared for us.''

Arteriel nodded. He had no other choice. It could be a trap, of course, but the commission at least had been genuine. He would have to trust in it. In this rebellion there would be many deceivers. Annaxion might well be another.

Provider Hummal Goresch wiped his mouth carelessly on his sleeve. His face was a sheen of perspiration, his eyes ringed, his hair matted. He slumped in his seat, making only a token attempt to rise as the Skryer entered the chamber.

Annaxion took all this in at a glance, noticing also the several armed guards stationed about the rim of the chamber. They were not as inconspicuous as they would like to have thought. It was evident that Goresch was a creature dancing to the tune of acute fears. His physical decline was advancing rapidly. Surely he knew what was happening to him?

"Well?" Goresch blurted. A flask of wine stood near him. There were puddles on the table.

"It is done," said Annaxion in a confidential whisper. "Our guest is safely housed. The commission has been executed just as expected. Zaer Phesmes will expect to be able to take delivery of his charge very soon."

Goresch belched carelessly. "Pity he'll be disappointed. Where is the Angel?"

"Leave it to me. I'll get him to Elevate Yvane at the appropriate time. It remains for you to speak to Provider Orvech. I'm sure he will want to convey word of your success to Elevate Yvane personally. He will wish to reward you." The lies slipped easily from Annaxion's tongue.

"And the hybrid?" Goresch could not keep the longing out of his voice. It was filled with the urgency of an addict.

Annaxion masked his disgust. "Of course. I will see to it. Soon the hybrid will be in your possession. Orvech has agreed."

Provider Sughai Orvech paced his chamber angrily. He could not believe the delays that were taking place. Could Goresch handle nothing without snarling it up? Ah, but at least he, Orvech, would soon have the pleasure of attending to the fool's execution. But perhaps it would be more entertaining to let him see how he had been betrayed, how his flesh was already degenerating. Yes, a slow death would be far more appropriate.

His thoughts were broken by the arrival of a courier. "Sire, Provider Hummal Goresch seeks an audience with you."

"Yes, yes," snapped Orvech testily, waving the courier away. Moments later Goresch appeared. His face was white, his body shivering as though with the cold, though this chamber was comfortable enough.

"So?" snarled Orvech. "Is the business properly concluded? The Angel Guards have brought the renegade to heel?"

"Indeed," said Goresch, allowing himself a smirk. But he did not feel at ease in the presence of this chilling rival. "The commission of my erstwhile master, Zaer Phesmes, has been executed, just as expected. Arteriel is here in Thousandreach."

"Does Zaer Phesmes know?"

"It is no matter if he does. I have had Arteriel hidden safely away. Word may have reached Elevate Zaer, but while he awaits delivery, Arteriel will be brought here. Your personal Skryer has taken charge of the matter. And has done so with supreme discretion, if I may say so."

Orvech had gone very still, his eyes narrowing. "My own Skryer? To whom do you refer?"

Goresch frowned. "Annaxion. He is one of Yvane's most able Skryers, is he not?"

"I have not seen Annaxion for some time. His business seems to have taken him to other parts of Thousandreach. I do not have absolute control of him. No Provider has that power over the Skryers. What has he to do with the affair of the renegade Angel?"

Goresch began to feel the cold creep of panic. "But is he not working for you?"

"On what matter?"

"On the matter of the blind Angel!" blurted Goresch. "He is discreet, profoundly so. Arteriel is in his charge. I would not risk delivering him to any other."

Orvech looked livid. "On whose authority did you deliver Arteriel to Annaxion? *Whose?*"

"The Skryer told me—"

"The Skryer, the Skryer? Whom do you serve?"

"Why, you know that. I serve you and Yvane. How have I angered you? I have delivered to you—"

"I have not seen the Skryer Annaxion for too long. Where is he now? Where did you last see him?"

Goresch thrust down his panic with difficulty. "In . . . my chambers. Not long since."

Orvech called for his couriers. Three of them came running to his side in moments. "Get word out to all my immediate staff. They are to locate the Skryer, Annaxion. I want him brought to me, *at once.*"

"What is wrong?" said Goresch, his voice dropping so low as to be almost lost. He watched as the couriers raced off to do Orvech's bidding.

"You are a fool!" snarled Orvech. "They have taken you in. Annaxion!"

"Surely you do not suspect him?"

"What did he tell you? That I had given him precise instructions? That you were to obey him, and him alone?"

"That I was to act through him, yes—"

Orvech sagged back suddenly onto his chair, hand going over his eyes. He shook his head. "As easy as it is for one to betray another, so the disease spreads."

"I cannot believe this of Annaxion!" blustered Goresch, though his voice held no conviction. "Why should he betray Yvane! The most powerful of all the Elevates!"

Orvech looked up at him, but much of the fury had drained out of him. "Powerful? Yes, Yvane is not lacking in power. But Elevate Zaer commissioned *all* the Angel Guard. Unprecedented. Do you know what it would have *cost? That* takes power."

"Enough, you think, to persuade someone like Annaxion to betray Yvane?"

Orvech nodded. The idiot could at last see it. "They won't find him. Nor will they find the renegade."

"But—"

"Oh, get out, you oaf! Get out of my sight!"

On returning to his own chambers, Goresch felt a deep cold settling within him, a certainty that he would hear from Orvech again soon. He would have to leave, and quickly. Throw himself on the mercy of Zaer Phesmes? How much did Zaer's spies know? Why, there was no reason for them to know at all! Stupid to panic. How could they know anything?

But reason forced its own answer. Since Annaxion was a traitor, Zaer Phesmes must know. Yet—how could Orvech have been so sure of Annaxion's defection?

As these and other blurred thoughts tumbled over in Goresch's mind, the door behind him opened. He did not see the figure at first. When he did turn, his mouth gaped as if he had been kicked.

It was the hybrid.

Softly it closed the door behind it. It wore nothing, its skin gleaming, oiled and sleek. It held out its hand, offering a thin roll of parchment.

A message? Dazedly, Goresch took it, fumbling it open while the hybrid watched him patiently, expressionlessly. The note was from Annaxion.

I promised you a reward for your service. The hybrid, as you know, will not disappoint you. Drink deep of your pleasures while you may.

The parchment fell from Goresch's fingers. Stumbling, he felt the hands of the hybrid on him, slowly removing his clothes. Its lips brushed his cheek, its breath fragrant. It was utterly irresistible.

But he felt only the calm before the storm. The hybrid closed its arms around him, tightening them like steel bands. It lowered its teeth, smiling as it began its final, terrible work.

35

There were times on the journey when Ruarhi thought he would lose his mind. Only very rarely was there any light; it seemed that the creatures that had been crammed into the vast hold of the craft preferred darkness, no matter how extreme. Sommoi was able to close himself off from it, spending endless periods in a kind of sleep. Ruarhi was amazed by his tolerance of the conditions, his patience. He himself could only partially block out the nightmare, though he knew if he succumbed to it, he would never recover his wits. Death would become desirable.

The craft moved on gently, no more than a hint of forward thrust to suggest that it moved at all. The motion became as monotonous as the darkness.

This combination of the darkness with its total fracture of time and the food he was provided began to create an almost hallucinatory effect on Ruarhi. He began to wonder if some of the conversations he had had were real or imagined. And the girl, had he made love to her, or was that, too, a dream, a feverish attempt by his mind to cling to reason, familiar desires? She did not speak of it, and he would not ask.

He was able to exercise a little: Sommoi insisted on it. Ruarhi paced along a corridor of bodies to a small chamber that served as a toilet. It was barely lit, but scrupulously clean, as though only used by a few. The press of bodies in the hold appeared to have other arrangements.

After one particularly deep sleep, Ruarhi was woken by Sommoi. He knew at once that the craft had stopped moving: the gentle pulse of its forward motion had ceased. Already the hold was waking to the fact, ripples of anticipation spreading through the packed creatures.

Light filtered inward. A door had been opened, possibly the great ramp. Ruarhi stood and stretched: even the dim twilight of the outer world would be a vast improvement on the misery of this hold. He and Ukar-Tiri and Sommoi allowed themselves to be pushed along by the exodus as the craft began to disgorge its occupants. Ruarhi could not see clearly beyond the huge doorway. There were vague shapes there, possibly buildings.

"We will be met," said Sommoi. "Until we are safely hidden among allies, say nothing. Pretend we do not know each other."

Ukar-Tiri nodded. In the wan light she looked particularly pale and drawn, as though the journey had sucked out of her the last of her resistance. Ruarhi would have put an arm about her and given her words of comfort, but he felt only a dull ache of awareness himself, as though he lived now in some afterlife, some nether region of humanity. He touched his hidden sword haft lightly: it gave him little confidence. The MagMannoch hell, if it existed, could be no worse than this place.

Ruarhi was pushed by the press towards the ramp, Ukar-Tiri beside him, though her eyes were fixed ahead of her, almost as if she had been drugged. Sommoi must be behind them. On either side, the beings came into sharper focus as the light improved. It was artificial, Ruarhi saw, and not the seeping twilight of the heavens. Globes burned softly on what could have been a quayside beyond and Ruarhi could hear gruff voices. He took them to be overseers, calling out commands, though how anyone could organise such confusion was beyond him.

As he reached the ramp and shuffled down it, still hemmed in by the press, he could see over the tops of the heads of those before him what he assumed were the buildings of Thousandreach. But he was disappointed by the view. All he could see was an immense wall, the stones of which were cut from unimaginably huge blocks. He had seen nothing like this in his own world, and he felt his spirits sinking even lower. What creatures could possibly have cut these monstrous blocks, and then set them upon each other to make a wall that was fit to divide a world?

He craned his neck, looking to left and right, but the wall stretched as far as he could see, as it did upwards, too dizzy to contemplate. A god might have built it. Ruarhi felt himself choking on the thought. He had come here with Sommoi to defy the gods of this world. Was he mad?

At the bottom of the ramp, Ruarhi turned, looking for Sommoi and some hint of guidance. Sommoi was there, lightly resting one hand on Ukar-Tiri's waist and the other on Ruarhi's. He deflected them to the right of the mass of bodies, which parted easily enough. Ruarhi could still hear the gruff voices calling out instructions in a language he did not understand. But those coming down the ramp knew what was expected of them and divided accordingly.

Sommoi turned Ruarhi and Ukar-Tiri aside and they now found themselves moving against the current of bodies, but still there was no opposition. Looking into the empty faces, Ruarhi felt a cold chill of disgust: they were like the dead, like so many corpses that had fallen in battle only to be reanimated and marched to a bleak afterlife.

It was a long trudge, but at length they were free of the press and moving down a narrow quay. Ruarhi saw figures ahead, near an opening in the huge wall. It was an arched alleyway cut through the stone like the burrow of a worm, though the precision of the cutting was too exact to have been made by a living organism.

"Transmutes. We are expected," said Sommoi, glancing behind him once to see that they had not been missed.

At the mouth of the alley, two of the thickset Transmutes were waiting. Abnormally large, they carried long rods, the edges serrated, and they wore steel masks that Ruarhi assumed had been moulded to their faces: the expressions were bestial, though no doubt this had been done for effect. One of them gestured with the weapon it carried, motioning Sommoi and his companions into the alley.

Sommoi went first, followed by Ruarhi and Ukar-Tiri. The alley was long and poorly lit. Ruarhi shuddered. It looked like yet another descent, this time into an even more forbidding realm. But Sommoi did not seem put out by the place, as though he knew it. He walked on quickly.

Movement ahead of him pulled him up sharp, but it was yet another of the masked warriors, its bulk almost filling the alley. It gestured with a short weapon to the gap from which it had emerged. Sommoi turned to Ruarhi and nodded, as if he had been expecting such a diversion.

Ruarhi and Ukar-Tiri followed him up the rough steps that wound around inside the huge stonework of the wall. There was a chamber within, and Sommoi was first to it. Ruarhi and Ukar-Tiri held back for a moment: darkness awaited them, and with it an unpleasant stench. Ruarhi recognised it: he could not mistake the reek of blood. He would have stepped back, but the Transmutes were close behind him, their weapons suddenly menacing.

Sommoi went into the room, and Ruarhi and Ukar-Tiri were forced to join him. The beings behind them exuded menace. Ruarhi's unease grew: could these be the allies Sommoi had expected?

Light fizzed into being, a torch flaring in its cresset. Sommoi was the first to see the horror that the room contained. There was a single table, coated in something that leaked over its edges, dripping steadily on to the stone floor, where a thick pool had coagulated. Blood. In the centre of the table was a massive, misshapen head, several steel shafts driven into it.

Ukar-Tiri screamed, the sound reverberating in the narrow confines of the room. She flung herself against Ruarhi, who automatically put himself between her and the abominable thing on the table. Another warrior stood beside it, though he wore no armour, no mask. His own face was richly tattooed, his mouth drawn downwards in a false, fixed grin.

"You have an appointment with the Collector," he said with a painful smile. He gently touched the monstrous head. "He is here."

Sommoi was very still, eyes locked with those of the *goad*. He said nothing.

"And these are your wards," said the *goad*, lifting his hand and examining the blood, then rubbing his fingers together idly. "The External. And the girl. What is she?"

Ukar-Tiri sobbed as if she had been prodded. Ruarhi could feel his blade pressed between her and his own flesh. Very slowly he moved his free hand down from her shoulders towards its haft. He leaned toward her ear as if speaking words of comfort.

"Ease away from me a little," he said into her hair. "The sword."

"Have you nothing to say to the Collector?" said the *goad*, his smile widening.

Sommoi's expression did not alter. He neither moved nor spoke.

The *goad* leaned forward over the table and its grisly trophy. "Those who interfere in the business of the Elevate Yvane Sephir do not fare well. *Where is the blind Angel?*"

For a moment it seemed that Sommoi would not answer. But he drew in a breath gently, as though weighing his answer. "I don't understand you."

"The servants of Elevate Zaer Phesmes who were awaiting your coming have been dealt with." The *goad* smashed aside the head with the back of his hand. It thudded on the stone and came to rest up against the wall. Sommoi's eyes never left those of the *goad*. "You understand me? *Dealt with.*"

Ruarhi began to slide the sword from its sheath. Ukar-Tiri was trembling like an infant, but she shielded what he was doing.

"You know full well the degree of torment that we can visit upon you and your companions," said the *goad*. "There is nothing we cannot drag from your mind. I have Tormenters at my disposal. But the Tormenters are novices, their skills trivial, compared to the personal talents of Yvane himself. Spare yourselves his attention. I say again, where is the blind Angel?"

Ruarhi felt the thundering of his heart, as though its sound would betray him in this cramped chamber. His experience of battle was small, but he knew if he hesitated he would never act. It had to be now. He freed his weapon, bent his knees and swung the blade in an arc. The edge of steel bit into the flesh and bone of one of the Transmute's thighs. It let out a gasp of agony, stumbling, its own weapon tearing at air as it made an instinctive but abortive attempt to defend itself. As it staggered, blocking its companion's view of the room, Sommoi thrust the table forward, pinning the *goad* to the wall, temporarily hampering his attempt to drag out his own weapon.

Ruarhi followed up his advantage by using the point of his blade under the Transmute's guard. Again he felt muscle and bone parting. Ukar-Tiri cowered back, biting her hand to prevent another scream.

Sommoi swung round and wrenched the long weapon from the Transmute that Ruarhi had spitted. In one sweep, Sommoi brought it round and thrust its serrated edge into the neck of the trapped *goad*. Blood pumped immediately from the ragged wound and the *goad* crashed on to the table, clawing at it, trying to drag air into his ruptured windpipe. Sommoi ripped the weapon free and swung it about, preparing to defend himself from further attack. He saw Ruarhi jump back to avoid the toppling figure of the first Transmute, which the second had now heaved aside in its determination to get into the battle.

Sommoi locked weapons with this second Transmute and the two of them struggled furiously. Sommoi knew that his opponent was far stronger: his glance at Ruarhi said as much. Ruarhi acted at once, chopping down at the wrists of the Transmute brutally. Again blood pumped as the sword sheared through flesh. Ruarhi had no time to marvel at the exceptional power of the blade. The Transmute dropped to one knee, but before Ruarhi could drive his blade for the neck in a killing blow, Sommoi crashed the butt end of his weapon into the side of the creature's face. It was knocked sideways, almost into Ruarhi. As it fell, already unconscious, Ruarhi ran the sword into its vitals.

He heard Sommoi curse, and at once knew why. The last of the three Transmutes who had brought them here was lumbering back down the narrow steps. Ruarhi snatched up one of the long weapons and was out of the door before Sommoi could stop him. Ruarhi rushed downwards, almost stumbling, mind racing with the sudden surge of the kill. There was no time for coherent thought.

He rounded a gentle curve on the stair: the Transmute was in view, yards below, about to twist around another curve. Ruarhi drew back the weapon and flung it, spearlike, with as much strength as he could summon. He watched as the weapon tore through the air and took the Transmute in the small of the back, smashing it forward into the wall, spinning it round.

Ruarhi almost toppled over with the effort of the throw, but felt an arm steadying him. It was Sommoi.

"Careful. There may be others below. Have you killed it?"

Ruarhi could see the Transmute sagging against the stone, fingers desperately reaching back, trying to dislodge the weapon. But it was embedded, its serrated teeth fixed. The creature's life leaked out of it slowly.

Behind Sommoi, Ukar-Tiri had stirred, cautiously descending the stair. Her face was streaked with tears, though she had controlled her distress. Ruarhi allowed Sommoi to squeeze past him and lead the way back, but he gripped his blade, prepared to use it again if he had to. It was only now that he realised he was shaking, his body reacting to the mayhem, the release of grim killing power. For a moment he thought he would retch, but he breathed deeply, easing his nerves. Ukar-Tiri touched him gently, as though in sympathy. He shook his head, then went down.

The Transmute Ruarhi had speared was dead. They clambered awkwardly over it. Beyond the stair, in the alley, there was no immediate pursuit.

"We'll be hunted now," said Sommoi. "Yvane will spare no effort to find us. It will be difficult to know who can be trusted. It seems that even Zaer's agents are susceptible to bribes."

Ruarhi didn't answer. He followed as Sommoi led the way up the alleyway, into the darkness of Thousandreach and what could only be a promise of greater horrors.

36

Annaxion had no way of knowing whether or not Arteriel trusted him, but he was sure he did not. One could hardly blame the Angel for that: at least Arteriel was prepared to be led. Arteriel remained silent, typical of his breed, his blind eyes fixed ahead of him, though from time to time his head inclined itself slightly, this way and that, as though each sound, each breath of air, discharged its secrets to him.

He followed the Skryer now, footsteps surprisingly sure in the narrow confines of the passage. Annaxion took circuitous routes up through the many convolutions of this part of the city. Thousandreach's upper citadels were vast, endless, fusing together mazes of stonework, columns and pillars, colossal chambers, minute anterooms: the dust of centuries eddied throughout them, and there were corridors that time had claimed for its own, often unvisited for generations, or used only by individuals who had accidentally stumbled across them. Legends existed of charts that divulged the entire mysteries of the upper citadels, but in spite of the best efforts of the Skryers, no such charts had been unearthed. Those fragments of the immense puzzle that were found were jealously guarded by their keepers. Skryers had died refusing to give up what they had gleaned.

Certain sealed places were better left unopened. There was a central shaft to Thousandreach, a mile wide chasm that dropped down into the guts of the world, the Utterlost, where machines older than the Lightbenders churned and pumped, fueled and worked by the mutated Menials who spawned and died there in their thousands, lives brief as flies'. Tunnels and corridors threaded around the great shaft, and some of them had fallen into disrepair and now opened out on to the shaft. Annaxion had seen it, but had not lingered: the stench from below, the sounds, spoke of another world, a place more dreadful than anything beyond the city under Skydown. The shaft itself rose up through every level of Thousandreach to the halls of the Lightbenders, though they were shut off from it, shut off, that was, until one of the Lightbenders wished to draw up from the well whatever fuel he sought for his pleasures. Annaxion knew that Yvane went further: he had descended to those haunted deeps, wallowing in the misery there.

Annaxion could feel the proximity of the shaft now; the devious route he had chosen to take him to his destination passed not far from it, and though a good thickness of stone separated him and Arteriel from the shaft, something seeped through the stone like a miasma. Torment incarnate.

"The heart of chaos," Annaxion murmured.

Arteriel caught the words clearly. "I have heard of that place. It is spoken of in whispers, even among Angel Guard."

"Far down under the city, the transformation takes place. Life gives life."

"So we are taught."

Annaxion had paused. He lifted his fingers, reaching out. But he could not bring himself to touch the stone. How many centuries had his people been indoctrinated in their beliefs, their obedience to a system built on a foundation of pain? But it was an enforced obedience. The mass of humanity under Skydown were not disciples. And the Angels, the military killers, strict adherents to the laws, they did not deviate. Yet here was one, apparently a heretic.

"Why do you pause?" Arteriel said, his voice cold. Even in his blindness there was power. "Touch the stone, or does it repulse you?"

Annaxion instinctively drew back his hand. "You sensed me reach out?"

Arteriel nodded. "I heard the whisper of your sleeve. But answer me, why do you pause?"

"You rely on your senses. Can you feel the wall?"

"Yes. It is like a live thing. My own discomfort at being entombed is nothing to the agonies locked inside it."

"They anger you? Your kind do not question—"

"My kind? I have no kind. If you are testing me, spare your energy. *Your* kind, Skryer, have other interests, other goals. The suffering of this world is immaterial to you."

"You find it so hard to trust me—"

"I do not take trust lightly. A god struck me down."

Annaxion could not argue. "Life is not something to be abused. Not a force to be drained for the pleasure of gods, or those who would be gods."

"Fodda," said Arteriel, but there was no contempt in his voice. "You think of it differently now?"

"It is hard to change one's views, generations of thinking."

"Why have you changed? Why should I?"

"Desire for revenge has changed you. Fodda is still fodda. Is that what you think?"

The blind Angel did not react. "Perhaps. Fodda can only change when it recognises itself for what it has become."

"Evil is relative. The Lightbenders are sustained by fodda; therefore, the concept of fodda cannot be evil to them."

"And what sustains the Skryers?"

Annaxion was taken aback by the directness of the question. "I suppose it is a hunger for knowledge."

"For power? All things thrive on power."

"Yes. That is part of it. I am taking you to another Skryer

now. His name is Tetraven. He lives in isolation. Like many Skryers, he serves his own causes first. But he is too useful to the Lightbenders to be disposed of.''

"And what does he seek? Is he another despairing voice against tyrant gods?'' This time there was contempt in the Angel's reply.

"I'll let him tell you himself.''

Tetraven seemed uneasy as Annaxion brought Arteriel before him into the round chamber of his tower. Annaxion himself had uncomfortable memories of the place, the things that had been dragged out of him here.

They sat, the old Skryer on a couch, Annaxion in a chair, and Arteriel on a stone bench, his back stiff, his posture almost aggressive.

"Are we mad?'' Tetraven sighed. "Do we really talk of resistance to the powers controlling Thousandreach?''

Annaxion studied Arteriel, but the Angel might have been cut from the stone on which he sat. "I'm sure we are, Tetraven. Perhaps it is the best point at which to begin.''

It seemed to amuse Tetraven, his ancient face creasing as he smiled. But the smile quickly faded. He leaned forward. "I have lived through a thousand deceits and treacheries. Why do you think I shut myself off from it all? I have turned to my own devices. Thousandreach thrives on mystery and duplicity. You, Annaxion, I trust: I've visited your mind. I know what drives you. But you, Angel, I know nothing of you, only what I've been told. You may be the secret tool of Yvane, or any other of those monsters who call themselves Lightbenders. I don't care any more! But before I die, I'll gladly strike a last blow.''

Arteriel's expression did not change. Annaxion wondered if he thought the old Skryer deranged.

"How, precisely, are we to act?'' Arteriel asked.

Tetraven sat back. He seemed indifferent to the Angel's company, which once would have filled him with unease. "We appear to be components. Elevate Zaer is the one who will fit us all together, himself fed by another power.''

"Skryers,'' said Arteriel, "are reputed to be sensitive to certain things. The future, for example.''

"Divination?" said Tetraven. "Yes, there is that." He saw Annaxion's involuntary shudder.

"But I suspect," Arteriel went on, "that the real key to your involvement in this matter is a more tangible force."

"Go on," smiled Tetraven.

"The Overlap," said Arteriel. "If you do utilise divination, it is to seek it out, to predict its course. That is what drives the Skryers."

Tetraven clapped his hands. "Excellent! An Angel who thinks! You are quite right, of course. The Overlap. An enigma, totally unpredictable. But if we could harness it—"

"What is it?" said Arteriel.

"It has been described as many things. Some schools of thought insist that it is a living entity, an elemental force possessed of a mind, a free will. But very few Skryers subscribe to this now. Others see it as a raw energy, like a current between worlds, acted upon by the natural forces of those worlds in ways we cannot understand or harness. A popular belief. A few Skryers still hold to the belief that it is a tool, directed by gods we cannot identify, mutual to many worlds."

"But what do you believe?" said Arteriel.

"I know what caused it," said Tetraven, but there was no amusement in his tone now.

Arteriel sensed the tension in Annaxion. Whatever Tetraven was about to reveal, it would be fresh knowledge to him.

"War," said Tetraven simply. "Whether it was here or on some other plane, or realm, I don't know. As Annaxion knows, Skryers sweep back and forth in time. In many times. The Overlap is the result of war. If you want me to describe it, words would be a poor tool. I could open your minds, pour in such visions—"

"No," breathed Annaxion. "There are things I have glimpsed."

"And you, Angel?" said Tetraven. "You have a clinical mind. Ordered and arranged, though perhaps not so ordered."

Arteriel's mouth twisted in something approaching a wry grin. "Your words will be adequate."

"War on a scale that taxes imagination. Armies, machines,

technologies, all vaster than Thousandreach could dream of. And war that stretched from the birth of a world to its airless demise. Millennia. As a potter takes clay and squeezes it, reshapes it, so the war took worlds, civilisations, and squeezed them, fused them, rebuilt them. Flung them through the warps of time and space. War that held all natural forces in utter contempt. In such a cauldron, this nightmare of gods, the Overlap was born.

"You ask me what it is. I can't give you a precise answer. But it is a disease. It is not constrained by natural laws, ignoring time and space. If it is a ship, it has no rudder, no pilot either. It has no discernible purpose, no destination. It exists."

"Why do you pursue it?" said Arteriel.

"The Lightbenders use it, through us, to open gateways into other worlds. Life under Skydown is finite. Left to itself, all life under Skydown would be used up quickly. Without it, the Lightbenders would perish, like a man without nourishment. So they open doors and suck life in. A dangerous pursuit, and one which has almost resulted in catastrophe. There are worlds which should be avoided, worlds where life has taken on immeasurably horrifying form."

"Why do you pursue the Overlap?" Arteriel asked again.

"I have to be seen to behave as other Skryers do. We are all united in our service to the Lightbenders, their search for nourishment. But under this guise, I study the movements of the Overlap for other reasons. I am a historian. I believe that somewhere in the past, in *this* world's past, there was a time when life existed in a very different form. There were no Lightbenders, no fodda. And there was light in its true form. I cannot believe that we have evolved into this travesty of a world by natural means! The war I spoke of, it warped us, created the creatures that feed on us, perhaps out of us.

"If I learned the truth, what would it profit me?" He shook his head despondently. "Little, I suspect." But he leaned forward again. "Ah, but if, *if* we could control the Overlap, or at least its movements, even temporarily, we could achieve something. In my estimation, the Overlap has potential as a weapon. A destructive force, at least."

Annaxion gasped. "A weapon? But on what scale, Tetraven? Surely you would not unleash it here?"

Tetraven shrugged. "It would have to be focused."

"On the Lightbenders," Annaxion said softly.

"It would take precise control. To open gates, to unleash powers from other places. But we would have to know what they were, how to return them to their worlds of origin."

Arteriel had been listening in silence. He broke the pause. "There is another use you could put it to."

Both Skryers turned to him, looking at the blind eyes which hid a keenness of sight.

"Elevate Zaer has already commissioned its use. Does it not open gates? Can you not release the people of this world into another? Not just the Angel Guard, as promised, but the entire populace? Without them, this world will shrivel up."

"The Lightbenders would never allow it," said Tetraven.

"What if they were diverted?" went on Arteriel.

"By this rebel god?"

"Is this why he draws us together?" said Annaxion. "To thrust at Yvane and all the others—"

"While the Overlap is opened," muttered Tetraven. "But that assumes we can control the Overlap—"

"Perhaps your rebel god can," said Arteriel. "Zaer has promised the use of the Overlap. If this *is* your rebel god's plan, he would hardly enlist us without giving us the weapons to fight for him."

Tetraven sat up with a start. "Of course! He cannot act entirely for himself, or his fellow gods would crush him. But by using us, how could they know?"

Arteriel was about to ask something further, when there came a sudden hammering on the doors of the chamber, which Tetraven had taken the precaution of locking. The old Skryer gaped at the doors as though he had seen something frightful framed in them. He stood up slowly, unable to speak.

Annaxion also rose, turning to Arteriel as if in denial of something. Voices came from outside, muffled by the thickness of the doors, but the anger in the voices was not lost. Arteriel stepped back into shadows.

"They'll break the doors in," he said. "You had better open them. Unless there is a safe way out?"

Tetraven shook his head. "I set guards—"

"They'll have been slaughtered," said Arteriel bluntly.

"How can you tell?" gasped the old man.

Arteriel did not answer. "Open the door," he told Annaxion.

Confused and afraid, Annaxion went to the door and slid its long bolts. Almost immediately the door banged back against the stone. Several *goads* pushed their way past him, long swords waving. As Arteriel had predicted, they were slick with blood. Another figure emerged from the shadows in the hall beyond the doors. Arrogantly it strutted into the room, facing Tetraven, who had stumbled back against the couch.

"Provider Orvech," he murmured.

Sughai Orvech bowed. "You'll pardon this intrusion, but Elevate Yvane has given me direct instructions in certain matters." He moved forward. On either side of him, the *goads* took up protective positions, while behind him the last of them entered, covering the Provider's back.

"Annaxion," said Orvech. "I was wondering where I'd find you. You seem to have been avoiding me."

Annaxion feigned surprise. "Avoiding you? What possible reason could I have for—"

The sound of the doors closing with a crash cut him short. They all turned to see Arteriel sliding home the bolts before spinning round lightly, blind eyes facing them. He had deliberately locked the Provider and his killers in, an apparent act of suicide.

However, Orvech grunted with satisfaction. "Well. You have proved inordinately elusive for one of such limited powers."

Arteriel had undone his tunic: he took from his belt two short, curved knives. He moved softly, slowly, and not at all like a warrior who had been blinded.

"Yvane wants you," said Orvech.

"Let the two Skryers stand aside," called Arteriel as the *goads* formed a semicircle intent on closing him down.

"By all means," smirked Orvech. "Though they will pay for their treachery, naturally. Yvane is extremely angry."

"How did you know?" stammered Tetraven.

"A process of elimination," snorted Orvech. "And by the furious defence of your tower by your servants. They were very determined to keep me out. And they fought commendably, to the last."

"You—left none alive?"

"I left none alive."

Annaxion had moved as far back as he could. He could not keep his rising terror down. Death was closing on all of them. Orvech would be brutal, merciless.

37

Zaer Phesmes sighed. Light coruscated in the polished glass of his visor. "How beautifully you dance, Nu-Ko-Te," he told the girl as she rose from the marble floor. He watched in fascination as she drew breath evenly, then used her hands to comb her thick tresses back over her shoulders. Her innocence was a part of her beauty: she was poise and elegance incarnate. *I could be so selfish,* he thought. *I could deny the world her splendour.*

She smiled, skipping nimbly up the wide stair to where he sat. Easily he lifted her, setting her on his knee as if she were a tiny child.

"Does your Consort Imprimis please you?"

"How could she not?"

She leaned back into the vastness of his chest, hands idly stroking at the flesh. She took delight in the way he responded, his skin shivering, though she would never have dreamt of abusing her power over him. It was simply a joy to please him; nothing else in her world compared to that.

"I want to explain something to you, Nu-Ko-Te," he breathed.

She nodded listlessly, as though she were about to fall asleep, completely at rest.

"Don't sleep, not yet," he chided, but very softly.

"I hear you, Zaer."

"What do you know of the great trees?"

She frowned thoughtfully. "I know of them. And sometimes I have dreams, though not always about the great trees of Thousandreach. Other trees, much smaller. Many of them."

"Forests?"

"Is that what they are?"

"Yes, I'm sure that's what you see. Tell me about these dreams."

She closed her eyes in concentration and began to speak, reliving some of her visions. As she did so, Zaer became very still and relaxed, as though entering her visions himself as a silent observer.

"I see many of the trees, clustered together, a forest? And I enter this place. The air is pure, oh, and the light! The sky is filled with light, bright light, but it doesn't hurt my eyes. I can see far into the trees, corridors of them. They are so eager for the light, they stretch up towards it. There are other creatures here, but they hide from me. Perhaps they are afraid of me. I hear the leaves above me, making their own sounds, like many voices whispering."

"What do they say?"

"I don't know. Always the words elude me. But they are kind. Like you, they are telling me good things. I am very happy in the forest. I sometimes touch the trees, their thick trunks. They are hard, but warm, alive. It pleases them that I touch them."

"How could they not be pleased, Nu-Ko-Te?"

She smiled. "I wish I could take you there, Zaer. You would love the trees as I do."

"Of course. What about the great trees?"

"Here in Thousandreach? Well, I have seen them, or part of them. How magnificent they are! Do they truly go beyond the city, up to the regions of Absolute Light?"

Zaer nodded his tattooed head. "Oh yes. They make the air that we breathe, and which fills the heavens. All creatures depend on the great trees. Without them, life would quickly perish.''

"Then they are sacred. Even the Lightbenders would not harm them.'' She spoke with open distaste of the Lightbenders now.

"Yes. No one may touch them, except for those whose duty it is to tend them.''

"They must be very old.''

"You are perceptive, Nu-Ko-Te. The great trees are older than any of us. They came before Absolute Light.''

She let out a little gasp. "Oh! Are they gods also?''

"In their way. The forests that you dream of, they were real once. Our world was covered in them. And the light you saw was no trick of your dream. It was real. Sunlight, daylight. There was no shield, no Skydown. Periods of daylight were followed by periods without light: night. The life cycles of the world revolved around them. And the trees breathed out so that life could breathe in, and what life breathed out, the trees breathed in.''

"Yes, I understand that. The trees of my dreams took from me my breath, and gave me theirs. And with it, they took my thoughts, and I heard their whispers. Were they their thoughts?''

"They were.''

"I wish I could hear what they say.''

"You would like to hear the great trees?''

"Of Thousandreach?''

"It is not given to many to understand them.''

"Can they truly speak?'' She was wide awake now, her eyes gazing up at him.

"They speak to those they choose to speak to.''

"Do they speak . . . to you?''

He smiled. "In their way. But I am not adept. They do not send me the beautiful dreams that you have, though I know of the forests, the time of light.''

"Was it a time . . . before fodda?'' she asked haltingly, afraid that he would be angry with her for speaking the now-forbidden word.

But he was not angry. Instead he nodded. "Yes. There was no fodda then. No Lightbenders.''

"How did it change?"

"War changed it. Conflict of awesome proportions. Out of war came the warping of worlds, of life itself. Light became a destructive force." He stopped speaking, turning away, his own thoughts suddenly dark.

Sensing them, she clung the more tightly to him. "Will it be as it was again?"

He paused. "If not, Nu-Ko-Te, we go down forever into the darkness and the cold." Abruptly he shook himself, and she jumped down, reading some new purpose in him.

"You must speak to the great trees," he said.

"Zaer, I am afraid."

"I have given you certain gifts. This is to be the greatest of them." His huge hands operated something she could not see, some device within the vast chair. It swung round silently, facing away from her. Zaer pointed to a thick drape at the far end of the chamber. "Go and open the curtains there."

Instantly she ran across the floor to the drapes, finding a thick rope that served as an opening cord. She had to tug hard on it, but she felt the curtains sliding apart. They revealed what she first took to be a blank wall, though it had been sculpted in a peculiar fashion, covered in broken lines and crevices that could have been a pattern of brick and mortar, deeply intricate and complex. The colours unusual for stonework, intrigued her.

Zaer moved his seat across the chamber, pausing a few feet from the girl. He faced the wall. "What do you see?" he asked her.

"It's like a tapestry in stone."

"Stone," he repeated softly. "Touch it."

She did so, but drew her fingers back at once, her mouth opening in surprise.

"Stone?" he asked.

She shook her head. Again she reached out, this time more slowly, the tips of her fingers exploring the whorls and channels of the wall. "It's warm. Like flesh. But hard, like stone. But it isn't stone, is it?"

"No."

She became bolder, pressing her palm to the surface. Now

she held it there, enjoying the strange sensations. She laughed in sheer delight. "It's wood! And it's alive."

"Go on. It should not be a mystery to you, Nu-Ko-Te."

She leaned against it, putting her ear close to it. Then she gasped, turning to him with a mixture of delight and confusion on her face. "I can hear it whispering, like the trees in my dreams."

"And do you hear its words?"

She listened again, and it was as though the wood opened up to her, speaking privately to her. Images began to tumble over one another in her mind. She saw one of the titanic trees of Thousandreach, *this* tree, its roots buried deep, deep down in the bedrock of the world, its branches soaring upwards through the shield of Skydown, beyond it to a place of dazzling light. Shapes moved there, invisible and possessed of immense power. She withdrew from them, listening instead to the voice of the tree, the fluid in its million arteries. After a long time she turned back to Zaer. But she could find no words to convey to him what she had experienced. Instead, her eyes filled with tears.

"You are pleased with the gift?" he asked her.

She ran to him and flung herself at him, his huge, pudgy hand gently resting on her back.

"There is nowhere in Thousandreach that the trees cannot reach, nowhere," he told her. "Not only with their thoughts, but also with their roots, their branches, their powers. And you, my beautiful child, are part of this magic. It is how you were designed, Nu-Ko-Te."

"But why?" she sniffed, wiping away her tears.

"You asked me how it is that I can pour scorn on the Lightbenders, and seek their downfall. It is because I serve the trees, and all that they stand for. They have blessed me. And they have put themselves into you. They have a majestic purpose, Nu-Ko-Te, and you are part of it. Silent and secret, unseen by the Lightbenders and their corrupt powers.

"You can go to the great trees and through them move anywhere in Thousandreach, or above it."

"But, the tree is as solid as the stone I took it for—"

He shook his head. "It only appears to be so. You can open it, travel through it as easily as you travel through the corridors of the city. You can open paths that are beyond the reach of the Lightbenders.''

She gaped at the wooden wall. "But, Zaer, I'm only a girl, your servant. How is it that you cannot do these things?''

He laughed softly. "I am an Elevate. And as such I am tainted, spoiled by the genetic path that gave birth to me. You were evolved far more carefully. I harm the trees. Oh, not willfully, I promise you. It gives me more pain to know my failings. No, you must be their servant. You are their fruit.''

"I will not abandon you," she said suddenly, her hands digging into his flesh.

But again he laughed gently. "You are not abandoning me! I will be with you, in my own way.''

"What am I to do? Where am I to go?''

"Softly, Nu-Ko-Te. Enjoy this new knowledge slowly, a little at a time. We are not yet ready to begin our work. There are others who must come to us.''

"Can they also open paths?''

He shook his head. "Only you can do that. But these others will travel with you. Together you will perform the work of our purpose.''

She clung the more tightly to him. "Zaer, I am terribly afraid—''

He stroked her head with infinite care. "I understand your fears, Nu-Ko-Te. But you are protected.''

"Are you, Zaer?''

"I am an Elevate. But you must begin the development of your understanding of the great trees. We have very little time to indulge ourselves as we have done. Go again to the wall. Listen to it. Learn from it.''

Reluctantly she climbed down from his lap and went to the surface of the great tree. As before, she put her hands to it. Already there was a familiarity to it, an acceptance. It was as though the tree wanted to draw her into it, just as Zaer had said. She swung round to him, her face glowing.

"Oh, Zaer, it's wonderful! I—''

He saw the abrupt change, her face falling. "What is it?'' He made as if to rise, his bulk quivering with effort.

She pressed her ear to the wood. "Someone is in danger.

The tree is trying to tell me. A fight. Blood.'' She drew back. ''What can it mean?''

''Who is in danger? Where?''

She listened again. ''Skryers.''

''Are there names?'' Panic threatened to surge in him.

She nodded. ''Tetraven. Annaxion. There's someone with them. They're afraid for his life. He's . . . blind.''

''Arteriel,'' Zaer whispered. *''Where?''* he gasped.

''The tree wants me to go there. Oh, Zaer, I cannot—''

''You may have to. Who is challenging the Skryers?''

''Warriors. *Goads.* And a Provider. Sughai—''

''Orvech. Sughai Orvech! Yvane's creature.''

She nodded. ''Yes, it's him. There is a fight. They have cornered the blind one. He is an Angel Guard!''

Zaer grimaced. ''They won't find him easy to kill. But he may not survive this.''

''What can we do?''

''You must trust the tree, Nu-Ko-Te. Is the fight at Tetraven's tower?''

She nodded. ''They are locked in. All Tetraven's servants have been killed.''

''I'll send help. But you must go there, through the tree.''

''But—''

''Do as I say,'' he said, trying not to snap at her. ''Let the tree guide you. You must.''

Shuddering, she closed her eyes, giving herself to the pull of the tree, the susurrations emanating from it.

38

''Don't kill him,'' said Sughai Orvech, seating himself casually on the divan that Tetraven had vacated. He watched as his *goads* closed in on Arteriel, their weapons inching forward. "But cut off his arms."

Annaxion and Tetraven said nothing, but their faces mirrored their terror: they knew neither of them would leave the chamber alive. Yvane would waste no more time on them than he had to. Orvech gave them a smug grin that confirmed this. He sat back, interweaving his fingers, secure in his success.

The first of the *goads* thrust with his long pike, but the blind Angel heard its hiss through the air and evaded it, using the curved blade in his left hand to snare it and drag it downwards with a ferocious pull. Taken unawares by the power of the movement, the *goad* was drawn towards Arteriel, who brought his right hand up in a blur. The *goad's* head flung back, and the creature stood stupidly for a moment before toppling over. His throat had been opened; blood ran freely, pooling on the floor where he fell. He groped uselessly at the wound, rolling over, spluttering.

The other *goads* hardly reacted, though they approached the Angel more cautiously, forming a semicircle around him. They knew he could not fly in this confined space: the contest should be heavily weighted in their favor.

Orvech sat forward, hands gripping the edge of the divan. He knew this blind Angel must be remarkable, but seldom had he seen a being move so fast. And *blind?* It hardly seemed credible. The Angel had known precisely where to strike.

The *goads* began their assault without delay, and suddenly there was a frantic flurry of movement as they prodded at their intended victim. But Arteriel kept their opening attack at bay in a whirl of arms and steel, ducking and deflecting the pikes. The *goads* depended on strength more than skill and litheness and in this confined area were clumsy. By attacking in numbers they rendered themselves less efficient, but Arteriel knew that Orvech would have no real idea about organised conflict. Providers were excellent fighters, but they did not make good troop commanders. Arteriel had gambled on being able to reduce this small party steadily. If there were more beyond the tower, at least they would be kept at bay.

He hamstrung another of them, who lurched into a third,

and for a moment there was complete confusion among a few of the *goads*. Arteriel used it to enable him to move away, but always he kept a wall behind him. He had no idea what this chamber looked like, or whether there were objects he could use to screen himself or confound the *goads*. He dare not attempt using his wings. If they maimed him, he would be lost.

Orvech cursed. "What are you doing, imbeciles! Seven of you and you can't cut him down!" He was on his feet, face suffused with anger.

Annaxion could not move, though he would have struck out at the *goads* if it hadn't meant certain death: he could never hope to match the speed and strength of the Angel, blind or not. He took heart from Orvech's frustration, but knew it could not last. The *goads* were merely being cautious: a really concerted attack would bring Arteriel to his knees.

Another of the *goads* staggered back, one arm hanging by a few tendons from its socket, where the Angel's vicious blade had almost severed it clean through.

Again Orvech cursed. He began to edge away from the divan. The doors—but Arteriel had locked them. Surely he did not expect to defeat *all* of these *goads*! But Orvech's face had become greasy with perspiration.

At last one of the *goads* got through the lightning defence of the Angel, and although his steel was knocked away from its goal, Arteriel's groin, it twisted between his legs. Arteriel stumbled, then dropped to one knee. Another pike caught him a sharp blow across the side of the head and he was knocked to the ground. His blindness had, after all, undone him, that and his supreme confidence.

"Don't kill him!" snarled Orvech, rushing forward to the edge of the group. His *goads* waited: it would have been easy for them then to plunge their pikes home, reducing the Angel to bloody ruin, but they hovered over him.

"I said his *arms*," Orvech told them.

One of the *goads* prepared to deliver the chopping blow that would remove Arteriel's left arm, but as he did so the wall behind Arteriel abruptly developed a vertical crack. There was a loud groan, the unnerving sound of stone being

ground on stone and a cloud of dust blew outwards. Arteriel
rolled aside as the hesitant swipe of the *goad* came down,
missing him and raising sparks from the stone floor. Something weaved in the opening crevice, a long tendril, bleached
and smooth. Like a serpent it swung outwards, wrapping
itself about the neck and shoulders of the nearest *goad*. Other
tendrils emerged, whipping forward, and more of the *goads*
were ensnared.

The floor abruptly heaved, the stone a webbing of cracks
which puffed dust before enlarging. Still more tendrils sprang
up: Orvech saw them and gaped in astonishment. They were
alive, like the roots of a huge plant, or tree. He felt the
ground beneath him moving and clutched at the nearest *goad*
to prevent himself from falling over.

Arteriel had pulled himself clear of the *goads*. He could
not see what was happening, but he could hear the protesting
of stone, the snapping of rock, the muted gurgling of the
goads as they were attacked by something.

Tetraven and Annaxion watched in utter amazement as the
tendrils—roots?—wrapped themselves avidly about the *goads*,
choking them, digging into their flesh like living creatures,
mutations. No normal roots could do this. Tetraven grimaced
at the destruction of Orvech's warriors. He glanced at Annaxion.

"Is this your doing?" he whispered.

Annaxion shook his head, eyes fixed on the massacre. "I
thought it yours—"

Tetraven also shook his head. He saw Arteriel move away
from the wall like a shadow. Could the Angel have done this?
After all, it had been he who had locked the door. Why had
he done that? To bring this horror upon his enemies? But he
had almost been taken: another moment and he would have
lost an arm.

Orvech was backing away, eyes wide, head shaking violently like a man in a dream, disbelieving what he is seeing.
His *goads* were all fallen now. They writhed on the buckled
floor before the wall, and among them the tendrils twisted
and convoluted like a nest of serpents. Dust began to cloak
the worst of the slaughter.

From out of the darkness of the wall stepped a slender

figure. Pausing only briefly to look down at the dead and dying *goads*, it came into the chamber. Dressed in a simple, brief tunic, it was a young girl, her dark hair falling over her shoulders in a shining wave that gleamed in spite of the dust. Her expression was one of surprise, though there seemed to be a suggestion of pleasure in it, as though she had performed a task well. She seemed far too perfectly formed to be from the lower city.

"Who are you?" said Tetraven, though he felt foolish, his unaccustomed terror now an open wound.

The girl looked at him as if only just noticing him and Annaxion. She smiled pleasantly. "I am Nu-Ko-Te."

"You—did this?" said Annaxion.

Orvech stood motionlessly beyond them, face a mask of shock.

Nu-Ko-Te nodded. "I think so. I was in the tree. Moving through it—" She seemed a little bemused, as if she had just woken from a deep sleep.

Her words puzzled the Skryers. "The tree?" said Tetraven.

"Yes. I belong to Elevate Zaer Phesmes." She heard Orvech grunt, but ignored him. "He taught me how to speak to the great trees. And they have shown me how to move within them. It is my special gift."

"What brought you here?" said Tetraven slowly.

"I came in answer to your call for help. Zaer's servants were in danger. I used the tree." She paused, looking back at the dead *goads* as if seeing their mangled corpses for the first time. She put her hand to her mouth. "Oh, did *I* cause that?"

Tetraven turned to Orvech, and was about to speak to him, when he saw the shadows move behind the Provider.

Orvech had drawn a short blade of his own and took a step forward. "So this is Zaer's work," he snorted. "Well, it won't save you, Tetraven. Nor you, Annaxion. Where is the blind Angel?"

"I am here," said a voice softly in his ear.

Orvech did not answer. He felt the two hooked claws of Arteriel's gloves fixing themselves like hooks in the flesh of his shoulders. Orvech winced at the pain, wanting to shriek in agony, but he could not.

"I may not have my sight, but my sense of smell has become very acute," Arteriel breathed. "I would know your stench in a thousand."

Nu-Ko-Te let out a tiny gasp of shock as she saw the dark figure that had suddenly materialised behind the Provider. She saw the frightful talon-gloves digging through material and flesh. The blind eyes of the Angel Guard were scarlet, but they looked through her and beyond her to some inner hell. Nu-Ko-Te had never seen such a terrifying face before, the face of a demon. She drew back. Was this a servant of her beloved master?

"Arteriel," said Annaxion. "What is happening? Who is this girl?"

"I don't recognise her voice," said the Angel. "And I can only guess at the powers she has used. I felt the wall and floor cracking. And the *goads*—"

"All dead," said Annaxion. He explained what had occurred.

Arteriel could sense the disgust in the Skryer's voice. "Either that," he said, his grip on Orvech never faltering, "or you would both be dead, and I would be without my arms as well as my sight."

Orvech slumped forward, head lolling as if his neck had been broken.

"We must get away from this terrible place," said the girl. She could not take her eyes from Arteriel.

The Skryers looked at her with a degree of confusion. She seemed remarkably innocent in some ways, and yet how could she be that when she had just arranged the casual destruction of the *goads?*

"We must go to Zaer," she added.

"Yes," nodded Annaxion. "Yvane will unleash all his powers to find us after this. What of Orvech?" he asked Arteriel. "Is he dead?"

Arteriel shook the Provider, holding him up. Orvech groaned, his eyes opening, pain filling them. He winced in further agony as he felt the claws in him, remorseless.

"Open the doors," Arteriel told Tetraven.

"You can't mean to let him go?" said the Skryer.

"Open the doors," repeated Arteriel.

Tetraven did not argue. He went to the doors and slid the bolts. Light spilled in, more dust. Beyond he could see bodies heaped in the corridor, could smell the nauseating reek of death. Orvech's *goads* had been thorough.

Arteriel shook Orvech once more. "Go back to Yvane. Give him a last message. Tell him he aspires to heights he will never reach."

Orvech tried to speak, but could not, his teeth clamping on his lips to prevent himself crying out. The pain in his shoulders was excruciating: he thought he must surely pass out again.

"Nu-Ko-Te," said Arteriel. "There is a safe passage to Elevate Zaer?"

She jerked as though he had touched her, nodding. But she realised the Angel couldn't see. "Yes. We go through one of the great trees."

"Take the Skryers and wait for me by the entrance. Is it here?"

"Yes. In the wall. It resembles stone, but it is not. The tree has many guises."

"Go there. And do not look back into the chamber. Better that you were all as I am, without sight."

"What do you mean?" said Tetraven, at once afraid.

"Go with her!" Arteriel shouted. He pushed Orvech forward to the door, claws still fixed. Blood was seeping darkly into the fabric of the Provider's tunic.

The Skryers hesitated, exchanging uncertain glances, but they followed Nu-Ko-Te, who stood by the opening in the wall. She motioned them into its darkness, its peculiar warmth, her smile suggesting that nothing within could possibly harm them. The massed tendrils had withdrawn leaving only trails in the thick layers of dust to show that they had ever been here.

When they had gone in, Nu-Ko-Te looked back, but it was as if the blind Angel could see her, his scarlet orbs fixed on her. Her eyes could not pull away. Something inside her twisted, a strange, unnerving emotion, something new. The Angel fascinated her, she realised. She could not move for wanting to look at him, his raw beauty. She should have been appalled by it but could not be. Ah, but what would Zaer say! At last she wrenched herself away, turning and entering the passage in the tree.

Satisfied that the girl had departed with the others, Arteriel began his grim work. He released his grip, but slid his gloved hands down over Orvech's shoulders, gripping his arms around the biceps. Again Orvech gasped in agony.

"Kill me swiftly," he murmured, face dripping with sweat.

"You called for my arms. You must not disappoint Yvane."

Orvech felt his heart pumping, as if Arteriel had taken hold of it with one of those merciless claws and was squeezing it like a sponge, draining the blood out of it.

"Take him something as a symbol of your defeat."

Abruptly the grip on Orvech's arms tightened, impossibly. He began to scream like an animal as Arteriel applied unbearable pressure, his strength beyond belief. Flesh parted, tendons pulped, until the claws reached through blood and sinew to the very bones. As they, too, began to splinter, Orvech passed out. He was still unconscious as Arteriel gave the final wrench that ripped both arms free.

In the tree passage, the Skryers shuddered at the screams behind them. Nu-Ko-Te stood very still, trying to close her mind to the Provider's torment. There was a crude fascination in the sounds: she forced it away, wanting Zaer.

She heard the Skryers hurrying away into the dark, and now she became aware of a pungent stench, the smell of scorched flesh. She did not want to imagine what it must be. As she heard the soft padding of feet behind her, she knew she would not be able to bring herself to ask the blind Angel what he had done. But she had to see: she could not help herself. His power, his forbidding power, snared her, though he could not have known. It was not power in the way that Zaer possessed it, but it was deep, primitive.

As Arteriel came up the passage, claws slick with blood, he felt the girl's eyes on him as surely as if he saw them. And there was a nameless hunger in her.

39

Ruarhi was stunned by what he saw in the lower levels of the city. The streets were narrow canyons, poorly lit, filled with the press of countless bodies, teeming with life that seemed constantly on the move, though there was so little noise. Few among the masses spoke or shouted, and there were so many glazed looks, grim expressions: everything was steeped in despair. Thousandreach seemed to be a centre of misery, a region beyond hope, a nation of slaves. As Sommoi took Ruarhi and Ukar-Tiri deeper into the infinite mazes of the city, they sometimes went inside, squeezing along filthy corridors, then out again, crossing over narrow spans that bridged dark, empty abysses. Far down below there were the sounds of thunder, of machines that ground on interminably, the very walls pulsing with their mysterious energies. Inside or out, it did not matter: to Ruarhi, Thousandreach was a seething cauldron, its life as cheap as that of algae in any stagnant pond. The weight of despondency in this place bowed him, and his own world seemed desperately remote. Better, perhaps, that he had died alongside Dromator. But he used his despair to feed his anger, nurturing it through those dim passageways and sudden, soaring halls. If there was to be a goal here, fury would be the spur to it.

Ukar-Tiri held his hand in silence, cowed by terror. Whatever unpleasantness she had experienced in the outer regions of the world shrank beside the potential horrors here. The creatures who lurched through the maze were sexless things, fodda in the true sense, like machines tuned to monotonous, soulless tasks. There was no time for them; the present stretched beyond them, unchanging, fixed. In the deeps there could be only worse things, and Ukar-Tiri reasoned that those

who trudged downwards, in an irresistible response to whatever summoned them, went to an afterworld that could only
mean torment beyond her imagination.

Once, Ruarhi pulled Sommoi back, pointing down into
one of the black chasms. "What is down there?"

"The flesh mills, the transformation factories. It is where
fodda becomes energy. For the Lightbenders. It is fed up
through all these layers to the heights."

"Fed?" repeated Ruarhi, unable to keep the disgust from
his voice.

Sommoi held out his arm, the hand that had regenerated
itself. "Just as blood courses through our veins, so energy is
fed up through the arteries of Thousandreach. To fuel the
Lightbenders."

Ukar-Tiri turned away, closing her eyes. But in a moment
Ruarhi had put a comforting arm about her and they moved
on. Sommoi led them through a series of tunnels that seemed
to be winding ever upwards, though the scenery never
changed. The streets widened in some places, the lighting no
better; all the buildings were cut from naked rock. The sounds
that came from them were little different from the mechanical
rumbles and grindings of the abyss, though on a smaller scale.
Passing through one such building, Ruarhi was appalled to
see scores of beings, linked to each other by thin ropes that
seemed to sprout from their flesh, as if it had been created
out of it.

"Not all fodda is used for food or energy," said Sommoi
when quizzed insistently by Ruarhi. "The Elevates use it,
too. For many things." He was spared the unpleasant task of
elaborating by the appearance of a number of beings on the
far side of the huge hall. "We must avoid them," was all he
would say.

He led his companions swiftly aside, up yet another set of
stairs. They had to squeeze past several broad-shouldered
automatons, who said nothing, as if mute, and whose eyes
registered the typical bleak emptiness of this place.

"There is possible sanctuary ahead, though it will be temporary," said Sommoi. He became silent, lips pursed in concentration. Ruarhi could read the anxiety in his face, the threat
of defeat, the collapse of the enterprise. Sommoi had seemed

resolute in his confidence until now. But Yvane's agents were powerful. And this was their terrain.

A wall rose up in front of them as they reached the top of the stairs, its top far beyond sight, looming right over them as though it would topple. The stones of the wall were immense, as if cut from entire tors, the stone black and solid, no mark upon it. A narrow path ran around the base of the wall which gradually curved away in both directions, hemmed in on the other side by yet more buttresses of stone. Set in the black wall was a door which appeared to have been cast in metal. There was a script of some kind etched into it and symbols, neither of which Ruarhi could interpret.

"A place of worship," said Sommoi. "We can take refuge for a while. They might not find us here." He took the wide latch of the door and lifted it. With an effort, he swung the door inwards. Ruarhi led Ukar-Tiri into the place beyond and closed the door, putting his shoulder to its weight. There was a latch, but no means of bolting the door.

Sommoi was already looking round. He pointed to a pile of rocks heaped up against the wall for no apparent reason, and Ruarhi helped him to drag the largest of them over to the door. They wedged it against the bottom of the door, satisfied that it would hold it.

"There's no other way out," said Sommoi. "But if we are trapped in here, we'd be killed. They won't interrogate us any further, unless they bring Tormenters."

Ruarhi nodded, hardly hearing him. Instead he was looking about him at the place they had come to. It seemed to be a garden of some kind, though the resemblance was superficial. It was walled in, the walls being equally as high as the black wall, and at the heart of the small area the trunk of a colossal tree rose up. It came up from the ground, which was itself stone and not earth, like a pillar, as if its base was somewhere far below, down among the nightmare chambers of the deeper regions. And it rose up smoothly, a few thick branches stretching out like a ceiling, tangled and twisted, though without leaves.

"It goes up to the highest parts of the city," said Sommoi, seeing Ruarhi's fascination. "And even beyond, to Absolute

Light.'' His voice changed as he spoke, and for the first time lost some of its hard edge.

Ruarhi wondered if this was reverence of a kind. He would have questioned Sommoi on this, but there was a movement among the shadows beyond the vast trunk. From among a cluster of huge, pale plants that grew there, a figure stepped. It wore a bright green robe that flowed out behind it like the gown of a warrior king, strangely ostentatious for this sombre place.

Ukar-Tiri drew back in consternation. The figure had no face, just a huge, sagging chin, with a single opening above it that served for a mouth. It looked like a gash, gaped like a dried wound.

''You have come to worship?'' said the mouth, opening as it spoke to reveal a pinkness, devoid of teeth, that made Ruarhi draw in his breath.

Sommoi alone seemed unmoved. He turned to his companions. ''This is an *arborate*. A tree priest, if you like. The great trees are sacred. You must not touch the trunk, nor speak ill of the trees. They provide the air that we breathe. All life under Skydown owes its existence to the trees.''

''Their roots,'' said Ukar-Tiri, her voice dropping so that they had to strain to catch it, ''are where?''

''No one knows, unless the *arborates* do. Somewhere far under the deepest levels of the city.''

''You have come to worship?'' hissed the *arborate*. It sounded impatient.

Something clanged against the outside of the metal door and Ruarhi swung round, his sword leaping in automatic defence of himself and the girl.

The *arborate* emitted a strange ululation, its hideous mouth opening wide, like the gaping jaw of a serpent without teeth. Sommoi stepped back, as though in awe of the creature.

''You profane the sacred grove!'' said the *arborate*. ''You bear weapons. And why have you sealed the door? Others may wish to enter.''

The door rattled. Someone pressed hard against it from beyond. Undoubtedly warriors, Ruarhi knew.

The *arborate* seemed to drift towards the door, lifting its arms under the robe, preparing to push the boulder aside. Ruarhi stood in its way, holding up the blade.

"Leave that!"

"You would harm me?" said the *arborate*. Even though it was eyeless, it was fully aware of the blade, as though there must be invisible eyes under its pale skin.

"You must not touch him," said Sommoi, perspiration glistening on his features.

"Before I let him open the door to our enemies," said Ruarhi, "I'll cut him down where he stands, priest or not."

"He is the voice of the tree," said Sommoi. "If you harm him, you harm the tree."

"If he opens the door, how long can we survive!" Ruarhi shouted. "Leave the door!" he said again to the *arborate*. It turned to him, its mouth opening and closing like that of a fish.

"If you are enemies of the tree," it said, "I welcome your own enemies."

"We are not enemies of the tree," Sommoi insisted, almost touching the sleeve of the *arborate*. But he withdrew his fingers, as though touching the creature would be like touching the tree itself. "We came here to worship, to ask for refuge."

"From what?" said the *arborate*, ignoring a further crash on the outside of the door. The boulder held firm against any intrusion.

"Those who would enter are enemies of the tree," said Sommoi. "They bring fire."

The *arborate* hissed and drew back as if it had already been scalded. *"Fire!"* it whispered. "This must not be! Fire is tree-death. The ultimate heresy."

"Don't open the door," said Ruarhi. "They'll gut this place."

"Why? Why are they enemies to the tree?" said the *arborate*, its voice incredulous, as though Ruarhi had described the act of lunatics.

"Certain powerful beings in Thousandreach are jealous of the powers of the tree," said Sommoi.

"Beings?" said the *arborate*. "Such as whom? You must tell me. The tree must be informed."

"Yvane," said Ruarhi, not waiting for Sommoi to consider an answer. "The Elevate. Yvane Sephir."

Sommoi's eyes flickered as if in annoyance, but he said nothing, waiting.

The *arborate* turned back to the boulder, the door. "These servants of Yvane must be dealt with. I will go to them, even though they carry fire."

Sommoi's eyes narrowed and he took a step back. Ruarhi could see that there was a warning in his subtle movement. He did not trust the *arborate*. If the creature was so afraid of fire, Ruarhi thought, why should it open the door. Could it also be Yvane's servant?

"Leave the boulder in place," he told the *arborate*.

The creature stepped closer, lifting the sleeves of its gown to reveal its arms. There were no hands, only a thick tendril with a gaping orifice that duplicated the mouth of the creature. Both arms reached out for Ruarhi. Instinctively he swung his weapon, the air hissing as its cutting edge passed within inches of the *arborate's* bleached flesh. It drew back its arms.

"Don't let it touch you," warned Sommoi. "Their touch is death."

"Then I'll remove the threat," said Ruarhi, preparing to do just that. But the *arborate* glided back on invisible feet towards the tree.

"You won't get close to it with a sword," said Sommoi.

Ruarhi scowled, infuriated, but then he bent down and picked something up. He showed it to Sommoi, who could not understand his intention. It was a small stone that had broken off from the boulder they had moved.

The *arborate* was very still, as though in priestly communion. Ruarhi watched it for any sign of sudden attack. Then he tapped the stone hard against his blade. In a moment he had succeeded in making sparks. "Arteriel is not the only one who can make fire. Bring me some of those leaves," he said to Ukar-Tiri. "Dry ones."

She eyed the *arborate* warily, but did as he bade her.

Ruarhi screwed the leaves into a ball, holding it by a long stem. He gave the crude taper to the girl and again drew sparks from the blade with the stone. In a moment the ball of leaves caught alight. Smoke drifted up.

At once the *arborate* lifted its bizarre head and gave voice to the peculiar ululation. The door rattled under a further assault, but it held.

"Get more leaves," said Ruarhi. "This fire won't last."

"But what will you do with it?" said Sommoi, who had drawn back from the flames.

Ruarhi was puzzled by his increasing anxiety. Fire? But he had shown none of Inkulke's concern at High Crofels when Arteriel had threatened to burn the place down. Yet now Sommoi looked almost aghast. "It'll keep that creature away from the door," Ruarhi told him. "In the meantime you'd better pile some more stones against it."

Sommoi nodded.

As he did so, Ukar-Tiri stood close to Ruarhi. "But how can we escape, Ruarhi?" she whispered. "Sommoi said the door is the only way out. There will be many enemies out there now."

"There is another way out," he said, his voice equally as low. "We can climb the trunk."

Her eyes widened as she studied it.

Sommoi straightened. "I know what you intend," he said. "It is high sacrilege." Again his uncertainty was clear.

Ruarhi nodded slowly. *It's the tree! For some reason he's afraid of the tree.* He tried to make light of it. "You don't have to come, Sommoi. You can stay here and entertain the priest."

Sommoi looked bewildered for once. He turned to the *arborate,* but the creature had gone, as though it had merged with the tree itself. "When it returns," he said, "it will bring other servants. They will not spare us."

Ruarhi shrugged. "Since we've offended the tree already, we can do no worse. I'll climb. And you, Ukar-Tiri?"

She shivered, thinking of the repulsive arms of the *arborate.* "I will go with you."

"Sommoi? Does our rebellion end here? Without a blow being struck against Yvane and his masters?"

Sommoi studied the tree apprehensively. "To touch the holy trees is forbidden. To climb them—forgive me, but something in me holds the trees precious. It is an instinct."

"If we don't climb, we die," said Ruarhi bluntly. For once

he was able to take the initiative, and ironically it gave him a flush of confidence.

40

Ruarhi reached down and gripped Ukar-Tiri's hand, tugging her gently up towards where he crouched on the bough. Her face was creased with effort, not fear: she had enjoyed the steady climb upwards, even though it had been dangerous. Ruarhi was more concerned about Sommoi. He had unquestionably lost his composure, climbing upwards slowly, almost gingerly, as if expecting reprisals from the surface of the great tree. Ruarhi looked over Ukar-Tiri's shoulder as he helped her up, and saw Sommoi some distance below, face pressed to the bark, as if he were listening to something. Ruarhi found his continued uneasiness disconcerting.

"Take your time," Ruarhi called down. He knew well enough the perils of climbing. Fear was the enemy, the greatest danger. But Sommoi was coming up once more, fingers digging into the flesh of the tree, feet finding a purchase on the pocked surface.

Ukar-Tiri swung up next to Ruarhi, face beaming, pleased at her own efforts. She looked around, but could see only the ever-rising wall beyond her, a circular wall that seemed to enclose the tree, no matter how high it rose. Ruarhi had climbed as comfortably as a spider might have, as though he had spent his life doing this, and she wondered about his world. It must be so much like the world she had come from, a world that contrasted so vividly with this one.

Sommoi reached the branch. Ruarhi would have offered him a hand as he had the girl, but Sommoi seemed able to manage without help. He swung onto the branch and sat astride it, drawing in air hungrily. He was conscious that

Ruarhi had the advantage: it was something else he did not feel comfortable with. But he nodded.

"Is there any sign of an exit?" Sommoi asked. "Or must we climb forever?"

Ruarhi shrugged. "The tree rises and rises. So does the wall around it. But we have all the time we need."

"I'm hungry," said Ukar-Tiri.

"Yes," said Sommoi. "We must find allies soon."

"We'd better rest for a while," suggested Ruarhi.

They stretched out on the wide branch, easing their muscles. As they were dozing, the branch seemed to tremble, as if something had climbed onto it. Ruarhi looked along its winding length, but could see nothing. The thick trunk behind them gave no hint as to the source of the vibrations.

Sommoi got to his feet, unable to settle. "We intrude here," he said softly. "The *arborate* is sure to attempt retribution."

Ruarhi's sword slid from its sheath, though Sommoi grimaced at its cutting edge, as though he feared damage to the tree.

The trunk seemed to shimmer for a moment, and then a shadow appeared in it, like a long slit. It had occurred so swiftly they hardly noticed the transition, as though the opening had been there all the time, but they had not seen it. They drew back slowly, expecting an *arborate*, or something worse, to emerge. Instead it was a girl of about Ukar-Tiri's age who stepped out.

She had skin the colour of Ruarhi's, as if it were used to true sunlight, and not the pale colour of the inhabitants of this world. Her hair was dark, her features very beautiful. She was about the same build as Ukar-Tiri, slender and graceful, and she smiled as if she had been expecting to see the intruders on the branch. Ruarhi felt his face flush: she was perfect, sculpted by a god who understood beauty. Ukar-Tiri may have noticed the way he gaped for a moment, he could not tell. But he recovered himself to speak first.

"Who are you?" he said.

"I am Nu-Ko-Te," she smiled, stepping forward lightly, as though she, too, was completely at ease on the branches of this arboreal giant. "I have come to take you to Elevate

Zaer Phesmes. He has been waiting for you. He thought you had fallen foul of his enemies.''

Sommoi was visibly relieved, nodding.

"You trust her?'' said Ukar-Tiri, eyes fixed on the girl as though she did not.

"Ukar-Tiri—'' began Ruarhi.

But Sommoi cut him short. "The girl is valid,'' he said. "She is from Zaer.'' He, too, could not help but stare at her beauty, though Nu-Ko-Te was oblivious to the attention they paid her.

"We must hurry,'' said Nu-Ko-Te, although she still smiled, as though all this was little more than a form of amusement to her. "Yvane's fury knows no bounds.''

"Yvane?'' said Ruarhi. "What of him?''

"He hunts you with all his frightful power.'' Even now she did not seem perturbed for herself, and Ruarhi wondered if she eased her own fears with some form of drug.

"Take us to Zaer,'' said Sommoi impatiently.

Ukar-Tiri pouted. Ruarhi tried to speak to her, but she had already turned away from him, as though he had somehow insulted her.

"Come with me,'' said Nu-Ko-Te, turning back to the shadow opening in the trunk. "I have made a path within for us. The way is dark, but it leads to safety.''

"How have you done this?'' said Sommoi, the first to reach her. He frowned at the darkness, his distrust obvious.

"It is Zaer's gift to me, though he says it is of the tree. Hurry, please.''

"Zaer permits this?'' Sommoi asked.

"Oh, yes. The trees acknowledge Zaer and his power. They bear him no ill will. Nor you.''

Sommoi nodded, though Ruarhi could see that he was astonished at what, to him, was evidently the granting of a significant privilege. Sommoi stepped inside the coolness of the trunk.

Satisfied that they were following her, Nu-Ko-Te led the way into the tree, which seemed enormous, its passage one of many that threaded both up and down its breadth. There was light of a kind, like insipid moonlight, though Ruarhi knew it could hardly be that, and they followed the girl as she took them higher.

"A little easier than climbing," Ruarhi said to Ukar-Tiri, but her frown showed no sign of dissolving. She evidently didn't trust the girl ahead.

Eventually, after a long journey that had almost exhausted them all, Nu-Ko-Te stopped and put her ear to a smooth wall. She seemed to satisfy herself about something, then stretched out both palms, flat to the wooden surface. To Ruarhi's amazement, it dissipated like mist before sunlight. A moment later he was looking into a chamber, a spacious room, lit by braziers and lavishly decorated. No MagMannoch monarch had ever known such luxury. Their riches were squalid in comparison.

Nu-Ko-Te stepped into the room, the enigmatic smile returning to her face. She gestured almost shyly for her companions to enter.

Sommoi did so, looking about him warily; he had regained much of his composure. Ruarhi followed, Ukar-Tiri close to his shoulder once more. Behind them, the wall of the trunk had remoulded itself, as though the passages they had traversed had been no more than a part of their imaginations.

As their eyes became accustomed to the brighter light of the chamber, they realised that there were others here. Ruarhi was immediately on his guard, but Sommoi put his hand on his arm gently.

"Be easy," he said. "These are allies." He went forward to meet the others.

There were five of them, and they were uniformly garbed in flowing robes. They bowed slightly at Sommoi's approach.

"Verusion," said the latter, inclining his head to one of robed figures.

Ruarhi guessed that this was a Skryer: he had the look of a holy man or priest, though he seemed frail, his skin parched, his eyes haunted, though alert. Indeed, there was a receptive keenness in them that was striking, a hint of power far beyond the mummery and trickery of the MagMannoch shamans. Sommoi clearly respected the Skryer.

Verusion was equally relieved to see him. "We feared you

were lost. Allow me to introduce Annaxion, formerly a Skryer to the late Provider Sughai Orvech.''

Sommoi stiffened momentarily in surprise. ''Orvech is dead?''

''He is.''

''By whose hand?''

''Not by mine,'' said Annaxion, ''I have never taken a life, though it would have given me pleasure to kill him. It was the Blood Red Angel, Arteriel.''

''It was a matter I had wanted to attend to personally,'' said Sommoi, with unusual bitterness. Then he seemed to dismiss his rising anger. ''And you, Annaxion. A change of loyalties?'' he added.

Annaxion was somewhat older than Verusion, although Ruarhi could see in him evidence of the vitality that flowed through Verusion. The elderly Skryer's expression lacked humour, as if something troubled him. Ruarhi wondered if the others trusted him.

''His loyalty is proven in other ways,'' said Verusion.

''Then I am relieved to have your support, Annaxion,'' said Sommoi. If he had temporarily relinquished command on the climb, Ruarhi thought, Sommoi intended to reassert himself in this company.

''This is Tetraven, of whom you may have heard,'' Verusion went on.

Sommoi bowed to the eldest of this group. ''This is a double honour. Your work is known to us. I had thought you independent.''

''As I was,'' agreed Tetraven. ''But you'll find me loyal enough now.'' He spoke solemnly and clearly, a distinct power in his voice, as though it had not aged as his frame had.

Verusion turned to the other two beings. ''As you can see, these are also Skryers. Gabrellon lately served Provider Warvan Darvas, servant of the House of Spiritores, while this is Eorvan, who yet serves Provider Ramman Lurish. We represent the core of Skryers, bound together in the cause of Elevate Zaer.''

The two Skryers bowed. They were almost identical, possibly the same age as Verusion, their eyes reflecting the same bright intensity, though they did not speak.

Sommoi drew in his breath. "Forgive me, Verusion, if I seem surprised—"

"On the contrary, I understand only too well. An alliance of this nature would have seemed unthinkable only a short time ago. But believe me, we are sworn to this cause."

The Skryers nodded, though their mood was one of unease.

Sommoi turned to Ruarhi and Ukar-Tiri. "This is the warrior, Ruarhi of the MagMannoch clan. The External."

Verusion looked at Ruarhi with interest. It was true what he had been told, the warrior was young, though he looked powerful. No creature bred under Skydown could have attained his physique.

"And this is Ukar-Tiri," Sommoi added. "She, too, was once an External."

"You are both most welcome," said Verusion.

Why? Ruarhi wanted to ask. Why are we really here? How can we possibly be of use to your cause? But he nodded casually.

"We are complete," Verusion went on.

"Not quite," Sommoi said soberly. "If we are to achieve our goal—" But he stopped short as another figure emerged from a doorway across the chamber.

Ruarhi caught his breath, as did both the girls. The Skryers turned, their own faces tight with uncertainty.

Arteriel had entered the room. His wings were folded behind him, an integral part of him, like a cloak. He had removed his clawed gloves, tied them in place at his belt. His hands were long and pale, almost bloodless.

Nu-Ko-Te shifted towards him slightly, as though drawn to him and the power that seemed to radiate from him. And the blind eyes of the Angel Guard paradoxically seemed to drink in the scene before him. He was relaxed, though everything about him suggested preparation, as if he was constantly alert to any act of hostility. His tension suggested that the slightest hint of aggression would trigger an instant response.

Here is the true warrior among us, thought Ruarhi. *They say they hold me in esteem for my fighting skill, but they're fools to think I am deceived. The Angel Guard is power incarnate. Among warriors I am a soldier from the ranks, while he is a prince of killers.*

"Arteriel," said Sommoi.

"Our paths here have been more diverse than we had expected," said the blind Angel in his rich voice.

"You are committed?" said Sommoi.

Arteriel's mouth opened slightly, his perfect teeth parting as if he were about to make a typically disdainful reply. But he merely nodded. "I am persuaded," he said.

"Zaer wants to speak to you all," said Nu-Ko-Te, with another of her insouciant smiles. But her attention remained focused on the Angel, as if in some way she found him irresistible.

"By all means let us join him," said Sommoi.

Again Nu-Ko-Te led the way, and the entire party followed her.

Ruarhi felt Ukar-Tiri's fingers close with his own as they walked at the rear of the others. "I'm afraid," she whispered.

He had no answer, instead squeezing her hand in an attempt to instill a little courage into her, though he could hardly deny his own misgivings.

They passed through more corridors and chambers, all of them magnificent, well lit, and extravagantly furnished, as if this must be some huge palace, a treasure chamber of riches culled from numerous wars over the centuries. Light was revered here, celebrated. Yet this opulence apparently made no impression on Sommoi and the others, while both Ruarhi and Ukar-Tiri gaped in mounting amazement. They could never have imagined such splendours: their worlds seemed empty and barren compared to this. Even so, they would gladly have gone back to them.

The walls of the final chamber that Nu-Ko-Te brought them to could almost have been made of glass. They sparkled and scintillated, and Ruarhi could see that even the Skryers took a while to adjust to them, unused to such light. Sommoi, too, seemed a little taken aback by the place. But Nu-Ko-Te was perfectly at ease, spinning around and smiling happily: this was her realm, her home, and she was in her element here among the pillars and huge statues.

"Welcome, at last," came a voice from above them. As one, they looked up. Elevate Zaer Phesmes sat before them.

They had not seen him at first, for he was like one of the great statues, a huge being who seemed to have been carved out of the chair in which he sat, an integral part of him. His naked flesh gleamed in the brilliant light, his tattooed head nodding now as he welcomed them. His eyes were hidden behind a curved shield that mirrored the light, creating a bizarre illusion, as if light discharged itself from the eyes, rays of power.

Ruarhi tried not to look stupefied. Of all the amazing things this world had shown him, this was surely the most bizarre. Was this creature, this demigod, human? Its ancestors may have been, but it had traveled far down stranger paths to become this immensity of flesh, this travesty of humanity. Ruarhi closed away his thoughts: this being was their hope.

Nu-Ko-Te ran to Zaer as lightly as a trained animal and sat with her back to one immense shin. Resting there, she seemed perfectly content, oblivious to the darkness that was gathering in the world outside this amazing palace.

Sommoi bowed. "Elevate Zaer. You honour us."

"Ah, the renegade Provider, Gundra Sommesch. You are particularly welcome. I had feared for you. You have endured intolerable odds."

"We all have, Elevate. But the time of tolerance draws to a close."

"You are right," said Zaer, his huge mouth curving in the grim semblance of a smile. He turned his attention to Arteriel.

"And the resilient Arteriel. I recently received a message from you. It said that you are my enemy. I have certainly been the cause of much of your discomfort. Can we put aside our differences in favour of our common aims?"

Arteriel nodded silently, though it seemed that of all the company, he yet needed convincing of the veracity of the rebellion.

"We begin at once," said Zaer. "And we act directly. Already Yvane gathers his horrors about us. He will know of the death of Provider Sughai Orvech, among others. I will inevitably be implicated. There will be a confrontation. Subterfuge can be dispensed with, that is, up to a point. You will continue to act discreetly, in shadow, while I take up a more direct offensive.''

Nu-Ko-Te at last seemed perturbed, turning to her master in concern. ''Zaer, you cannot—''

''Listen to me!'' he hissed, his huge bulk quivering. He was addressing all of them, not just the beautiful girl. ''I have already set a chain of events in motion. I have delivered to Yvane a personal challenge that he cannot ignore. A private battle between us. I have offered him an opportunity to meet with me, alone. To fight to a conclusion.'' He left no doubt as to the implications of the statement.

''Master, you cannot!'' cried Nu-Ko-Te, rising.

''Elevate,'' said Sommoi, ''I fear she may be right. You would be risking your life—''

''The outcome of the battle does not matter, provided it creates the necessary diversion of Yvane's attention. I may well perish, but if I delay Yvane, even wound him severely, I will have succeeded. While I engage him, you will begin the real tasks of our rebellion.''

There would have been more protests, but Arteriel stepped forward, silencing the audience with a single gesture.

''You have promised the Angel Guard a path to worlds beyond this one.''

''And shall fulfill that promise,'' Zaer asserted.

''You are bound by it.''

''It will be done, Arteriel. Do not doubt it.''

''And just what are these tasks you speak of, Elevate? What miracles do you expect of us?''

Zaer laughed softly. ''Miracles? Perhaps you are capable of such things. Well,'' he sighed, leaning back. ''You must go beyond this level, to the place of the Lightbenders. Kaizu must die, as must all the others.''

Arteriel waited for a rational explanation, but the others looked as though they were about to hurl question after question at the Elevate.

''There are powers that will help you,'' said Zaer. ''I would hardly use a single cup of water to douse an inferno.''

SIX

THE LIGHTBENDERS

It is a common belief among men that immortality equates to godhood. I would accept that if there is such a thing as godhood in the truly divine sense, it must exist outside time.

Immortality should not be confused with longevity. In my experience, all that does attach to longevity is wisdom, although even this, in time, degenerates into senility.

It is quite clear that immortality exists not only outside of time, but also outside of the flesh. Flesh is finite. Flesh is subject to the laws of time. Flesh decays.

No true god would need flesh. No true god could die.

ZAER PHESMES—*The Book of Renunciation*

41

Zaer waited in absolute darkness. How he abhorred it. Light was something to be cherished, revered, whatever one's religious commitment. It gave life, life as it should be. But here, in this cold, stinking hall, this cavern of despair, darkness was, paradoxically, an ally, a rare comfort.

The hall was truly immense, so much so that countless pillars held up its enormous domed vaults, pillars as thick as trees, though no tree passed anywhere near this sterile place. Now fallen into disuse, it had once been a slaughterhouse, a place where the largest hybrid products of the failed Lightbender experiments had been disposed of. There were mercifully no records of how those creatures had been dealt with, nor of what had become of their flesh and blood. But it had not gone back into the system, had not been pumped upwards to fuel the powers that ruled a world. Fires, perhaps, had turned the flesh to running blubber: there were dark stains on some of the pillars that Zaer had seen on his one earlier visit. And there were drains to pipe away any waste to the deeps far below.

Abandoned now, the hall still reeked of carnage, the stones imbued with the fluids of the things that had died here in their seething masses. Yes, reflected Zaer, it was the ideal place to meet with Yvane Sephir. He of all the Elevates would not be able to resist it, this shrine to Kaizu, who would have heard in its screams a paean to his glory.

Word had been sent by secret means. And word had been received. Yvane would come, alone. This was to be to the death.

Zaer tried to shut from his mind all thoughts of the strange allies he had trawled and fused together in his grandiose design, but he saw their faces in the dark. Nu-Ko-Te's stood out from them, distraught, uncertain. He had tried to hide the truth from her, but she must have known. Yet she would do his bidding. They all had their given tasks now. Already they would be hurrying to perform them. The Skryers would be welded together under Verusion and Annaxion: their combined powers were unique, but would they be enough? And how dedicated was the blind Angel? Could he be trusted? Was his hunger for vengeance enough?

I must concentrate on my own work, Zaer chastised himself. He watched the dark. Was that a distant light?

It was. Yvane approached. Far across the hall, screened by a forest of pillars, the huge bulk of an Elevate drew closer. Yvane had brought light, fire. He torched the ancient braziers by the far wall. They burned a dull red, their glow suffusing the hall with ominous crimson light.

Zaer kept very still, though his own bulk would doubtless be visible to his enemy.

Yvane slithered forward. His arms were enormous, thick bands of flesh that were out of proportion to his body. Already the transformation in him was well advanced. His neck had disappeared, his head an immense dome that thrust up from his shoulders, folds of flesh hanging from it in wattles, gleaming obscenely in the fire-glow. His eyes were great, circular orbs, bulging in a perpetual, horrified stare: there was no fear in him. His massive chest bulged over his abdomen, which spread out, misshapen and gross beyond con-

ception. The legs had been absorbed, the lower half of the
Elevate like the final segments of a worm, tapering to a point,
a whipping tail. His weapons, then, would be his hands, those
swollen fingers, and the tail.

His mouth opened. A tongue slapped against the scarlet
lips; there were no teeth. Yvane fed on a liquid diet, fastening on his food with that leech's mouth and converting it to
fluid, flesh and bone alike. Yes, he was well advanced. Soon
he would turn completely.

Zaer glanced down at himself briefly. *And what have I
come to?* he asked himself. *Am I any more lovely than that
slithering monster? Nu-Ko-Te thinks so. Ah, but it is so unfair. I have made her what she is. Just as we shape all life
around us, funnel it to ourselves. How could one so divine of
form as Nu-Ko-Te hold me in kind regard?*

Like Yvane, he was immense, but he still retained something of his original form. His body was gross, but not so
bloated as Yvane's, and he still had all four appendages. But
his legs were useless: they would be the next to alter, drawing
up into his bulk while his abdomen swelled outwards, shaping its own tail. It would be inevitable. Nothing could reverse
the process. Evolution dictated it, and they had warped the
rules, made them strict.

"I see you, Zaer!" came the expected roar of Yvane's
voice. "There is no darkness that can hide you from me."

Zaer operated his chair, that mechanically grafted part of
himself, sliding it forward over the stone floor. Light fell on
him, reflected from his curved visor. "I am alone," he said.
"As I promised. We want no witnesses."

"I agree," snorted Yvane, wriggling forward, his hands
flat to the stone. They faced each other, fifty yards apart, but
their voices absolutely clear. The thick carpet of dust and the
festoons of cobweb did nothing to distort the acoustics.

"Our Lord Lightbenders would be furious with us for
meeting like this," said Zaer. "But I knew you would come."

"Your challenge surprised me. You realise what it will
mean?"

"Oh, indeed. It was not thrown down lightly."

"When I have killed you, I will be glorified by Kaizu. He
understands well enough the intrigues in which you have en-

gaged yourself. Do you really think that Subran of the Des Aubach House can overthrow the Da Sangravilles?''

I must let him think what he will. I merely buy time by being here. Already Sommoi and the others—but no, I *must* not think of them. ''We all have our ambitions, Yvane. I stand in the way of yours, and you mine. I thought that we could dispense with prolonged and tedious subterfuge.''

''A direct confrontation? There are no records of such a thing happening in the past. Elevate against Elevate, in such open contest.''

''You speak of the prize, should you survive. Kaizu would embrace you, move you closer to Absolute Light.''

''I am almost ready,'' Yvane nodded, his entire bulk quivering. ''You can see that in me.''

''You will risk everything?''

Yvane laughed, but there was a degree of apprehension in the sound. He knew that no Elevate would be easy to destroy. ''You have been subtle until now,'' he said. ''You have embarrassed me, eliminated certain of my servants. It is the way you fight best, Zaer, this war of attrition. I prefer more direct means. You know that. Which is why I wonder about you. I have not come here like some blundering oaf, eager to plunge into conflict, though my blood sings at the thought of it! How can I trust you, who should be wary of my physical power? Why have you tossed away your own skills in favour of more dangerous solutions?''

Zaer felt a stab of unease. Had he underestimated Yvane? Had he, after all, set up a trap? Would he fight?

''I cannot take your challenge lightly,'' said Yvane, sliding closer, moving this way and that to avoid the pillars. ''But I cannot refuse it. Are you alone?''

''I am. No one knows that I am here.''

''You trusted me to come alone?''

''You are a warrior, Yvane, a destroyer. Your pride would not let you bring support. You are alone, and you believe you can destroy me, no matter how well I fight.''

''But somehow you must also believe that you can destroy me!'' Yvane laughed.

''I have looked ahead, considered the possibilities.''

Yvane's grotesque smile twisted into a glare of annoyance,

intense suspicion. "The Skryers! You have perverted them. That incompetent moron Orvech told me as he died how even Tetraven had swung his loyalties to you. Tetraven! That gatherer of relics! So what have your prophets seen? My death here?"

"They have given me no special knowledge. I tried, of course. But Skryers are all alike, as you know. They cannot agree on the path of the future. Just as they cannot predict the coming of the Overlap."

"Then when you say you have looked ahead—"

"I have considered my future, how it might go. And I have considered that of my master, Subran. Whichever way I examine the possibilities, Yvane, one thing is clear. The Da Sangravilles will have absolute mastery. Kaizu will be supreme. If Subran and his family fall, I will follow."

"And so?"

"Better to eschew the slow fall to such an end in favour of this conflict."

Yvane looked puzzled. "Then you expect to die by my hand?"

Zaer smiled. "I won't make it easy for you. If I can kill you, rest assured, I will."

"I am sure of that. But this is too simple an explanation. Zaer Phesmes, most devious of Elevates? Come, you insult me, dullard that I am. Have you so readily tossed aside all your plots? You have thrived on them for so long."

"They will come to nothing, I fear."

"You astound me."

"It's very simple, in spite of your misgivings."

"If I kill you, your plots die with you."

"Naturally."

"It would be a pity to kill you without knowing something of what you planned. I am intrigued by the way in which you have thwarted me recently in certain matters."

Zaer tried to remain calm, but he could sense Yvane's determination to have satisfaction in this. "Matters?"

Yvane leaned forward, eyes bulging, scarcely holding back his frustration. "What is the significance of the blind Angel? Why is he so important to you?"

Zaer knew he would be asked. "I underestimated him. He

should be crippled. In effect, he is far from it. He remains a brilliant warrior. I thought he would make a fine assassin. Who would take a blind warrior seriously? But word of his skill has spread throughout Thousandreach like a plague.''

''Assassin? Who would he have killed?''

Zaer feigned surprise. ''Why, Yvane, you of course. Who else? You were always my target.''

''He would never have been allowed near me,'' Yvane retorted contemptuously.

''No? You would not have wanted to see him, to discover for yourself what a strange creature he has become, what power he has? One slip, Yvane, one small opening. I am patient. So are my servants.''

''But not any more?''

Zaer sighed. ''It has become too open, this plot. Destined to fail. I told you, defeat beckons me, as it draws in the Des Aubach and the Spiritores.''

''Then if I kill you here, what of your servants? This blind Angel?''

''Oh, he's yours. None of them will matter to me if I die.''

Yvane drew in a deep breath, as though contemplating all that he had been told. He would either take up the challenge, or leave. But if he left now, Zaer knew there would still be time for him to discover and thwart the others.

Zaer watched him as he shifted his bulk. Yvane leave? How could he? How could he resist the bait? His love of violence and conflict was a drug to him. Just as Zaer's servants had used the weaknesses of others, their lusts, their failings, so would Zaer play Yvane.

''Perhaps you doubt your powers?'' Zaer said softly, but his voice carried. ''I had wondered about them. You are not invincible.''

Yvane reached out and put his fingers around part of a pillar. His face contorted with effort as he squeezed. Stone groaned, cracking, as the pillar moved. But Yvane withdrew the pressure before the pillar could be dislodged.

''I think we have wasted enough words. We are alone. I accept your challenge, Zaer. Begin when you are ready.'' He slithered to one side of another pillar, coming forward gradually.

They were near the centre of the hall, a wider oval area that had once served some dark purpose, its stones pitted and chipped as if they had known machinery or weapons. The two Elevates approached each other from either side of this oval. Neither had weapons. Zaer's chair droned quietly as it carried him across the flagstones.

"I cannot leave it," he told Yvane as the latter scowled at it. "But it is harmless. No weapons."

Yvane grunted. He was the first to slide into the makeshift arena. "I am ready."

They had no need to say anything further. Zaer guided himself into the oval. He eased himself forward a little, arms ready. Yvane weaved towards him like a massive serpent. At the last moment he swung round, his tail whipping out. His intention was clear: he meant to smash Zaer from his seat, overturn it.

But Zaer had anticipated this and slipped backwards quickly, the tip of Yvane's tail slicing the air inches from his face. Zaer's hand shot out in an attempt to grip the tail, but it had flicked away before he could snare it. Yvane swung round once more. He came forward, huge arms reaching out, but there was nothing lumbering in his movements: there was no grace, but he was fast and adaptable.

Their hands locked and they struggled titanically, grunting as they heaved and twisted. Yvane's head ducked and drove hard for Zaer's chest, bringing a huge gasp out of the latter, as though his thick hide had barely absorbed the shock. The chair rocked back, and Yvane gave another tremendous heave, raising the chair onto its side. But Zaer brought a knee upwards under Yvane's bulging abdomen and found a soft place. Yvane squealed and released his victim, sagging back. The chair crashed down, but Zaer moved it away from another lunge.

They stared at one another for a moment, each massaging bruises that spread darkly across his pale skin. Then Yvane renewed the assault, this time using the nails of his hands, extending them like knives, tearing a chunk of flesh from Zaer's right arm with one sweep. Zaer retaliated by punching hard into the face of his assailant. He felt bones snap under the thick folds of flesh. Yvane spit blood, again drawing back.

Zaer's right arm throbbed, blood dribbling in thick rivulets over his lap. Yvane glared at it in triumph, his mouth opening hungrily like that of an animal eager to feed.

Again he swung his tail, a lightning move. Zaer was slower to react and the end of it caught his chair, rocking it. Yvane followed up swiftly, this time using his shoulders to slam into the chest of his enemy. Zaer could not prevent the chair from tilting, feeling himself pressed backwards. The chair was up on its back rollers, skidding crazily across the oval. It smashed into one of the pillars, sending Yvane over Zaer, his head cracking on the stone. Yvane tumbled aside as the chair righted itself. But Zaer knew the motors were ruined. The chair would only operate manually. He put his hands on the floor, trying to swing the chair away, but needles of pain shot through his damaged arm.

Yvane shook himself and struggled up, again using his tail like a ram to bludgeon the chair. Irresistibly he sent it toppling; Zaer was flung out, spilling across the stones. Yvane watched as Zaer used his arms to right himself, dragging himself to his knees. But he could not stand.

Yvane reached for the broken machine and lifted it with an effort. He flung it and it bounced off another of the huge pillars before crashing to the ground, sections of it breaking off and rolling across the flagstones. Zaer watched it in silence. As he struggled for balance, blood began to leak from a dozen ruptured feeder pipes which had been linked to the chair.

Yvane saw the pooling blood and paused.

Zaer nodded. "You can watch me die, Yvane. Or finish me. My life depended on the chair."

Yvane snorted. "Let us finish this." He slithered forward, striking out with his huge hands, one of them chopping through Zaer's own defence and smashing him on the side of his head. He reeled, his other hand trying to steady himself on the stone, but Yvane's tail flicked out and knocked it aside, snapping bones with the tremendous power of the blow. Zaer fell, sprawling.

With a grimace of pleasure, Yvane dropped on him, hands reaching for the neck. As he did so, Zaer squirmed over onto his back. His glass visor was broken, fragments lodged in his hidden eyes, blood welling in twin pools. But his ruined abdomen fastened onto Yvane's, and something within it sank into flesh, barbed and cold, dozens of tiny steel tendrils.

Yvane gasped at the shock, reaching down in an attempt to knock these hooks free, but Zaer's arms pinned him, wrapping around him, dragging him chest to chest, chin to chin. Like lovers they rolled across the flags, locked in each other's grip. Yvane could not free himself. He cracked Zaer's head against the stone, crushed him with his weight, but still Zaer's grip had him fast. He felt the abdomen of his enemy holding his own like a huge leech, a score of tongues probing his flesh, hooked in, immovable.

And then he felt himself being drained.

"No!" he screamed, the sound of his voice rocking the high ceiling. He flung about in a fury of desperation, trying to dislodge Zaer, but to no avail. Zaer was dying, his arms and torso thick with blood, his face a ruin, but his body had become one with Yvane's in a hideous parody of copulation.

Yvane banged his face down into Zaer's, shrieking obscenities, calling upon Absolute Light to save him. When he paused for breath, he realised that Zaer was dead. But in death he clung as fast as he had in life. Their flesh had *fused*. Yvane bent backwards, ripping free of Zaer's lifeless arms.

He groped for the flesh that had snared him and clawed at it, ripping and tearing. Blood gushed around them, thick and hot. At last Yvane had torn free. Howling with an almost insane glee, he made to rise, but as he did so, a thousand agonies shuddered through him, In tearing free, he had opened himself: he gaped in horror at the huge, irreparable wound in his own abdomen, from which the organs were already tumbling.

He inched himself across the oval, leaving a thick trail of blood behind him like some immense mollusc. The hall was vast, the door remote. He dredged up his reserves of strength, but in the end never covered more than a fifth of the distance.

42

Nu-Ko-Te led them upwards in silence, no more than a glimmer of light to guide her, though her surefootedness was uncanny. The near-darkness of the inner tree closed tightly about them, but there was nothing sinister nor hostile in its embrace. In fact the fragrance of the air was unexpectedly soothing, a dramatic contrast to the smells of the city outside. There was a danger, Ruarhi thought, of complacency, of becoming almost drugged by the closeness of the air. He was continually amazed by what Nu-Ko-Te could do: she simply touched the flesh of the huge tree and it parted like a curtain before her, revealing paths and curling tunnels that wound ever upwards through the very heart of the titanic growth. Its dimensions were awesome. Somehow the girl and the tree were linked, and Ruarhi could only think of how men of his own race had achieved a particular harmony with their wolfhounds, almost as though mind spoke to mind. He understood that Sommoi possessed something of this skill, but even he seemed stunned by the curious relationship between Nu-Ko-Te and their bizarre surroundings. And he was clearly mesmerised by the girl, Ruarhi could see, as if Sommoi noticed no one else.

Ruarhi was also aware that Ukar-Tiri was full of mistrust. Either she feared Nu-Ko-Te or she harboured other, equally sour, emotions. Jealousy, perhaps? Ukar-Tiri was very fair to look upon, but Nu-Ko-Te was exceptionally beautiful; it was impossible not to look at her in a way that men did. No doubt, Ruarhi told himself, it was unreasonable of him, but if Ukar-Tiri really was jealous, let her be. Either she wanted his attention or she did not. He had still not been able to fathom that particular puzzle. He would like to have dismissed it altogether, but he could not.

Nu-Ko-Te, he sensed, was very uneasy about this part of their journey. Not so much because they were now moving as fast as they dared upwards towards the regions of the Lightbenders, but because she feared for the safety of Zaer Phesmes. Her face, at first calm, vaguely amused, was now grave, her lips pursed, her eyes close to tears. What had her precise relationship with the Elevate been? Surely she could not have been his lover. A creature such as Zaer and so beautiful—but Ruarhi shut out the thoughts. It was unfair of him. What did it matter that Zaer had the body of a monster? The Elevate had shown himself to be unexpectedly compassionate, extraordinarily so. The future of his world meant everything to him. There could be no denying the sacrifices he was prepared to make for it.

Zaer had spoken to them all in turn, with a strange calmness, a strength born of his complete conviction, his longing for justice in a world of extreme evils. He had made no demands but by his very tone had commanded respect, a willingness to comply. Ruarhi had been surprised at his own reactions. Throughout his sojourn under Skydown he had been suspicious of the inhabitants, angry at their calculating assumptions that he would be their tool. But when Zaer spoke of what needed to be done, Ruarhi could not deny him. It had suddenly struck him that he had been subjected to all these indignities in order to understand what *fodda* really meant, to have his disgust directed towards the destruction of a corrupt system. If he had needed a final conviction, he had it in the blind Angel, the enigma of whom they were all afraid.

Arteriel said very little at any time, no more than was absolutely necessary. His own contempt seemed intense, as if he held life very cheaply. Certainly before he was blinded he must have been typical of his kind: created as a controller, an upholder of the cruel laws of the system that regulated the world under Skydown. One did not converse with fodda. Someone, the invisible ally, had attempted to reduce Arteriel, to humiliate him. They had not achieved that, but they had given him a taste of the emotional traumas fodda suffered.

Ruarhi wondered if it meant anything: all he saw was a warrior who had been fired with killing anger, with a burning desire for revenge. Zaer had read it all, and shaped it with uncanny skill. Ruarhi had known priests of his clan who could mesmerise whole armies, convincing them that there was only one purpose, a single, united will. Zaer had been far more subtle. And believable. Whether or not the blind Angel accepted what Zaer had told him, Ruarhi was not sure. How could he judge? But Arteriel was with them still. When it came to a confrontation, Arteriel would not flinch, and in him there lurked a destructive force beyond contemplation.

Nu-Ko-Te stopped, her head snapping up as though she had heard sounds behind them. But the twisted tunnels were utterly silent.

"What is it?" said Sommoi.

"Two things," whispered the slender girl. "Firstly, the hunt for us is gathering momentum. Kaizu himself has unleashed every force at his disposal."

"The tree?" said Sommoi, his reverence still firm.

Nu-Ko-Te nodded. "It feels these things, transmits them to me. Far below us, creatures stir. They will race through the chambers of my master. Kaizu was never so open before. But he knows of the threat to him. He will no longer care for subtlety. We must hurry. But the tree will not admit Kaizu's dark spawn."

"What else?" came the soft voice of the Angel. In the unnatural glow of the passage, Ruarhi thought he resembled a demon: how Dromator would have shuddered at this incarnation of his nightmares.

"Zaer has met with Yvane, his enemy," said Nu-Ko-Te, shivering. "He cannot hide it from me. They will fight. It will divert Kaizu's attention, just long enough for us to reach the upper heights of Thousandreach."

"You fear for him," said Sommoi hesitantly. "I feel it like a cold wind. You—have seen Zaer's death. Are you like the Skryers?"

She shook her head again, fighting to keep her tears at bay. "He did not have to tell me. I know my Zaer. Better than he. Yvane is far too powerful for him."

They stood in silence for a few moments, and even Arteriel

seemed thoughtful. But Nu-Ko-Te urged them on with a sudden movement. "Come!" she snapped, annoyed at her own sorrow. "We must not fail him now."

Ukar-Tiri nudged Ruarhi's arm, and he jumped. His mind had been fixed on the remote scene that was being enacted somewhere below them. Zaer and the formidable Yvane, locked in mortal combat.

"This is madness," Ukar-Tiri whispered. "What can *I* do? And you, with a sword, Ruarhi?"

"Zaer believed we could bring Kaizu down. It is all that matters. Zaer has probably given his life. We may have to give ours."

She looked at him as if she thought his words empty. "You believe that?" she whispered incredulously.

As so often with her, he struggled to find the words to answer her. What mattered to her? Her freedom, of course, but this quest? It seemed to him that it was the culmination of all her life's miseries, a hopeless outcry that would not even be heard.

"The Skryers are ready," said Sommoi abruptly, also concentrating on the air, as if it brought silent messages to him. Curiously he had accepted Nu-Ko-Te as the leader, the word of Zaer.

Ruarhi grunted an acknowledgment, trying to ignore Ukar-Tiri's frustration. It was true, her own purpose had never been made clear. She felt cheated. She had looked to him for succour but he had led her to no better a fate than she could have expected at the hands of Festubul. Surely she could not have expected him to flee with her into the wilderness under Skydown. But he must think of other things here.

What would the Skryers do? Ruarhi asked himself for the dozenth time. Zaer had clearly managed something of a coup when he had fused the group together: Verusion, Annaxion, and the others had specific powers when they were pooled. Zaer had known it, as had Verusion. But when Zaer had prepared everyone for the assault on the upper regions, he had given the Skryers their detailed instructions privately. Of course, they must be the group's shield, Ruarhi knew. Like Zaer, they would screen the spearhead formed by Arteriel and his group. But there must be more to this. Perhaps, at this stage, it was better not to know. Maybe Ukar-Tiri was right and they were insane to think of rebellion. But they were committed.

Sommoi was satisfied that the Skryers were in place, ready. Perhaps he used his powers to speak to them. Mind linking with mind was in some way an accepted phenomenon under Skydown. Ruarhi doubted that he would ever get accustomed to such a notion, but he had to believe in something other than physical force: they had so little of that.

Nu-Ko-Te moved upward with greater determination, almost recklessly. Rather than narrowing, the tunnel, or vein, or whatever it was, had opened right out, so that the party were now climbing the inside of a vast shaft that must be the inner wall of the tree. Other tunnels ran off it, most of them pitch-black, forbidding. Ruarhi did not look back, nor down. The tree must be even more gigantic than he had imagined. Overhead, shadows clustered like the sky: their destination was totally obscured.

Across the central void, they could see the far wall, partially hidden in darkness. Up from the depths, thick vinelike growths threaded their way heavenward, each of them wrapped around with smaller growths, rootlike protuberances, the bearers of life-giving sap. A number of similar growths emerged from the wall beside them, fused with the wood, contorting upwards like the pipes of an immense engine. Ruarhi could hear the sap flowing within them. He was reminded of something, concentrating his memory. When he had closed on the elusive concept, he stumbled.

Sommoi was beside him at once, sensitive to his thoughts. "What have you seen?"

"These growths," said Ruarhi, indicating the nearest of the thick veins. "They're just like the pipes in the fodda farm."

"It's an illusion," said Sommoi. "This is a living tree—"

Ruarhi answered him by tugging from his belt the length of pipe he had kept. He held it out.

"It is an artefact," said Sommoi. "It transported converted fodda—"

Ruarhi lifted it and brought it down against the thick growth

on the wall. The sound that rang out made them stand very
still. "Metal on metal," said Ruarhi.

The thick pipe he had struck gleamed. Sommoi went to it
and touched it gingerly, bringing away fingers that were slick.

Nu-Ko-Te was beside him at once. "What are you doing?"

"It is fodda," said Sommoi, as if he did not quite understand.

"What does it mean?" said Arteriel. "Metal on metal?
What metal? We are within a tree."

"Yes, what does it mean?" said Ukar-Tiri sarcastically,
suddenly letting her anger flow, her eyes widening, her hands
clenching.

"The *tree* feeds the upper reaches?" said Sommoi.

Nu-Ko-Te seemed momentarily confused. "Wait," she
said, listening in to private sounds the others could not hear.
Then she shook her head. "No. These pipes are not part of
the tree. It is the way the Lightbenders use the tree. The tree
is convenient. The pipes are fed into it and up through it.
Like vines, they have made themselves part of it."

"Like parasites," said Sommoi. "An abomination."

"The trees are abused," said Nu-Ko-Te, as though the full
implications of the pipes were only now striking her. "Ev-
erywhere. All of them." Tears were forming in her eyes as
she spoke.

Sommoi drew back from the pipe. "How do the trees tolerate this?"

"They are powerless to prevent it," Nu-Ko-Te answered.
"For as long as they can remember, they have been used by
the Lightbenders, forced to accept their burden. It is metal.
It resists the tree."

"The Lightbenders have desecrated the trees with metal?"
said Arteriel.

"Yes!" said Nu-Ko-Te bitterly. "The trees have resisted
all efforts by the Lightbenders to channel the pipes into them,
into their own sap-stream. This tree tried once, long ago, but
it is dying. It remains erect, but is like stone, solid, almost
lifeless. The Lightbenders dare not use all the trees this way,
but their greed for power overrides caution. All the trees will
die in time."

Arteriel made a sound of scathing disgust as though only

now had his quarrel with the Lightbenders been given its true perspective.

"What if we were to destroy these pipes?" said Ruarhi.

"There are far too many," said Nu-Ko-Te. "And they are protected. Even the *arborates* have become corrupted, slaves to the Lightbenders' will. We have very little time to act. Even now, Zaer struggles for his life."

"You are right," said Sommoi. "We must hurry. Lead us on, Nu-Ko-Te."

They moved on as one, silent again, each lost in his or her thoughts, but all conscious of the silent suffering of the monstrous trees. It seemed to add to their united will. Even Ukar-Tiri felt a pang of horror at the thought of the mighty tree's maltreatment.

Nu-Ko-Te led them away from the endless climb, going instead down one of the branching tunnels. It was narrower, more confined, but she stopped before it began to taper inwards too tightly. "There is something you have to know about the pipes. They lead ultimately to the palaces. We must use them to enter."

"You mean, go *into* the pipes?" said Ukar-Tiri incredulously, her disgust evident.

Nu-Ko-Te nodded, aware of the other girl's animosity. She looked puzzled, baffled by it. "The Lightbenders would never expect an infiltration through the pipes. Besides, the pipes will be defended."

"By what?" said Arteriel.

"I cannot say. But the tree warns me."

"How do we get in?" said Ruarhi. He did not relish the thought.

But Nu-Ko-Te held up a hand to forestall further questions, her eyes closing in concentration.

"Zaer," she breathed. "The battle—"

"Can she really see it?" whispered Ukar-Tiri to Ruarhi.

"She can," said Arteriel, almost beside her. "But we already know the outcome. Yvane will kill him. They are ill matched."

"Zaer buys us time," said Sommoi. "He has got us here."

"We are followed," said Arteriel as if he had not heard him, stepping back towards the opening of the branch. "Kaizu's warriors, whatever they are: they come. I can hear a great number of them. They, too, have the power to move within this tree. We cannot linger. If you can open the pipe," he told Nu-Ko-Te, "then do it quickly."

Sommoi reached out, preparing to touch Nu-Ko-Te, break her from her apparent reverie, but suddenly she let out a cry, clapping her hands to her head.

"Zaer!" she shrieked, and the word seemed to reach into all their minds, a cry that staggered them. But there was something more, a deeper power. All of them were shaken by it, as if a bolt of energy had crashed among them.

Arteriel fell back against the wall of the passage, hand automatically going to his eyes, as though it were possible for him to be blinded again. Sommoi dropped to his knees, hands, like Nu-Ko-Te's, covering his ears. Ruarhi and Ukar-Tiri clung to one another, gasping for air.

There was a roaring in all their ears. They could hear Nu-Ko-Te shouting Zaer's name again and again. Like the abrupt breaking of a storm, sound washed around them, filling the air with its turbulence. Then, as suddenly as it had come, it was gone.

When they were able to gather themselves at last, Sommoi went to Nu-Ko-Te and tried to console her. She was sobbing uncontrollably.

"The battle is over," said Arteriel. "Zaer is dead."

Ruarhi felt the echoes, like distant thunder, within his skull, as though someone was shouting far away, above the receding din.

"You hear it, too?" murmured Ukar-Tiri.

"Inside?"

She nodded. For a moment they seemed to share a strange unity, and Ruarhi felt an almost overpowering wave of desire for the girl. Then he noticed that Sommoi was looking at them strangely. He touched his head inadvertently, as if expecting to find something there.

"Power," they heard Nu-Ko-Te say. "Zaer's legacy. It is true, Yvane has killed him, but Zaer has released his last gift to us." She turned to the blind Angel. "And you, do you feel it?"

"I remain blind. But something else has lodged in me."

"Yvane is dying," said Nu-Ko-Te. "But Kaizu is aware. He knows he is being attacked. His hunters gather. Quickly. We must enter his territory." She stretched out her hands over the curve of the wide pipe and Ruarhi watched in amazement as the surface quivered like the withers of a stallion. Then something was leaking from the metal, like an opened wound. Shadows deceived the eye. Nu-Ko-Te had done to the metal what she did to the tree. It was open.

Carefully she climbed over the lip of the aperture she had made. Darkness beckoned them all, the stench of decay. The way up to the palaces stretched like a gullet.

43

Inside the pipe, the air was thick and musty. The pipe itself was dried up, its sides caked solidly, in places so thickly that it was difficult to pass. If it had once been used to pump vital fluids upwards to the Lightbenders, it had either fallen into disuse or had been ruined by disease, a metal canker that had shriveled it, coagulating its contents, drying them out like rock. A trickle of muck ran down its length from above, making the floor slick and dangerous, gleaming in the phosphorescent glow of the metal. Like maggots inside a corpse, the party crawled upwards. They were silent now, and whatever uncertainties they had about their mission crowded in on them, every fear pricking them, probing raw nerve ends. It would have been easy to go back, but they moved mechanically, set.

They stopped only to eat, wedged against the dried contents of the pipe. Ironically they would never have been able to climb the almost vertical shaft if the sides had not been so thick with solidified matter. Their food was inevitably fodda, the simple, cheeselike wedges that Ruarhi had first eaten out on the road. His hatred of it had become no more than a dull ache, pushed to the back of his mind.

When Nu-Ko-Te finally decided that they had climbed high enough, they were close to exhaustion.

"We should rest here," she said. "Once we leave the pipe, we will be in constant danger. While we are here, we will not be found. This pipe is dead. Outside it is the tree." She smiled with sudden realisation. "It is the tree that has done this. The pipe hurts the tree, in time kills it, but this tree has strangled the pipe in its folds."

They nodded in silence. In spite of their precarious position, they found sleep easily.

When they woke, stiff but refreshed, Nu-Ko-Te again opened the metal. There was faint light beyond, and the welcoming smell of wood, the body of the tree. They emerged into a curling corridor that appeared to follow the insides of a massive branch. Being free of the pipe filled them with strength they could hardly have anticipated. Arteriel, face drawn, was visibly relieved to be out of the congested shaft, eager to be on with the assault.

Nu-Ko-Te touched the whorled surface of the wood before her. "I think we should exit here."

"What lies beyond?" said Sommoi.

She shuddered. "They are there. In their palaces. Once we go in, the hunt will intensify."

"Open it," said Arteriel, stretching his arms, the fabric of his wings rustling as if he longed for flight.

Nu-Ko-Te nodded, then used the tree's gifts to open a way through its flesh. When she had done, light spilled in, bright and dazzling, so that for a while the company had to step back from it, eyes smarting. Although Arteriel could see nothing, even he reacted to the light as though he could feel its intensity.

"It will be all right," said Ruarhi. "It's no brighter than the light in my own world. It just takes time to get used to it." He stepped to the breach that Nu-Ko-Te had made, squinting. Beyond he saw another passage, its walls smooth and transparent. He touched it: the surface was like living flesh. Something gushed along inside it. Another huge pipe, though not made of metal: this was like a skein.

"How do we pass?" said Ukar-Tiri.

Nu-Ko-Te also touched the glasslike surface. She was either listening to the sounds trapped within, or something else. The echoes of Zaer's voice? Ruarhi wondered.

"We must open it," Nu-Ko-Te said. "Though it is not as the trees."

"Must we enter?" said Sommoi, voice dropping with sudden loathing. "You know what that is inside."

Ruarhi glanced at him, though he knew the answer.

"A fodda stream," said Sommoi. "This is one of the principal feeder ducts. It probably leads to a reservoir."

Nu-Ko-Te nodded. "Yes. It goes eventually to feed one of the Lightbenders. We are in the House of the Des Aubach. The only safe way into its labyrinth is along this duct, then out before it empties in the pool of its *amniot.*"

"I don't understand the word," said Sommoi.

"It is what Zaer calls the Lightbenders."

"Why must we enter this duct?" said Ukar-Tiri, wrinkling her nose in disgust at the thought. The decayed pipe had been nightmare enough, but the thought of entering the living pipe was revolting.

"The Regulators will find us if we are not careful," said Nu-Ko-Te. She chose her words carefully, as though constantly listening to advice before speaking. The others knew why, although Zaer's ghost said nothing to them. Even so, Ruarhi sensed something close to him, on the edge of his thoughts, more than just an echo of the huge Elevate.

"They serve the Lightbenders," Nu-Ko-Te went on. "They attend to the ducts, the mechanics of the Houses. If they discovered us, they would kill us instantly."

"Then you'd better open the duct," said Arteriel.

"I cannot," said the girl, frowning anxiously, her hands already feeling its surface. "It is not like the trees or metal."

Arteriel reached out with his gloves, the taloned hands. "Show me where to make an incision."

Nu-Ko-Te hesitated only momentarily, then put her hand on his wrist, her eyes widening as she felt his flesh, its warmth. She drew closer to him, her fascination for him undisguised. Did he realise? Ruarhi wondered. For a moment she paused again, then she guided his gloved hand to a place on the transparent wall of the duct that was level with his blind eyes.

They turned to her briefly, but his face was expressionless.

"Try here," she said, breathing the words.

Arteriel leaned forward, exerting himself, dragging the claw downwards slowly. At first it seemed that it had had no effect: there were no marks on the smooth surface. But as he stood back, the watchers could hear a soft hissing, as of air escaping, and the slow tearing of the material as it unpeeled itself. Arteriel frowned, then pulled Nu-Ko-Te back.

"Stand back, all of you!" he snapped. They obeyed at once, just as the wall of the duct burst outwards, diverting a gush of the liquid stream within it. It was thick and oily, with a sweet stench that they all found offensive. But after the initial rush, the stream steadied, only partially overspilling the bottom of the circular duct.

Arteriel turned, facing the way they had come. "Whatever creatures protect the tree tunnels," he said, "they will emerge soon. Get into the duct."

Nu-Ko-Te was the first to do so, stepping gingerly, dropping into the thick flow, which reached her upper thighs. She used the convex wall of the duct to steady herself. Ruarhi and Ukar-Tiri followed her, the latter gripping Ruarhi's waist with one hand. Sommoi dropped down behind them, and Arteriel was close after him.

"Move!" he called.

Somewhere beyond, they could hear roaring, as if the liquid suddenly plunged into a deep pool. They were loath to go forward, but saw the necessity of doing so. It was difficult to go down the duct quickly. The flow increased as the gradient sloped downward, and the floor was like glass, dangerously slippery. More than once one of them nearly stumbled, and only by gripping each other's hands were they able to prevent a disaster. Only Arteriel did not join the chain, but for all his blindness, he was the most surefooted. They dared not turn and look back, having to concentrate on the slippery descent, but they thought they heard something above the roar of sound ahead of them, where the stream tumbled away to its destination. The pursuit was unquestionably closing, invisible but sure as death.

Nu-Ko-Te gave a gasp, lurching and almost sliding away into what was now becoming a fast flow. "We have to get out," she gasped as Ruarhi dragged her back to her feet. "If we go on, we will fall into the reservoir. There would be no escape from it if we did."

Ruarhi called Arteriel forward, and the Angel struggled through the muck, now almost waist-deep. "Watch behind us," he said to Sommoi, who nodded grimly.

Turning, Ruarhi saw something coming along the stream, distorted by the strange light of the chambers beyond the walls. There were various scarlet shapes, vaguely anthropomorphic, eyeless, the spiderish, elongated arms strung out across the duct, pressing the walls for support as the creatures slithered onwards in pursuit.

Once again, Nu-Ko-Te guided Arteriel's claws, and he tore open a section of the duct wall, this time into the chambers beyond. The flow gushed out as the wall of the duct parted suddenly and Arteriel had to dig his claws into the fleshlike wall to prevent himself from being smashed into the chamber. But he swung outwards and dropped, balancing with uncanny precision. Nu-Ko-Te went out almost at once, stumbling on the slick floor, but Arteriel's arm shot out and steadied her. Again she looked up at him in amazement.

Ukar-Tiri alighted more comfortably, with Ruarhi right behind her, and they both helped Sommoi down.

He wiped filth from his face. "They're close behind us," he said anxiously.

Ruarhi positioned himself beside the ripped duct wall. As when they had entered, the steady flow of liquid spillage soon ceased, the main flow gushing quickly now towards the drop. Ruarhi had drawn his blade. He motioned for the others to find cover while he defended the gap against the first of the pursuers. A fight of some kind seemed inevitable. He could see through the duct wall the first of the creatures pulling itself forward.

As he waited, he saw the wall of the duct starting to seal itself, healing up like a wound, almost instantly. He gaped at it, stunned by the speed of its recovery. Beyond, the first of the pursuit made a grab with its long fingers, like a fleshly spider falling upon its prey. The mutated hand banged up against the wall of the duct, scrabbling at it. But the fingers were without nails or claws. They slid impotently on the duct's surface. Unlike Arteriel's clawed gloves, they could not effect a fresh rip.

Ruarhi stepped back, watching the horrors in the duct in amazement. Like great scarlet spiders, they threshed in the muck that was the flow, a dozen of those elongated arms swinging and beating at the wall. But to no avail. The creatures were heaped up against each other by the flow, forced slowly downwards until suddenly, with one last gush, the flow had its way and bludgeoned them past the place where Ruarhi watched. Tangled up like one monstrous mutation, the creatures passed out of sight to the inevitable plunge.

Ruarhi almost whooped with relief. He swung round, only to see Sommoi cautioning him to silence. For the first time he studied his new surroundings, and almost choked on the sight.

They were in an immense chamber, the ceiling of which seemed at first glance to be open to the sky; and it was a very different sky from the one under Skydown. Then they were above the shield! Ruarhi realised. He studied it for a long moment: it was like the midday sky of his own world on a cloudless day, the sky azure and lit by a brilliant sun, somewhere beyond the rim of the building. As he looked, he realised that there was a ceiling, a vast dome made out of what must be glass or crystal, held in place by enormous spans of metal that themselves gleamed and sparkled.

Ahead of him, the others were grouped under the shadow of a huge stone pillar, its thickness comparable to the combined thickness of hundreds of men. It rose up to the ceiling, one of its main supports. Other such titanic pillars rose up, and among them Ruarhi could also discern the dark wood of the tree trunks, the immense growths that seemed to rise up forever, even beyond the glass dome itself. Beyond the nearest pillar there was a maze of ducts and pipes, some of them even thicker than the duct they had left, others far smaller, the thickness of a human wrist. Some of them were translucent: the viscous flow of liquefied fodda squeezed through them endlessly. And over all this vastness of construction and piping, a deep silence reigned, as though this was not a great palace but a mausoleum.

Sommoi was beckoning Ruarhi over to him urgently. Quickly and silently, Ruarhi did as bidden.

"The pursuit—" began Ruarhi.

But Sommoi was nodding. "We saw. But there'll be others. The Regulators."

"What are they?"

"Wait and you'll see. They are sensitive to the slightest change in here. The Lightbenders live in a world that is very different from that of our kind. Everything must be regulated. The slightest change, the slightest intrusion, must be dealt with quickly."

He had barely spoken, when they heard something beyond the pillar. It sounded like the slap of naked feet on stone, slow and ponderous. Ruarhi and the others moved back deeper into shadow, following the curve of the great pillar around to where a wall of some kind rose up beside it.

Ruarhi watched as the Regulator emerged. Some eight feet tall, it was humanoid, its ovoid body supported on two almost comical, squat legs, its arms by contrast ridiculously thin and spindly, as though the creature had been designed ineptly. Its head was a bald, neckless dome, its features almost an afterthought; the eyes were minute, as was the gash of a nose and the lipless mouth.

It shuffled with apparent effort to the duct and the place from which the intruders had lately emerged. Its bizarre hands reached out and began to probe: they were clearly far more sensitive and effective as tools than they looked.

"It must be destroyed at once," whispered Arteriel. "And swiftly."

"It will be difficult," said Nu-Ko-Te. "It is not like us. It has no vital organs. It would absorb any sword stroke," she added, with a meaningful look at Ruarhi.

"Can't we just run?" said Ukar-Tiri softly. "It looks too slow to catch us."

"No," said Nu-Ko-Te. "It will warn others. There are many of them. They would smother us. But if we kill it here, in its own sector, our trail will be hidden."

"Then how do we kill it?" said Ruarhi, watching the Regulator as it bent down and touched the dark pool on the floor, lifting its soiled hands to sniff at them like a hunting hound.

Arteriel pulled out two of his short, curved instruments. "Ruarhi, hold up your sword." As the latter did so, Arteriel ripped a length of his outer garment, tossing it to Ruarhi. "Bind it around the blade as best you can. And another."

Baffled, Ruarhi did as asked. He saw the Regulator turn, its eyes suddenly falling upon the group. At once it swung round, ponderous and hideous, mouth sagging open like that of a huge fish under water, and plodded forward, its intent unmistakable.

Once Ruarhi had bound the strips of cloth around his blade, Arteriel stepped closer to him and struck his two instruments together. They shed a tiny rain of sparks, which ignited the cloth almost at once. Ruarhi needed no further instruction: Arteriel's intention was obvious.

With a grim smile, Ruarhi went out to meet the oncoming Regulator. Its arms opened in a mock welcome, but Ruarhi ducked down, plunging the blade into the bulging abdomen. The cloth was burning in a fiery blaze, threatening to consume itself in moments, but its effect on the Regulator was spectacular. The flesh of the creature caught at once, and fire tore across it in trails, black smoke churning upwards. Its mouth opened wide in a mute scream that was all the more horrible for its silence.

Ruarhi leapt back as the creature beat at itself uselessly. The fire roared, devouring its victim incredibly swiftly. Fat hissed and spat, until, toppling, the carcass exploded, gobbets of it continuing to flare. The sword was flung away by the detonation: it skidded along the floor, resting accusingly at the feet of Ruarhi. He bent to pick it up, but winced at the heat in its haft.

Both of the girls had turned away from the sight of the blazing Regulator, but Sommoi watched in silence. His face was a mixture of fascination and disgust.

"Is it done?" whispered Arteriel coldly. To him it seemed a minor thing they had accomplished, almost of no consequence.

"Yes," said Ruarhi.

"Then we had better begin the real work."

Ruarhi grimaced, wondering what hellish task it was that Zaer had given the blind Angel to do.

44

Verusion and the renegade Skryers were secreted in another ancient and disused part of the city, a tower that was in a dangerous state of disrepair, shunned for that very reason. They knew that whatever the outcome of Zaer's confrontation with Yvane, the latter's minions would hunt remorselessly for their enemies. Nowhere would be safe. Kaizu himself would have taken a very special interest in the strange events that were unfolding in the lower levels: the mighty Lightbender might even feel moderately threatened by what was happening. But this tower, at least, would be passed over initially. Later, as with every other tower, it would be combed, its every stone pulled apart if necessary. Zaer's purpose had been to buy his servants time. In that he had succeeded.

The Skryers had listened deeply to the words of the Elevate. Zaer had revealed certain things to them that had shocked them, things that they had not been able to guess at in their work. Not even Tetraven, with all his accumulated understanding of history, could have known the secrets Zaer passed down to him. Annaxion, too, already confirmed in his desertion of his former master, was taken aback by the scope of the revelations.

These things bonded the rebels more tightly. Whatever disasters were about to befall Thousandreach, they could not shy from setting them in motion.

The crumbling chamber in which they gathered was circular, the heart of the old tower. Above them, lost in immediate shadow, a shaft rose upwards, presumably to the very guts of the upper palaces. In the centre of the chamber

there was a well, yards across, which also plumbed an un-
fathomable darkness. Distant rumbles, the thunder of remote, immense machines, came up in occasional waves. In
the centre of the well there was a circular disc, suspended
over the drop by chains as thick as a man's waist. Annaxion
had carefully crossed over to the disc.

He disrobed himself and sat down, his arms folded across
his chest, his eyes closed, already beginning the meditation.

Verusion and the other three Skryers also disrobed and
they sat equidistant from one another around the rim of the
well, facing inwards. Every detail had been given to them by
Zaer: he had described this place vividly, every stone, as
though he knew it intimately and had visited it often. He also
described the ritual the Skryers must perform. His words echoed in all of their heads, locked there now as if repeating
themselves in an endless mantra.

They waited. The world beyond them faded completely.
The chamber became everything. Below them, the drone
faded, closed out.

Into the combined darkness of their minds came the first
tremors of conflict. Zaer Phesmes and Yvane Sephir had met,
had begun their dire struggle. Zaer had told the Skryers ex-
actly what would happen, how Yvane would destroy him. It
was, he had said, inevitable but necessary.

"My physical being is a pitiful thing, as you can see. If I
lived on, it would undergo an even greater transformation.
Alive, I could not avoid it. Unlike my contemporaries, I am
glad to reject this," Zaer had told them.

Verusion could not see the battle that was raging somewhere else in the city, the two huge Elevates writhing in a
final dance of death. But he felt the agonies of his master, as
did the others. They maintained their postures with difficulty,
holding their heads, gasping. Mercifully, the worst of the
contest did not go on for very long. They felt the life suddenly bleed out of Zaer, the flesh collapsing in on itself.
Something fled from it though, bolts of energy, thought,
power: an intangible force that leapt across gulfs of space
and mind and smote all of them, almost knocking them flat
to the ground.

For a long, silent time each of them squeezed himself into

a tight ball of mental anguish. Like men long trapped in utter darkness, they began to test a new daylight, slowly opening their eyes on the miracle of a sun. They glanced across at one another, at Annaxion on the disc, but none of them spoke.

The bloody battle was over. Zaer's flesh was dead. Yvane's, too. Somewhere in the sprawling immensity of Thousand-reach, their two carcasses sprawled. They would rot where they lay, fodda for spiders, rats, vermin.

Again the Skryers waited. They felt the breath of something monstrous on their shoulders, but would not move. The power would instruct them in its own time. This was not a place for questions.

Verusion closed his eyes and at once caught a glimpse of figures on his inner eye. Nu-Ko-Te, the perfect child, led her party of assassins up into the high reaches of Thousandreach. The diversion had screened them: they were pursued by monstrous forces they could not begin to understand, but they were through the barriers that should have protected the Lightbenders' realm. Verusion watched as they entered the fodda duct, reopening it to step out into the palace of the Des Aubach. Very soon they would be ready to receive what Zaer had prepared for them. Through the Skryers.

Something of Zaer had survived, some primal essence. He had known it would be so, shaping his existence around that conviction. It was not an inner voice that spoke to Verusion now, but something directed his thoughts, injected new ones into his mind. He shivered: there was an exhilaration in this. He opened his eyes and looked about him. Each of the other Skryers nodded in turn: it was a shared experience. Zaer had promised this.

"Let us concentrate," said Verusion.

They did so, minds linked by Zaer's intent. As one, they watched the progress of Nu-Ko-Te and the others. And as one, they saw the stirring of the first of the Lightbenders as it brought its own mind to bear on the sacrilegious intrusion. Its power was inestimable, but the Skryers had to ignore any fear engendered by it. Fear could swamp them, Zaer had warned. Fear could uproot their sanity, shred it.

"Find the Overlap," was his clear instruction. "Feed on

what I leave you. Use your own skills, fuse them, everything you have acquired. The Overlap will be drawn to you. It will not be able to resist.''

Verusion no longer needed to speak. Each of them was a component of one force. Like Zaer, they had abandoned their flesh. Energy centred on Annaxion, his own peculiar talent, his future vision.

"Select one of the many branches," Zaer had told him. "Fix it clearly. The Overlap will respond. It is rudderless, but present it with its own tangible future, and you will steer it.''

Annaxion moved effortlessly onward into the darkness that was the way to forever: he did so with more ease, more certainty, than he had ever done before. Previously he had been like a crippled child, incomplete, staggering, reaching blindly for goals which constantly eluded him. Now he moved with godlike confidence, soaring, mocking the shadows. Ahead of him huge vistas were flung wide: there were so many choices. But he knew what he sought.

For Verusion and the others it was very different. Their own search was conducted in a shadowland, a merging realm of endless confusion, world upon world, link upon link. Like a tapestry that had been unraveled and reworked aimlessly, the chaos of worlds churned. It was in this entropy that the Overlap writhed, itself a crippled force, struggling for answers, for cohesion.

Zaer focused the will of the Skryers. They were his eyes, the power he had lacked.

And through Annaxion, they found the Overlap. It, too, searched, like a prisoner in a labyrinth, beating on walls of stone with bared and bloody hands, tearing at every chink in the stone, every possible clue to egress.

Something in Verusion recognised it for what it was: not a nameless, accidental quirk of nature, a freak power, but an *intelligence*, an entity. It was no more corrupt and mindless than the essence that Zaer had become. It was a slave of time, a survivor of eternity, a mutation, product of the wars that had warped past and future alike.

It sensed the kindred that had come for it. Like a man about to go under the waves for a final time, it reached in utter desperation for the hand that would save it. The Skryers felt the linking. For a moment there was a searing white light, then nothing. Absolute emptiness. Absolute silence.

Absolute light.

Zaer's essence saved them from panic, steadied their reason. A multitude of thoughts fought for precedence within each of the Skryers as they forged the link with the Overlap. But the realisation of what it was threatened to overwhelm them.

"I told you that not all of the so-called gods were of a like mind," came Zaer's controlling thought.

"The rebel god. The ally," Verusion said aloud.

"Yes. Driven out for his rebellion, his rejection of their contemptible system. For his condemnation of their creation: Skydown, the evolution of the Lightbenders, their perverse methods of control. He could not be destroyed, merely set loose to become a victim of chance."

There was no answering thought from the Overlap, but like a secret craft, it had moored alongside them.

"They could not subvert his thoughts, nor alter his purpose. He could not work from above, so he has worked, slowly, from the depths, far under Skydown."

"But they have used him: *we* have used him," said Verusion, with a sudden feeling of horror. The Overlap had been the means by which innumerable beings had been brought into this world, wrenched from their own worlds to be made victims of the system here.

"You never exercised control, nor were you ever able to. But it amused the Lightbenders to use the Overlap as you have said, and the gods found it truly ironic. A fitting punishment, they thought, laughing at the futile efforts of man, the everlasting despair of the exile.

"We are one now," Zaer's thought continued. "Our flesh has become as the fodda that our world produces so single-mindedly. But we still have need of flesh. We remain tied to it. It is still the tool to the craftsman, the sword to the warrior."

Verusion knew to whom Zaer referred. He could envisage the small group of assassins as they toiled closer to their goal somewhere in the palaces of the Lightbenders.

"First, the Lightbenders," said Zaer, and in the ocean of light that flooded them all, there was a tremor of response, a shudder of pleasure, of anticipation. The Overlap gathered itself like a serpent gathering its coils about its prey.

They were moving along a narrow channel between two walls, one of stone, as it seemed, the other the side of a colossal glass tank. This latter was filled with fluid that could have been water: it gleamed in the radiance of sunlight from the dome far overhead. There were numerous pipes and ducts leading from under it, some of which curled upwards and across to the stone wall, burying into it like the ganglia of monstrous creatures.

Nu-Ko-Te led the group again, and Ruarhi wondered how it was that she seemed to know where to take them. But neither Sommoi nor Arteriel demurred, as if they had faith in her.

"Other Regulators will come," said Arteriel. "This place will be infested with them. We cannot fight them in numbers."

"What are we searching for?" said Ruarhi impatiently.

"The way to the House of the Da Sangravilles," said Sommoi. "It is obvious. Kaizu must be our prime target."

Ukar-Tiri, who had been constantly looking over her shoulder, suddenly sagged back against the stone wall, her hand over her mouth, her eyes bulging in terror. She was looking up at the tank. She pointed.

Something vast had moved into view on the other side of the glass. The colour of bleached flesh, it was elongated, immense in girth, and had a number of protrusions on either side of its gargantuan body. They flapped in the fluid, guiding it like paddles. But they were grotesque hands, with webbed fingers longer than a man's body. There was no head in the human sense, merely an extension of the tubular body, and long, pulsating gills either side of it that acted like mouths.

As the group watched, transfixed by the monstrous vision, one of the pipes linked to the underside of the tank shifted as if by its own volition, and within the tank a thick cloud of dark liquid blossomed where the pipe entered. Avidly the monster in the tank swung round, the blunt end of its body opening to reveal a scarlet maw. It sucked in the dark cloud and as it did so, two lids flickered upwards to reveal the creature's eyes. Like twin moons they gazed, rapt with the pleasure of feeding, as if indifferent to anything beyond the glass wall.

"Fodda," breathed Sommoi. "This is where it is pumped."

"What in all the gods is that abomination?" gasped Ruarhi, his fingers white around the haft of the sword he had retrieved from the scene of the Regulator's slaughter.

"Even though I am blind," said Arteriel, "I can feel what it is that lies beyond."

"Imahal," said Nu-Ko-Te. "An *amniot.*"

"One of the Des Aubach heirs," said Sommoi. "Is this him?"

Ruarhi watched as the huge creature used its repulsive handlike fins to guide itself back into the heart of its huge tank. *"This* is a Lightbender?"

"It is what all life under Skydown strives to become," a clear voice within him told him. Zaer. As if he sat beside him, guiding him still.

Ruarhi could not speak, and he felt the hand of Ukar-Tiri take his. He was glad to grip it and hold on to it, as though her touch was the only real link he had with sanity, a world far removed from this hideous, unbelievable realm.

45

Arteriel swooped upwards, crossing the open spaces between the upper trunks and pillars that bisected the palace of the Des Aubach Lightbenders. The others had agreed with some reluctance that it would be sensible for him to attempt to discover the safest way through the maze, just as they had agreed that they ought to make their prime target the palace of the Da Sangravilles. They must find Kaizu before his powers found them.

The blind Angel Guard could feel the intensity of the light beyond the dome that his companions had described to him. The trees, they said, grew beyond it, spreading their green canopies into the very realm of Absolute Light. Somehow, as the light speared down inside the palace, it made shadows with the trunks and the pillars, and Arteriel read the patterns unerringly, as though the power to do so had been implanted within him. He guessed this was the doing of Zaer, but he was unable to communicate with him in the strange way that Nu-Ko-Te still seemed to do.

Thought of the girl weakened his concentration on the flight; he wished that he were able to see her. Something in her voice, in the sounds that she made as she moved, deeply intrigued him. It was unexpected, this fascination. He could sense the danger in it, and smiled to himself. Ironic that he should be here, in this most hostile of environments, and yet his fascination for Nu-Ko-Te should afford him more concern!

He knew that she could not keep her own eyes from him. Often he had sensed them, studying him as if he were something from a dream. His power, perhaps, attracted her. The smell of blood, the knowledge that he had killed: it was nectar to some. But the thought of her being drawn to him for this was suddenly repulsive. What he did was necessary. To take pleasure in it, savour it, was the Lightbender disease. Yet Zaer had bred her, created her. And he had been forced along evolutionary lines, shaped for higher things. Zaer rebelled, yes, but were there traces of his heritage still in him, passed on to Nu-Ko-Te? Could such things be eradicated completely?

Arteriel twisted in midflight, narrowly missing one of the pillars. Concentrate!

Beyond the next pillar he sensed an orifice, air billowing from it as if from a vent to outside the building. Hovering, almost motionless, he tried to estimate the size of the opening, what it might lead to. A passage, but to where? Another palace? Possibly. He would have to bring the others here.

Swiftly he rose up and recrossed the upper palace. As he

did so, he became aware of movements below him, stirrings as of fluids, waves striking on surfaces. And within the numerous deep pools of liquid, shapes, gently rising. And with them rose a miasma of malice, as of creatures avid for blood. Something lashed the air below his feet. He swung upwards, knowing that death was closing on him.

Flight saved him, and an aerial ballet conducted at terrific speeds, a weaving between more trunks, extended branches. He almost came to grief on them in his effort to avoid whatever it was that sought to snare him and drag him down into those awesome vats. But he was free of them, dropping down into the cool shadows of a steel corridor, beyond the area of the tanks.

"Arteriel!" It was a whisper, but it came through the air clearly. Nu-Ko-Te.

He hovered above her and the others. They had been hidden under a buttress of piping.

"There is a passage, a possible exit. But we must pass through many more of the tanks. They seethe with life."

"The Skryers have begun their work," called Sommoi. "They have summoned power, through the Overlap."

"How can you know this?" said Arteriel, dropping lightly to the ground.

"Zaer was not destroyed in his conflict with Yvane," Sommoi answered. "He was merely converted into another kind of energy. It links us to the Skryers. And it links them to the Overlap."

"Can they control it?" asked Arteriel.

"I think so. They will direct its power here, to the palaces. But they must do it before Kaizu realises what is happening."

"We must get to the palace of the Da Sangravilles," said Nu-Ko-Te suddenly. "We are the key that will unlock the power of the Overlap. All of us."

Ukar-Tiri shrank back, but Ruarhi tried to calm her. "We'll be destroyed!" cried the girl.

Ruarhi nodded. "She's right. How can we be of use to such powers?"

Nu-Ko-Te scowled. "I don't know. But we have to go there. Without us to focus upon, the Overlap cannot function. It could not find Kaizu."

"The Overlap functions through *us?*" said Arteriel, stunned.

"Yes," nodded Nu-Ko-Te frantically. "Through Zaer, the Skryers, and us. We are all components. The Lightbenders could never have known. Arteriel, you must get us beyond this place."

"It will take time. The palace is a vast maze. And the Des Aubach spawn—"

"Even so," said Sommoi. "You must lead us."

Arteriel rose up slowly. He knew the direction he needed to take and began the gentle flight, allowing the others time to follow as they threaded their way through yet more banks of piping. They were able to move a good way through the palace in this fashion, sometimes squeezing through the narrowest of openings, sometimes crossing an open divide between huge pillars, but keeping always to the shadows, and mercifully avoiding the huge pools that increasingly interlinked the vats.

At length, however, they came to an open area. It was like a huge sunken pool at the heart of the palace, with a number of wide slipways dropping into it. Something gleamed on the nearest of the ramps, as if a creature from the pool had either just entered or left it.

"I can't see any cover around this pool. It's wide open," said Ruarhi, scanning the edges as far as he could see on either side.

Sommoi nodded. "You are right. And we cannot cross the water."

A hundred yards across the pool there was an open area, devoid of any furnishing, broken only by more of the pillars. A single pipe ran across it, twisting back on itself before opening into the huge pool. But nothing ran from the pipe.

"We will have to try and skirt the pool," said Nu-Ko-Te. "There is only one way round, even though it is exposed."

"Where's Arteriel?" asked Ruarhi.

"Here," came an immediate answer. The Angel Guard stood above them on a cylindrical stack of piping. He seemed to be scenting the pool, as a hound would have. "I've tried to find a path through the piping, but I cannot. This pool is walled off. But if you expose yourselves—"

"Have you flown over it?" said Sommoi.

Arteriel nodded. "There's a Lightbender in it, possibly asleep. I think it may be Subran himself."

Ruarhi pointed to the area directly above the centre of the pool. High overhead, set in the dome, a wide funnel of glass rose up towards one of its many apexes. "What's that for?"

Arteriel had not been aware of it, listening to Ruarhi as he described it. "It could be a vent," the Angel Guard said. "I will find out. You begin going around the pool. The passage I saw is beyond it." He took to the air at once, and Ruarhi again marveled at the gracefulness of his flight.

Nu-Ko-Te urged them on, and they went out onto the glistening slabs that formed a lip around the pool. The waters were a brilliant blue colour, very still, and for the moment there was nothing to suggest life within them. Slowly the party moved around the rim.

Arteriel arrowed upwards, investigating the funnel that Ruarhi had seen. Directly beneath it, he felt the stirring of air. There was an uncanny freshness about it, a unique coolness: the air of the outside? But it was a far purer air than the air he knew under Skydown. The funnel was possibly a way out, to the realm of Absolute Light, but he had no mind to find out. Besides, the others could not hope to climb up here.

Sounds below drew his attention and he swung away, arcing downwards. Something was moving through the pipe maze, homing in on the small group that was edging around the pool. Although Arteriel could not see them, he guessed what they were: a score or more of the Regulators. They had been summoned away from their vectors, drawn here, possibly by Subran himself. The Lightbenders knew there were intruders in their realm. The purpose of the Regulators was also clear: they intended to block off the retreat of the party.

As Arteriel made to drop down, he felt the fluid below him stirring, as surely as if he could see it. Something monstrous moved there.

Ruarhi and Sommoi saw the rippling on the waters at the same moment. They heard Arteriel's warning not to turn back.

"Run!" called the Angel Guard. They needed no second

bidding, the four of them breaking into an immediate sprint
along the slippery slabs. Out in the pool, something dark
broke the surface, moving parallel with the runners, swift
and silent. It was barely visible, being hidden by the water,
but it gave an impression of immense size.

Beyond the group, a shape floated up out of the pool, a
perfect sphere, twice the size of a human head, trailing
threads beneath it that seemed to be comprised of the fluid
itself. Another followed, then another, until a dozen of the
gleaming spheres wove a pattern in the air, to and fro, like
creatures too nervous to approach the intruders. Others were
sliding up from the water, scores of them, varying in sizes,
none larger than the first, the smallest of them no bigger than
a fist. They had ranked themselves, spreading in a defensive
formation that cut off the intruders from the rest of the pool;
the end of the line of floating spheres moved forward and
hovered over the path around the pool.

Ruarhi turned, warned by Arteriel of something behind
him. Onto the slabs where the group had emerged from the
pipeworks, a number of Regulators were coming.

"We're trapped!" cried Ukar-Tiri. "They'll kill us!"

Nu-Ko-Te alone seemed to remain calm. "Arteriel, what
did you find up there?"

"It's like a vent. Possibly to the outside. But you can't get
out that way. Unless you can see a way to climb up."

"We cannot get out," said Nu-Ko-Te, "but something
could get in."

Sommoi looked at her in bafflement. "That way leads to
Absolute Light. It would incinerate us."

"The Skryers must begin the unleashing," said Nu-Ko-Te.
"Subran will have to be the first."

Ruarhi was watching the Regulators. With slow but purposeful movements, they were coming along the rim of the
pool. He gripped his weapon. This time there would be no
fire to use.

"Prepare yourselves!" cried Nu-Ko-Te.

The others all turned to her, but their eyes were suddenly
wrenched away by the sight of the great shape lifting itself
from the central deeps of the pool. Water cascaded from it
in thunderous falls as it broke the surface, sending out waves

across the pool that converged on the group, threatening to sweep it into the water.

Verusion felt the tug in his mind, as strong as a river's current. The Overlap strained for direction, release. The Skryers spoke to each other as one, minds sharing the knowledge of the Overlap as it focused its attention on the palaces of the Lightbenders, the small human force gathered there, the intended lens.

Kaizu knows! came a thought like thunder. *He cannot prevent the unleashing, but he will deflect power.*

Verusion and the others understood, the images tumbling over one another wildly, uncontrollably. Kaizu had discovered what it was his would-be assassins intended, the power they would set loose upon him. To avert it, he had woken Subran, sent his own discharges of power into the amniotic fluid that held Subran.

The Skryers could feel the agonies of the Des Aubach ruler, and sense his bloated body cramping as the pangs seized it.

Subran nears his time for elevation! Verusion felt his mind shout, only to be echoed by the others. *Kaizu brings on this birth prematurely. In the madness of his pain, Subran will destroy everything around him.*

The Skryers knew why. In the chaos, the power of the Overlap would be sent to shield the assassins. It might be enough to save them. But even if it was not, Kaizu would be spared. Ironically, he had bought himself time with this treachery, just as Zaer had bought time with his death. While the House of the Des Aubach crumbled, and utter ruin spread among the Lightbenders, Kaizu's own birth upward to the realm of Absolute Light would be uninterrupted. He would sacrifice a world to achieve godhood if he had to.

But there would be countless others for him to savour. He had dreamed of them for an age.

46

Ruarhi brandished his sword, adrenaline pumping through him. He indicated the swaying globes ahead of them. "We'll have to go forward," he shouted above the swirl of the waters as they threatened to wash the party from the walkway around the pool. A number of small waves had broken over the slabs, buffeting them, but they clung together. Behind them, still struggling along the walkway in pursuit, was the group of Regulators, but the sluggish waves had struck them, too, halting their progress.

"I agree," Sommoi called. "We can't fight the Regulators." He was watching the centre of the huge pool. Its inhabitant rolled and shook like an ocean leviathan, but the monster did not seem intent on attacking the creatures at the edge of its pool. If it had noticed them at all, they were far too insignificant for it to concern itself with. Yet something had disturbed it, and disturbed it terribly. It seemed to be in turmoil.

As the four figures worked their way precariously around the ledge, mindful of the globes ahead of them, Nu-Ko-Te at last understood what it was they were all witnessing.

"It's Subran!" she cried.

Sommoi watched the light from above the dome bathing the huge being, gleaming on its flesh as the creature turned and thrashed. Did the light disturb it? But surely not: the pool had been designed to be fed by the light. The creature should be glorying in it.

Ruarhi was again dumbfounded. The Lightbenders were not human at all, even more grotesque than the Elevates. *This* was what Zaer had meant by transformation. Human form ended with the Elevates before they began the change.

There was no time to speculate further, for the line of globes moved in, shimmering and weaving. Ruarhi met the first of the globes with his blade, unleashing his frustration and anger in a manic swipe that struck the globe full on. To his amazement, it shattered into hundreds of glittering fragments, and he thought he heard a scream of pain as it broke over him. Encouraged, the youth swung at another globe. It evaded him, but the sword caught part of it and it dropped downwards, unable to prevent itself from crashing into the walkway. Like the first of the globes, it burst, and this time its cry of pain was clear.

The other globes, now an angry swarm above the group, hung back as if they had seen the destruction of their companions. Ruarhi called the girls to him, and they were quick to duck down and obey, Sommoi bringing up the rear. He had no sword, but Ruarhi tossed him his own.

"Here, use this!" he shouted as another fist of water sluiced over the walkway into their knees. It was thick and oily, as if Subran bled profusely from innumerable wounds, and its smell was unpleasantly sweet.

"I've this," said Ruarhi. He held up the length of pipe.

Sommoi managed a wry grin, his fingers closing uncertainly around the sword haft. It was evidently a weapon with which he was neither familiar nor comfortable. But he swung it at the first globe to hover close to him. Like an angry wasp, it darted out of range. But the globe swarm realised that to come too close to the four figures below meant destruction.

Ruarhi urged the girls on around the walkway. He could see that the huge creature in the pool would not attack. But something was wrong with the Lightbender: there could be no doubting its agony.

"What is it?" Ruarhi shouted to Nu-Ko-Te.

She and Ukar-Tiri were holding on to each other, helping each other forge through the swirling waters to keep up with the youth, and Ruarhi grinned as he realised that Ukar-Tiri had put aside her prejudices for the moment.

Nu-Ko-Te answered him with a cry. "Kaizu is doing this. Subran is under attack. By stirring him up and throwing the entire Des Aubach House into turmoil, Kaizu has screened himself."

Ruarhi had no time to ask anything else. One of the globes had swooped down, pausing as another wave lashed at the party. Ruarhi stumbled, and the globe dropped toward his head. He knew instinctively that if it had struck him, he would have been killed. He swung wildly, but lost his balance and went down. The murky wave burst over him, mercifully protecting him. He thought he heard Ukar-Tiri scream, but he was fighting for his breath as the waters dragged back and tried to suck him out into the pool. He clung onto the pipe, knowing possession of the weapon was vital. But it meant he could not grip the slippery floor of the walkway. Within moments he was out of his depth.

He thrust the pipe in his mouth and clamped his teeth on it, waiting for the right surge in the waters. When it came, he struck out for the walkway. The next wave gathered itself up behind him and shot him forward. He was almost crushed up against the wall beyond the walkway, but managed to grab hold of something that protruded from it.

When he was able to see clearly again, it was to watch Sommoi whirling the sword overhead in wild defiance of the globes. The girls were waist-deep in the waters, struggling to avoid the next swoop of the globes. Ruarhi looked back to where the Regulators had been, but they were no longer in view. Either the waves had pulled them under, or they had made it back to safety beyond the pool.

Ruarhi waded along the walkway, using his pipe to smash another globe from the air. Its glittering disintegration seemed to deter the other globes, and they swung back as one, reforming out over the pool. Where was Arteriel? Ruarhi was mentally shouting. But he had no time to look, instead gripping Ukar-Tiri and pulling her with him along the walkway.

There was an opening in the wall, a dead end, but it promised a step up to a higher level. Ruarhi forced Ukar-Tiri into it, urging her to climb in spite of her exhaustion. When he had got her up, he swung round. Nu-Ko-Te was almost behind him, protected by Sommoi, who had himself smashed another two globes from the air. They now appeared to have completely regrouped, wary of the danger of attacking.

Ruarhi pushed Nu-Ko-Te into the opening and Ukar-Tiri reached down from the ledge above and tugged the girl up with her. Sommoi was almost knocked from his feet by yet another wave, but Ruarhi caught him and swept him into the opening. He turned, ready to defend himself from another attack, but still the globes held back. There was no sign of the Angel Guard. Ruarhi slid back gently, and in a moment he, too, had clambered up onto the ledge. It was some sort of lintel, but whatever door was beneath it was immovable. It would serve as no more than a temporary haven.

"There are too many of them," gasped Sommoi, coughing up water as he hung on grimly to a metal spar.

"They'll only attack us in force if they think we'll attack Subran," said Ruarhi.

"Yes, but they think *we* are responsible for Subran's agonies," Sommoi retorted, doubled over.

Arteriel suddenly appeared on the structure above them, his head cocked on one side as if he were listening. "Are you there?" he called down.

"We can't get out along the pool's edge," Ruarhi shouted. "The waves are too strong. Sooner or later those globes will take us. Isn't there a way we can climb up?"

Arteriel seemed to ignore Ruarhi, turning away with his customary contempt. Ruarhi swore obscenely, but Sommoi gripped his arm.

"He hasn't abandoned us yet. Look." He pointed. The Angel Guard was hovering in the air, trying to assess the strength of the globes, though being blind he looked dreadfully vulnerable. He was lowering something, a thin length of wire.

"Can you grip this?" he called.

"Swing it this way," Sommoi called back.

Guided by the voices, Arteriel brought the wire closer to Sommoi's grasping fingers, until at length he took it. Above him, the Angel Guard had dropped back onto the top of the metal construction that formed the near side of the pool's wall. Once in position, he tugged on the wire.

"You go up," Ruarhi told Sommoi. "Arteriel needs covering. If the globes attack him, he'll be knocked off the edge. I'll send the girls next."

Sommoi swallowed hard, but nodded. His unease at having to shin up the vertical wall almost unnerved him, but as the waves crashed against the ledge, still rising, he began the climb. Arteriel held the wire firmly, hauling Sommoi up like some bizarre catch. At the top, Sommoi stood shakily, but in a moment had gripped the sword with a new determination, facing the renewed threat of the hovering globes. Still they did not attack.

"Ukar-Tiri!" Ruarhi called. "You saw how he climbed. Now you."

But she shook her head and pointed to Nu-Ko-Te. "She goes next."

Ruarhi cursed, but Nu-Ko-Te was already climbing, using her hands to pull herself amazingly dexterously up the wire. Ruarhi stood below, watching. He felt Ukar-Tiri's eyes on him. Nu-Ko-Te reached the top, where Sommoi safely pulled her upward.

Ruarhi turned to Ukar-Tiri. "This time, no arguments. You go up. I'll follow."

She smiled in her infuriating, enigmatic way, but started the climb at once, moving with the same speed and grace as Nu-Ko-Te. Ruarhi caught his breath. Gods, but if only they ever could get away from this insane world.

He climbed, and as he reached the top of the wall, could see that the globes had given up the idea of attacking.

"There's still a distance to travel to get to the opening away from this palace," Arteriel told them. "But I can no longer tell you the best route. This flood has confused everything for me. You will have to guide us." He pointed in the direction of the opening, but all the party could see was a mass of tubing, pillars and trunks.

They were able, however, to traverse the wall. It was wide enough to be safe, but on the side opposite to the pool it rose up in metal sheets that were polished and unclimbable. Slowly they made their way along the wall, policed at a distance by the globes.

Sommoi led them, closely followed by Arteriel, who allowed himself to be guided by Nu-Ko-Te. Ukar-Tiri followed her, with Ruarhi bringing up the rear. His eyes scanned the pool, where Subran yet thrashed and heaved, sometimes diving deep below the surface, far from sight, only to come soaring up again in a welter of spray. But it was mindless, and mercifully there was no hint of an attack from the pool. Other creatures seethed in its heaving waters, but their attentions were fixed on the Lightbender.

"He's dying," said Nu-Ko-Te. "Can you not feel it?"

Ruarhi ignored her, turning to look back along the twisting wall. The Regulators could not have given up so easily. There would be a further chase. But he could see no activity outside of the pool.

He was about to comment, when something rose up under him, driving for his groin. His instincts saved him, but the blow, which took him inside his thigh, sent him spinning. He tumbled, barely hanging on to the wall. Someone screamed, and he swung round to find himself confronted by one of the Regulators. It had climbed up through an opening he had not seen. Before he could get to his feet, it groped for him in its clumsy way. He smashed down at the fingers, his pipe bouncing off them as if they were made of springy wood.

In a moment it was on him, long arms trying to wrap around him. He brought his knee upward and used his strength to pry its hold free for a few precious seconds. In that time he was able to use the pipe to crack down on its elbow. Its head dropped as it stumbled, but its slack mouth fastened on his lower leg. Instantly the pain seared him and he beat at the head with the pipe. But the Regulator was like a maddened hound: it would not release him. Tears sprang from his eyes as it closed its jaws. He felt blood running freely, and his muscles parted as the thing bit harder.

Arteriel realised what had happened, and brushing Sommoi aside, took to the air, measuring the distance from the sounds of Ruarhi's cries of pain. The Angel Guard seemed to glide in on the fight, then swung both feet unerringly. They connected with the head of the Regulator, snapping it back, forcing it to loose its prey. Ruarhi was too weakened to add a blow of his own, but he had the presence of mind to roll out of the way. Arteriel swept past, one taloned glove reaching down, hooking into the flesh at the shoulder of the Regulator. With amazing strength, the Angel pulled the Regulator to the side of the wall, and with a vicious twist, swung it out over the waters. He released it and it fell with a splash, disappearing beneath the surface. The waters heaved as if something else swam beneath them. The Regulator did not reappear.

Sommoi had found the opening and the steel ladder that the Regulator had used to climb up. He slammed the trap shut, then turned to find both girls bent over Ruarhi.

"Is it bad?" he said. Behind him he sensed Arteriel's soft tread as he, too, waited for their answer.

Nu-Ko-Te turned, her face grave. "There is much blood," she said, for once unsure of herself.

When Ukar-Tiri looked up, her face was streaked with tears. She could not speak. Nu-Ko-Te understood her distress at once, recognising the mirror of her own. She put her arm about Ukar-Tiri in an effort to comfort her. Ukar-Tiri did not resist.

Sommoi bent down. Ruarhi's skin was grey with pain. "The bone," he gasped. "It's broken."

Sommoi studied the leg, the bloody mass of pulped muscle and bone. The Regulator had been thorough. The damage was far worse than Ruarhi realised: the lower half of his leg had been torn off below the knee. Ruarhi was lying in a thick pool of blood: the terrible wound threatened to leak more blood if something wasn't done to staunch it quickly.

Sommoi hunched over it, ripping strips of cloth from his tunic, binding up the limb, trying to ignore Ruarhi's gasps of pain. But the youth sank back with a final moan, passing out.

Ukar-Tiri saw what had happened and lurched forward, drawing in air for a scream, but Sommoi put a bloody hand on her arm.

"He's alive."

A shout of alarm from Arteriel alerted him, and he turned.

The Angel was listening to the pool. "What's happening to Subran?" he asked.

Sommoi rose unsteadily, chest heaving with fresh horror at what he saw. The Lightbender was rising up from the pool, the enormous dome of its head streaming water, immense eyes straining wide with pain and madness. A curving mouth opened, spewing tons of fluid, to reveal a cavernous pink maw.

In spite of his colossal pain, Subran was propelling himself through the water with distinct purpose, bearing directly down on the intruders. In moments he would be upon them and that silent, gaping orifice would swallow them.

47

Verusion and the Skryers watched through the medium of minds the events in the palace of the Des Aubach, and saw the sudden rising up of Subran, his intention to destroy those he thought responsible for his agony. Kaizu's ploy had worked perfectly.

They'll die! came the thunderous mental words. The Skryers heard them simultaneously. *Release the Overlap. Subran must be stopped, otherwise Kaizu will elude us. Everything we have planned for will be in ruins.*

Annaxion felt the nearness of the Overlap, a huge presence that was not here in any physical sense, but which hovered right beside the Skryers' tower as though moored alongside it on another plane. It was alive with energy, primed for its work.

A gate! came the command. Whether it was Zaer, the Overlap itself, the combined powers of the Skryers, or all of these things, Annaxion could no longer distinguish. It did not matter. He simply directed power as he was able, focused it.

And drove it like a shaft upwards towards the palace of the Des Aubach. As it speared away, a trail of blinding light, Annaxion felt the other currents surging into it, feeding it like torrents feeding a river in spate. Vast energies flowed into the shaft. His mind looked back along the shaft to its source, his eyes unharmed, his physical being untouched by the mental bolts of fantastic power.

He was aware of the orifice, the whirling fury that heralded the coming of the Overlap, the gateway to another world that it was opening, linking one realm to another. Beyond the portal a strange darkness gathered, like a storm, but of impossible proportions. The storm was fueled by visions of something else, too terrible to look upon. The Overlap had opened the door to a forbidding world of chaos: its horrors boiled, about to spill through the gate, inundating this world.

Use them! Bring them through at once! again came the cry.

Annaxion and the others knew what they had to do, in an instant redirecting their powers, sending a fresh wave of energy to the palace.

Sommoi felt it first. Like a sudden explosion of light inside him, it set his entire body glowing. He felt an unbounded elation, crying out with it. Nu-Ko-Te and Ukar-Tiri felt it too, and cried out with the shock of it, as if they had been plunged into freezing water.

"The Overlap!" shouted Sommoi. "It is here! We must use its power."

Arteriel staggered as he, too, felt the tremendous jerk of power. He steadied himself.

Direct the power at Subran, came the command from within each of them.

Together they faced the monstrous bulk that bore down on them, the hideous, gaping mouth, the scarlet orbs that bulged in parody of a madman's.

Open a gate! was the roar.

Light cascaded down from above, using the funnel to the world outside the dome, as though the Overlap hovered beyond, pumping energy down the funnel at Subran himself. The Lightbender's immense body was bathed in the brilliant glow, deflecting as much of the light as it could, sending out scores of beams in all directions. Where the beams struck the walls, machines and tanks of the palace, they burst, exploding in showers of yet more light and fire.

Subran was momentarily checked in his plunge towards the company, suddenly sinking below the waves as if they would save him from the attack.

What is wrong? came the voice within the company.

Sommoi understood at once. It was Ruarhi. He had to be a part of this. To complete the cycle, he must be revived. Sommoi bent to him, but Ruarhi was still unconscious.

"We must revive him," he told Ukar-Tiri and Nu-Ko-Te who had also come to his side.

"Hurry!" called Arteriel. "Subran will rise again. This time he will be before us."

Sommoi bent right over Ruarhi, and Ukar-Tiri watched in horror as the long tendrils at the back of his head swung forward like living things. They fastened on Ruarhi's neck. It was too much for Ukar-Tiri. With a cry of protest, she made to throw herself at Sommoi, but Nu-Ko-Te pulled her back.

The two girls struggled with each other, barely able to keep their balance. Arteriel dared not turn back, trying to gauge what was happening in front of him, whether Subran had risen again.

Sommoi ignored all this. He felt himself linked to Ruarhi, felt the flow of blood into the youth, the transfusion of power. It seemed to take an infinity, but at last Ruarhi opened his eyes. A questioning horror was in those eyes as they stared directly into Sommoi's, but then the young warrior tried to rise.

Sommoi detached himself at once. "Subran is upon us," he said. "The Overlap needs us all."

Ruarhi raised himself on his elbows, gaping at the two girls, who were still struggling with each other.

"Ukar-Tiri!" he shouted, his voice cutting the air like a knife. "Stand still!"

Direct the power! came the voice within them again.

Sommoi and Arteriel focused it, and at once Ruarhi linked his own mind to it, unable to prevent the flow. The girls were swept into its flood, and this time the five of them poured energy towards the Lightbender as he rose up like a god before them, only yards from their haven.

As light streamed down through the funnel from outside, a searing white beam, it struck Subran with the force of a dozen electrical storms. His huge body twisted around as if lifted by another force, beyond imagining. Before he could crash down on the company, obliterating them in seconds, he was flung with contemptuous ease out into the pool, right under the central focus of the light.

Ruarhi felt an awesome stream of power burning within

him, directing it out at the Lightbender, and he saw the others similarly directing power outwards. The Skryers were feeding it through them, guided by Zaer.

The Overlap! It was here. And not out of control, but *in* control, fusing all their energies to its purpose. There was nothing mindless about its actions.

Subran was picked up and tossed like a dead thing, his huge mouth opening and closing, blood pouring from it, as if every internal organ he possessed had been pulped. As he turned over, his endless tail smacking into another section of wall beyond the rim of the pool, Ruarhi marveled again at the size of the being. Huge fragments of skin were sloughing off him, like plates of armour, to reveal a white skin beneath, the veins throbbing, rupturing as the light struck them.

As Subran came under the heart of the beam from above, something began to emerge from the tunnel, a contrast to the light, like long plumes of jet black smoke, creeping tendrils that groped into the palace. Emissaries of the world beyond the Overlap's gate, they clawed hungrily for whatever denizens of this world they could find.

And settled on the dying Lightbender.

Ruarhi concentrated on delivering the power focused through him, but he was appalled at the malefic powers seeping from these intrusions. Like living ropes, they bound Subran. All around him the globes had come in force, hovering and darting, but each time one of them touched the swirling darkness from beyond, it shattered.

Drive them back! came the inner command. *Subran is almost dead. Drive back the intrusions.*

Immediately the company altered the flow of power, attacking the darkness that even now threatened to seek out more of the palace's life. As light swept into the tendrils of darkness, they recoiled. But their grip on Subran never wavered. They lifted his dripping carcass, blood and flesh tumbling from it in crimson cascades. Directly below, in the murky waters of the pool, other shapes writhed.

Subran was hauled up towards the funnel, which was now in total darkness, but the intruders from beyond the gate were withdrawing. They had their prey and would remove it as an eagle removes its prey from the scene of the kill. But something sucked at the waters of the pool like a whirlwind, churning them, tugging them upwards, and as the waters fountained in a sudden burst, the other creatures, servants of the Lightbender, were drawn up to their doom. Clouds of globes were drawn in, the sound of their explosions, their screams of agony, clear above the din of the storm.

Ruarhi sagged back, relinquishing the power. The others, too, were momentarily exhausted. Ukar-Tiri almost crawled to his side. She looked haggard, her eyes raw.

"Ruarhi," she murmured.

He put out his hand weakly, but was too drained to speak. Their fingers barely touched.

He doesn't realise, she thought. *His leg—*

Sommoi gazed down at Ruarhi. "We can't stay here," he said. "The Overlap will suck up into the gate everything in this palace. Every other Des Aubach will be destroyed. The vengeance of the gods is absolute. If we don't get out quickly, we'll be drawn upwards as well."

Nu-Ko-Te was nodding. "The process can't be reversed now. Not until the gate is closed."

"Kaizu," said Ruarhi. "He's still free."

Although they spoke their thoughts aloud, they knew that each of them was tapping into a single thought, fused for the moment by the incredible powers of the Overlap and Zaer, who seemed to have become one with the renegade.

"We must help you," Sommoi told Ruarhi.

"I'll be all right," Ruarhi tried to grin. He heaved himself up on his elbows again, twisting over, about to attempt to stand. It was only then that he understood what had happened to him. He gaped at his ruined leg.

Ukar-Tiri let out a sob, her hand covering her mouth.

Ruarhi saw the tears welling in her eyes. Horror, true horror, clawed at him then. He felt his mind veering. "My leg," he gasped. "My leg—"

Sommoi gripped his arm. "We *must* go now. We cannot remain. There is more to do. Kaizu will escape—"

Ruarhi gazed dumbly at him, for a moment speechless. Then he used Sommoi's arm to haul himself up, hopping, trying to close out the nightmare. *My leg!* his mind shrieked, over and over. The others felt the raw terror in his unspoken cries.

"Lead the way!" called Arteriel impatiently, as though Ruarhi's disability meant nothing to him.

Ukar-Tiri glared at him as if she would fly at him, but if the Angel was aware of her fury, he did not show it.

"Our work is done here," Arteriel said. "Now we must get to the Da Sangravilles. Everything is wasted if we fail."

Sommoi nodded, putting an arm about Ruarhi's waist. "We can't move quickly. Ruarhi cannot walk without help. He has—" But his words trailed off helplessly.

Ruarhi gritted his teeth. "My leg, Arteriel. It's damaged badly."

Arteriel's face clouded, his eyes narrowing. Something in Ruarhi's voice warned him of the extent of the damage. But he had become the complete predator, the lure of the kill driving all other thoughts from him. "To delay means to fail," he said evenly. "Even now, Kaizu is readying to leave his palace."

"To go where?" said Sommoi. But he knew.

"If he reaches Absolute Light before we stop him, he will warn them. He will be one with them. And they will unite. They did that before."

And exiled the renegade, the Overlap, thought Ruarhi. "Then you must go on," he said. "Leave me here. I'll follow as quickly as I'm able."

"Don't be foolish," cut in Nu-Ko-Te. "Without you, our powers fail. We would not have destroyed Subran had Sommoi not revived you. You cannot be left."

Arteriel stood before them as if he would force them to his will, as if he had given up everything for his fanatical desire to destroy Kaizu. But his words took them by surprise, lacking his usual harshness. He directed them at Nu-Ko-Te.

"You speak wisely," he told her. "Forgive me for not doing likewise."

Nu-Ko-Te stared at him, shocked by the unexpectedness of the change. His fierce beauty drew her, but coupled with compassion it was even more compelling. At that moment she yearned to reach out to him, but something prevented her.

"I must search for Kaizu," Arteriel went on quickly, aware of the sudden tension between them. "Help Ruarhi. Bring him as swiftly as you can. But if we travel together, slowly, we will not find Kaizu. If I go ahead, I may be able to delay him."

Sommoi nodded, also surprised at the sudden change in the Angel's tone. Perhaps the powers that worked through them had effected other changes. "So be it."

"Follow me when you can," said Arteriel, more curtly, then took to the air. Within moments he had swooped away over the pool and out of sight.

Ruarhi gritted his teeth against the crushing debility of his wound. He tried to push the real implications from his mind, but already a darkness welled up there. No amount of power from beyond could hold it down forever. He saw his life in fragments before him.

"This way," said Nu-Ko-Te, who had elected to lead them across the precarious constructions to the far side of the pool. It churned yet, a red column fountaining upwards into the funnel in the dome as the gate drew into it the spoils of the storm.

48

Arteriel felt the tremendous concussions as the whirlwind of air was sucked into the hungry mouth of the gate, ripping up sections of tank, pulling at the buckling pillars that supported the huge dome of the Des Aubach palace. Somehow he managed to keep airborne, swerving and dipping, streamlining himself against the terrific flow of air. He could feel the force of the invisible Overlap, guiding him, lending him something of its inestimable power. It had to be that, otherwise he would never have been able to prevent himself from being smashed to pulp by the drag of the gate. He moved at dizzying speed, but something compensated him for his blindness. He heard the pillars and the trees as he arrowed past them on either side, but when he reached the passage that led out of the palace, he was miraculously unscathed.

He hardly had a moment to think of the others: he had to assume that the Overlap, Zaer, whatever, would lend them the same strength, guide them through the tortuous currents of the storm. As he dived down and into the wide semicircular passage, Arteriel could hear creatures being dragged along it by the air current, pulled into the gate from outside the palace. He ignored the bellows, the alien cries, shutting his mind to everything but the express need to reach the palace of the Da Sangravilles.

He kept to the upper apex of the passage, where the air was less turbulent. His wings slightly grazed the smooth stone, but he made intricate adjustments, keeping to the fine balance between skill and recklessness. Something flapped up towards him, shrieking, but he swiped at it with a claw and felt a soft presence come apart. Whatever it had been, it fell away as swiftly as it had come.

Ahead of him he felt the passage open out into another huge, domed area. He emerged cautiously and instinctively curved upwards, hovering, testing the air. It was not still, but as yet was not being sucked away at the same frenzied rate as the air in the passage.

An antechamber to Kaizu's palace, came the inner voice. He knew it at once at Zaer's, though it had altered strangely. *Let me be your eyes,* it told him.

He nodded, as if Zaer were somewhere below him and would see him. At once the voice of the Elevate issued instructions, guiding him through the new maze of pillars. Overhead he could hear the groaning of the dome as its superstructure began to weaken. Spars were cracking, glass shattering. The immense power of the gate that the Overlap had opened was drawing into it everything that was near it.

The palaces of the Lightbenders will not be able to resist, said Zaer's voice. *As the gate feeds, so it will grow. Nothing can withstand its draw.*

"What of Sommoi and the others?" Arteriel shouted aloud.

Already the wind in this part of the palace was beginning to swirl, gathering speed as it whirled away to the Des Aubach palace.

The Overlap protects them. They will come through the passage as you did. Without them, we cannot destroy Kaizu.

Arteriel said nothing more for the moment, content to be guided through further parts of the maze. He had to drop down to a place where the ceiling dipped much lower, supported on scores of stone pillars that were closely packed. It was dangerous to fly between them at any speed, but time was slipping away. He guessed Kaizu was attempting an escape of some kind: Zaer knew this, but still seemed unprepared to reveal what it was that the Da Sangraville master intended.

This passage takes you to his palace. We will need to open another gate there, just as in Subran's palace. You must contain Kaizu until the others come.

Arteriel could only attempt to follow Zaer's guidance. Below him he could feel a growing army of beings; they bayed and shrieked at him, and he knew they were striking the air with claw and steel in their lunatic efforts to carve him from the air. But he came unscathed from the corridor and out into yet another huge area. Above him he could feel the heat of natural light coming through the dome. He sensed that he was surrounded by a forest of pillars, even more immense than the ones he had seen previously. There were again numerous tanks, and in their swirling waters he was aware of other creatures, some huge, their malevolence rising up at him like heat from a furnace. Yes, this was the private hell of the Da Sangravilles, and it seemed that every living thing here was bent on ripping the intruder from the air.

They'll not reach you, Zaer told him. *None of these abominations are capable of flight.*

Arteriel would have asked many questions, but before he could frame any of them, he was distracted by something ahead of him. Intuitively he knew what it must be: the heart of the Da Sangraville palace, the pool of Kaizu himself.

The Angel swerved, hovering and listening. The wind was now a distant roar, though it was drawing inexorably closer as the gate groped for further substance. Below, in the reek-ing pools, creatures, Da Sangraville spawn, thrashed and heaved, boiling the waters. And directly ahead of him, Arteriel could feel the palpable presence of Kaizu.

The creature was awesome in its girth, and had risen from the waters of the vast pool. Arteriel could imagine the Lightbender's proportions vividly, even though he could not see it.

He has opened his funnel to the skies beyond the dome, said Zaer. *Just as the Overlap used you and the others to open the funnel above Subran, Kaizu has used his own powers to open this one. We should have come here first, but he knew our intention. Thus he sacrificed Subran, drawing off the Overlap's strength.*

"But if the funnel is open," said Arteriel, "why does the Overlap not attack him here?"

Bring the others and it will. Another gate can be opened, and Kaizu will be sucked into it, disposed of. He could not resist the pull of the dark worlds. But the gate has still to be opened.

"Why has Kaizu opened the funnel?"

Because he can rise through it to the outer skies. Once he is there, we will have lost him. He will have joined Absolute Light. They have long since banished the Overlap. They would never permit it to enter their world. Once outside, Kaizu would be one with them. He would be under their protection.

"What is happening now?" Arteriel could hear the sounds of water heaving and thundering, cascading down off the immense being, as if it were rising upwards. Kaizu himself made no sound: no roar escaped whatever mouth he must have possessed, no bolts of mental anguish flashed across the void to strike at the Angel's mind.

Do not be deceived. He hears you, said Zaer.

"And you?"

No, not me. He knows the Overlap is close, but thinks it is tied to Subran's palace. He is not afraid of you alone, Arteriel. You are an insult to his dignity. His many minions will seek to bring you down, but Kaizu will ignore you.

"How am I to detain him?"

There was an unnerving silence, as though Zaer had not considered the problem. But at last he spoke again. *He rises.*

I will try to give you something of the power you used jointly against Subran.

Again Arteriel nodded. He concentrated, slowly winging closer to where he knew the huge Lightbender would be. Arteriel drifted upwards, searching for the funnel, using its heat source to guide him. He was aware that Zaer must be moving him, utilising his subconscious, but he did not feel manipulated. He flew in an elaborate pattern that Zaer could only have designed to thwart the probes of the enemy.

It must be now, came Zaer's voice, and in it there was a hint of anxiety, of uncertainty. Arteriel steeled himself. He had not come here to shy away. Everything he had suffered had been the doing of this monster before him.

"Show me!" he almost snarled.

Zaer directed power into the Angel: Arteriel felt the surge as he had felt it back in the palace of Subran. He jolted, but then focused it, himself directing it at Kaizu. It was like throwing a spear of concentrated heat. Arteriel marveled as it streamed from his arm. Somewhere beyond him he heard it strike home. There was no bellow, no scream of agony, but the Lightbender reacted. Taken unawares by the suddenness of the attack, it lurched, sending up a fountain of spray that Arteriel felt. But Kaizu recovered quickly.

It is not enough, said Zaer, and there was a hint of panic in his voice. *He deflects it easily.*

Arteriel waited for further instructions. He knew he dared not go in close. Against the Lightbender his usual powers would be pitiful.

Beyond him, rising upwards again, Kaizu began to writhe, twisting his huge bulk this way and that as if sudden spasms of pain racked him. Arteriel could sense the bizarre movements. Had the power found a weakness in him?

But he felt a mental shudder as Zaer answered him. *No. He is beginning the change. He is going outside, leaving the cocoon of flesh that has housed him in this palace.*

Arteriel heard a booming sound above. Kaizu had attached part of himself to the lower end of the funnel. The Lightbender began dragging himself laboriously upwards, swinging the huge bulk of his body from side to side, its skin parting, tearing, to reveal a new form beneath.

Zaer's concern communicated itself inevitably to Arteriel: if Kaizu was not stopped soon, he would be free. The effects of the storm in Subran's palace would not reach him. Arteriel felt himself clenched by the force of his own fury. Ignoring the silent warnings of the Elevate, he flew upwards to where he sensed the lip of the funnel must be. Kaizu could be no more than yards away: the Angel could smell the stench of his flesh, as if it rotted on him, sloughing off to reveal new layers beneath. If eyes turned upon him, Arteriel could not feel them, but something rose like a miasma from the bloated Lightbender, a fog of loathing, a threat of slaughter.

Arteriel shouted out commands to the whispering presence of Zaer, demanding that he send him power. Zaer obeyed, caught up in the mental fury of the Angel, only now aware of the depth of its force. The Angel flung light at the monstrous Kaizu, directing it at the part of him that was struggling for a grip on the funnel, the shaft that would take it to the skies beyond the dome. Arteriel could hear the raw power fizzing like fire, striking at the Lightbender. It shook, the entire construction of the funnel rocking, but Kaizu held firm, the glands under his thick neck secreting a steaming ooze that glued him to the funnel. Yard by yard, he rose upwards, dragging his squirming belly into the orifice.

Arteriel pumped more power at the Lightbender, but it did no harm. Nothing could prevent the monster from hauling itself upwards. Thick peelings of skin slipped from it, tumbling back out into the palace and down to the pool, where the waters seethed, choked with Kaizu's minions. They seemed to have gathered to celebrate Kaizu's rise, his elevation to godhood. Arteriel could feel Zaer's revulsion, and was glad that he could not see them himself.

Kaizu's entire bulk was now in the funnel, wriggling ever more quickly up its narrowing tube, leaving behind a slick trail, clotted with skin. Arteriel was forced back to the mouth of the funnel, hovering, waiting. He thought of fire, but knew it would be hopeless: Kaizu would deflect it as easily as he had deflected light.

"Where are the others?"

Zaer was silent for a while. Then he spoke. *Coming. They are shielded from the worst of the storm. Subran's palace is beginning to collapse about them, dragged into the gate. But a vortex has been created for them. They will get through.*

"But we cannot stop Kaizu. They will be too late."

Zaer did not answer. Arteriel felt despair seeping through his mind. But it served only to infuriate him further. He craned his neck, as if he would be able to see up through the funnel. He could hear Kaizu receding, drawing nearer his goal.

"Then I'll follow him," he said. "You hear me, Zaer, wherever you are, whatever you have become? I'll follow Kaizu."

I hear you, came the reply.

"Guide me through," snapped Arteriel, rising again. As he lifted on the still air in the funnel, he sensed the heat above, the natural heat of sunlight beyond. Kaizu had disappeared over the lip of the funnel. He was outside.

Arteriel flew upwards, avoiding the treacherous sides of the corridor, the secretions that would have held him.

"Be my eyes," he told Zaer. "I can feel the light."

In a moment you will be outside. Above Skydown. And yes, I will be your eyes.

Arteriel felt the abrupt intensity of the daylight. It threatened to burn him, but he adjusted quickly to it. How fierce it must have been! How brilliant. To see it—

It was only then that he realised. It came to him with the light. Only the Lightbenders, Absolute Light can bear it. It would have burned out my eyes. So to prepare me, they blinded me.

"For this," he murmured. "The Overlap blinded me so that I could fly above Skydown—"

You have overcome your blindness, Arteriel. You have learned to exist without your eyes. You are still a superb warrior. If you had come here as you were, you would never have survived the light. The shock would have reduced you to nothing. As you are, you remain an effective assassin.

"And I carry—what? Your mind?"

You did not see me, but the others must have described me to you. No Elevate could come here. Not unless, like Kaizu, they went through the transformation. I had too many ene-

*mies: they would never have permitted me here. Besides, I
am an iconoclast.*

"Then you knew the company would fail?"

*No. But we could never be absolutely sure that Kaizu would
be trapped and sent through a gate. We had to have a way
of following him if he eluded us. As he has. You are our last
hope.*

"You can see in this realm?"

*Through you, I can. I will open your mind to it. Neither
of us will be harmed by the light. We must follow Kaizu.*

"And kill him?"

Somehow.

"Somehow," Arteriel murmured. And waited for the
stream of images to begin. Zaer felt the unnerving hunger.

49

As the Angel took to the skies, Zaer felt a shudder of elation.
Although Kaizu's flight threatened disaster, Zaer was inca-
pable of controlling the emotional surge brought on by his
being here above Skydown, his mind locked with that of
Arteriel, physically experiencing this realm with him. And
Zaer could see for both of them.

The light was strong, its source a golden ball, a sun too
strong to look at directly; it was this brilliant orb that would
have blinded the unwary who studied it. But the miraculous
glow that bathed the world, dazzling at first, became glorious. It was just as the Overlap had said it would be, a world
of shimmering colour, without the drab greys and blacks of
the underworld. But Arteriel's own eyes, evolved through
generations of dwelling in twilight, would have failed him in
such a glare.

Above the vast domes of Thousandreach, there was a landscape, though to Zaer and Arteriel it seemed almost ethereal, a vision from a dream, cloaked as it was in drifting banks of cloud. The lower portions of the domes were hidden in this sea of cloud, which lapped at them, swirling gently around them in ever-shifting patterns, slow-moving surf and spray. The cloud ocean was the shield, Skydown itself, generated by the mighty trees but forged into the shield by the power of the gods of this realm and held in place by their Light-bender servants.

Zaer marveled at the domes as they loomed up from their white beds. Polished until they dazzled with reflected sunlight, they had been shaped in glass, and from out of them the upper branches of the great trees emerged as though they were a natural extension of the domes. Vast areas of rich green verdure hung from the branches, the broad leaves drinking in the sunlight.

Beyond the domes and in the rolling cloud banks between them, other treetops emerged, some of them isolated, others in clusters. Their leaves whispered in the hint of breeze that fanned this world. Zaer wondered if there were ever storms here, and if so, did the powers of Absolute Light control them as they did under Skydown?

Do you see? Zaer asked Arteriel.

The Angel flew on effortlessly, but he drew breath to speak. "I see," was all he said, but even in so few words there was awe. He swung round gently, facing another of the domes, recognising it at once as the central part of Subran's palace.

Zaer watched as the thick plume of darkness that was the gate rose upwards into the vault of the sky overhead. It was like a whirlpool of dark air, a long cord that stretched away into invisibility. Faint sounds came from within it, faraway thunder. Its grim work went on, and would not be staunched until the Overlap closed the gate.

"If we find Kaizu," said Arteriel, "do we drive him into that tunnel of darkness?"

No. It is impenetrable from here. Just as Skydown is. We will need another gate.

Arteriel did not reply, but Zaer could read his thoughts, his sharpened will. The hunt began.

As they flew across the domes, they could hear them groaning and protesting in their milky beds as the devastating force of the gate generated more implosions, sucking out of them the creatures that thronged within, pulling apart the superstructures. Glass shattered, the sounds carried with remarkable clarity across the air above the city. But Arteriel ignored them. The need to find Kaizu monopolised his thoughts.

Zaer did not need to control Arteriel. Their purpose was a shared one, their trust a bond. Zaer knew that the Angel felt no bitterness towards him, nothing that would have weakened their alliance. His hatred, his controlled fury, were for the Lightbender, as intense as the searing light.

Shapes moved at the edge of Zaer's vision. Cautiously he studied the horizons. He knew what it must be. Not Kaizu, but one of the denizens of this realm, one of the so-called gods. He caught a glimpse of something but deliberately and deftly shielded Arteriel from seeing it. There was no need for the Angel to be distracted. But Zaer could not help but react to the creature.

It was magnificent, even seen from this distance. In some ways it was like a bird, though in others it was more like a fish, with vast wings that lifted and sank in easy, flowing movements; there was a long tail that trailed behind it, its rudder, straight and pointed, though as the creature flew, so the tail gave a slight twist to the side, or up and down, directing the flight. If the creature was aware of Arteriel, it made no sign of recognition. It veered away in its slow, comfortable sweeps, merging with the mists of distance, omnipotent in its freedom.

There were others, but all of them swam through the skies at the very edge of vision. *They may not be gods,* Zaer thought to himself, *but they have the supreme beauty and perfection of form one would expect in a god. If that is what we become—*

"I have found him," said Arteriel, his words rasping along a nerve of guilt in Zaer's mind.

Zaer concentrated. Arteriel was right. Ahead of and below them, an enormous silhouette moved against the curling cloud landscape. Its flight was ungainly, in direct contrast to that of the creatures Zaer had seen. Yes, this was the fleeing Kaizu.

Arteriel swooped, but he was careful to keep well above the Lightbender. Kaizu would hardly be expecting to be followed to this realm. As the Angel dropped lower, Zaer saw the continuation of Kaizu's transformation. Most of the thick cocoon had sloughed off, though shreds of it still clung to the underbelly, impeding the flight. Revealed was a white body, still to undergo the last change. Soft and vulnerable, it was nevertheless huge. Once it had completed its metamorphosis, Arteriel would be utterly powerless to harm it.

The wings that were unfolding from Kaizu's white body were clumsy, though they had taken on enough of their finished shape to enable him to fly. They were transparent, almost gossamer-thin, but gradually they would become the graceful wings of the creatures Zaer had seen. For the moment Kaizu was flying as close to the cloud as he dared, vulnerable until the change was complete.

Arteriel followed a flight path that took him almost directly above Kaizu, a short distance behind him, where he had still not been seen. The Lightbender was truly huge: it would have taken several chapters to destroy him. But Zaer had seen a way to harm him.

The wings. That is his only weakness until the change, he told Arteriel.

The Angel understood. If an army had closed in, Kaizu would have been aware of it and would have unleashed a devastating counterattack on it. But one assailant could get through. Possibly.

Arteriel selected a point, dived.

As he drew closer to the fabric of the huge wing, he saw the fibres knitting, the skin taking shape rapidly, as if the very sunlight acted as an agent for rapid growth. He landed on Kaizu's wing, bending his body against the rush of air, steadying himself. There was no movement to suggest the huge Lightbender had noticed him. Arteriel felt the slow, ponderous beat of the wing.

He reached down and used his talons to tear into the fabric. It was like a tough skin, but unexpectedly thin. Like cloth, it ripped easily. Arteriel remained calm, resisting the urge to go at his task madly; he worked systematically, slicing deliberately across the wing in a way that would do the most damage. He had a perfect understanding of the structure of a wing and Zaer marveled at the way the Angel chose his areas. As the flesh of the wing opened, the wind added to the destruction, guided into the rents by Arteriel's precision.

At last Kaizu was aware that something was wrong. The wing faltered, the Lightbender began to drop towards the cloud. Arteriel took off, falling behind in a controlled break, before diving forward again. In spite of his inferior size, it was easy for him to keep up with the Lightbender.

Kaizu's flight slowed, the damaged wing evidently giving him pain. He had almost stopped, stretching the wing out, then pulling it inwards.

"It will heal if I don't damage it further," said Arteriel. He waited until the wing was extended again. Kaizu adjusted his flight, the flat head turning, the slitted eyes searching for the assassin, eyes that were like the eyes of a reptile, now grown venomous and malefic.

Zaer could only feel the Angel's emotional charge: it was not for him to attempt to guide it. He felt Arteriel tighten his resolve, then suddenly plummet, talons spread before him like a diving bird of prey. Even over so short a distance, the Angel built up great speed. Zaer knew what he intended: a strike at the weakest part of the wing. It was a dangerous ploy, but Arteriel had calculated carefully, and had absolute trust in his work.

When he struck the wing, his claws tore through flesh and fibre, ripping a deeper hole, plunging on into a brief darkness that smothered Zaer in unaccustomed panic. The wing reacted, rising up against the air, inadvertently serving to drive Arteriel through it like a missile. He emerged into the light, falling away and steadying himself.

As he watched the stricken Kaizu through Zaer's eyes, Arteriel wiped at the blood that clung to him.

Stunned, Zaer saw the Lightbender fall, spinning dangerously. *You've wounded him sorely,* he gasped. *If he falls through the clouds, he'll be destroyed.*

"Are you sure?" said Arteriel.

I cannot be. But it is Skydown. If he goes through it—

Arteriel finished cleaning himself and said no more. He went into another fast dive, following Kaizu's plummet. As he closed, he saw something else reaching up from the clouds, like the withered arm of a supplicant. It was part of another tree, though it looked dead, as if charred. As Arteriel closed with it, the details of the structure became clearer. Blackened branches spread out against the pure white of the cloud.

Kaizu swerved towards them, seeking succour, barely able to guide his clumsy flight. But he crashed onto the huge network of branches, wings outspread. Some of the branches snapped under the impact, and part of the trunk split, but the tree held, partially impaling Kaizu.

Arteriel flew around the stranded monster.

It is not enough, Zaer warned him. *He'll recover. Soon he'll be totally healed. We have very little time. We need the gate.*

"Call the others. Use the Overlap."

There is only one way to create a gate.

"How?"

The Overlap must enter this realm. But if it does, it will be exposed to all its enemies. The gods will swarm here.

"Can the Overlap enter this realm at any point?"

Zaer felt a jolt at the words, as though he had been struck by Kaizu's anger. *I am a fool!* he said. *Of course! It no longer moves randomly. We can direct the Overlap! The Skryers can still help us. We can bring the Overlap here, with absolute precision. But—*

"Why do you hesitate?"

It will open the gate, but it would be at the cost of its own existence.

"We must open the gate," said Arteriel. "Summon the Overlap."

Zaer shielded Arteriel from the anguish he felt, closing part of his mind as once more he reached out for the presence of the Skryers. Somewhere in the realms far below him, under Skydown, Annaxion and the Skryers felt the probing mind of the Elevate. They, too, knew remorse, but they began their new work instantly.

There had been numerous times when Sommoi was convinced that they would never reach the far side of Subran's collapsing palace. Apart from the tremendous drag of air from the mouth of the funnel, the gate, there were other hazards to negotiate. Whole sheets of metal, artefacts, chunks of broken pillar tumbled end over end through the ruins towards the dark maw. Regulators and other inhabitants of this bizarre palace, their bodies mauled and bloodied, fought for a grip on anything that would prevent them from being sucked up into the tendrils of that other world. And overhead the glass dome was being pulverised by forces that also threatened to thrust it into the gate. Huge shards of glass plummeted down into the pools that had burst their banks and made a lake of the entire floor of the palace, their waters thick and oily, congested with the wounded and the dying.

The Overlap somehow protected its own, diverting the destructive forces around the small company, just as the Lightbenders had deflected light. Subran was gone, drawn beyond, and most of the Des Aubach had followed him, totally unable to resist the immensity of the powers set against them. In the neighbouring palaces of the Spiritores and the Da Sangravilles, similar mayhem was erupting.

"The passage! That must be it," shouted Ukar-Tiri above the almost deafening roar of the gate. She pointed to the semicircular opening ahead of them. One arm supported Ruarhi, who had limped here with her and Nu-Ko-Te's help as Sommoi watched for any possible assault. But the creatures and servants of the palace were only interested in self-preservation.

Ruarhi moved as quickly as he could, urging the two girls on, though his efforts had taken a dreadful toll. His face was sickly pale, the sweat dripping from his face. He had hardly spoken, and Ukar-Tiri dared say nothing.

He would rather have died, she thought, but forced the words away. His pride alone would never let him survive this.

Sommoi helped them across the broken palace floor, wading through feet of thick, murky swell. But the waters were receding, like everything else sucked upwards in a spiral waterspout.

In the passage they were able to move a little more quickly, threading through more debris and broken forms, shapes that flopped like beached fish, limbs waving aimlessly. It was like the aftermath of a disastrous war, the corpses flung mindlessly this way and that by forces that had run amok. The stench was nauseating, but the four figures moved on through the passage, pausing only briefly to rest.

When at last they emerged into what had been the palace of the Da Sangravilles, they were staggered by the extent of the destruction. Most of the glass dome had fallen in: they had to shield their eyes from the light that speared down from the smashed dome. It had acted like fire, searing all flesh beneath. It would be unnecessary for the Da Sangravilles to be sucked up through the gate to the hell opened by the Overlap. Hell was already here: corpse after immense corpse hung from the sides of the ruptured tanks, split open and steaming where the light had burned into it.

Sommoi guided the others through shadows, avoiding the direct sunlight. It was difficult to progress through so much carnage and destruction, but eventually they came to the huge pool, the amniotic fluid that had been Kaizu's second womb. Exhausted, they slumped down by its side.

"Gone," said Sommoi. "We are too late."

Nu-Ko-Te pointed upwards to the funnel, where shreds of Kaizu's former flesh hung. "He rose, as Subran did. But he has gone to Absolute Light."

"What of Arteriel?" said Sommoi, though he spoke to the air, as if listening for its answer. All he heard were the sounds of continuing havoc in the Des Aubach palace.

Ukar-Tiri leaned back, stretching her arms, the stiff muscles. "You must let me examine your leg," she told Ruarhi, hardly able to look into his haunted eyes.

He shook his head. "Later." Would that be her duty from now on? To nurse him? He shivered. Why could she not believe that even as he had been, he had needed her?

Nu-Ko-Te suddenly stood up. "Arteriel!" she said, the word filling the air.

"Where is he?" said Sommoi.

"He is desperate for help. We must open another gate. We must link as we did before." She dropped down beside Ruarhi, holding her hand out to Sommoi. He reacted at once, coming to her, taking her fingers eagerly.

Huddled together, they waited for the inner presence, the combined power of the Skryers, the Overlap and Zaer. It came with the suddenness of a great wave breaking on a shore, and they rocked with its concussion.

EPILOGUE

Paradise is a concept that man frequently misunderstands. It should never be confused with physical ecstasy, which is necessarily a temporary thing.

Paradise is a state of mind, as lasting as a mood. Build a world on a promise of paradise and you build on clouds.

ZAER PHESMES—*The Book of Renunciation*

50

Zaer felt the power of the Overlap locking into him, to the body of the Angel Guard, directed and focused by the Skryers. For a moment the darkness closed in and he felt Arteriel's uncertainty as he, too, was temporarily plunged back into his blindness. But the darkness heaved, then crackled with fresh power.

In the crumbling tower in Thousandreach, Verusion felt himself stretched by the renewed demands on his strength, and his pain was echoed by the circle around him as the other Skryers fought to sustain their efforts. Above them, beyond the tower, thunder detonated. Jagged spikes of light tore through the fabric of Skydown and the air hummed with their discharge of energy.

"Will it come?" Arteriel said into the darkness that now enveloped him as he hovered, almost motionless above the domes.

Concentrate! admonished Zaer.

They were one mind again, Zaer, Arteriel, and the others, and with slow but deliberate precision, they brought the Overlap closer to its goal.

Arteriel felt an abrupt wrench, something tearing apart. The gift of sight, through Zaer, returned in an instant, daz-

369

zling him. But he recovered and saw below him the spread-eagled form of Kaizu, still caught on the vast tree. But the Lightbender would not be held for much longer: already his wing was healing, the flesh strengthening, taking on a new shape. It was no longer delicate, but muscular and powerful.

Zaer knew it for what it was, the wing of a golden imago, a lord of these skies. Kaizu's transformation was almost complete. And with it would come a new strength, powers far beyond the physical abilities of the creatures below Skydown.

"Is it coming?" said Arteriel.

Zaer was about to answer, but they both saw the turbulence that had begun in the clouds below Kaizu. The white shapes were swirling, moving in their listless, sluggish way at first, but then gathering speed until they had formed a colossal spiral of cloud. It accelerated, becoming a cyclone, pulling into it more and more cloud, revolving into a deep well, discoloured now, grey churning to darkness down in its deeps.

"The Overlap," breathed Arteriel, staggered by the sudden appearance.

It's a gate, corrected Zaer. *But it is here. So close. So close.*

The drag of the cyclone gate was beginning to create fierce currents of wind. Already Arteriel was finding it hard to hover as he was pulled downwards. He beat with his wings, pulling back.

He and Zaer could see the tree that bore Kaizu beginning to rock as the cyclone swirled directly under it, like the maw of a gigantic leviathan, several times greater in girth than even the Lightbender. Kaizu shook himself, lifting his upper body from the tree. His new form had repaired itself, his golden splendour complete. He rose, yard by yard, into the sky. Zaer repressed the sense of wonder that rose in him: this may not be a god, but in all history had there ever been such a fabulous creation?

Arteriel was forced to turn and struggle back towards one of the domes, the winds howling around him. The drag from the gate of clouds intensified, far greater in magnitude than the first gate's power had been in Subran's palace.

Zaer was aware of the other shapes, moving at the rim of

vision, summoned by the alien force that intruded in their
world. Their combined strength could easily nullify the gate.

"What are they?" said Arteriel.

You see them?

Arteriel's unease at discovering the aerial beings was
matched by his anger at Zaer's attempt to hide them from
him.

Absolute Light. Gods.

Arteriel's scorn burned through him, and Zaer sensed it.
But it mirrored his own rejection, his own angry rebellion.

*They will care nothing about Kaizu's past, his injustices
and cruelty. They are beyond such things. He is imago, as
they are. They look after their own.*

Zaer could add no more, for he and Arteriel were forced
to bend every effort to resisting the gate's pull. Arteriel beat
his wings like a swimmer in a flood tide, struggling against
it. He glanced back once. Kaizu was being pulled inexorably
downwards, his magnificent new body unable to prevent the
whirlpool of cloud from taking him.

Arteriel saw what might have been an eye, a searing half-
moon of hatred, casting this way and that for a victim. And
it was as though beams of pure evil radiated from it. Kaizu
was aware of his enemies, stabbing out in random sweeps
with bolts of mental energy that would have smashed Thousandreach itself to rubble.

The Skryers deflected the worst of the assault, but their
own strength withered: Verusion knew they could never sustain it. He felt a judder, a shrill cry. Tetraven, the eldest of
them, had succumbed. The circle was broken for only a moment; the Skryers repaired it quickly. The assault went on.
Another of the Skryers fell.

Zaer knew that Kaizu's efforts were immense, but the
Lightbender was doomed, sinking through the gate. In its
swirling darkness, shapes were writhing, shapes far more terrible than those which had reached for Subran. The Overlap
had opened a world of nightmares. Zaer sensed the sudden
tension in the air around him. The very gods of this world
drew back at sight of the things that hungered in the gate.
Their hesitation was brief, but it was enough.

Kaizu fell below the lip of the gate. His lower end was

engulfed in the darkness there. His great mouth opened, screaming in silence as he twisted and heaved in a final effort to rip free. Blood fountained up from his mouth.

Arteriel began to lose his battle with the winds. They were inching him back steadily. The gate summoned him, voracious and indiscriminate.

Zaer felt the death of Tetraven, then of another Skryer. One by one their lives were being pulled into the well. Kaizu clung tenaciously to his own life, using the lives of the Skryers to sustain him longer. Zaer knew that he would take them all if he could.

The gate began to swallow the Lightbender, his body attacked on all sides by the crawling shadows. As he sank down out of sight, Arteriel also fell, righting himself, but swept along by the winds. He braked himself, again beating with his wings to pull away, but the whirlpool was irresistible.

Kaizu dies, Zaer's voice whispered.

In the broken tower, Annaxion and Verusion felt the chilling hands of death take hold of them, closing, closing. An utter coldness grew, the coldness of the gulfs beyond the stars. Then numbness. Oblivion.

Arteriel closed his mind to everything. The last thing he was aware of was the dome some way ahead of and below him. He fixed on it, again trying to beat his way against the wall of air. But it showed no sign of weakening, even though the gate gorged on its prize.

Silence filled the dome. Nothing moved. Light flooded down from above, glittering in the pools. They, too, were still.

Sommoi was the first to lift his head. He gazed about him as if seeing the ruined palace for the first time. Those of Kaizu's servants who had died here and had not been dragged through the maze beyond to the first gate were sprawled in heaps, already stiffening. None of them had survived.

Nu-Ko-Te also raised her head. She and Ukar-Tiri were huddled together with Ruarhi a few feet from Sommoi. Like animals uncurling from a hibernation, they stretched themselves.

"Has it stopped?" said Ukar-Tiri.

Nu-Ko-Te nodded. They had all blacked out. But they had seen.

"He's dead," said Sommoi.

They knew he meant Kaizu. In their minds now there was only an emptiness. Zaer, the Overlap, the Skryers. They were gone.

"What about the others?" said Ukar-Tiri, asking what her companions could not.

Sommoi shook his head. "I felt the Skryers slipping away, like water through our fingers. They gave their lives' energy."

Nu-Ko-Te stood up and gazed towards the open sky. She had to shield her eyes against the glare, but she watched for as long as she could.

"I think we have lost him," Sommoi suddenly said at her shoulder. He reached out and touched her arm, and to his surprise her fingers closed on his.

"We have lost them both," she murmured.

Behind them they heard a gasp. They turned slowly to see Ukar-Tiri on her knees beside Ruarhi. He was still unconscious, and the girl had been examining his leg. She was gazing up at Sommoi and Nu-Ko-Te, astounded by something.

"What is wrong?" said Sommoi.

Ukar-Tiri could not speak. She pointed to the leg.

Sommoi bent down. The crude bandages had been pulled aside. The leg was restoring itself, even the foot was complete.

"How could this happen?" murmured Ukar-Tiri.

"It is the gift of this world," Sommoi told her. He studied his hand for a moment, the hand that Ruarhi had once cut from him. "Regeneration."

"Fodda," said Nu-Ko-Te. "Fodda does this."

Ukar-Tiri drew back as though the healing leg had somehow offended her, a blasphemy. As she did so, Ruarhi opened his eyes, yawning and stretching his arms. He saw Sommoi, blinked, and sat up.

"The gate—?"

"Kaizu was taken."

"Destroyed?"

Sommoi nodded. "But we have lost the Skryers. And I think we have lost Arteriel and Zaer." He pointed to Ruarhi's leg. "But you—"

Ruarhi's eyes widened. He looked at the leg as though this was a trick. Very slowly he touched it, then gasped in amazement.

"Fodda," said Ukar-Tiri, who had pulled away. She seemed unable to say more, as though she had uttered a curse.

Curb your anger, Ruarhi heard the voice. It was Zaer. *You would never have survived under Skydown had you not adapted to it. It has repaid you. Soon your leg will be complete.*

Ruarhi stood up warily, as if unable to trust the limb, stretching it, touching it to the floor. It was as though he had never lost part of it, the nerves alive. "Zaer," he said softly.

Nu-Ko-Te almost pounced on him, realising that he alone was in contact with the Elevate. "Where is he?"

Ruarhi was concentrating. "They are being drawn to the gate. The Overlap cannot seal it quickly enough. And there are other powers up there, closing on them."

"Can't we help?" said Nu-Ko-Te. "Why doesn't he speak to me!"

Ruarhi understood. Zaer considered his own cause and that of Arteriel lost. The gate would take them. Ruarhi shook his head. "We must try," he said aloud. He turned to the others. Even Ukar-Tiri responded at once. They formed a circle, hands touching hands in renewed concentration.

As they directed power outwards and into the skies, they linked with Zaer and Arteriel almost instantly, rocked back by the suddenness of the onslaught of air. Arteriel was flying in the teeth of a hurricane, pushed ever backwards. Beyond him the swirling circle of the gate loomed.

Zaer's voice shouted defiance. *Save yourselves! If you perish with us, we have only partly achieved our goal! Go back. You have so much to do!*

Arteriel said nothing, directing all his energy into fighting the current, though his wings beat less steadily, exhaustion threatening to engulf him.

Ruarhi felt himself conversely growing in strength: his leg was healed! Gods, but it was an indescribable relief! Whole!

And the Lightbender had been destroyed. Ruarhi forced power out of himself, forging the others to it. He reached out with an invisible hand, closing on the groping claws of the Angel as though reaching for a man who was about to sink forever under a heaving sea.

As he did so, an image bobbed up to the surface of his thoughts. Dromator. Ripped open like a slaughtered bull. All the callousness of the Angel Guard, his cold, chilling arrogance, welled again before Ruarhi, incident by incident. Murder shone in Ruarhi's eyes, fed by the hell he had endured under Skydown, every indignity, every sorrow.

Spare him, Ruarhi, said Zaer's voice, growing as faint as a whisper. *Like you, he is a victim.* Then the voice was gone, all energy spent. It would not be heard again. There was only the mind of Arteriel, its determination not to give in blazing like a beacon.

Ruarhi felt the clawed talon as surely as if he clung to it physically, his flesh bleeding where it bit into him. He began the struggle, tested to the limit of endurance. The grip of the storm began at last to relent. Ruarhi felt it loosen. But his own hold on the Angel could not last: his flesh was not strong enough.

They waited, slumped down together in the shadows. They could not speak, wanting only to collapse. They tried not to let sleep claim them, knowing they must get away soon. If they slept, they might never find the will to rise. But it was inevitable. One by one they succumbed.

Much later, Ruarhi woke. Sommoi was still asleep, chest rising and falling gently. Beside him, incongruous in the mayhem they had witnessed, the sword had fallen from his fingers.

Ruarhi could not see either of the girls, but he was too weak to look for them. His hunger gnawed at him. He reached into his pack, pulling out the last skin-wrapped wad of food. He stared at it. Fodda. Zaer was right. It had made him a part of this world. Not only had it changed his flesh, the way it protected itself, but it had sharpened his mind, made it available to Zaer's. He understood it now. Resentment was pointless. And he had no energy for it.

Besides, somewhere along the way, in the maelstrom of the final upheaval, Zaer had imparted the rest of his design. Ruarhi and the others had their part in it, and had from the beginning. The echoes of Zaer's words came back to him as he ate.

The world under Skydown is dying. Destroying the Light-benders will not save it. But the Overlap can open gates for its people before it, too, dies. If the people under Skydown go through to other worlds at random, they could soon perish. They must go with care. They will need envoys. And strong rulers.

Your world, Ruarhi, is wild and barbaric in many ways, but it is young and free of the darkness that claims so many others. You will go back, I promise you. You will become a king. You will sire a dynasty. With Ukar-Tiri.

Sommoi will weld together the disparate peoples under Skydown. When he brings them through to your world, you will make a place for them, you and your sons. It will take time, lifetimes. You may not see its conclusion. But it begins with you, and with Sommoi. And with my beautiful Nu-Ko-Te.

As Ruarhi began to eat, chewing slowly, he felt the gradual seeping of strength back into his tired limbs. Sommoi moaned in his sleep, turning over, then subsiding. Perhaps he dreamed, also hearing Zaer's words.

Some distance away, across the ruined hall, Ukar-Tiri looked down into the lifeless pool. She, too, reflected on Zaer's words to her. They had made her angry. She had been used from the start, never allowed to choose her own path.

"Will it be so hard?" she heard Nu-Ko-Te say.

"Do we still invade each other's thoughts?" she retorted.

Nu-Ko-Te shook her head patiently. "No, that is over. But I read your face. You are angry."

"Since I was a child, I have been used. Through all this—"

"We have all been used. But can you question Zaer's vision?"